THE
LAST DITCH

THE LAST DITCH

ROY BRADFORD

BLACKSTAFF PRESS

Bradford, Roy
    The last ditch
    1. Title
    823'.914[F]   PR6052   R25/
    ISBN 0–85640–258–3
    ISBN 0–85640–259–1 Pbk

© Roy Bradford, 1981

Published by Blackstaff Press Limited
3 Galway Park, Dundonald, BT16 0AN

Printed in Northern Ireland by
Belfast Litho Printers Limited

My Lord, my country is indeed in danger, but there is one way never to see it lost and that is to die in the last ditch.

William, Prince of Orange, rejecting the peace terms of the English invaders in 1672.

They had taken longer than expected to track down the informer. At the family's council house on the vast, bleak Cregagh Estate, they had drawn a blank. A local gave them a lead to a drinking club in the centre of Belfast. Eventually, they had picked him up at a nearby disco. Now, the battered Vauxhall Victor pulled up at a shuttered store in a side-street parallel to the main artery known as The Avenue. A dirty dim-lit desolate street, a mixture of back-to-back houses; some occupied, others blocked up waiting demolition, a couple of shops with boarded windows separated from the store by a burnt-out shell.

Four men got out of the car: first Blondie, thinning bleached hair framing the sharp face, then two helpers in jeans and jerkins holding the accused, who stood silent as Blondie opened the door with two keys, mortice and Yale. Cropped brown hair, the rubber-soled boots and ankle-length denims of the 'Skins', about nineteen. An urchin's face spotted with pustules, the top teeth protruding slightly. The brown eyes were hostile and bright. There was still an air of defiance about him. One of the helpers pushed him into the store, a converted shop piled with cartons of tinned goods. The door closed behind them as Blondie pulled two light switches and snibbed the Yale lock. They went through the front area into a back room stacked with cartons of vodka. The rear window was boarded up and secured with metal strips. A naked bulb shone harshly on the metal table, chairs, electric fire, and the dirty cups on top of a row of cupboards.

'Gimme the bag,' said Blondie.

A helper handed him a canvas grip which they brought with them. He unpacked it on the table – a blanket, thick nylon cord, an electric drill with a long length of cable. He dropped the bag on the floor and handed the cord to the helpers.

'Tie him up.'

At the sight of the electric drill, the accused had uttered a sudden whimper. His face went deathly white.

As they moved towards him he darted in panic for the door. He got halfway, and two vicious swipes from the heavily be-ringed fist of one of the helpers scored a gash under his eye and smashed his lower lip. He

1

lay moaning. The two men, both in their twenties, their faces flushed, shouted curses while they kicked him until Blondie called them off.

'Stop! The bastard's gotta talk.'

The accused had managed to shield his head from the worst of the blows. He was dragged, half-sobbing over the table. He could not see Blondie remove the electric fire and plug in the drill. Blondie moved to one of the cupboards, took out a bottle of whisky and tumblers which he filled well up. Giving one to each of his helpers he told them to drink up! They drained the glasses in one gulp. There was a loud knock on the front door. They froze and waited. Two distinct double knocks followed.

'It's Reg,' said Blondie, taking out a packet of cigarettes. 'Let him in.'

As Reg the Quartermaster entered, his eyes fell on the electric drill. He could not repress a groan.

'Aw Christ! Is that what you're up to?'

Blondie made no reply.

'Has he coughed?'

'Sure, we fuckin' know it was him! But he's got to admit it. Turn him over.'

The accused was lifted to a sitting position on the edge of the table. Blood oozed from his mouth and from the gash below one brown eye. The pimply face was very young and drained of expression. Some mother's son, brought up to hunt with the pack, hate with the tribe, bully the weak, bow to the strong – the old Christian codes of school and Sunday school had never impinged on his boyhood years. He had grown up with violence and murder. The loyalties of the street-gang, the soccer team and, once, of the organisation, were the highest he had ever spired to. But then they had beaten him for keeping a few quid he had collected from a pub, while all round him his superiors were driving cars and buying clothes for their girl-friends. He had got his own back. To come out the winner was the only credo of his desperate generation.

Reg caught him by the chin and shook him. 'What did you tell them?' The eyes dropped. Again nothing.

Blondie's face changed – the whole skin tightened. 'Leave him to me.'

He motioned to the helpers. They turned the accused face down on the table, unbuckled his studded belt, and pulled his grubby denims down below his knees. Blondie inserted a long thin bit into the drill and tightened the chuck. He pressed the trigger in the grip and the high-pitched whine cut the atmosphere like a knife. The effect on the accused was galvanic – he twisted round like a terrified animal. 'No. No. No.'

2

He was howling in broken bursts.

'What did they pay you? The Branch? What did you tell them?' The bit was now touching the skin at the back of the knee. He shrieked. 'No. No . . .' But the rest was muffled as the blanket was thrown round his head and Blondie, his face ecstatic, leaned on the drill. The point broke through the soft resilience of the skin and the bright blood from the popliteal artery spurted out under the bit as if propelled by the beat of the pulse. Under the blanket the screams rose and fell. The body squirmed and writhed like a snake, the volume of blood increasing all the time. But the helpers, grunting with a mounting excitement, held it down, one by the shoulders, the other pressing on the legs and buttocks. There was a strangled screech. The note of the drill changed as the steel slipped through the tendons and bit into the back of the knee-cap. Blondie gave a moan of feral fulfillment as the synovial fluid flowed out — the water mingled with the blood. Suddenly the gluteal muscles tightened. The blotchy buttocks heaved and sagged, exploding in a flood of molten faeces as the tortured bladder and bowels gave way. The stench hit their nostrils in a gust. Recoiling, the helpers let go their hold, and Blondie, cursing, lost his grip on the slippery trigger.

The whine stopped and in the momentary silence the bloody desecrated creature rolled over, moaning. Reg Nimmo, the Quartermaster, felt the burning vomit mount in his throat. The days when he had been a fitter in the foundry seemed light years away. There was a child's weak cry and the creature slumped off the table onto the floor. As it fell, a leather wallet, drenched in ordure, slipped from the hip-pocket of his crumpled denims. It was one of those made by the prisoners in the Maze, inscribed in poker-work 'For God and Country'.

It was coming up to 10.30 a.m., the regular time for the Thursday Cabinet meeting. As if in salute, the cantilevered security boom rose to admit each car on to the terrace in front of the Castle. As it did, the policeman on duty outside lifted his arm in casual unison. The vehicles swung round so that the passenger doors were next to the stone steps. Purposeful, lethargic, depending on how much importance they attached to their image, the ministers leapt out or laboriously detached themselves from the seats.

The Ford Granadas predominated; that of the Minister of Agriculture well streaked with mud, befitting a working farmer who already that morning had been half-way up a mountain inspecting sheep. The Daimler of the PM with the police escort Vauxhall was already parked against the grass verge – had been since 9.30. The Jaguar XJ12 of the Minister of Home Affairs earned a crisp salute at the barrier. Deemed because of his office to be more at risk than some of his colleagues, he was accompanied by a Special Branch man as well as the hand-picked police driver. Close behind followed a Vauxhall with two more Branch men on board.

There was a touch of panache in the way the Jag pulled up, with the detective out and opening his master's door almost before the spraying gravel had come to rest. The head of the Minister emerged, the columnar neck enclosed in a high white collar. Looking all of his forty-two years, the dark hair thinning at the temples and lined with grey, the jawline heavier than it should have been. But he held himself well, and below the slightly drooping lids the bold blue eyes illumined the whole face. This ex-rugby three-quarter was known as a snappy dresser, the shirts ordered from Turnbull in Jermyn Street, and the suit, Chester Barrie, but bought in his own constituency, a nice balance between personal vanity and practical politics. How often at meetings had he been greeted by admiring female supporters.

'Seen you on TV last week Mr Carson.'

'Oh yes, what was I talking about?'

'Och I dunno, but you were lookin' terrible well!'

Impact was half the battle and Desmond Carson had always held it as

4

a basic maxim that if you wanted people to listen, you had to predispose them to want to listen. Now he looked out quickly at the Castle steps. No reporters: it was officially just a routine meeting, but you never knew. He got out of the car slowly, brushing away cigarette ash, and waited for his colleague, Education, who had arrived at the same time and was hurrying over to meet him with just that hint of eagerness which established their relative positions on the greasy pole.

'Well Cecil, how was your meeting last night?' The enquiry was polite but uninterested. Cecil McFee smiled his smile of resignation and struck his forehead. He was given to gestures of a somewhat evangelical nature. His father was a lay preacher, and the son was constantly tossed between moral certainty and social insecurity.

'Need you ask? As soon as we set foot in the hall I could see what we were in for. Three rows at the back, and then two rows of them at the front and nearly every man-jack with a Bible, of course.'

They reached the top of the steps and the main glass doors opened.

'Did Arthur get a word in?' As of right, Desmond Carson marched straight through ahead of his colleague. In the entrance hall, the two messengers by the desk, clad in government navy blue with gold crowns on the lapels and the desirable strip of campaign ribbons, sang out together, 'Morning Ministers!'

They passed into the spacious lobby hung with Sir John Lavery landscapes of Tangier Bay, and his portrait of Craigavon.

'Arthur? Wait till you hear! As soon as he entered the hall, most of the audience jumped up, clapping like mad. The boyos, Wylie Mullins' lot with the Bibles, sat their ground of course, and you could hear a steady groundswell of "Traitor" and "Papish-Lover". They were really working themselves up and *I* was due to go on first.'

Carson turned to him with an amused smile.

'Yes,' McFee grinned. 'That's what I thought too. But the wee chairman – what's his name? The Christian business man?'

'Harrison.' Carson knew them all.

'That's him. Well, what does he do? As soon as the din settles a moment, hammers the table and asks them all to rise for prayer. So of course they had to get up and shut up. Well he prayed and he prayed. He prayed for Ulster. He prayed for guidance. He prayed for all present, and by the time he'd finished, they were punch-drunk with supplications!'

'So?'

'Well, he put the PM on immediately.'

5

'And they listened?' Carson's interest was waning.

'He read his script. Arthur's not the world's greatest in a rough-house, as you know, but he got away with it. Kept mumbling, which was a great help. Anyway . . .'

But Carson's mind was on other things. With a muttered excuse he hastened on into the inner hall where Tom Lefaux, the Minister for Information, was talking to his Private Secretary. He looked up expectantly as Carson approached.

'Have you heard anything?' He spoke quietly.

Carson shook his head.

'Nothing more this end,' said Lefaux. 'The PM is playing it very tight. All I know is what I told you last night. Home Affairs is definitely involved.'

'Thanks Tom,' said Carson, and squeezed his colleague's elbow. 'No doubt all will shortly be revealed.' And no doubt – he said to himself as he moved on – the event will be less dramatic than the build-up. So many of these storms blew up in official teacups. Yet Lefaux, a level-headed fellow, was worried. One would just have to play it by ear.

Ahead he spied Willie Burton, the Minister of Finance, who was trying to avoid his eye. He had a bone to pick with Master Willie!

'Morning Cecil.' Someone grabbed McFee's arm from behind. It was big Edmund Martin, Agriculture, who had just emerged from the cloakroom rubbing his hands on a handkerchief. 'Not a bloody towel in the place.' The broad red face split in a grin. 'It's you ecumenicals driving good Protestant staff away. It wouldn't have happened in the old days, I can tell you that.'

But McFee was serious and suddenly subdued. 'Look Mun, what's supposed to be happening today? Cabinet Office rang my secretary last night. Funny he never mentioned it?'

Mun Martin smiled again; the smile of someone in the know and who knows it. McFee stroked back a lock of his greying hair.

'It's a bit thick you know. My people have been working for weeks on this maintained schools scheme. The First Reading is already well behind schedule. I've got to get approval.'

'You've already got it, haven't you?' Mun's smile was tighter.

'What do you mean?'

'Well, I hear your friend the Cardinal is very happy. A hell of a lot happier than our people, I can tell you.'

'Oh, come on now, Mun . . .' McFee looked worried.

But the Minister of Agriculture had already broken on the blind side and was hailing the Minister of Trade, James Gillan. Disconsolate, McFee moved slowly towards the Cabinet room swinging his black brief-case as we went. As he passed, Willie Burton the Finance Minister turned uneasily from his soft-voiced but intense conversation with Des Carson, to nod and smile. Willie greeted everyone, always, in accordance with his deeply held conviction that you always need a man twice and you could never tell when that second time would be. Willie had not remained in the Cabinet under two Prime Ministers and after three re-shuffles without learning by rote the small print of survival. At that precise moment he would gladly have engaged McFee in small talk. Carson was pressing him: pressing him to express a definite view, to come out in public in support of tougher action by the police. Willie abhorred being tied down. With the fixed look of an agonised Atlas, he continued to nod gloomily and murmur. 'Yes, yes I know. It's difficult, difficult.'

Preoccupied, McFee acknowledged the greeting without a smile and continued on his way. The black brief-case, that mark of ministerial status which, like a metronome, swung in tune with his moods, felt more and more leaden with every step. Mun Martin was not only Agriculture. He was the grass-roots and he clearly didn't like the education deal. Mun, like Carson, was an old stager. McFee was a comparatively new creation, owing his place to the Prime Minister's need to surround himself with compliant and grateful adherents. Martin must be propitiated. He could be a real trouble-maker. Perhaps there might be an opportunity to go along with him in Cabinet, to butter him up. All the signs were that something was brewing up for today's meeting. Carson had been preoccupied, edgy. But why hadn't the PM given McFee a hint last night? Probably keeping his options open: otherwise, he would have had his supporting cast lined up long before now; a discreet word from the Cabinet Secretary, perhaps even a flattering invitation to drop into The Room for a drink round about six o'clock, the hour when the All-Highest permitted himself to relax with his personal staff. But there had been no approaches. It was worrying. Life was worrying. McFee entered the Cabinet Room, once the grand salon of Stormont Castle, now seat of the Government of Northern Ireland. A fire blazed in the massive dog-grate. From above the mantelpiece Disraeli, the apostle of One Nation, presided over the scene like some unlikely ikon.

When Carson entered the room, several of his colleagues were already at the table. Lefaux was checking a press hand-out with his

Secretary. Fred Butler, Minister of Labour, who had formerly been Carson's Parliamentary Secretary in Home Affairs, was stolidly puffing at his pipe, gazing out through the wide French windows at the smooth lawns with the conservatories beyond. An October day, calm and clear, in a world where God was in his heaven and the order of things seemed as perdurable as the sandstone blocks of which the Castle was built. A morose McFee was unstrapping the black brief-case in his accustomed place. He sat to the right of Home Affairs, who faced the Prime Minister.

'Cheer up Cecil! They tell me there *is* a life before death!' Carson smiled and clapped his colleague on the shoulder. Then he turned to have a diplomatic word with Fred Butler.

The room was filling up. James Gillan, the dark, darting little Minister of Trade and Development, came in, listening intently to Mun Martin. He paused to make a point as they came through the doors, and so avoided being overheard. They took their seats side by side, nodding briefly to Carson. Then Gillan exchanged greetings with each of the rest of his colleagues. It was a nicely judged correspondence of recognition which defined the pecking order of the various participants, a delicate dance on the Cabinet Table of Precedence. But Carson detected an extra bonus of bonhomie which made him think. Were these the overtures in another bid for the leadership? Did Gillan discern an opening that Carson was as yet unaware of? Every Cabinet discussion was a thinly disguised battle for supremacy. This one might well dispense with the camouflage.

As the company, in desultory order, settled round the long baize-covered table, the climax of the ritual, like the alarum in Shakespearean drama, sounded without, or rather in the adjoining room, the private sanctum of the Prime Minister. The well-muffled crash of a flushing lavatory, located in what he called his 'thunder-box' which had been installed exclusively for his personal and private use, presaged the arrival of Sir John Arthur Montgomery Packham, PC KCB, Her Majesty's First Minister of Northern Ireland. Minutes later, and the man himself appeared through one half of the French doors. He was followed by – a surprise this for most of those present – *the Attorney General* and as usual by Sir Stewart Taylor, the grey Cabinet Secretary, and his bright-eyed Assistant Secretary, Ronnie Fine. It was Fine who, referring to the Premier's habit of disappearing into his 'thunder-box' when he wished to postpone decisions, had said, 'My master, alas, tends to stall between two stools.' Fine was the script-writer, the re-drafter, the ideas man; Taylor the stabiliser, the shrewd counsellor, with that rare quality known in the trade as bottom.

Together with Billy, the veteran Party secretary, they functioned as a think-tank, central policy committee and Kitchen Cabinet to their jealous and unpredictable lord. As the four men entered the room, most of the ministers made the gesture of attempting to struggle to their feet.

With a brisk 'Good morning, gentlemen' and a 'Please . . .' Packham waved them to their seats and took his own in the elbow-chair at the centre of the table. No chit-chat at all. As they settled down, he studied the green folder which the Cabinet Secretary had placed before him. In the stillness which followed he removed his spectacles, rubbed his right eye and looked round the table.

'You are aware that the Secretary to the Cabinet has been discussing during the past week or so with officials of the Home Office, possible additional measures which we might consider adopting to deal with the growing unrest in the Province. These measures – a tightening up of the command structure of the police, a review of the present system for the allocation of council houses, some form of Complaints Commission or Ombudsman and so on – were set out in a memorandum and considered in Cabinet last Thursday. Discussions at official level with the Home Office, were, as I understood, proceeding smoothly and without undue disagreement.' He paused. Mun Martin caught the eye of James Gillan, Trade, beside him on the right and swiftly looked away. There was a general fidgeting. Only Carson stared fixedly at the wall behind the Prime Minister's head. He could feel it intuitively – bad news. Tapping his left hand with his gold ball-point pen as he carefully chose his words, the PM continued.

'Then yesterday evening at about 5 o'clock, I had a personal call from the Home Secretary. They had just held a special Cabinet meeting in Downing Street and he had been asked by the Prime Minister to convey to me the conclusions they had arrived at. He then asked me to scramble and I instructed the Cabinet Secretary to listen on the extension, and to make a verbatim note of the conversation. What I shall tell you now, is the gist of what he said.' He stopped for a moment. 'I have to tell you, gentlemen, that we are faced with an ultimatum.'

Round the table the faces turned towards him, all except those of Gillian and Mun Martin seated side by side to the Prime Minister's left. It was clear to Carson that they knew something. McFee was so tense that the pen he was fiddling with dropped with a thud on the table. In some confusion he recovered it. The PM lifted his head and spoke

9

deliberately. 'First, they propose to remove nearly all our powers in the field of security and of administration of justice.' Brows furrowed in disbelief. 'They intend to vest control of the police in the Home Secretary.' Round the table, faces reddened. There were disjointed mouthings of incredulity. Gillan and Martin exchanged a long, hard look.

The PM held up his hand to still the murmur of indignation. 'They have decided to,' he searched for a word, 'stand down the B Specials and replace them some kind of gendarmerie under Army control.' He paused, conscious of the impact of his words. 'That, in essence, is what they require us to agree to.'

From the less self-assured members of his Cabinet there came grunts of stage defiance. Carson, Home Affairs, the man whose fief was directly threatened, sat tight-lipped. His eyes switched around the table to check reactions. There are two ways of swinging a Cabinet discussion. One is to bide one's time, let the others have their say, and then when – in Asquith's phrase – the argument takes on a favourable curve, intervene and whip it hard for the finishing post. The other way is to move in right away with total conviction and with such persuasive logic that the opposition is forced on to the defensive, hesitates, and is lost.

For the moment Carson was letting the hare sit. He had not bargained for this. He needed time. Gillan was better prepared. He had thought hard about how to play it, ever since, just sixteen hours previously, his own special tendril on the Castle grape-vine had alerted him that crisis was in the wind. Surely Packham, for all his agility, must be wrong-footed this time.

The Prime Minister too, was letting the hare sit. That was his form by nature. He was a Fabian, a delayer. Coldly he observed his Cabinet in their mental splutter, reacting emotionally, trying to work out the implications of what they had just heard. It was Mun who kicked off.

'Prime Minister, I'm sure I speak for everyone round this table, when I say that I find it hard to believe my ears. That we should be faced with this ultimatum – you certainly used the right word – is nothing short of outrageous, monstrous! It is clear to me that they are employing some kind of shock tactics in order to soften us up. So I take it, Prime Minister, that this is a kind of package of which the ingredients are negotiable?'

Slowly the Prime Minister shook his head from side to side. 'No, Minister. No. So far as Downing Street is concerned, it was made quite clear to me that the British Government sees no grounds for discussion on what they regard as a firm policy decision.' He turned to the Cabinet Secretary seated at the small table behind him. 'Stewart?'

Sir Stewart Taylor leaned forward deferentially adjusting his glasses as he did so. 'Yes sir, I'm afraid that the officials at the Home Office were at pains to stress that the proposals were to be regarded as a firm . . . request.'

Mun Martin stared at him. 'Request? Aye the way I request a load of bullocks to come down to the abattoir.' He didn't smile. Nobody smiled. 'It's just not on, Prime Minister. The country won't stand for it. There'd be a massacre. If we let them take away the police, *and* the Special, *and* the courts, what authority have we? We may as well shut up shop. We can forget about law and order. We'll have completely, completely lost every shred of credibility. The thing's monstrous. It's . . . it's unbelievable. I cannot see how any British Parliament will go along with undermining a democratically elected government.' He stopped and glanced at the faces opposite him: Tom Lefaux, the plump equable Minister of Information, McFee, Carson, and Fred Butler who avoided his eyes. He was losing them and he sensed it. Angry with himself, he became truculent. 'As far as I'm concerned, Prime Minister, it's totally unacceptable. It's time we dug our heels in.' He looked round again seeking endorsement. Gillan nodded emphatic agreement. McFee, caught unawares, smiled nervously in sympathy.

Over beyond the Prime Minister, Willie Burton gave an agonised toss of his head that could have conveyed anything from despairing dissent to whole-hearted accord – Willie was waiting for the PM to show him the way. Des Carson was next. He had decided to take the bull by the horns. But cautiously, knowing how vulnerable was his position if he lost his cool.

'The Minister of Home Affairs,' intoned the Prime Minister.

Carson cleared his throat. 'I am sure, Prime Minister, we all share the sense of shock expressed so well by the Minister of Agriculture, for let us make no mistake about it, what these proposals amount to is nothing less than the abolition of the government of Northern Ireland, and a total disregard for the democratically expressed will of its people.' For a moment his voice instinctively rose, anticipating and invoking the burst of approval from the back of the hall.

McFee was moved to murmur, 'Hear, hear'.

Gillan sat impassive . . . how was he going to top this?

'It saddens me,' said Carson, 'that any British Government should

11

not only contemplate such an imposition, but should apparently feel confident of carrying it through. I would be grateful for the Attorney's view on the constitutional position, but I myself am strongly of the opinion that this kind of unilateral edict is *ultra vires.*' He looked at Crossley, but the Attorney General was doodling on the pad in front of him and his face seemed, if anything, to convey dissent. 'Certainly Sir Ivor Jennings, in his work on the Constitution, takes the view that in matters affecting law, order, and good government, the Parliament of Northern Ireland is sovereign. In attempting to abrogate our powers in this field, the British Government is clearly acting unconstitutionally, and we should tell them so.'

'The country won't stand for it,' burst in Mun Martin, who had been working himself up over what he regarded as a lot of legal clap-trap. '*That's* the point. Not the constitutional position. What we should be doing now is not arguing the toss, all the pros and cons about *ultra vires*, but deciding what we're going to do about it. We're sittin' here and . . .'

'Just a moment, Minister,' the PM cut in firmly. 'Just a moment. We've heard your views. And no doubt we'll hear them again' He gestured across the table to Carson. 'Home Affairs? Have you . . .' The sharp rebuff to Martin was a straw in the wind which was lost on no one.

Carson, half-smiling. 'Thank you, PM. Two points. First, I think it *is* important to have some idea of the thinking behind this extraordinary list of demands – what do they hope to achieve by them? Secondly, I take it they hope to use us as cats-paws, bearing the brunt of the reaction and pretending that the decisions are in fact ours?' He stopped and waited for the Prime Minister to reply.

'As regards your first point, Minister, I shall try to deal with it in a few moments . . . in so far as I am in a position to do so. As for your second point, we have been given the firm impression that if *we* don't act, they will.'

'Very well,' said Carson, 'in which case we must play it cool. The demands they make on us would be unacceptable at any time. In the present climate, they are totally divorced from political reality. We need time to consider our position and to mobilise our forces. We, therefore, must insist on a meeting with the Prime Minister, certainly with the Home Secretary, to seek further elucidation. Such a meeting they can hardly refuse since – assuming even that we were willing to go along with the changes . . .'

'What?' snorted Mun Martin, rather overdoing the drama. Beside him, Gillan found it necessary to frown heavily in solidarity with Mun, though as yet, he himself was entirely preoccupied, deciding on the best initial line to take.

'I said, *even assuming* that we were willing to accept, there would have to be further discussion on how to implement such fundamental changes.' He was spelling it out, as to a child. 'Therefore, I was saying, they cannot refuse to meet us. That gives us breathing space, and time to get into a dealing situation.' He turned to Mun. 'That's the point I was making. Right? I trust the Minister of Agriculture didn't seriously think that I was advocating surrender!' He gave Mun a smile with just a tinge of condescension, and leaned back in his seat. He had given nothing away. He had spoken firmly and he had made them think without shutting down any options.

Both Willie Burton and Fred Butler gave him emphatic nods of approval. Willie Burton had made his little obeisance to a potential leader, but also to a contribution which he gratefully interpreted as committing no one to anything. Butler, as a former Parliamentary Secretary in Home Affairs, had in some measure adopted the role of faithful retainer, relying heavily at times on Carson's good offices within the Party. The son of an Englishman, Fred Butler was conscious of the need for such a hybrid strain to cling closely to the strong stock of Orange orthodoxy. So he jumped in, convinced that he was landing on firm ground.

'I think our colleague can put his mind at rest. The last thing we would associate with the Minister of Home Affairs is surrender. And I know that he will agree with me one hundred per cent when I say that the last thing we could even contemplate is surrendering the Specials!' At once, there was a spontaneous and solid growl of support right round the table, with only two exceptions – the Prime Minister and the Attorney General. On this favourable wind, Butler sailed on. 'We all know the Specials are the backbone of our security. They're the one thing the IRA are afraid of. They know the countryside. They know the people. And they know how to shoot! Our people rely on them. Prime Minister, to think of disbanding the Specials would be political suicide. The Party just won't stand for it.' He was running out of steam but pressed on, the lurking Lancashire vowels more and more marked under stress. 'Any road, quite apart from that, where are you going to recruit the alternative? Do you think the Catholics are going to rush into this new force they're talking of setting up? Huh!' His grunt of dismissive disdain would have warmed the heart of any Orange gathering. 'You'll get the same men volunteering once again for the new force – if you're lucky, if they're not so disgusted at the way they've been treated that they decide to take the law into their own hands – and sometimes I, for one, wouldn't blame them!'

The Prime Minister frowned and looked hard at his Minister of Labour. The Attorney General jerked his head in sharp disapproval. Carson raised his eyebrows, but with a reassuring smile.

For Butler had gone too far. He was not in his Orange Lodge now. Hastily he went on. 'It's a real danger, Prime Minister, and one that we must take account of. Once men are freed from the restraints of service discipline, anything can happen. You and I know that, Prime Minister.'

'Yes, yes, but the Special Constabulary is, after all, a part-time force, an emergency force.' Arthur Packham, ex-Brigade of Guards, hardly concealed his distaste at being bracketed with the Royal Army Education Corps in which his colleague had once served.

'They may be part-time, but they're loyal, Prime Minister, they're loyal. They can be trusted. I say again' – he was finishing on a high note – 'at this time, to disband the Specials would be political suicide and we as a government shouldn't touch it with a barge pole.' Anxiously Butler looked round for favourable reaction. His contribution had been received with less than rapture. He should have stopped the first time he mentioned the 'B' Specials. Carson alone gave him an encouraging nod. That was what friends were for.

The Prime Minister moved into the hiatus. 'Perhaps it would be helpful if, as Home Affairs suggested, I outline what I believe to be the reasoning behind this . . . this series of demands from Her Majesty's Government. We have known for some time that they were far from satisfied with the present system of control of the security forces. Instead of the Cabinet Security Committee, chaired, as you know, by the Minister of Home Affairs,' he inclined his head briefly towards the man sitting opposite him, 'and attended by the Inspector General and the GOC, the Ministry of Defence have been pressing for a greater measure of overall control to be given to the army. This pressure is partly due to the familiar allegations made by our opponents – that the police are a sectarian force, undisciplined and unacceptable to the minority etc, etc – but it is also due to the fact that we are not getting results.' He held up his hand pacifically as Carson frowned and made to answer. 'I am making no criticism, no criticism. I am simply stating the facts, that we are not getting on top of the IRA – in fact the situation, as we know, has been deteriorating. For that, we must all share the responsibility.'

'So they restore the situation by totally demoralising the police forces!' Carson was bitterly on the defensive. He could not take this lying down. He went on: 'And how, Prime Minister, does taking over the judiciary improve matters?'

The Prime Minister paused and fanned out his hands in resignation. 'The whole package, I suppose, must be regarded as "the new initiative", which those hostile to us, both at home and in Westminster, have been demanding more and more insistently. The British Government is not prepared to give us a free hand. They refuse to allow the army to do so. They insist on maintaining a bi-partisan approach in the House of Commons. That means waffle. So faced with charges of inaction, of fiddling while Belfast burns, they unveil what they will wish to present as a radical transformation of the whole security scene. The areas of controversy: judicial appointments, sentencing, the direction of the police and army on the ground, is to be taken out of our hands. Thereby, they hope to mollify our opponents, win the allegiance of the minority, and, having demonstrated that all is sweetness and bi-partisan light, mobilise a united Ulster against the IRA. You will forgive the irony, gentlemen. Nevertheless that is, I believe, how they envisage the . . . I believe it's called the scenario.'

There was a moment's silence. Carson lit a cigarette. Willie Burton cleared his throat, nerving himself to take the plunge. He had to speak soon or forfeit all claim to precedence as a senior minister.

But McFee, who had been showing increasing signs of emotional agitation during the Prime Minister's remarks, burst in before him. 'Prime Minister, I am appalled. I am *appalled*. I ask myself. What have we done to deserve this? Have we refused to introduce changes? Of course we haven't! Everyone round this table knows that we have pushed through reforms against the stiffest opposition in our own Party. And got little thanks for it! You and I, Prime Minister, had enough evidence of that at the meeting last night – we were in Lisburn, in what used to be an absolutely solid Unionist area, and the Prime Minister was hardly allowed to speak, *hardly allowed to speak*!' As he repeated the phrase he nodded emphatically to each of his colleagues to underline the enormity of the incident.

But it was apparent to the practised observer that Arthur Packham did not entirely relish this suggestion of waning popularity. 'Oh the usual Mullins yobbos – we know them, we know them,' he said testily.

McFee redeemed himself quickly. 'If I may say so, Prime Minister, you handled the situation magnificently.' He turned to each side of the table. 'He really took them on and shut them up. You certainly did, PM, you certainly did. But that just makes my point. How have we got to this pretty pass? Because for months we have been taking the brunt of the criticism and the British Government has been getting the credit! Not that we're looking for thanks, but we do expect a little recognition of the realities of the situation. Can't they see that the Republicans are just as much against them, as against us? We have been fighting the UK's battle all along. Can't they see that if it's Belfast bombed today, it could be Birmingham tomorrow? We've just got to make them see sense. If they insist on going through with this, the situation will be ten times worse. We must do the right thing. We must not surrender or shrink from our responsibilities. No one ever came to harm doing the right thing. If we stick to our guns, the country will back us, Prime Minister. I know they have the whip-hand, but never mind. We, Prime Minister must do what we *believe* . . . is right!' He sank back, as though virtue had gone out of him.

Arthur Packham turned to Shane Crossley, the Attorney General, seated at the end of the table. During the previous contributions, the bald head had been bowed as he made notes with an old-fashioned fountain pen. His only reactions had been those of dissent – the occasional frown or deliberate shake of the head. He was not normally present at Cabinet meetings, only when legal or constitutional matters of importance were being discussed. 'The position of the British Government has been raised several times. Can you tell us, Attorney, just how strong is the constitutional ground on which they appear to be standing? I think we should know that before we go any further.' There was a general murmur of agreement.

Shane Crossley had made his name at the Bar as an advocate rather than as a jurist, a lawyer's lawyer. Despite the distaste he affected for the business of politics, he was a most assiduous constituency Member, attending meetings, social gatherings, cultivating his officers through small gifts and favours for their friends, even lunching them at his club, a social milieu which most of them would never have aspired to. Crossley knew the levers. He knew the gossip and the shifting popularity ratings of his colleagues. He knew, too, that they knew that his sole ambition was to get on to the High Court Bench. Meanwhile, his colleagues suspected that he maintained a strongly pro-British Government line because it was with the Lord Chancellor that preferment lay. The broad, mobile face was suitably grave, as he nodded deferentially to the Prime Minister.

'The powers of Her Majesty's Government in relation to Northern

16

Ireland are quite clear, specific and unequivocal. They are set out in the Government of Ireland Act 1920.' He lifted a red-backed booklet lying in front of him. 'I have it here. This Act established the State and Parliament of Northern Ireland. The Parliament was given a general power to make laws for the peace . . .' He paused. ' "The *peace*, order and good government of the state, subject to certain specific reservations, conditions and safeguards, in particular relating to the Armed Forces, the Crown and international relations." But from the point of view of our present discussion, the relevant Section of the Act is Section 75. I quote: "the supreme authority of the Parliament of the United Kingdom shall remain unaffected and undiminished over all persons, matters and things in Northern Ireland and every part thereof".' He had read the words slowly, and with great emphasis. 'In other words, Westminster is sovereign. We are a subordinate government and in any conflict, subject to, and bound by, the decision of the Government of the United Kingdom.' His words – spoken with authority – had a depressant effect.

After a moment Carson spoke, injecting into his voice a confidence which he hoped was convincing: 'But surely, precedent is important. Sir Ivor Jennings is quite definite in stating that precedent in similar situations throughout the Commonwealth is against central government over-ruling the local parliament. And surely Westminster cannot remove our powers under the 1920 Act without our consent.' He realised he was on shaky ground.

Crossley showed just a flicker of irritation. How long would he have to spell out the basic grammar of political life to those who regarded themselves as 'A' Level?

'I have read Jennings. My view is that none of the precedents which he cites has any relevance to the issue before us. The 1920 Act from which I have just quoted, was enacted by the United Kingdom Parliament. They can change it, repeal it, re-enact it, do as they will with it. They have "Supreme Authority". They no more need our consent than they do to pass a Drainage Bill. That is the reality. But we have a precedent which is, I think, instructive. In 1931, Craigavon, the Prime Minister of Northern Ireland, clashed with the British Government over a matter of rates. In that confrontation he recognised the reality and . . . kissed the rod. As he said at the time, the only alternative was to leave the Kingdom, make in fact a Unilateral Declaration of Independence.'

It was the opening the Prime Minister had been waiting for. He took his time. 'Thank you, Attorney. I don't think you need expand on that any further. You have put the choice before us very clearly. If we reject these proposals out of hand, we could find ourselves on a road leading to a head-on collision with Her Majesty's Government. We could find ourselves in a constitutional crisis of the gravest kind, the consequences of which it would be impossible to foresee. Such a crisis on top of our present economic difficulties would be disastrous for the country. We must act responsibly, gentlemen.'

He stopped. That was enough for the time being. A lead but not too binding a lead, one that left room for manoeuvre. He wanted first to see what way Gillan, his Minister of Trade, would go. Give him enough rope and he might just put the noose in the right place. He turned to his left where his colleague was moving his mouth convulsively, a sort of chewing action, which he unconsciously indulged in when he was agitated. But Willie Burton, with a stammer of relief, was already snatching up his master's bait.

'Prime Minister, I entirely agree. Above all else, we must act responsibly. As Unionists we cannot defy the Queen in Parliament. If we did that, we would be completely undermining our moral position. We'd be nothing but rebels, rebels. On the other hand, if we accept these demands, we are cutting our own throat, because I cannot see the Party or the country accepting them. It's been bad enough selling the new housing scheme, not to speak of defending the security situation. We've got to take our time, Prime Minister. You put your finger on it when you said that we must, at all costs, avoid getting into confrontation with HMG, because that's one we can't win. I know, I know. Some of you are shaking your heads, but you heard what the Attorney said. They hold all the cards. If we take them on, we're heading for humiliation either way – a total climb down or . . . or . . . we resign.'

The word 'resign' dropped on the Cabinet table like an unspeakable excrement. Each in his own way, the men at the table backed away, shuffling papers, muttering to the immediate neighbour. Willie had uttered it. And his Prime Minister was well satisfied. The warning shot had been fired. That should sober them up and bring the stragglers to heel. Aware of, and gratified by, the unexpected impact of his words, Willie continued to align himself on the side of the angels.

'So, I don't see that we have much choice. We shall just have to try and go along with them. Having made it absolutely clear just exactly where we stand. That's the way I see it.' Willie subsided with relief. He, no more than his listeners, had really any idea of exactly where he stood. Except that, for the moment, he stood by the PM – he stood by his bread and butter. Nobody was in the slightest surprised.

It was Gillan's turn to speak. They had all been waiting for him, especially Carson and the PM. To the first, he was simply the rival, the man he had to beat to get to the top. To the latter, he was the conspirator: able, scheming and omnipresent. All three shared the same presentiment – that matters inexorably were coming to a head. In the background sat the Assistant Cabinet Secretary, Ronnie Fine, his antennae quivering to all kinds of signals, already planning his master's tactics after the Cabinet meeting, for the battle he was certain would come. So all eyes were on Gillan: the sleek dark head, streaked with grey; the eyes, the mouth, never in repose. He began, matter-of-fact, a man in control of events. Carson appeared to be scribbling disinterestedly on the pad before him.

'I am sure we all share the sense of outrage so well expressed by the Minister of Agriculture and by the Minister of Education. The whole manner of the British Government, in springing these demands on us without a word of warning, is not only in breach of the normal courtesies as between governments, but in a matter so vital as this is downright disgraceful!'

'Hear, hear,' echoed round the table. He was striking the right note from the word go. 'Having said that, I ask myself whether we are not over-estimating the strength of Downing Street? If we stand firm, I do not think for one moment that they have the nerve to push it through. They may seem to be attacking us at the point where we are most vulnerable, because our opponents have chosen the legal system and the security forces as the main targets of their most virulent criticism. But it is precisely the ability to maintain law and order and protect its citizens which is the very essence of a government's authority. And it is control of the forces needed to fulfil that task, which distinguishes a government from a County Council. The Prime Minister has said that we are not getting results against the terrorist. We are not getting results, because we have not got control, real control of the security forces – the Army, instead of backing us up, is hamstrung by the Ministry of Defence.'

Again a murmur of warm approval led by Mun Martin. Carson doodled impassively on.

'The Party, inside the House and outside it, are aware of this, and they are restless. I'm sure we all deplore the kind of reception which the Prime Minister got last night in Lisburn, but it's an indication of the state of feeling in the party and in the country. They are looking for a strong lead and we have got to provide it for them. If they get a lead, they will back us to the hilt. They will see this ultimatum from Downing Street for what is is – an attempt to castrate this government, to take away the instruments of our authority, and reduce us to puppets dangling on Westminster's string. That is why I cannot go along with the Minister of Home Affairs, when he talks of getting into a dealing situation. On the issue of whether we continue to govern or abdicate our authority, there can be *no* compromise! Surely, Home Affairs, you can see that, if we allowed this through, your Ministry would virtually cease to exist! So far as I'm concerned, let us seek no meetings with the Prime Minister or with anyone else. I believe . . .' he dropped his voice and spoke with dramatic slowness, 'I believe that they are trying to manoeuvre us into a corner. They see us either capitulating or . . . resigning – as Finance was shrewd enough to perceive. In either event, they assume effective total control. But there is a third choice . . .' He was certainly dominating the table. The eyes of the Prime Minister were even more hooded than usual, his demeanour that of a chairman waiting impatiently to get on the next business. Gillan was now in his 'strong man' role, giving a lead.

'It is this. We stand our ground. As my friend here said – we dig our heels in. We go public, put it to the country, explain our stance and tell Downing Street in the most dignified, responsible way, that we refuse to commit suicide, and that we, as the democratically elected government of this country, supported by the vast majority of its citizens, have no intention of abandoning our posts.'

Mun Martin was exultant, broadly smiling. 'That's more like it. Yes, sir!' There was, indeed, an involuntary straightening of backs round the table, a mood of prognathous determination. Carson acknowledged it with clinical appreciation.

Gillan was certainly laying it on – *and* taking the waverers with him. Now he was into his peroration. 'Gentlemen, this is an issue on which we cannot give way. As Craigavon said in 1925' – his expression changed to one of grim resolution, 'and I quote him with all the seriousness at my command, "We give nothing . . . not an inch".' He held his pose, leaning across the table, his eyes roving slowly across the faces. He had them. At his table, Ronnie Fine savoured the moment. It was quite a little tour de force. From Martin, McFee, Fred Butler, there was a rumble of affirmation.

Willie glanced to his left – his chief remained impassive – Willie remained silent. The line-up was emerging. Carson looked pensive – he would have to come in again.

Only one man had not yet spoken – Tom Lefaux the Minister of Information and Acting Chief Whip. He hardly needed to, for this plump astute ex-journalist – a brief spell on a provincial Co Antrim paper before establishing his own advertising and PR company– owed his political start and subsequent advancement to the Packham interest. But whether they liked him or not, depending on their own allegiance, his colleagues agreed that he earned his keep. Throughout the troubles he had managed to keep on cordial terms with media of all political persuasions. If Lefaux wanted coverage, he got it, though, as he once said, the number of bar-hours he had clocked up would have totted up to a Johnnie Walker Centenary!

His master turned to him now: 'Information, have you anything to add?'

'Well, Prime Minister, our colleagues have covered most of the angles, but what has been made very clear to me – I go along with Home Affairs on this – is that this is something we cannot rush. I frankly have not yet made up my mind as to the best course. But of this I'm sure – this is a make or break situation for us as a government. To take a decision on a matter as crucial and all-important as this, we need breathing space – to find out how far Downing Street is prepared to push this. How does the Parliamentary Party stand? I need time to talk to our colleagues. How far will the constituencies back us if we act tough?'

'The whole way,' said Mun Martin emphatically.

'You say so,' went on Lefaux, 'but I'd like to be sure, before I took that road. Once we embark on it, we want to be damned certain that we have the back-up to carry it through. Have we the money to run this country if we cut the traces? It's a solemn thought, gentlemen, and I am not in a position to take that kind of snap decision at this moment. I don't think that any of us are.'

He had dampened down the mood of euphoria which had seemed to exist after the Gillan intervention. His Prime Minister approved. Packham authoritatively took up the reins.

'I think we'd all agree that that's sound sense. I don't propose to try and sum up this discussion. We've had first reactions, understandably heated in some cases, in view of the unprecedented nature of the situation which faces us. But first reactions need not always be the best-advised.'

He was lulling them now, in well-modulated, sedative phrases. 'Let us sleep on it, and meantime, I shall have a quiet word with the Party Chairman, without – and I emphasise this – without being specific as to

21

the precise nature or extent of the proposals – simply a radical shift of control of the security forces, I shall call it. What has been discussed here this morning is on the basis of the strictest confidentiality and I would ask you, therefore, to be especially careful that this time there are no leaks. If, before we, as a Cabinet, have decided on how we are going to face up to this situation, there is any premature disclosure of what is in the wind, then the consequences could be disastrous.' He removed his glasses and looked unwinkingly round the circle of his colleagues, driving the point home. There was a slightly embarrassed silence. Leaks from that room had not, in the past, been unknown; even on matters of the highest classification.

Lefaux spoke. 'You can be sure we accept the need for the tightest secrecy, Prime Minister. In view of that, I must tell you all, that the Press have already got some idea that a new British initiative is on the way. I have already mentioned this to the Prime Minister.' He glanced warily at his chief, who nodded confirmation. 'I was concerned when, just before Cabinet this morning, I had a call from the *Guardian* who was obviously following up a lead from London. He had nothing harder than "a new initiative". I was able, in all conscience, to assure him that so far as I was concerned, there was nothing to it, but the fact that he was so insistent convinced me that someone had been pointing him in a certain direction. To cover myself, I told him that there might be something in this renewed chat about an all-Party conference, but to kept it firmly off the record. I am saying, in fact, that they have, as yet, no suspicion of the real issue, but they're sniffing vigorously. So the name of the game is extreme vigilance, kick for touch on everything.'

There was some fidgeting movement round the table, as several of his colleagues assumed an expression of Sphinx-like inscrutability. But Carson was clearly unhappy.

He knew that Crossley's cold exposure of the constitutional reality had dented his authority. His rival's posture had been much more clear-cut. The damage had got to be repaired at once.

'Surely, Prime Minister,' – his tone demanded attention – 'since the story could break at any time, we cannot leave this meeting without any decision whatsoever. This government has honourably tried to discharge its responsibilities. There is no need for breast-beating. All right, I accept the Attorney's view that, in a constitutional confrontation with Downing Street, we go naked into the council chamber. So did Craigavon in 1931. But there's no need for a strip-tease, no need to revel in our lack of cover. It's psychologically wrong. It's bad for morale in the country. Above all, it's unnecessary. So what do we do? I believe that we must open up contact at once. We make it clear that we are willing to consider any reasonable changes in control of the police. We are prepared to negotiate, but we shall not negotiate with a pistol at our head.' He stopped, looking straight at the Prime Minister and waited. There was a silence.

Fred Butler jumped in. 'Yes, I agree. Either we say no or we try to get them to negotiation. Isn't that the long and short of it?'

No-one else spoke. Gillan and his ally, Martin, had been caught off balance. Carson's re-entry had been unexpected. Now that they had the full facts, they needed time to assess and assemble their troops.

Each of the others was too concerned about his own personal position, and how best to protect it now that the wind had started to blow, and looked like reaching Gale Force before it would be all over. The Prime Minister cleared his throat. He had known it was going to be a difficult meeting. He had been prepared for some hard pounding. In the event, he had got through amazingly smoothly. He had known that his Minister of Trade would try to wrong-foot him. Carson had not been too unhelpful, despite the fact that it was his department which was principally under threat. No, he had never felt under intolerable pressure, despite some bad moments. He would live to fight another day. Wind it up. Decisions would have to be taken, crucial decisions, but not here. He donned his glasses, looked round in elaborate interrogation.

'I should be very happy to continue this discussion if my colleagues so desire. There seems, however, to be a general feeling that we cannot take it any further at this moment. I think that is the wisest course. I propose to call another Cabinet for tomorrow morning, when we shall have to arrive at an agreed line. I shall endeavour, in the meantime, to find out as much as I can of the thinking in the Home Office in London. We should then be in a better position to determine whether there is any possibility of modifying the proposals – as the Minister of Home Affairs has suggested.'

This deference to Carson's views was not lost on his colleagues, especially since it was directly opposed to the Gillan thesis of 'no surrender'. Fred Butler's relief that his man's stock had risen again, showed in a pudgy smirk.

'As soon as we have reached decisions, it is essential to bring our colleagues along with us. I took the precaution of asking the Party Secretary to call a provisional meeting of Parliamentary Party for

23

tomorrow afternoon. Can I stress again the need for total discretion? I think that is all for the moment. Thank you, gentlemen.' He rose, gathered up his folder, smiled an all-embracing benevolent smile, and turned towards his sanctum. Then, as if by an afterthought, he stopped at the end of the table beside the Attorney. 'Oh, can I have a word with you, Shane?' Ronnie Fine scurried ahead to open the double doors. The Prime Minister; his Attorney; Stewart Taylor; and Fine, ducking apologetically, as if he should not be part of such a distinguished company, disappeared into the Prime Ministerial suite. The doors closed behind them.

At once there was a brouhaha of banter and forced jokiness from those who remained.

'There's a turn-up for the book. Looks like they're trying to make you redundant, Des!' said Willie.

Carson smiled grimly. 'Yes, I'll get you to handle my compensation claim.' Willie was by profession a loss adjuster.

Mun Martin, who had been talking in low tones with Gillan, broke away and took Willie by the arm. 'Oh Willie, can I have a word with you sometime?' Willie winced. He knew full well what was afoot. He was going to be got at, pressured, persuaded into believing that his true interests lay with the Gillan camp. Curiosity and apprehension contended within his soul.

On his side of the table, McFee observed Lefaux and Des Carson in serious exchange, with Fred Butler hovering on the fringe. Once again on his own, unwooed, unwanted, McFee was conscious of a sense of anti-climax. This thunderbolt intelligence from Westminster. The world shaking around them and yet nothing had changed. The conspiracies, the little intrigues, the shifting pattern of allegiances still danced across the Cabinet table. Why was no one whispering to *him*? Like a man in a position of authority, who had never been offered a bribe, he felt it as a reflection on his power to deliver. He sighed and bent over to buckle the straps on his brief-case. A hand touched his shoulder. 'Bad show, Cecil. We're in trouble. I'd like to talk to you about it. Can you spare a moment sometime?' It was Gillan. Gillan, who never did more than pass the time of day with him, was looking for his support.

'Sure James, sure,' he said, casually. He was no longer on the touchline.

As the door to the Cabinet room closed behind him, Arthur Packham put his arm on the Attorney General's shoulder. 'Well Shane, what did you think of that? Eh? That little shit thinks he's back in 1912. "Not an inch", if you please. He'll be drawing up another Ulster covenant – to be signed in orange juice no doubt!' His entourage grinned dutifully. 'What'll you have, Scotch, isn't it?' On a satinwood table at the end of the room stood the usual array of bottles and cut glass. 'Sit down.' He indicated the long cream-coloured sofa in front of the fire – logs from the Castle woods. He himself sank into the armchair on the left hand side of the chimney. Behind him was a window that looked out across the lawn towards the Antrim hills.

Ronnie Fine was going out through the second door that led into the adjoining office, when Packham called to him. 'Tell Billy I want to see him in about ten minutes.' Fine nodded, smiled and left the room. 'Yes Shane, that's what I want to ask you,' said Packham. 'What is the position if we did dig our heels in and refuse to resign?' Taylor handed each man a whiskey and poured in the water from a bulbous silver jug.

Crossley took a sip. 'Assuming that they had suspended Stormont?'

'Well, what would the sequence be?'

'First, a very short Bill repealing the 1920 Act and instituting direct rule from Westminster, probably with a separate Secretary of State for Northern Ireland. If we tried to continue in office and administer the country, we should be an illegal government, in rebellion. I don't think they would attempt to arrest us or occupy public buildings with the army. They wouldn't have to.'

'Why not?'

'Messy and unnecessary. Simply turn off the financial tap. All kinds of sanctions they could impose, without using force. In any case, I don't think the senior civil servants would wear it for a moment. Quite apart from their oath of allegiance to the Crown, their pensions would be at risk – we couldn't guarantee them.'

Packham sipped his drink reflectively, and put it down on the table at his elbow. 'I thought as much. But he knows it's just the kind of hard-line, atavistic stuff that goes down well in Armagh.'

'And on the Protestant Shankill,' added Crossley.

'Yes, the old independence, anti-British, "Ulster will fight and Ulster will be right" mentality is never far below the surface. What makes him dangerous, is that I believe he actually suffers from the dementia himself. Real Unionists are scarce enough in Northern Ireland, and in the Unionist Party, a very small minority!' Packham stared moodily into the fire for some moments. 'It's going to be a hell of a job . . . even

25

attempting to sell this package.'

'Yes,' said Crossley. 'I can see that. Especially the Special Constabulary. They're part of the Ulster mythology and that's a dangerous thing to tamper with. If I may suggest something . . .?'

'Of course.'

'Why don't you try a little bluff – counter-bluff if you like, for as someone said, they may well be testing our nerve. Build up the possibility of a massive Protestant back-lash. In such a situation the forced resignation of the government could lead to anarchy. You could never be a party to it . . . and so on. See what they say to that. At least it will test the measure of their resolve. It's either that or piecemeal capitulation.'

'I agree. We have little choice.' Packham turned to his Cabinet Secretary who was busy with papers at a small writing table in the corner. 'Stewart, could you . . .' A nod was enough. Stewart Taylor rose and left the room closing the door quietly behind him. 'Shane.' Packham leaned forward towards his colleague and fixed him with a steady look. 'There's one other option we haven't mentioned.' Crossley raised his eyebrows. 'Even I cannot sell the unsaleable. You can't really see me presiding over a puppet show, can you?'

'Good God, Arthur. I never dreamt that you were thinking along those lines. Surely we are not anywhere near that point yet?'

Packham smiled. 'Gillan thinks we are. Couldn't you see the way his mind was working? The strong man who was prepared to lead!'

Crossley held up his hand, moving the palm gently back and forward towards the Prime Minister reassuring, assuaging. 'Yes, yes, of course. He sees himself in your shoes, but if *you* couldn't sell it to the party I couldn't see *him* doing it.'

Packham screwed up his mouth sceptically, not convinced. 'I dunno. The little bugger's as cute as a fox. He might even make a great show of defiance and intransigence while sliding in all kinds of changes by the back door. He has always been adept at talking tough and acting soft. He's a salesman, a soft drinks salesman. The family money comes, after all, from lemonade. Still, never mind. I am not resigning yet, and when I do, you can be bloody sure that he won't be my nominee – that's if there is anything to succeed to; which I am beginning to doubt.'

'I would share those doubts,' said Crossley.

'Well,' Packham finished his drink and rose to his feet. 'Whatever happens, you're all right, Shane. The Chancellor likes you and we have still *some* friends at court.'

26

'I assume nothing,' said Crossley, rising.

The Prime Minister led him to the outer door. 'Thank you for your help Shane – I'll think over your suggestion about calling their hand. I'll have a word with Des Carson. Not a bad lad, basically, but unpredictable. You might have a word with the Rooster. He should be beholden to you, now you've made him a Crown Prosecutor.'

'Means little, I'm afraid, he's a law unto himself, but I'll see what I can do,' said Crossley.

'Do you realise,' said Packham, 'that they are determined to remove us nearly all our little areas of patronage!' He smiled. 'Not much point in being an Attorney is there? Or a Prime Minister.' They laughed together. 'By the way,' continued Packham, stopping, as he was about to open the door, 'my own position – it was just a passing thought. So not a word.'

'My dear Arthur, put it out of your mind. *I* shall.'

In his office on the first floor of Parliament Buildings at Stormont, Desmond Carson was also listening to the news. He lay back with his feet on a large desk of heavy mahogany covered in blue leather. There was a tray with coffee, and as he listened, he munched a sandwich. It was a routine enough bulletin. A bomb discovered in time and rendered harmless by the army in a controlled explosion; three men from Andersonstown convicted on arms charges; a councillor fulminating against an increase in electricity charges – no mention of initiatives. His mind turned back to the Cabinet meeting less than an hour before. If it came to the crunch, was he going to let Gillan make all the running, or was he going to throw his hat into the ring? He had a feeling it might be his year . . . there is a tide in the affairs of men which taken at the flood leads on to . . . what? His father, a country doctor near Banbridge, had combined his practice with a fanatical dedication to the Unionist Party, on whose central executive he had served for many years, and whose local branch he had nurtured and expanded, until he became its life President. With such a background, the young Desmond had absorbed the Unionist ethos, its silent code of pride and prejudice, its infinite network of tribal signs and allegiances, as naturally as he learnt his mother tongue. His mother, too, had been a party activist, running the sales of work, the annual fair and coffee mornings, enlisting the help of her ewe lamb to swell the party money chest. At his boarding school, Portora, in County Fermanagh, he had captained the rugby Fifteen, and gone on to play for the province. At an early age, he had automatically been enrolled by his father into the junior branch of the Orange Order, the Protestant framework round which the Party had been built.

At Queen's University, Belfast, already known as a rugby player, he had toyed with Medicine before switching to Law. He had revitalised the university Unionist branch and come to public notice in a series of rowdy debates on the perennial theme of a united Ireland. A successful campaign to force the university authorities to fly the Union Jack on 12 September – the anniversary of the signing of the Ulster Covenant of 1912, and a red-letter day for Protestants – had also brightened his political prospects. The one gap in his impeccable credentials was filled when he joined the Army Territorial Reserve. From then on, as a Unionist, he was armed cap-a-pie.

It was this background of solid Protestant orthodoxy, 'sound on the constitution', as the phrase went, which had brought about his swift translation from Assistant Whip, to the Chief Whip's office, to Ministry of Home Affairs. The Civil Rights agitation, growing like a menacing cloud, had added a new dimension to the maintenance of public order. With strange concepts like subversion, non-violent protest and civil disobedience, entering the public vocabulary, Packham had seen the clear need to reassure his police force. He did so by appointing as their political head a man with whom they could identify, one of their own, of themselves, only writ larger. It was a role Carson revelled in: defender of the faith and of the human instruments entrusted with its keeping. The RUC and the B Specials had no more eloquent champion. In this new and alien world of shifting values, they repaid his steadfast loyalty with devotion. And yet things had not gone well.

Packham was right. They were not getting results; were being outplayed in a whole new ball-game. Frank Kitson had called the process of defeating terrorists 'a sort of game based on intense mental activity allied to a determination to find things out and to an ability to regard everything on its merits without regard to customs, doctrine or drill'. That was Kitson's text, and Carson was never tired of quoting it. He had got to know Kitson during the latter's time in Northern Ireland in command of 39 Brigade; first at the Joint Security meetings, and later, on a social basis. He had been deeply impressed by the pale impassioned soldier who, single-handed, was attempting to drag the army through a revolution in its thinking as profound as that effected by Cardwell a hundred years before. So he had read *Gangs and Countergangs* – Kitson's earlier work on guerilla operations, and had been singled out for an inscribed complimentary copy of *Low Intensity Operations*, after the author had left Ulster.

This intimacy had given Carson enormous pleasure. Despite his provincial background, he had always regarded himself as something of an intellectual. Even in rugby he liked to think he played with the head, and 'psychops' – the battle for the mind – was as much the basis for success in politics as it was in more lethal encounters. He had tried, in the short time available, to introduce changes in the training programme at the depot, but a force which is undermanned and constantly under pressure is not disposed to take easily to new tricks. And he was always aware that by trying to instil new attitudes, he was

29

adding to the burdens borne by both officers and men, and further reducing efficiency. It was a vicious circle made worse by the way in which the army had usurped the police role, so that in many operational situations they were merely observers. Morale was low. All in all, the domain over which he exercised his jurisdiction was in poor shape. As he leaned over and switched off the transistor, his mind clicked back to full cock on the Cabinet meeting. Just as well his plea for immediate decisions had fallen on deaf ears! If this thing went through, his ministry would be decimated. He would be the Emperor without any clothes; a figure of fun. But how to fight it? At one time he had convinced himself of Jennings's thesis that Westminster was not in all things supreme, but as he had listened that morning to Crossley's cold demolition job, he had found himself admitting to a hopeless case. Defiance, as in 1912, was at the heart of the Unionist paradox. It was one thing drumming up Dutch courage in an Orange Hall, but for a Unionist, an upholder of the Union, to defy the Queen, was a nonsense and he knew it. Let Gillan go that way if he would – it was a cul-de-sac.

But how could he be a party to relinquishing control of the police, to doing away with the Specials? His whole past reputation, his credibility . . . no, it was not on. He was boxed in. The enormity of his situation was becoming horribly clear. Unless he moved, and moved decisively, he, Desmond Carson, would be the major casualty. He was by nature sanguine and after twenty-five years in the business, he had learnt that political science was, in essence, escapology. Tight corners, blind bends, skid row – there was always a way through if you held on and kept your nerve.

There was so little time. He needed time to create space for manoeuvre, to blur the cruelly sharp definition of his present plight. One thing was clear: he would have to move out of Home Affairs sidways or . . . upwards . . .? Already his mind was clutching at outside chances. He must talk to Brian, his faithful henchman, who functioned as a part-time agent. He must talk to his own little squad; get Butler moving among their party colleagues to sound out support. The lobbying, he knew, was already under way – that had been clear from the whole trend of the meeting and the soft-spoken exchanges afterwards. He pulled his feet off the desk, brushed the crumbs from his clothes with his handkerchief, and, reaching for his cigarettes with one hand, touched the intercom switch with the other. 'Robert?' It was not the voice of his Private Secretary that answered, but a girl's.

'Robert is at lunch Minister. He'll be back in about fifteen minutes.

He's just up in the canteen . . . Can I help?'

Carson found himself suddenly speaking with constraint. 'No. No. It's all right, thank you.'

He let the switch click back and slowly took the Dunhill lighter from his pocket. He lit the cigarette. 'Christ! That was unexpected!' Since she had come to the Private Office just three months previously it had not been easy. Not that he came into official contact with her all that often. She was in an outer office two rooms away. But he was too aware of her presence. For she was not just another secretarial assistant. Her appointment had been, in its way, historic. He remembered all too well the gravity with which Arthur Jones, his Permanent Secretary, had broached the matter. It might have been a major political decision, and in a real sense it was, because she was the first Catholic ever to have been employed in the Private Office of a Stormont Minister.

To understand the implications of such an appointment, an outsider would need to know the functions of a Ministerial Private Office. It is the channel through which all information flows from the various branches of the Department to the Minister's desk. It is both a filter and a watch-dog, controlling and monitoring the papers and persons that reach him. It is privy to the most confidential matters, and to the contents of Cabinet Papers. Although it is in theory non-political, it is aware of, and frequently services, his political activities, including party and constituency business of a most sensitive nature. Craigavon, first premier of Northern Ireland, had once summed up the three qualities needed in an official working for his Private Office: 'To keep his mouth shut, to keep his mouth shut and to keep his mouth shut.' Blunt but to the point – trustworthiness was of the essence. And Ulster Catholics, as a whole, because of the legacy of grievances, often real, often imagined, felt that they owed little loyalty to this British statelet founded against their wishes. Indeed, as a community, they resented its continued existence. In a Unionist administration, even in one more open-minded than its predecessors, Catholics in sensitive political positions, especially in Home Affairs, were regarded as a potential security risk not only because they might be less inhibited or less guarded in discussing government business, but because, during the ever-recurring IRA campaigns, they would be much more open to blackmail and intimidation. That was the public rationalisation. The private emotional charge was different. Most of Carson's constituents would have said, 'Sure you couldn't trust one of them as far as you'd throw them. The only good one's a dead one'.

So when Arthur Jones had informed him that there was a vacancy in the Private Office, and that he had a candidate who was in every way qualified for the job – intelligent, efficient, conscientious – but with one serious question-mark, Carson had faced his moment of truth. It was not just that she was a very pretty girl with an open friendly manner – though that was no harm – no, it was a vague uneasy feeling that had been crystallising inside him for some time, something that was compounded of conscience and proper pride. It was the growing realisation which he had been half resisting as a weakness, as a softening of his principles, the awareness that if he, in a position of power, was not capable of opening doors and showing trust, then there could never be any hope of breaking out of the Northern Ireland impasse. This high-minded view he had confided to his Permanent Secretary. He had been less frank about the feeling of pride that he, Desmond Carson, would be the one to make the break-through, the hard-liner with the inflexible sense of justice. While all those soft-centred liberals in the party went on prating about ecumenical gestures, he, Carson, was prepared to act. Anyway, she had been well vetted: her father, a prosperous wholesaler in the Belfast licensed trade; her mother from a hard-line Republican family no longer politically active, substantial farmers in Co Antrim. Josephine Scanlon – her name alone revealed her tradition – educated by the good Sisters at St Mary's Convent in Ascot, followed by Sussex University, then eighteen months as an assistant with the EEC in Brussels, before returning to enter the Northern Ireland Civil Service.

Carson got to his feet. His finger moved again to the intercom switch but hesitated as he stared at the box. Then he went to the door at the end of the room that led to the adjoining office. He opened it and looked through. This was the office occupied by Robert, his Private Secretary, and John, the Home Affairs Press Officer. Filing cabinets; a cupboard with a pile of green folders holding Parliamentary Questions; two desks facing each other, covered with an orderly clutter of papers and reference books; the intercom; four telephones – two green, one red, one black – and on the far desk, a small portable typewriter. The office was empty except for her. Her brown hair was pulled back in a chignon and her dark eyes expertly shadowed; the kind of oval face that looks well framed in a head-scarf; a beautiful mouth. She looked at him as he opened the door.

'I wasn't sure that you were alone,' he said quietly. 'Come in a moment.'

He turned back into the room. She rose and followed him. He shut the door behind her as she entered, and then very deliberately took her in his arms. They kissed naturally and hungrily. He moved his mouth away from hers and held her tightly as he nuzzled her ear like a puppy-dog.

'God, why do I have to?' he whispered into her hair.

'What is it darling? What's wrong?'

She pushed both hands against his chest so that she could look into his face. Suddenly anxious, her eyes searched his.

'Nothing sweet, nothing.' He gave a half-laugh to reassure her. 'They're just trying to crucify me, that's all. I'll tell you later, later.' He kissed her again with great tenderness. 'I needed that,' he said.

She took his hand and put it to her mouth. 'I'll say a prayer for you,' she murmured.

'Oh no, not that!' he laughed. 'Just offer it up!' He threw his arms round her again and lifted her off the floor.

'Des. Behave yourself!'

'Right, back to unreality!' he said.

'Here, just a moment.' Solicitous, like a mother, she took from a pocket in the swirling pleats of her skirt a small handkerchief, spat on it delicately and proceeded to carefully remove the lip-stick from his mouth and chin.

He waited like a child while she adjusted his tie and smoothed the lapels of his jacket. 'OK?'

'Yeah.' They fell back into their official roles.

'Get Brian, will you? Tell him to come up here as soon as he can. Ask him to find out where Harry Harrmon will be this evening.' He caught her hand. 'I'll try to get round to you before ten – scrambled eggs and a drink, all right?'

She nodded. From the adjoining office came the sound of someone moving. 'Very well, Minister,' she said in clear tones. Quickly she tore her eyes away from him and left the room.

He stood for a moment looking after her, then turned towards the window. Four stories below him the broad steps sloped down to Lord Carson's statue. Beyond, the main avenue with its distinctively reddish surface fell away arrow-straight to the ornate entrance gates a mile distant. Behind squatted the purple hills of Castlereagh. It was a magnificent vista reminiscent of the Paris of Haussmann, designed for the ritual of ceremonial parades and protest marches. The first massive demonstration of the Ulster Defence Force had been held there, ten thousand strong. He had addressed them from the balcony below the room in which he stood. 'Ulster salutes you for your sense of duty and will to serve her. Ulster expects from you,' he had roared, 'the greatest restraint and discipline.' He had ridden the rhetorical tight-rope between condoning and condemning, between the safety-valve and saving face.

Instinct, amply justified by subsequent events, had told him not to align the government in any sense with such a heterogenous crew. But they had their uses. He had since made it his business to be of discreet assistance to their leader, Harry Harrmon, the shrewd ex shop-steward and spoilt evangelist, who had risen with the movement from scratch. What muscle there was on the Protestant side resided there. Already forming in his mind was the vague idea that somehow the Harrmon organisation might ease his problems; a diversion maybe, a shot across the bows of Downing Street signalling real trouble if they moved ahead too fast. Far be it from him to contemplate enlisting the help of paramilitaries, but the heat was on – he had to create space at any price. Anyway, a word with Harrmon, without commitment, would do no harm. Especially if Gillan took to the barricades. His colleague in Trade would look very silly if Harrmon refused to become involved, or indeed had decided to back another candidate.

The more Carson considered the UDF angle, the more possibilities it seemed to have; especially when he contrasted the potential for pressure which Harrmon and his cohorts represented, as against, say, the officers of his own Constituency Association, a mixture of place-seekers and dedicated party workers who provided him with his power-base but were themselves without wide influence. To sway the apolitical masses outside required commandos.

His intercom buzzed. 'It's the Castle, Minister. Mr Taylor.' This time it was Robert his Secretary speaking.

'OK put him on.' He lifted the black telephone. 'Yes, Stewart. Yes. Yes. Right. I'll be down at 4.30.' He replaced the receiver thoughtfully. So the PM wanted to see him. That could be interesting. He pressed the intercom. 'Robert, come here a moment.'

His Private Secretary entered, carrying a clip-board. The son of a foundry-worker from West Belfast, a bright boy – only high-fliers were found in the Private Offices – Robert was unusual in that he had come into the service direct from grammar school at eighteen, and not, like most of his colleagues at a similar level, after university. But he knew intuitively the feelings and reactions of the Ulster working class, especially that of Belfast. Carson had taken him into his confidence before deciding to bring Jo into the Office. At first, his Secretary had demurred, but a strong sense of fair play had carried him through. They got on well together. He was intrigued by the exotic tinge imparted to the Office by this Catholic girl, yet astute enough to have realised that recently there had been a new and, to him, disquieting element introduced into the pattern of his Minister's days. But it would take more than that to dent his devotion to the man he served, a dedication that went far beyond the demands of the job, and had something almost of the nature of a family tie.

Now he ran down the Parliamentary Order Paper. 'Two questions down Minister, both on last Saturday's procession, and of course it's coming up on the adjournment.'

'Look, Robert,' Carson fixed the young man with a steady gaze. 'There's something serious in the wind. I'll talk to you about it later. But I need all the time I can get this afternoon.'

Robert shifted his glasses on his nose. 'The PQs are no problem. All you need to say is that you will deal with the whole matter in detail on the adjournment. You needn't come back to the House at all until then. Mr Gillan's got his Industrial Development Bill, and that's bound to go on till six!'

'Yes, that will keep *him* tied up at least,' said Carson. 'I want a word with Mr Butler. Get him for me now will you, and check with Jo that she got hold of Brian.'

'Right Minister. The car's waiting to take you down to the Castle. I'll try Mr Butler now.'

Carson sat motionless for a few moments looking at the closed door. Then he turned his gaze to the large oil painting on the wall to his left. Some ceremonial occasion, a triumphal return with, as its centrepiece, a regal figure in seventeenth-century costume mounted on a prancing white charger. King William III returning from the Battle of the Boyne – a common enough subject in Ireland. In the style of the period, there was a number of tutelary angels blowing trumpets and hovering benignly in the sky over the happy monarch's head. But the picture had one unusual, indeed unique feature. Prominently perched on the largest whitest cloud was the unmistakeable figure of a mitred Pope holding a crozier in his left hand. With the other he was clearly blessing the group beneath, including the arch apostle of Protestantism and architect of the final defeat of the Catholic and national cause in Ireland. True, history records how a Te Deum in Catholic Vienna celebrated William's victory

35

over James and his patron Louis, but myth does not marry well with historical fact. When the picture had hung in one of the public chambers of Stormont during the 1930s, an Orangeman, incensed at this slander on his hero, had slashed the canvas with a pen knife. Skilful restoration had remedied the damage and Carson had rescued the picture from the obscurity of an admin store and had it mounted in his office where it proved a never-failing conversation piece. He had enjoyed shocking Protestant and Catholic visitors alike with selective titbits on the two protagonists; the homosexual tendencies of William and the unbounded nepotism of the Venetian Ottoboni, enthroned as Pope Alexander VIII. But recently he had found the picture an irritating charade, an unwelcome reminder of his own situation, where an upbringing in the puritan moralities had proved small anchor against the undertow of the eternal feminine. Painted kings and painted popes – cardboard irrelevances in the cataract that seemed at times to thunder through him. Was he schizophrenic? Strange how suddenly he had felt inadequate. Agonising too much? The Puritan conscience was a hard task-master – it coloured the purest chance as retribution. Things crowded in as they were crowding in now. Sometimes, in a moment of sharp anxiety, he wondered if he was losing his appetite for politics. But he knew no other, could conceive of no other existence. And now, when he needed all his wits about him, he was emotionally in disarray. The black telephone rang. Instinctively he straightened his back and stubbed out the cigarette. 'Yes. Wally? I want you to do something for me . . .' He was brisk, forceful, back in the business he knew.

The Prime Minister took his glass and poured himself another whiskey. The handsome old bracket clock on the mantelpiece said 12.30. He turned towards one of the front windows. Outside two RUC men, with Sterlings slung over their shoulders, paced up and down.

It was a pleasant room. Previous occupants had given its fine pilasters and cornice the glitter of white and gold. He had transformed it into the library of a country house. The satinwood bookcase with calf-bound tomes and the coloured dust-jackets of today jumbled together, the jardiniere of yellow chrysanthemums from the Castle hot-houses, the log-basket and scuffed fire-irons – all that was lacking were the dogs on the hearth-rug. The exotic clutter on the mantelpiece – a chunk of fool's gold; a fistfull of coloured pencils in a beaker of polished yellowing ivory, a memento of a Rhodesian safari; the battered silver cigarette box incised with the signatures of his wartime mess – these were part of the inventory of his life.

He preferred this room to the apartments down the hill in Speaker's House, 'buried in dank rhododendrons', as he had once remarked. It was bright, personal and over the shop. And Arthur Packham had not tired of trading just yet. The door from the offices opened gently and as the head of Sir Stewart Taylor tentatively appeared, he motioned him to enter. There followed Billy Dixon, the Party Secretary, stocky, breathless, smoothing back his thick dark hair which shone with lotion, and Ronnie Fine, oiling his way in like some mohair-suited Groucho Marx.

Dixon greeted the Prime Minister respectfully but informally – they were clearly comrades of long standing. 'Before we get down to business, what's in the House this afternoon, Stewart?'

Taylor glanced briefly at the Order Paper on the clipboard he was holding. 'Industrial Development Bill; the Opposition are bringing up the banning of last Saturday's procession on the Adjournment and – this concerns you directly, sir – there's a Private Notice Question asking for a statement on a possible British initiative – from Maguire.'

'Trust Maguire,' said the PM.

'He must have got it from the *Guardian*, but Tom Lefaux says there's no reason to think that they're any wiser than they were earlier this morning,' said Fine.

'All the same,' said the PM, 'it shows how little breathing space we have. Have you got the draft answer?'

'It's being typed sir,' said Taylor, 'playing the whole thing down – speculation.'

'Right. Now!' Packham indicated the drinks table. 'Help yourselves. What time is it? We mustn't miss the five-to-one news just in case someone has taken it further. You might drum up some sandwiches Ronnie; smoked salmon for me.' Fine went to the telephone on the writing table.

They settled down in a semi-circle, facing their master in his armchair. Only he and Billy Dixon were drinking. Dixon drew from his inside jacket pocket a buff envelope on which was a list of scribbled names, some marked with crosses. The Kitchen Cabinet was about to go into session.

'Now Billy, Stewart has put you in the picture I take it?' Dixon nodded. 'Right, we've got to have maximum support at the Party meeting. Above all we must fix Gillan. What I'm concerned about, is that he doesn't get a bandwagon rolling.'

37

Dixon thought for a moment. 'Are you sure PM, are you *sure* that they're going ahead with this. The courts, the police and so on, we might get away with, but doing away with the B Specials – that's going to be murder.'

'I know, I know,' said Packham, 'but for the time being we have got to work on the assumption that they'll go the whole way. If they don't, then it's a bonus and we get the credit for standing firm. But I don't intend to let that little bastard hang his hat up on this one. You can be sure he'll be stumping round the country at the first opportunity, so we need to gut him at the Party meeting, before he gets going.'

Billy Dixon got the message. There was no mistaking the neurotic insistence. He was to put a contract out for Gillan. 'PM, I think the first thing you've got to do is have a word with Des Carson.'

'I intend to.'

'If you get him you have another five along with him.'

'The trouble is,' said Packham, 'that I can hardly expect him to acquiesce in his own extinction. If this plan is adhered to, Home Affairs will virtually cease to exist. Nothing left.'

'Fire Brigades and Dog Licences,' said Ronnie Fine. 'Unless, PM, you could provide him with something more desirable . . .'

'What do you mean?' asked his master.

'Well, Home Affairs, in the last few years, has been very much a bed of nails, and I'm sure that Des Carson would not be averse to Trade.' The PM smiled indulgently at his licensed aide. 'After all, you were talking the other day of the need for a new look. In the re-shuffle you move Trade to Finance – the senior ministry after all.' Packham laughed. Even Taylor allowed himself a broad grin.

'All right. It's a possibility, I admit – but only in extremis,' said Packham. 'I'll speak to Carson sometime this afternoon, Stewart.' Taylor made a note.

'Right!' said the Prime Minister. 'What's it look like, Billy?'

Dixon studied his list. 'I think I can handle most of them. If I have any problems I'll let you know. I won't bore you with the details, but at the moment, I make it about thirteen. If we get the Carson clique, that makes it eighteen. The two boyos you're seeing should be twenty. That's out of thirty-five, or thirty-three excluding the Speaker and the Chief Whip.'

'Willie?'

'When I tell him the way the wind's blowin' – what do *you* think?' said Dixon bluntly.

'Good' said Packham. 'I'll leave you to get on with that. Now the actual handling of the meeting. We must know exactly the line we're going to take. How do you see it Ronnie?'

Fine was suddenly serious. 'PM, our room for manoeuvre is very limited. That is clear. Defiance is out, even as a tactic, because it would strengthen enormously their moral position and correspondingly weaken ours. Apart from the fact that we couldn't win. As I see it, we must therefore agree in principle and play for a phased introduction of the changes, pleading the need to neutralise those elements in the Party who will favour a confrontation.'

'That's all very well,' broke in Dixon, 'but I don't care how you phase it, you just cannot tell the Party that the B Specials are being disbanded. They won't wear it, PM. You know that. It would be bad enough if we even looked like getting on top of the IRA, but with another policeman shot this week – and the bombing, how can you do away with the one force that our people have confidence in? We might as well all pack our bags here and now. It's serious, PM. It's really serious.'

'I entirely accept what Billy says.' It was Taylor, soft-voiced and diffident, pushing his head forward as if he were fighting for air-time in a studio debate. 'But need it be presented so starkly as that? Surely it will be recognised that the B Specials with their Point 303s, and essentially rural skills, are seriously in need of modernisation. Let us give them better weapons, and the better equipment they need and deserve. This is not a quesion of disbanding, but of re-fitting, of stream-lining, of integrating the Special Constabulary into the whole security machine – of transforming them into a new anti-terrorist force packing a real punch!'

'Bravo, Stewart, bravo!' said Packham. 'You were waxing quite eloquent. And I think you have something.'

Dixon grunted a grudging approval. 'That would put a better face on it certainly. But if they're going to have a new name, it had better be a good one.'

'At least,' said Fine, with a grin, 'it puts us on the side of the angels, while the apes are banging away at the Orange drum.'

The PM brightened. 'I think we're beginning to see a chink of light. Oh!' He glanced at his watch and motioned to the shining transistor on the side-table. 'Turn that thing on. I want to hear what's happening . . .' The Kitchen Cabinet directed its entire attention to the BBC five-to-one news. When it was finished the PM rose from his chair. 'Well, no mention. That's something.'

39

Stewart Taylor came in from the office. 'Desmond Carson will be here at 4.30.'

Billy Dixon looked at the Prime Minister anxiously. 'I'll make a point of running into him later, just to check that all's well.' In political persuasion Dixon did not admit the concept of 'overkill'. 'I'll have a word with Fred Butler too. He's mad keen to get that Commonwealth Parliamentary trip to . . . you know, Ceylon?'

'Sri Lanka,' said Fine.

'That's it. I'll make sure he earns it. But Carson's the key.'

The Prime Minister nodded. 'Something occurred to me just now. Supposing, supposing we gave them both barrels. Introduction of the proposals in easy stages, as gradually as possible, playing up the brave new deal for the security forces – I think that could ease matters – but at the same time . . .' He paused. 'At the same time, we go hard on the danger of Protestant reaction, of a rising even, if London pushes too fast. Well?' He turned to his Cabinet Secretary.

Taylor twitched apologetically. 'I honestly think, PM, that we can't get much further until we have some idea of public reaction, and I don't think we'll have long to wait. I'm sure your suggestion is basically sound. We can't improve on it at the moment. What worries me is that the initial reaction may be worse than we think. Especially if the Minister of Trade is whipping up feeling. Whatever happens, we must take the initiative and hold it.'

'Obviously!' said the PM testily, the mention of Gillan not improving his temper.

Taylor coloured slightly. 'I was going to suggest, PM, that I have a word with the Home Office, emphasising our fears of what might happen on the Protestant side and putting before them, in the starkest terms, the options which they may find themselves facing.' He waited a second. 'May I take it sir, that I can direct official minds to the situation which would face them in the event of a mass resignation of the government here?'

'I see no harm in that Stewart.' The PM was mollifying. 'The blacker you make it the better.'

There was a silence. The previous euphoria had evaporated. They were all very much aware of the battle ahead. It was a question of survival. Not just for the politician. The three officials knew that new brooms, like new measures, more often than not, meant new men.

'Let's get on with it,' said Packham. 'I take it Home Affairs has alerted the army, just in case. A word in their ear, Stewart, and we can be sure they'll be straight on the blower to Whitehall! I'll probably want you this evening Billy.'

They filed out, Billy Dixon nodding sympathetically as though to the head of a bereaved household. Packham patted him on the shoulder.

'Cheer up, Billy. We've got a good head start. Just think of what the opposition have to cope with! We might even push the little bugger into Home Affairs eh?'

The mood lightened as they laughed.

One of the office staff waited deferentially till the Prime Minister watched Dixon disappear. 'The clergy are waiting for you, sir.'

Packham closed his eyes. Another delegation from the combined Council of Churches. The sapient sutlers of the Lord. They would express grave concern at the deteriorating situation. They would lecture him on the need for action in terms that could spell only inaction.

'Yes, yes,' murmured Packham. 'Here beginneth the forty-first lesson . . .'

That afternoon the process of winning friends and influencing people was gaining momentum at all levels. Mun Martin strolled into Burton's room on the third floor of Parliament Buildings where the Ministry of Finance had their main offices. Mun, whose Ministry was located in Dundonald House, a vast office block at the bottom of the hill, had his own Parliamentary pied-à-terre on the ground floor near the Commons Chamber, but he was coming to Willie. The Mountain was making sure that Mahomet wouldn't give him the slip. One of the secretaries in the outer office waved him through. His coming had been announced. Inside, Willie rose to greet him.

'Well Willie,' said his visitor with a quizzical smile, 'I thought it was about time we got together.'

Willie laughed nervously. 'Sit down. Would you like a cup of tea? I've just ordered some.'

Mun sat down in one of the blue leather armchairs and stretched his legs. He had the unhurried approach of the countryman. He looked round at the dark mahogany; the bookcases; the imposing desk; the table and dining chairs for conferences, and the conventional pictures, including a Paul Henry and a William Conor on loan from the Ulster Museum. He looked at the silver booty on the desk-top: the ink-stand, the small salver, contractors' presents from topping-out ceremonies, official openings. 'You've got a lovely set-up here, Willie. How long has it been? About eight years isn't it? You've done a good job in Finance, Willie. I'd like to see you stay here a few years more.'

41

Willie had expected something like this. But his smile was a little forced. 'Oh I think on the whole that the PM is reasonably satisfied with the job I'm doing.'

'I'm sure he is.' Martin looked at him hard. 'But how long is he going to be PM?'

'Oh, c-c-come on now, Mun! I don't see anyone shifting him at the moment.'

Mun rose to his feet, and placing his hands on the desk, leaned forward until his face was a couple of feet from Willie's. 'Look Willie. He's on the way out. He has no chance, *no* chance of selling this. As soon as the country hears that they're taking the Specials away from us; that they're taking away control of the police; the balloon goes up. The only way is to stand up to them. You *know* that. And the only man that's got the guts for it and the support in the country, is James Gillan. It's all over bar the shouting, and Willie . . .' His voice dropped, taut with conviction. 'I want you to be on the right side.' This was the approach direct. 'What do you say?'

Willie's mouth formed into a strained half-smile. 'Let's see what happens at the Party meeting. You remember the last time you made a move?'

'That was a completely different situation, completely different. Look! Arthur's not going to take on Westminster. He's going to try and waffle through, saying one thing and doing another, like he always does. If it doesn't work – too bad! He gets a fat PM's pension – not that he needs it. He's got over 500 acres, and God knows what else besides.'

'I'm not on the breadline.'

'Of course you're not. But the Gillans have been good to you, haven't they?'

'What do you mean?' Willie coloured.

'They push quite a bit of business your way, don't they?'

'What if they do? I don't mix my business and my politics, Mun. I'm not on anybody's pay-roll.' Willie bristled with moral indignation. 'If James Gillan wants to take his business elsewhere, he can do it tomorrow. I won't starve. I won't starve you know.'

'Easy, easy, Willie. Nobody's saying you'll starve. I know you don't need Gillan to send you business. You'd probably get it anyway. All I was saying was . . .' Mun spread out his hands apologetically. 'He hasn't done you any harm has he?'

'No, no of course not.' Willie was only too glad to be mollified. He had never any stomach for rows, especially with Mun Martin whose

42

instinct for the jugular was well known.

A girl arrived with tea, which eased the tension and gave Mun a moment to amend his tactics. He had handled it badly, stroked him up the wrong way. He debated with himself whether to play his trump card now, or leave it. But time was too short, and he had Willie alone, softened up, Mun guessed, through a natural reaction to having lost his temper. Time for the honest man-to-man approach.

'Willie, you know what I'm here for. I want your support for Gillan. Why? Because he speaks for the people of Ulster. If you doubt that, go into your constituency tonight and tell them that the British Government is doing away with the Specials *and* taking away control of the police. See what they say. No, no I don't want you to comment. I just want you to think about it. But there's something else I want to say to you, Willie, something *I* know that you don't know, something your friend Arthur hasn't told you.' He paused. His man was all attention. 'There's going to be a re-shuffle. And the chances are that someone else will be offered Finance. That's not a story, Willie. That's a true bill.'

It was not a story, rather a surmise based on intelligent guess-work. Gillan's grape-vine had faithfully transmitted, within the hour, Packham's parting sally to Billy Dixon. If a shuffle were in the air, then the Gillan camp could work out the limited permutations without trouble.

Willie looked sceptical. But his nonchalance was not convincing. 'There are always rumours floating around. If they were all true, there'd be a new Cabinet every week!'

'This is not a rumour.'

'Who told you then? Has the PM taken you into his confidence?'

'Willie! Use your head! You heard this morning. Carson is not going to fight. But he's not going to stick in Home Affairs without a Ministry. So he's moved – where? Trade or Finance. If he gets Trade, Arthur would have to offer Gillan Finance. Where does that leave you? Even if you were prepared to take Home Affairs – and what a climb-down that would be – he'll give it to a lawyer, one of his budding back-benchers. Even the Rooster. It makes sense, doesn't it, Willie . . .?'

'How do I know this isn't all pure speculation?'

'Willie, I give you my solemn word that Arthur has been discussing changes this very afternoon. More than that I cannot say. You've no time, Willie, no time to wait and see. Because if you wait to see which way the cat jumps, it'll be too late . . . won't it? Come with *us* and you're safe. Stay with him and . . .'

43

Mun threw open his hands. Willie said nothing. His visitor rose from his chair.

'Think it over, Willie. I know you don't like committing yourself, but, believe you me, it's all up for grabs now, Willie. It's time to stand up and be counted. I'll be in touch.' At the door he turned and looked long and hard at the Minister of Finance. 'Thanks for the tea.'

When he left Willie sat motionless, trying to work out his best course of action. Was it a try-on? Yet Mun seemed very definite, and was astute enough to realise that, once forewarned, he, Willie, would leave no source and no shoulder untapped until he had checked up on the re-shuffle story. It was disturbing. He steadied himself. If he was worth all this to Gillan, he was worth something to Packham. He'd take the bull by the horns. Have a word with Dixon. Let them know he wasn't a sitting duck. He pressed a switch on the console.

The headquarters of the Ulster Defence Force was, as usual coming up to five o'clock, very busy. The organisation encompassed all kinds of activities. But the appearance of the building from which its operations were directed gave little clue as to their extent. Once a doctor's residence and surgery, it was situated in a cul-de-sac off the Albert-bridge Road in East Belfast. It was the only occupied building in the truncated street. Beyond it was the blank rear wall of a factory. Opposite, two derelict artisan houses, doorways and windows walled up with breeze blocks, the tiny front gardens patches of rusty grass, littered with the accumulated rubbish of the streets. Beyond the two houses, an entry led to the adjoining maze of streets, the terraced red-brick of nineteenth century Belfast. The HQ was stucco that had once been painted grey, three storeys, with the third lit by dormers in the pitched roof. The downstairs windows were covered with stout iron grilles. The front door, giving straight on to the street, was open. There was a porch with an inner door which was covered in metal sheeting and was usually kept closed. A bay window on the ground floor gave a field of vision up and down the whole street. A fish-eye lens in the inner door took care of anyone who penetrated as far as the porch unobserved. The security precautions were discreet but unconcealed, the only policy for a responsible organisation working daily for and with the public. It was not public knowledge that, after nightfall, there was a look-out posted in the upper room of one of the houses opposite, equipped with an RT set and any other hardware he required. Outside, a Cortina and a Mazda 1800 were parked. Inside the Cortina were two men, one in the driver's seat, the other in the back. These were the Harrmon escorts – he discouraged the use of the term 'minders' because of its connotations. The interior of the building was as shabbily Spartan as the exterior. Off the hallway to the right, was the guard-room, or reception as it was usually referred to in the presence of visiting journalists – the UDF was a bit schizophrenic in its attitude to nomenclature. A cheap desk with three metal chairs and a space heater. The duty man, with one foot resting on an open drawer, was on the telephone. On the walls, a map of Belfast, and a large heraldic shield with the Red Hand of Ulster carved in wood. It bore the legend, *Ulster Defence Force*, picked out in gold paint on a scroll. There was a pin-up calendar from a tyre company, a notice-board covered with business cards, and a typewritten list of telephone numbers ranging from the Housing Executive to the local RUC and army barracks.

Two youths in jeans and leather jerkins stood smoking in the hallway. The decibel level in the waiting room opposite reception, indicated a full house. Most were waiting for the Welfare Office with requests for housing, or on behalf of Loyalist prisoners in Long Kesh. A sales rep underlined the involvement of the organisation in the business life of the city, especially in the licensed trade, where because of the Troubles an increasing number of publicans were only too ready to lease their premises on favourable terms. A transistor, belting out the local pop station, and the shrill voices of little children raised in protest from the cloakroom; it all made for an atmosphere of warm multifarious humanity – an animated page from the *News of the World*.

In the front office on the first floor over the waiting room the Commander was aware of, but well insulated from, the commotion below. The tufted brown carpet was laid on two thicknesses of rubber felt. The effect was so springy that it was referred to variously, by his subordinates, as the whore's arse or the bloody trampoline. The Commander's desk was fittingly large, with two telephones; filing cabinet; drinks cupboard; easy chairs in PVC – Harrmon had demanded 'proper office furniture'. The walls were painted cream, except for the fireplace side which was papered in a bold geometric pattern. The elaborate electric fire had simulated coals. A large TV set completed the furnishings: A transistor stood on the mantelpiece – the UDF was very media conscious. Further proof of its cultivation of a public image adorned the walls. There were numerous press photographs of the organisation in action; drilling, masked and serried ranks in its initial and tense brinkmanship confrontations with the army; its Commander despatching a busload of children to a holiday camp; waving women, setting off in UDF transport, to visit their menfolk in the Maze Prison compounds. There was one sombre note, an enlarged portrait of the previous commander, who had been killed in mysterious circumstances. The picture carried a bow of black crepe.

There were five men in the room. Harrmon at the desk, his unzipped anorak showing the open-necked check shirt, a small cheroot in his fingers. Four of his aides faced him, one perched on the arm of a chair.

Reg Nimmo, the Quartermaster, white-faced and sucking furiously at a cigarette, was under the gun.

'For Christ's sake, I couldn't get him outa the store. He was bleedin' like a pig. And the whole district was crawlin' with bloody army.'

'What the hell was the army doin'?' asked Harrmon.

'Bomb-scares. They were there half the night!' The QM was on the defensive, almost shouting.

'That's right,' confirmed someone, more calmly. 'They done two shops in the Avenue last night.'

Another broke in angrily. 'But when you *did* get out, why the fuckin' hell didn't you dump him? And burn the car? Jesus! That car must be plastered with prints!'

The QM was stammering. 'It was Blondie and the other two left him in the car.'

'Jesus Christ Almighty. What a cock-up!' The critic, known as Big Charlie, was an ICI textile worker from Carrickfergus, whose corpulent fifteen stone and close-cropped hair was reminiscent of a US movie cop. He appealed to Harrmon. 'Christ Harry. They'll be stampin' all over us – police, army, the whole fuckin' lot! We got to do something!'

'Like what?' asked Harrmon coldly.

The big man blustered. 'Like that Blondie merchant, for a start. He's a fuckin' nut-case!'

As the other two neutrals joined in denunciation of Blondie, Harrmon raised his voice, and they gave way.

'Look! Blondie got the OK from us to go ahead. It was a Council decision. We had to make an example of him, right? Reg was the officer in charge. So far so good. Then the balls-up.' He looked straight at the QM. 'That drill. You let them go too far. Then you should have dumped him – *not left* him in the *bloody car*!'

'That was the idea,' stammered Nimmo, 'only when we went back in the morning, at about six o'clock, he was dead. I told them to dump him in the Short Strand, and report back. I stayed to clean up. When they got to the Short Strand there was still police around so they dumped the lot down by the cattle market. I mean I thought that . . .'

'OK, OK!' Harrmon cut in, now in control. He thought a moment. 'He was found – what time?'

'About two hours ago.'

'We gotta move,' said the Commander.

'Jim!' He turned to the young man on the chair. 'Get someone to report the car was stole. Where does Blondie keep it?'

'On the street.'

'Get him to report that it was missing this morning. With a bit of luck, this rain should have made things dicey for the forensic boys.'

'What happens,' asked Big Charlie, 'when they start askin' around, and find that Blondie and the helpers were lookin' for him?'

'Jim!' said Harrmon again. 'Tell Blondie to make sure they fix an alibi – a good one – and keep their mouths shut!' He smiled grimly at Big Charlie. 'Don't worry. Blondie'll keep them in line. He may be a nut-case, but he's all right. Billy! You go along with Jim, Reg! Get down to the family in Cregagh. Have a word with them. You know what to say. Tell them we'll give him a good funeral. We pay for the lot. OK?'

The QM hesitated.

'Get movin' for Chrissake! All right?' Harrmon's tone was half-angry, half-affectionate, as he jerked his head dismissively.

Reg Nimmo left the room, followed by the other two. As the door closed Harrmon sighed. 'Stupid bastard. But he's straight, Charlie. He's straight. You'll have to shift that stuff for him.'

'We moved it last night – Monkstown.' Charlie gave a smug smile.

'Two thousand bloody quids worth! A hundred and twenty for an Armalite – spares are gettin' dearer all the time.' Harrmon was musing on the harsh economics of existence.

'Not like Reg,' said Chairle. 'I dunno what come over him.' Reg Nimmo was in charge of hardware, transport and accommodation. He had joined the movement early on in its existence. An honest man, he was moved by the need to show himself and his family that he was not, as he put it, 'going to let Ulster's bone go with the dog'. He was close to Harrmon. Both still believed that the object of their organisation was to make war, not money, despite the compromises they had been forced into during the first heady days of the Loyalist renaissance. In Harrmon's book, Reg Nimmo was straight. Absolute trust in one's associates is something that only a fool aspires to. In the country of the blind the one-eyed men are kings.

Harry Harrmon had not been elected, but had emerged as one of the champions of that demi-monde of street politics, fundamentalist religion, and loyalist institutions, that seethed in the Protestant quarters of Belfast. To the inarticulate and impotent tide of resentment and frustration at IRA outrages, he and his mates had given direction and purpose. His trade-union background in the Sirocco engineering works, had taught him how to organise and manipulate. Five years in the North Irish Horse, a Territorial Regiment, had given him a military edge. But it was his Calvinist fervour, which on occasion could raise him to surpringly passionate flights of demagogy, that lifted him head and shoulders above the ruck; first of all to Deputy, then on the sudden death of his Chief, to Supremo. In the process, the gospel fervour had somewhat faded, and shaded into agnosticism, and the fanatical dedication to the organisation he had helped to found, had grown colder and more clinical. He had acquired the habit of power: power he would use so that his tribe should prevail. But the sinews of power required money, and Calvinists always had an eye to business. The empire expanded, becoming more and more an end in itself. Those who were not for him, were against him. And those who, in his terms, turned out to be other than straight, were dealt with ruthlessly. All the time he grappled with the basic dilemma of the Ulster Loyalist: how to maintain a credible posture, while regarding the forces of the Crown as your enemies. Only they, unlike the politicians, had to face it in its roughest and most concrete form. When in pursuit of their task of defending their community, and of allegedly attacking the IRA, they came into conflict with the security forces, it was no war-game. The ammunition was live. The outcome was not defeat in the lobbies or in the television studios, but long-term imprisonment or, in some cases, death. From this fundamental conflict flowed all kinds of uncertainties. Did passing on UDF information to the army constitute as grave a betrayal as it would for a member of the IRA? Since the organisation professed to co-operate with the security forces, at what point did co-operation become disloyalty to the cause? Such questions weighed less and less with a hard-pressed commander, whose priorities were to maintain some measure of discipline among his lawless forces and prevent his more covert operations from being penetrated and exposed by the police. There had been too many prosecutions of his members already. The integrity of his organisation was paramount. He did not shrink from the most brutal measures to preserve it. The writ of the Force was accepted throughout the working-class Protestant areas, and even its most unsavoury exploits condoned simply because it was the only Protestant team on the field, at a time when the Catholic goal average in terms of political successes was provocatively high.

Harrmon was conscious that the UDF was marking time. The isolated act of retaliation was not enough. Anyway, it was impossible to claim credit for most of the acts perpetrated by the lunatic fringe, even if association with some of those acts, such as bombings in the Republic, had been desirable. He walked the tightrope of legality, and the price he

49

paid was a constant exposure to infiltration of the kind he had just been dealing with. What was urgently needed was an issue, something big he could latch on to, and behind which he could throw the weight of the organisation, something that would put fire in the belly of his troops, and ensure the right kind of publicity.

'I had a telephone call today.' Harrmon lit another cheroot and twirled the packet in his fingers, tapping it against the table before he continued. 'From Brian Kedge, Carson's side-kick. Wants to see me tonight at his place. What d'ye reckon he's after?'

Big Charlie grinned knowingly. 'Maybe yer man Carson wants a job done!'

'He's a fly bastard. Always keeps his distance. I dunno. Maybe he's worried.'

'How do you mean?' asked Charlie.

'There's all kinds of chat, that the Brits are trying to get this organisation banned – there's no votes for Carson if he goes along with that.'

'Are you going?'

'Why not?'

Harrmon was not going to admit that he had found the invitation not unwelcome. It was a step nearer to the Establishment. He affected to despise the conventional politians, but secretly he envied them. He envied them their status, but he hated them for their aloofness. This could be the chance he'd been looking for. If they needed him, if they were prepared even unofficially to bring him in from the cold, he would come – but at a price.

James Gillan sat alone on the Front Bench in the Stormont House of Commons, a clipboard on his knee, ostensibly taking notes. He had made his opening statement on the new industrial incentives. At most, there were a dozen members in the House. Nobody was interested. Even his civil servants, in the Officials' box behind the Speaker, were finding it hard to concentrate. The Hon Member for Armagh was droning on about the years of neglect his area had suffered at the hands of this Government, about how admirably suited it was, with its abundant supplies of fresh water, as a location of one of these new American man-made fibre plants.

'A God-forsaken country of hills and snipe-grass,' thought Gillan, remembering the occasion when, as a pure public relations exercise, he had dragged a reluctant tycoon from Georgia to view the terrain, criss-crossed with country lanes. 'How you-all goin' to get the stuff out? By helicopter?' had been the comment. The Member was now expatiating on the inexhaustible reservoir of willing and adaptable labour which was awaiting the enterprising industrialist . . .

Upstairs in the public gallery an elderly man staggered up the stairs to the exit. The Deputy Speaker shifted his weight to the other side of his chair. The Clerks at the table below him continued catching up with their paper work. Stormont was fulfilling its statutory democratic functions, as it had for over fifty chequered years. Gillan looked at his watch. Two more down to speak. Should be finished before six. He wondered how Mun was getting on. Must get the bandwagon rolling. The story would be in the *News Letter* in the morning. He'd make sure they'd get straight on to him. Grab the initiative from the word go. Dixon would be beavering away, of course. Promising jobs all round him! By God! He'd gut that sleekit slob as soon as he took over.

'Mr Patterson,' intoned the Deputy Speaker.

Patterson rose on the benches behind him. A GP who practised in his own constituency – an infallible combination, medicine man and family confessor at one stroke. He was congratulating the Minister on his Bill . . . further useful addition to his armoury . . . the drive for new industry . . . magnificent achievement to have maintained some momentum . . . present unrest . . .

'Friend of Willie's,' thought Gillan. 'Must get Mun to have a word with him.'

At the Castle, Stewart Taylor showed Carson into the Prime Minister's room, closed the door quietly and left them.

'Good of you to come down, Desmond. A drink? Bit early maybe. Sit down.'

Carson took the chair on the other side of the fire, so that he could talk face to face. He lit a cigarette to calm the tension he was feeling.

'I thought it might be helpful to have a quiet word with some of my senior colleagues. You are the first I've seen, because you are very much in the firing line. There won't be much left of Home Affairs if this goes through.'

Carson nodded assent.

'But then we are all very much with our backs to the wall. It's the moment of truth which no Prime Minister of Northern Ireland has ever faced head on. Craigavon's confrontation in 1931 was only a skirmish, and the 1912 revolt is pre-history. Do you see a way out?'

51

It was a good question, and the rhetoric of the Cabinet room would provide no hiding place. 'Frankly, at this moment, no. I've thought about it. If we defy them, there's only one way we could survive . . . and that's a deal with the South.' It was a foolish thing to have said, and the incredulity that registered in Packham's face made Carson swiftly add, smiling to underline the point . . . 'That's the kind of lunatic logic we'd finish up with.'

The Prime Minister's face relaxed. That kind of talk, even in jest, shared the nature of obscenity.

Carson pressed on, at a loss to understand why the idea had occurred to him, out of the blue, intuitively, as a realistic option. It was so alien to his normal thinking. Pillow talk; subliminal suggestion? Was this what she was doing to him? He heard himself saying, 'There is no magic way out. I still stick to what I said this morning. We must get them to take it slowly if they won't change their minds. Gradually, piecemeal, maybe under the guise of a radical shake-up of security, *maybe* I say, it might be possible to get by. But I'm not too sanguine, in any event.' He had thought about this one on the way down to the Castle and now, on impulse, decided to play it. 'I don't see how I can possibly remain. I have identified myself with the RUC. I believe I have gained their confidence. For me to acquiesce in the changes proposed would be unthinkable. I think it better that I tell you this now than later.'

The die was cast. He had not intended to go so far, but the politician had taken over. He had not been able to resist the *sound* of the gesture, and now, in his nostrils, was the stench of burning boats. He waited.

The Prime Minister looked directly at him. 'I thought you might feel like that Desmond. I understand your position. Indeed, it may come to the point where the only credible action the Government can take, is to resign en masse. But I don't think we have reached that point yet. And I urge you not to be too despondent. I must tell you now, that before this whole thing was sprung on us, I had been considering the question of a Cabinet face-lift. Governments are as subject to sag as any other body. I have not, as yet, come to any decisions, but frankly, I have had your position very much in mind. You've borne the heat and dust of the day for . . . over two years now. That's a long time in a very demanding, gruelling job. And no one could have done it better.'

Carson muttered his modest demurrer.

'No, I mean it. You have taken a great load off my shoulders. We've had some rough moments together in the past two years . . . and I trust . . . that you will not find me unappreciative.'

52

This was better than Carson could have expected. He was being offered a life-line. 'Arthur, the last thing I want to do is rock the boat. But I cannot see how I could preside over the disbanding of the Specials. I am as aware of their shortcomings as anyone – more so probably – but to the public they represent something which it's hard to put a name to – the last line of defence, the last remnant of the old certainties. Apart from that, I have a feeling of personal responsibility towards them. I have defended them in the past. I cannot desert them now.'

'Of course you can't. None of us can. There can be no question of anyone . . . presiding over their disbandment. But surely it must be generally accepted that a body equipped with 303 rifles, however good their marksmanship, is hardly suitable for modern crowd-control . . . not to speak of dealing with massed gangs of young thugs pitching stones and petrol bombs. No, I've been giving this a lot of thought in the last few hours, and I believe that if we get London's co-operation in timing and in presentation, we might just pull it off. And I'm forced to admit that, forgetting the politics of it, I see merit in what they are proposing. The problem was very different in the Twenties and in the late Fifties. The security situation *does* need a new approach. As regards the other aspects: by centralising more control in the Home Office, we are moving more into parity with the rest of the Kingdom, thereby strengthening the Union!'

Carson could not resist laughing. 'You make it sound almost desirable!'

'Exactly!' The PM held out an open hand. 'Presentation! It's nine-tenths of the battle.'

Carson was sober again. 'Yes, yes, but isn't this really a bit unrealistic? Can you really see us selling this line at a meeting in North Belfast or . . . like the one you were at last night in Lisburn?'

The mention of Lisburn was unkind and he regretted it, but the Prime Minister's euphoria had really been getting out of hand.

Packham's face hardened. 'Those meetings are a waste of time. They're usually packed by the hardliners. You never contact the people you *want* to talk to. No, television is the thing that really makes an impact. Television and radio. That's the way to get to the people: in their homes. And no possibility of the papers blowing up some minor incident into a major fiasco. As you know, they're only too ready to knock us, given half a chance. No, in future, I'm cutting right down on these meetings. Some, I know are unavoidable, but the minimum, the minimum!'

'Oh no!' thought Carson. There it goes again; the antipathy to the hustings, the paranoia about the press. This was the new neurosis at the top; the Prime Ministerial sickness that seemed to inflict every administration, of whatever complexion. A sickness fed, had Carson but known, in the previous hour by the clerical delegation, who had urged the Prime Minister, in the words of the daily House of Commons prayer, to 'forgo all partial affections', and to speak directly to the great silent majority. To Arthur Packham this meant one thing, the warm uterine capsule of the TV studio, wherein all was hushed and safe from interruption.

'You're good on the box Arthur. I've always envied your natural-ness.' Carson meant it. He himself preferred and needed the response, the highs, the play-back from a live audience. But he had allowed himself to be side-tracked. 'Certainly,' he went on, 'if we can get the media on our side, get the tide moving for us, then that's our best hope. It's a matter of mobilising our support, getting them off their backsides.'

'The Protestant back-lash is our safest bet,' said Packham. 'They won't like that.'

'It's my feeling that it won't require any exaggeration,' said Carson, soberly. 'It could be a very real threat. There's been a lot of crying "Wolf" in the past, but we must be very near the last straw by now.'

'Anyhow that's the plan,' said Packham briskly. 'The task now is to get it accepted by the Party, and then in the country.'

Carson hesitated. 'I'm sorry Arthur but . . . it still leaves my problem unsolved.'

Packham smiled wryly. 'I can see that. I'm afraid it's one of those things that only you can decide.'

'Was it for this,' thought Carson, 'that he brought me down here?'

But the Prime Minister had not yet finished. He leaned forward for emphasis. 'I can promise you this. If you stick with me, I won't leave you holding the baby for very long. I think you take too pessimistic a view . . . I know, I know,' he smiled, 'I'm always being accused of exactly the opposite.' Suddenly serious again and speaking slowly he continued, 'I believe, that if we get the timing we want from London, and if we get the presentation right, that the reaction over the Special Constabulary will be containable; especially if someone else is entrusted with actually implementing the changes. And that would be very understandable. A new man for new measures. Given your association with the traditional Specials, you would naturally wish the changeover, however essential, to be undertaken by someone else. Would that be so

54

out of the way?'

Packham waited for a reaction. 'Yes, that might ease the situation. I am grateful to you for the suggestion, Arthur. I have no wish to resign. Who has? And I would like to be as helpful as I can. May I ask exactly what . . .?'

The Prime Minister broke in quickly. 'Please don't press me, Desmond. I'm doing what I can, as you see, but at this moment I cannot be more explicit. I'm sure you appreciate the position. The whole thing was blown up so suddenly and we are talking about . . . major decisions. I know you understand.' He smiled his warm smile. 'For a Prime Minister, Desmond – I can talk to you like a father, because I can give you twenty years or more! – the one quality he looks for in his colleagues, and the rarest, is loyalty. And loyalty begets loyalty. You may have cause to remember that one day. Oh, one soon finds out who the devious ones are, the schemers, the congenital conspirators. They're a fact of life. One lives with them. But, when the time comes, one can hardly be expected to feel any sense of obligation.' He spoke with some bitterness.

Carson remained silent. There was nothing he could say.

The PM continued after a moment. 'You can go a long way Desmond, and I don't say that to flatter. Think over what I've said to you.'

The Prime Minister rose from his chair. The meeting was over. Carson was rather taken aback, conscious that no real conclusions had been reached. But that was the Packham style. You planted an idea and then gave it time to germinate. Or you put someone in the picture, but left it partially painted, inviting the subject to guess at the final outline. The Prime Minister saw his colleague to the door of the room and clapped him on the shoulder.

'Give me a ring tomorrow morning before Cabinet. I shall be in the office at nine o'clock.'

Carson moved out into the inner hall from which the main staircase led to the upper floors of the Castle. He was wrapped in thought, wrestling with the elliptical utterances of his Chief. Was he being kept sweet with pie in the sky? Or had he been offered something? If so, what? And that bit about having no sense of obligation – that was clearly a dig at the Gillan camp – and the one firm commitment that he would not be left long with the baby. Could it be Trade that was being dangled before him?

'Minister. How are you?'

Down the stairs came tripping Sir Stewart Taylor. He liked Taylor;

55

an honest man, a strange character who had eschewed alcohol until he was fifty but now drank only champagne. Liberated and buoyed up on Bollinger, he had been known to perform acrobatic feats astonishing in a man of his years, and unbelievable, when one encountered the grave, erudite and self-effacing civil servant the following morning.

'Can I offer you a cup of tea?'

This was deferential officials' code for 'can I have a word with you'. Taylor had known him, and had been unfailingly helpful, since Carson had been on the back-benches. Socially they had long been on Christian name terms but Taylor insisted, on all official occasions, on the nominal master-servant relationship.

The Cabinet Secretary had something to ascertain or to convey. Carson followed him into his office. As he did so he noticed that George Patterson, a back-bencher, was being escorted by a private secretary towards the PM's room.

Clearly the cohorts were being lined up for the fray.

'Well, Stewart. Tell me all. No tea thank you!'

'How did you get on with the PM?'

Carson shrugged. 'Oblique as usual. But anxious to be helpful. My position is not all that wholesome, you know.'

'I realise that. I just wanted to say to you, if I may, that I hope you won't take any precipitate step, because I believe that the prospect for you is nothing like as bleak as it may appear.'

'What are you trying to tell me Stewart?'

Taylor looked embarrassed. 'I think it's obvious that a lot is going on behind the scenes and you know I can't comment. I can only confirm what you must have already guessed. It looks as if Trade is taking the gloves off and there's no knowing where that will lead. One thing is sure – the PM will insist on collective responsibility. If the Cabinet line is fixed tomorrow morning, then he will expect total solidarity. Anyone who breaks ranks, goes, and that's that. In any case, as you know, there's not much love lost between the two of them. So I urge you to hold your hand and let others do the resigning, that's if there *is* any resigning. I'm always sceptical! I think the next few days are going to be rough. Incidentally, I've been on to the Home Office, and if the thing breaks prematurely, they have agreed to play it very low key: discussions still going on with us; regular review of security etc etc. Sir David and his officials are being as helpful as they can. It's the Prime Minister, apparently, who is baying for blood.'

'He may get it too,' said Carson grimly, 'and not quite in the way he

56

wants it. I've asked the GOC and the Inspector General to come up first thing tomorrow afternoon, just so that they are not taken by surprise. It's a ready-made situation for the Roundheads – real "No Surrender" material.'

'I take it the PM gave you the sort of line we intend to take tomorrow. Are you reasonably happy?'

'What means happy? I think it's a lot better than I'd anticipated.'

Taylor's face brightened. 'Good. Good. I'm glad that you feel things are more hopeful. With your weight behind us, we can really stand up to this "go it alone" nonsense.'

'I didn't say . . .' Carson began, and then started to laugh. He couldn't be angry with Stewart Taylor. Anyway, he had the feeling of being able to move again. Space was being created; the sense of being hemmed in was not so acute. As he turned to go, the telephone rang. Taylor took it and motioned to him to wait. It was a call from Robert, to tell him that Gillan was winding up, and that the Adjournment would be twenty minutes earlier than expected. His agent Brian Kedge was waiting for him in the bar.

Back at Stormont he turned sharp left out of the lofty, ornate central hall, lined, like all the public precincts, with Roman travertine, an ironic touch, in what had once been called 'a Protestant Parliament for a Protestant people'. The new bar was on the first floor. It consisted of two rooms, the tall windows taking advantage of the fine outlook at the front of the building. The larger bar was for visitors, clerks of Parliament, journalists, with an unwritten laissez-passer for senior officials. The smaller and under-used room was reserved for Members only, the theory being that there they could discuss affairs of state and 'the high benefit and commodity of the kingdom' without intrusion from prying reporters. But it was a gloomy room, decorated in dark browns by a trendy liberal MP whose service in the House had been short-lived. All the crack, the gossip, the intrigue was with the fourth estate in the general bar – politicians, even when reviling it, cannot leave the press alone. That was the door that Carson pushed open, and the brouhaha of chatter and laughter gave some indication of the lack of interest in the proceedings below. Ducking the invitations to have a drink, he caught Brian's eye.

Brian Kedge was a tough young quantity surveyor of farming background who had been, as Chairman of his Young Unionist Branch, and as an influential Orangeman, a devoted Carson supporter long before he had taken on the job of part-time agent, not for the token salary, but because of his fanatical belief in his own brand of basic Unionism. It was a sad fact which all politicians had come to terms with, that energy, drive, sheer dedication, and a readiness to put one's money where one's mouth is, were found, not in the ranks of the high-principled liberals or moderates, but among the fundamentalists. There lay the staying-power. In a huddle in the corner Carson got the state of play.

'I got Harrmon. My place at 8.30. The Green Street Branch are meeting tonight. Two of the constituency officers will be there, talking about the electoral roll. I thought you might drop in about 7.15. I know you can't say anything, but it'll give you a chance to test the water. Maybe you could give an indication of . . . you know . . . of what's coming up. They always like to think afterwards that they were in the know all along. All right?'

'I'll think about it. This Harrmon meeting.'

Kedge was hesitant. 'Are you wise?'

'You didn't say I was coming?'

'No, of course not. But he must know damn well that you're behind it.'

'I've got more important things to worry about. Has Fred been in touch?'

Kedge looked round. 'He was here a few minutes ago. He's getting round the lads alright.'

'He's not the only one.' Carson threw his eyes up, indicating the area behind him where Mun Martin was in earnest conclave with a Member usually referred to as the Rooster, possibly because of his tuft of sandy hair, prominent nose and well-documented randiness.

From modest beginnings the Rooster had established a reputation as an extremely effective advocate, with a surgical line in cross-examination. A loner, he sat for one of those typical Belfast areas which are half heavy – industrial and half residential – bourgeois. His constituents either detested or idolised him. He was unattached to either wing of the Party, in Dixon's terms unreliable, but because of his debating skills, he exercised considerable influence, especially among the hard-liners whose views he articulated best. Yet his professional association with the Attorney, Shane Crossley, in whose chambers he had been a pupil, remained close, and was the main reason why he spared the government when, so often, it was open to attack and especially since he found the Prime Minister, with his air of patrician breeding, far from *simpatico*. Vain, though short-sighted, he always tended to remove his glasses in attractive female company. Ambitious to make money, and there the political ladder helped, he was prepared to listen to Mun. He was curious to know more of the little gathering which was to meet at Gillan's house that evening, where he would hear, he was assured in Dickensian terms, something to his advantage. His instinct told him that Mun really *did* know something.

'It's this so-called initiative, isn't it?' said the Rooster bluntly.

'That's unimportant,' said Martin, playing for position. 'Good God! Was it all round the bar already?'

But the Rooster's next remark reassured him. 'Hot pursuit round the clock . . . new army tactics, undercover SAS . . . what the *Telegraph* was talking about the other day, eh?'

Mun gave his cryptic smile as he moved on. 'That's hardly our department. See you then. 8.00?'

As Carson was leaving the room, Mun grabbed hold of his arm.

'Got a moment Des?'

Carson pulled him to one side and spoke quietly. 'You're being a bit obvious, aren't you, Mun? People can see you coming a mile away. You're doing yourself and your friend more harm than good.'

Martin was taken aback. "So you're really going along with it.'

'I thought I made it clear this morning that I saw no point in running our heads against a brick wall.'

Mun smiled his tight, unpleasant smile. 'You've changed, Desmond. You've changed. Ah well, we'll just have to see, won't we?'

They parted in an awkward silence.

'That should slow him up a bit,' thought Carson. 'I must find out from Fred just how many he's been round already.' He wound his way down the stairs again. Robert would be waiting with his papers. The adjournment would just be another instalment of the debate which had gone on for the past five years. When was it right to ban a procession? How to reconcile the seemingly insatiable urge to walk endless miles in some sort of uniform with the right of the non-marcher to be protected from riot in the streets. The great moral issues of citizens' rights had long ago been overtaken and engulfed by the demands of political expediency. The big battalions would continue to march: the smaller platoons would have to take their chance, on the day. The price of liberty was time-and-a-half for a couple of thousand policemen.

Robert was waiting in the rear corridor behind the Chamber Chair. A brief exchange. He took the file and entered the Chamber once again. The blue leather, the mace on the table, the daylight that was always artificial. Gillan was at the box, rocking backward and forward on his heels, fluent and emphatic. Carson took his seat on the front bench behind him, with a quick glance up at the Public Gallery. On with the motley. He reflected that Jo had never seen him in the House; grave, composed, Her Majesty's Minister of Home Affairs.

In the corridor, which ran outside the front entrance to the chamber, was Dixon's den, officially known as the Whips' Room. By some obscure arrangement dating from the distant Thirties when the ruling party made all the rules, the secretary of the Unionist Party was always on the Parliamentary pay-roll, with the official title of Superintendent of the Whips' Office. At this moment, the Superintendent was faced by an irate Minister of Finance.

'I thought you were coming up to see me?' said Willie, closing the door behind him.

Dixon was casual. 'I couldn't get away. I was sorting out next week's questions. What's your problem.'

'What's all this about a re-shuffle? Am I the last to know?'

'Re-shuffle? News to me. Who told you that?'

'Never mind. What happens if Carson goes?'

Dixon was at a loss. Willie, he knew from of old, was always flying off at a tangent at the slightest whisper of possible changes in government, but where had he got hold of this one? Suddenly he recalled the half-serious exchanges while leaving the Kitchen Cabinet. Bloody hell! Was that starting to leak too? No, it was just coincidence – someone simply playing on Willie's insecurity. 'Who's been getting at you? Mun?' His spies had already informed him that Mun had been seen on the Finance floor, well outside his normal beat. The look on Willie's face was confirmation enough. 'He's feeding you a load of bloody nonsense. Sure he's been up there in the bar all afternoon lobbying everyone but the barman! If that's the way you want to go, you go, Willie. So long as the PM knows where you stand.' 'That'll fix him,' thought Dixon. 'After all we've done for the sod – slippery bastard.'

'Now look, Billy, I'm not going anywhere. You know that. The PM has always had my support.'

Dixon went on scribbling on the blue Order Paper and spoke without lifting his head. 'Fair enough, Willie. I'll tell him that.'

Willie was staring unseeing at a photograph on the wall, a shot of some long-forgotten Parliamentary golf-outing. He turned round, the aggression gone out of him, uncertain. 'But what happens if Carson goes, Billy?'

Dixon eventually condescended to look at him. 'Why should he go?'

'He's not going to have Home Affairs cut to ribbons. He couldn't wear it.'

'Who says he has to wear it? We might decide to fight, we can still get a deal. Anything can happen.' Dixon wagged his finger in admonition. 'But your position, Willie, is simple. All you have to do is decide one thing – whether you're going to stick with the PM or whether you're going to sell yourself to a man who'll be as much good to you as the full of my arse of roasted snow!'

Willie's face reddened, but he suppressed his anger. One day he would get his own back on this jumped-up corner-boy.

Dixon, sensing that he had gone too far, switched from tough to tender. 'Willie. Put yourself in my position. I've stood up for you time and again. You can believe me or not, but it was touch-and-go the last time round, whether you'd stay where you were. But I told the PM that you'd always played the game, and that I couldn't let you down.' Dixon was now in the realm of fantasy in which he functioned as a grey eminence making and breaking cabinet ministers. But he had enough real influence at the Castle to make his pretensions plausible enough to those outside the magic circle, more so, since the Prime Minister recognised that the putative patronage of his Party Secretary was his handiest weapon in maintaining party discipline. So Willie, though with a pinch of salt, was prepared to accept his indebtedness.

Dixon sensed it. 'So what does it make me look like, Willie, when the PM hears that you've been playing footsie with Gillan's lot? Makes me out a fuckin' Charlie, doesn't it?'

Willie was now thoroughly wrong-footed and hastened to make amends to the aggrieved Dixon. Mutual apologies. One of those unfortunate misunderstandings. Willie had never, for one moment, wavered in his allegiance to the Prime Minister. His assurance of support was unnecessary, but he repeated it gladly. One hundred per cent! As the door of the Whips' Room closed behind him, Dixon muttered half-aloud, 'Until the next time.'

Outside the bell was ringing, the signal that the House was up for the day.

Green Street was near the market place in the town which was the centre of Carson's constituency. Originally in the County Down countryside, serving a prosperous farming community, it was gradually being absorbed into the so-called Greater Belfast Urban Area, a popular shopping centre for the growing numbers who shunned the daily disruptions and traffic problems of Belfast. Unionist meetings were held in the Orange Hall in Green Street, largely for reasons of tradition, rather than because of any very active link between the Constituency Party and the Orange Institution, which was regarded as too plebian by the more snobbish members of the Party, even though they might not be totally unsympathetic towards its aims. There was also a small but growing movement within the Party, to dissociate formally from the Orange Order, a reflection both of ecumenical changes and of pressure from the liberal wing of the Party to open up its ranks to Catholics. Until very recently, Carson had not concerned himself very much with this uphill struggle to drag the party, screaming, into the second half of the twentieth century. Now, because of his personal circumstances, he bitterly regretted his failure to pull his weight earlier. Green Street Branch, like much of his constituency party, was largely un-reconstructed Unionism with the odd courageous sally by the largely middle-class moderate element.

The Orange Hall was a two-storey building of yellow brick, with stucco surrounds to the doors and windows. High up on the gable was the date 1887, the period of an earlier Protestant back-lash, when Gladstone's Home Rule Bill resulted in a swift and massive expansion of the Orange Order throughout Ulster. The upstairs room in which meetings were held had a high-pitched roof. On the walls were lithographs of William the Third and Mary, flanked by pictures of former Orange dignitaries. Two deacon poles – ceremonial Orange staves – were crossed behind the high-backed, heavy mahogany chair in which the Worshipful Master presided over meetings of the Lodge. It had been moved to one side and the dais was occupied by several officers seated behind a table draped with the Union Jack.

As Brian Kedge entered shortly after 7.15, the proceedings were in train. To an audience of about fifty or sixty people, a small, ferrety, grey-haired man was holding forth on the perennial subject of security. Sammy Suffern, North Down District Councillor and storeman at the local Short Brothers factory, took the English language by the throat and throttled it into submission. 'The whole of this consistency, in fact the whole country, is cryin' out for something to be done. I tell you all most sincerely, lookin' at the "entermas" of the whole question, if the army don't get off their backsides, the people of this country are goin' to do it for them. I mean, look at the moral ethnics of the situation. These terrorists in the IRA are layin' down the law to the government. And I'm telling you in all sincerity – I mean this most sincerely – the signs are there for all to see. The signs are corruptin' out all over the consistency. The people are not goin' to stand for it. Why are they keepin' the B Specials in the background? Why are they not usin' the men that can do the job?' There was a burst of sustained applause from all round the speaker. 'I say that the present security policy "mittelates" against the interests of the people of Ulster. The people I represent are lookin' for action. What the government has got to do is to study the traces of the ordinary workin' man and really consider the discourses at their disposal, so that they can protect him. They have got to devolve a new policy – I say this most sincerely. It's the workin' people that is bearin' the brunt. Take that wee woman from Comer Street – now the day she was hit with the bomb . . .'

The chairman of the branch, a sales representative with a lively, cheerful manner, attempted to stem the flow. 'Excuse me, Councillor Suffern, I know that what you're discussing is important, very important to all of us, and we are all very grateful to have your views, as a man who keeps closely in touch with the people, but two of our constituency officers have kindly come along to discuss the new electoral roll, and they'd like to get away for another meeting. I know you'll understand. There will be an opportunity later on under "Any other business" . . .'

Sufferin, who had remained on his feet, reluctantly gave way, but not without a peevish parting shot. 'All right, Mr Chairman, all right . . . but only in deferment to our guest speakers. But I warn you. I'm not finished.' He sat down.

'Thank you, Councillor,' said the Chairman, and was turning to the papers in front of him when there was movement at the back of the hall: a scraping of chair legs, as people swivelled round to glimpse the new arrival.

At the sight of Carson, there was sporadic applause, as he strode up the central gangway smiling and exchanging greetings. One stout party worker rose and gave him a hug. 'This is *my* man. This is *my* man,' she repeated.

'All right, Emma, all right. We've got work to do. Pleasure later!' He extricated himself, grinning, and leapt on to the platform, shaking hands with, and greeting the officers in strict precedence, starting with the branch chairman.

Greetings over, the chairman rapped the table and called the meeting to order. Then after a quiet aside with Carson, went on. 'We are delighted to welcome our member, the Minister, here tonight in Green Street. He's a very busy man as we know – he's got a special security meeting at eight o'clock, so I feel sure you would like to hear him right away.'

Good applause as Carson rose. After brief introductory courtesies to the platform, he went straight in. 'Ladies and gentlemen, fellow Unionists, I have always tried to keep you in touch with the latest developments and the latest thinking in the Party and in the Government, and I have taken you into my confidence as far as I legitimately could. You all appreciate, I know, the delicate position in which someone doing my job can find himself.' At that there was a murmur of sympathetic understanding. He spoke with gravity. 'Tonight I find myself in an even more difficult position than usual, and I ask for your indulgence if I am not as explicit as I should like to be.' His audience registered the tension he transmitted. 'Within the next twenty-four hours, there will very probably be reports of new developments, changes in, among other things, the disposition of the security forces. These changes will no doubt be exaggerated and indeed distorted by the media, in their usual fashion . . .' A growl of indignation indicated short shrift for the media if they ever penetrated as far as Green Street. 'But I want to say this to you: don't believe all you hear! Don't jump to conclusions. The Government will keep a firm grip on the situation. We shall not be stampeded into anything which we believe to be opposed to the real interests of Ulster – whatever the pressures from Westminster!' Again warm and sustained applause.

He developed and repeated the theme that the only changes the Government would ever agree to in the field of security would be changes for the better. He touched on the need to take a tougher line with protest marches, that could so easily turn into confrontations, and stressed the need for more policemen – they were still sorely under strength. Then he drew to a finish.

'The army are doing a great job under difficulties – we know that.' Perfunctory applause. 'But what I want to see, and what I know *you* want to see and what this whole province wants to see, is *Ulster* men – *and* women – defending Ulster!' Oh yes! Immediate approval; the thunder of feet drumming on the floor. 'But we cannot expect our own people to do the job unless and until we give them the tools to do it with. Our police force is a fine dedicated body of men that any country would be proud of. But I shall not be content until they are not just the best in the UK but the best *equipped* in the UK. We must see to it that their training and weaponry is second to none. That may mean change, change in organisation, in tactics, change in role but only, *only* so that they are better able to carry out the task which we are asking them to do.' The applause came again, but muted. They were uncertain as to what he was driving at. He had gone quite far enough, almost given the game away. Capitalise on it! He dropped his voice and again spoke deliberately. 'My friends, because I am here in my own constituency, among the people I know and trust, among the people who have known me for many years now, I have gone further than I intended. But believe me when I say this – and I speak as political head of the security forces in this province of ours. Whatever lies before us, be sure that I shall accept nothing which is not in the best interests of the RUC and of our Special Constabulary; nothing which you yourselves would not accept in my place.' Warm applause, warm, encouraging, fortifying.

As it died down, he added as a throwaway: 'And I know I can say the same for my successor, whoever he may be, when the time comes.' Leave it at that. Just to avoid the impression that he was a fixture at Home Affairs – two years in the turbulence of today's Northern Ireland must seem a long time. His last assurance had passed without impact. On the platform and in the body of the hall were smiling, nodding, approving faces. The chairman rose, and pledged their confidence and total support in whatever steps he would see fit to take.

As he leapt off the platform and strode down the hall, Emma once again threw her arms round him. This time her message had more point. 'Whatever you do Des, don't let any more Papishes into the RUC – keep the RC's out!'

Amid warmly applauding constituents struggling to their feet to do their Member honour, it was a chilling note that no one else was apparently aware of, nor found remarkable. It struck him fleetingly that not so very long ago he himself would have felt the same. He was smiling again. The show was on the road again. Brian Kedge fell in behind him as he gave a last wave round on leaving the hall.

'Well,' said the agent, as they tripped down the stairs to the waiting cars, 'They seem solid enough. It was a good idea wasn't it?'

'What would I do without you?' said Carson, and thumped him on the back. Outside the Hall, Carson's cars were waiting beside Kedge's yellow BMW. Carson looked at his watch. 'I'll tell you how we play this. I'm going straight home. When Harrmon arrives, get him chatting. Tell him there's a move to mess around with the police and that it might be an idea if he had a word with me. I've been thinking about this. There are no secrets in this game, as you know. It's all right for him to come to see me at his request, but it's not all right for me to meet him, even on neutral ground – and your house is hardly neutral. Right? Give me a buzz before you come.'

One of the escorts was waiting by the rear door of the Jaguar. 'There's a lot of traffic on the main road, sir. We'll go over the hills.'

He nodded and got into the back seat. The RT under the dashboard muttered and crackled. The detective beside the driver spoke briefly into the hand microphone and they moved off, the Vauxhall behind. Security, security. It made private living very difficult, he reflected. At the traffic lights, cars were two abreast on each side. Thursday night, late shopping, the city setting out for a night's entertainment in the music pubs and roadhouses that had mushroomed in the outlying areas – safer, plenty of parking, the feeling of getting out of Belfast, away from it all.

The big car surged forward. It had begun to rain. The susurration of the wheels on the wet road was sedating. He pulled down the armrest and lay back, trying to work out what he would say to Harrmon. But his thoughts like a compass needle swung back to her. He would see her tonight. At first it had been once a week, then twice, now he seemed to be arranging his life, postponing, cancelling, drawing up his programme around her. It was becoming more and more difficult. Robert was clearly getting sceptical about the reasons given for failure to do a meeting, speak at a dinner, even attend a charity ball where his master's presence would have been a political bonus. Carson could not in theory spend many more evenings at home working on speeches, since the net result in terms of words produced was negligible. But Robert, as always uncomplaining, cancelled, re-jigged with only the occasional mild reproof. It was even more difficult with security. He had had Crosbie Knox, the Inspector General himself, telephoning from the RUC Headquarters in Knock, complaining that the Minister would have the

Head of Special Branch round the bend, with his habit of dismissing his escort and driving himself round at night in his private car. With respect, the IG hoped that the Minister would appreciate that officers assigned to him were under strict instructions to be in attendance at all times – except, of course, when he was at home, where there was a regular guard round the clock.

The phrase 'setting an example' had even been employed at the RUC end. Carson had already been stopped once in his private Mercedes by an army patrol of the Welsh Regiment, newly arrived in the province. A Corporal, sensing Carson's impatience to dispense with the routine examination of boot and engine, had turned bloody-minded and held him while they contacted the nearest depot at Hastings Street to check his identity. Only a passing RUC patrol had saved him from further embarrassment. After that, he had given instructions to install a radio-telephone link in his car in case of similar incidents, or indeed – sometimes it struck him as he drove alone by night through the city – in case of a real emergency. He sometimes carried a PPK Walther pistol, and the feel of the weapon offered some reassurance, but he was under no illusions as to what his chances were if they really decided to get him. His wife, who had long since got used to his comings and goings at all hours – his practice of sleeping in a dressing-room to avoid disturbing her late at night was proving an easement he had not originally bargained for – even she was asking why he could not use the official car at all times, and pestering him as to where he might be contacted when he took off on his own. He accepted that his personal driver and escort had more than a suspicion as to what was behind his nocturnal excursions and he hoped to God that their discretion was as total as their loyalty. But he recognised that it was only a matter of time before the whispers grew. As if his life were not complicated enough. It was all a mess. And yet, and yet, he had never known such elation before. The desire was intense, precise, unique, but when he came to define it to himself, he became bogged down in waffle, imprecision. He had projected himself so completely into this Catholic girl that when he was without her, he felt lost, unrecoverable. Somewhere he had read that there is no pleasure like that given by a woman who really wants to see you. He had never got closer to it than that. And yet he had known her hardly three months.

At the time of her appointment, because of its special nature, he had talked to her at length. Even at that first encounter he had felt exposed, not entirely in control. The alternation of sophisticated withdrawal, apartness, and then, swiftly, the warm childlike even malicious frankness had even then, he now recognised, begun to exercise its potent attraction. About a week after she had joined the office he stopped the car at the Massey Avenue entrance where she was waiting for a bus. On the pretext that he wanted to find out how she was getting on in her new job, he took her for a drink to the nearby Glenmachan Hotel where they always served him in a private sitting room. She knew by instinct his interest was not professional and very soon he knew that she knew. The unforeseen improbable force that pulls and then fuses together two disparate human beings – elective affinity, biochemistry, call it what you will – had them in its thrall.

They met again several times. A month after their first meeting she hired a car and they drove to part of the Glens behind the Antrim Coast Road and went walking across the moors. That had been dangerous – Carson's face was too well known. Wherever the transmission lines of the Electricity Board strode in their seven-league pylons across the remotest hills, the public faces peered from the flickering box. But they had got away with it. Carson, with a tweed hat and sunglasses – a disguise which he soon doffed, because they never saw a soul – and a shopping bag over his shoulder, had taken her hand and talked and given himself up to sheer enjoyment, like a schoolboy. Every now and then they stopped and hugged each other and kissed long, long, and laughed out of pure *joie de vivre*. Was it the fact that she was from a different tribe, an exotic creature whose responses and attitudes, in all the unsensual things, were strange to him although they both had their roots in the same small plot of earth. Sometimes he felt inhibited for fear of offending her, especially when politics shaded inevitably into religion. After half-an-hour's walking, well away from the road, they began to look for a place to picnic. As they searched for a sheltered slope facing south-west and the sun, rejecting this heathery hollow, that bank of wiry grass, there was the unspoken sense of mating animals seeking a lair, a den in which they would not be surprised by chance observers. The place they found was under an outcrop of shale partially overgrown with silvery turf and giving a superb view out across the North Channel. Away to the east was the granite hump of Ailsa Craig, to the south the Maidens Lighthouse, and beyond that the coast of Scotland. The slate-blue sea flowed with an effervescent radiance in the sunlight. Below on the road was the hired blue Escort, less conspicuous than his own Mercedes. Even the simple act of deciding where to park and the change-over into the Escort had been magnified into a cloak and dagger operation – the excitement of the meeting enhanced by the real risk of discovery.

With a field of vision all around the hillside no one could approach them unawares. They flopped down on the grass and lay silent, she utterly motionless with arms by her sides, he with his head supported on his cupped hands, staring out at the sea. Suddenly they were aware of what they were doing. The constraint between them was painful, palpable. He moved to take off his jacket, muttering that the sun was so hot. She opened her eyes. They looked at each other in silence, and in that second, they knew that they had smashed into each other's innermost being a window that would never be replaced. It was the first time they had made love and as he kissed her breast, she lifted his head. 'Technically I'm not a virgin, but – darling does this sound funny? – I feel I am.'

For four hours on that warm August afternoon they had embarked on that never-ending, dangerous, heart-breaking, dazzling, delirious exercise of peeling off the onion skins that enclose each separate being, the laboriously acquired layers that are both impediment and armour. What had been an exciting flirtation, an adventure, had that afternoon solidified into an all-engrossing love affair. Forbidden fruit had become the essential bread, the panis angelicus.

The Jaguar braked suddenly as an oncoming lorry swerved to avoid them, its lights on full beam through the driving rain.

'Bloody! Sorry about that sir,' said his driver. 'Some cowboy . . .!'

Carson muttered agreement and returned to his reverie. He was conscious of hunger. She would feed him tonight. Like all passionate women, she loved food and took a meticulous pleasure in preparing it. Even on that first unforgettable day on the mountain it had been smoked salmon and a pie made by herself, which she had produced from the shopping bag. 'Better than Fortnums,' he had said, ashamed of the very ordinaire vin which had been his contribution to the feast. The car stopped at traffic lights coming into the city. An ambulance, its siren braying, sped towards them up the Ormeau Road. Two fire-engines followed, bright with bells, leaving the traffic lines spread-eagled in their wake.

Carson lurched back to reality. 'Find out what's up, Joe.'

The escort in front reached forward and lifted the blue RT microphone on its expanding cord. He switched on. 'Tango Four to Aztec. Can you tell us about a fire in the South Belfast area, Carryduff direction?'

A slight pause. 'Aztec to Tango Four. Hold on a moment.' Then after about ten seconds. 'Tango Four? A new pub near Dundonald Hospital. They had a warning and cleared it. A small charge attached to incendiaries apparently. That's all we have at the moment.'

'Thank you, Aztec. Out.' The policeman turned round to Carson. 'Must be a big one, sir. Those engines were coming from the Lisburn Road Station. Central is nearer, unless they're very busy.'

'Could be,' said Carson, non-committally.

There was nothing he could have done in any case. Only a major disaster now required his presence, and that as a political gesture: a public relations exercise to show the flag and commiserate with those involved. Army Bomb Squad would be there, too late this time. Uniformed men from Dundonald Division would be in charge, controlling the bystanders, though the rain would ensure only minimal interest. They would endeavour to cut down the inevitable looting, and secure what remained, if anything, of the premises. But they knew as he did that, short of a twenty-four-hour guard, nothing would prevent the invisible locusts descending in the night and picking the carcase clean. Anything moveable, saleable or consumable: copper piping, liquor, utensils, furniture, even the wash basins, would be gone by dawn. In the morning, Forensic would appear, taking statements, scratching and scraping through the blackened debris, searching for clues as to precisely where and how the devices had been planted and detonated, looking for a familiar pattern or a new departure, knowing that the chances of tracing and catching the perpetrators were heavily against. In the morning, too, the official surveyors of the Ministry of Finance would appear, to estimate the damage. But others would be there; roving loss assessors and commission men, vultures touting for business, eager for a fat percentage of the compensation claims that already totalled over two hundred million, shamelessly pressing their services on some manager or owner, weary and distraught after a night of havoc. A booming new Ulster industry which Carson and his colleagues had often reflected they could well do without.

Now the car was turning off the main road into the avenue in which he lived. As they drove through the gates and halted in front of the large semi-detached Edwardian building, two B Specials emerged from the darkness at the side of the double garage, re-slinging their Sterlings as they came. He returned their greetings, stayed a moment to talk to them and then dismissed the cars.

'I don't intend to go out again tonight, Joe.'

'You can always contact the pool, sir.'

'Of course. See you at 8.30 then. Keep your head down.'

He raised his hand and entered the house through the side entrance which was always open. A lobby led to the kitchen which functioned as an unofficial guardroom during the hours of darkness and to the front hallway where the lights were on. He glanced offhandedly at the mail on the hall table, opening those letters that looked personal or with the stiff outline of an invitation card: official paper, bumph, constituency stuff that would be dealt with in the office, bills, a statement from his estate agent enclosing a cheque for ground-rents, two joint invitations, both already opened by his wife, one to dine with friends, the other to a charity dance. He considered fleetingly the possibility that Jo might arrange to be present. They had done that once before, but even the one occasion on which they had been on the floor together had excited comment. A Minister may dance with one of his secretarial staff, but when she is very pretty and a Catholic and when they remain for ten minutes on the same corner of the floor in close conversation, then he had gone too far. Eyebrows had been raised at his table and when he returned to it, his wife, Janet, had asked, 'Is that the Catholic girl there was such a fuss about in your office?'

On Thursday his wife was at a university evening class. Now that their only daughter was at boarding school in Kent, Janet devoted her considerable energies to bridge, fund-raising organisations for Cancer Research, and courses of cultural lectures which culminated several times a year in educational visits to places like Italy or Greece. Her apparent self-sufficiency somewhat eased his guilt complex, but her honesty and lack of deviousness had now become a standing reproach to the Puritan sense of retribution which had been inculcated in childhood and which, despite only a token adherence to religious obligations, he would never totally lose. When he had first met her (the only daughter of a well-to-do Belfast solicitor and educated in England) she had seemed an Irish version of the English rose. Now, at forty-two, she was somewhat etiolated. But twenty years ago, when she was riding to hounds and possessed of a self-assurance which he envied, she had seemed to him a most attractive girl, and to his family and friends a most desirable match. For her, this young rugby player, with intellectual pretensions and already quite a personality in political circles, offered something of a challenge. She had no great beauty but she had something to offer him – style, and, through her father's practice, an invaluable boost to his professional career with a lucrative partnership

71

to follow. After her father's death the practice, which handled business for many of the old-established landed families, and did little criminal work, was run by the two other partners, leaving Carson, now senior, to devote all his time to politics. Theirs was, on his side, a marriage of convenience; on hers, an emotionally undemanding relationship which tolerated her husband's occasional philandering. He appreciated all she had done for him and the impeccably acceptable background which she still provided. Her admirably staged dinner parties had done him no harm. There were unkind tongues murmuring that she had catered him into the Cabinet. He got his kicks out of politics and international weekends in London or Scotland with 'the boys', friends from his rugger days. But the pattern of these prolonged undergraduate 'piss-ups' had begun to pall, even before his personal thunderbolt had destroyed it. He was glad that Janet was not at home. He would not have to make excuses. With a bit of luck he'd be away before she returned. He left the mail on the table and went into the cloakroom to wash. He was having a pee when the telephone rang. He took his time shaking off the drops. No, it couldn't be Brian. He would hardly be home yet. What line to take when Harrmon came? He still wasn't clear in his mind. In the study, he lifted the receiver. It was Ricketts, the night editor on the *News Letter*.

Carson listened for a moment, his mouth tightening, then: 'Sorry Sam. I've got someone with me. Ring me back in about ten minutes. Right?'

Christ! He hadn't been ready for that one! They'd got the story, or part of it. And Carson was in little doubt as to the origin of the leak. The tie-up between the Gillan entourage and the *News Letter* night-staff was well known. It was Gillan beating the gun and running hard already. In theory Ricketts would have rung him up for a quote – the first reaction from a member of the Government and a splash on the front page next morning. Some sub would then ring up the BBC, and Gillan would be quoted on the midnight news and grab the lead on all the morning bulletins. Carson knew the drill – he'd played the game himself. He paced up and down, hitting his fist into the palm of his hand. Ring the PM? No, that would only tie his hands. Packham would tell him to say nothing, to wait until the Kitchen Cabinet had drafted a statement. No, he had to play it for himself. He would take the everything-above-board line, and try to turn things in the right direction. Yes, discussions had been taking place and certain proposals were being considered. He, Carson, had been concerned for some time about the need to keep the RUC and the Specials abreast of the latest developments in weaponry and training. Weaponry always sounded good! He had been concerned, too, about the need for better co-ordination of the different arms of the security services. In the near future, the Government would hope to make, jointly with Westminster, who – he could hear himself saying it – are, as you know, responsible for overall defence, including the army . . . Wait a minute! Where the hell was he? Yes, jointly with the British Government they would make their recommendations known. That sounded all right. No pressure. No panic. It depended of course on what Gillan had said, but Carson was sure that his colleague would be careful to keep his personal reaction non-committal, waiting for public indignation to build up. It flashed through his mind that it might be easier to deal with Harrmon now that the cat was out of the bag. He felt edgy and nervous and made for the fridge. His exits and entrances were so unpredictable that Janet seldom arranged for a meal to be provided. But there was always cold stuff. Munching a piece of pie as he went, he poured himself a beer in the dining-room and then went back to the study. He had to get the Harrmon operation right. It could come very unstuck. He was about to dial Fred Butler to find out what was happening on that front (telephoning always gave the comforting illusion that he was on top of a situation) when it rang. It was Brian. They were coming over.

'Drive straight up to the front door – it's your car, isn't it? I'll tell the guard you're coming.'

He had hardly replaced the receiver when it rang again. Ricketts back. Carson let him talk. The easier one came first. 'Changes in the legal set-up? There has been talk, I know. You'd better ask the Attorney General about that. Yes, all I can say is that if we come more into line with the system operating in the rest of the Kingdom, then as Unionists we can hardly complain. I'm sorry, the Attorney's your man. The police? They certainly *are* my responsibility. Yes, discussions have been taking place . . .' Carson stuck to the line he had decided on, pooh-poohing suggestion of sensational change of any kind. Had Ricketts been onto anyone else for reactions? Yes, he'd been on to the Castle. The PM was not available. The press man on duty had promised to chase things up. Lefaux, the Minister of Information, was not available. But, surprise, surprise! The Minister of Trade had been good enough to give him a quote when telephoned. Naturally Mr Gillan had not wished to comment on what was after all speculation, but he had said – and Ricketts read out his note to Carson: 'I am convinced that any proposal to scrap the B Specials would be totally unacceptable to the great majority of the people of Northern Ireland.'

'Would Mr Carson agree with that?'

Carson weighed his words. 'I would certainly agree that any such proposal which involved a radical reduction of our security forces, would be totally unacceptable to the people of Northern Ireland.'

The editor pressed him no further. It was useless, Carson knew, attempting to quiz Ricketts on the source of his information. Sources, like facts, were, in theory, sacred.

'What about the opposition? What are they saying?'

'I'm just going to try them. I have the feeling they'll be pleased,' said the editor cryptically.

Carson took out his pocket diary and looked up the number of the direct line to the Castle. Now that he had cleared his own lines, he had better inform the Kitchen Cabinet.

They were finishing dinner in the first-floor flat which the Prime Minister used when he was not at his home in Armagh. Whatever the state of the nation, whatever the upheavals of the day, dinner-time was sacrosanct. A sandwich snatched between engagements at lunch-time, but in the evening, he insisted on a decent dinner taken at leisure, so that the political batteries could be properly recharged. Even on the rare occasions when he spoke at an evening meeting in the country, it was the duty of the Chairman or Member concerned to see that his distinguished guest was accorded the ritual hour and a half in congenial company with a bottle of reasonable wine. On this October evening, as the rain beat against the windows of the Castle on the hill, all was snug in the dining-room upstairs where a fire burned in the grate. At the round table sat Packham with Taylor and Fine. Lefaux, who had just taken Carson's call, had joined them with the news that the word was out. Miss Montgomery, the resident cook-housekeeper, was clearing away the remains of an apple and blackberry tart, the Prime Minister's favourite pudding. Before that she had provided mushroom soup and a roast of mutton. Nothing fancy: solid gentleman's fare. The bottle in the coaster said Chateau Lascombes 1961. She now placed a piece of Stilton on the table and a decanter of port.

'Coffee is there sir,' she said, nodding towards the hot plate on a side table.

'Thank you, Miss Montgomery. Excellent dinner,' said the Prime Minister, gloomily. As the door shut behind the housekeeper he added, 'Trust that little shit . . .'

'It was bound to happen anytime, PM, even if he hadn't,' said Lefaux, adding more cheerfully, 'I think Desmond took the right line. Don't you?'

'Yes. Yes. I'd have preferred him to have said nothing for the moment, but I suppose that's asking too much,' grumbled Packham.

The other three exchanged covert glances. Lefaux had already gathered that dinner had been devoted to drafting a statement to cover the contingency which now faced them, but that none of Ronnie Fine's formulae had met with his master's approval. Now willy-nilly, they had

75

to go along with Carson.

'This fellow Ricketts . . . was he co-operative?' asked Packham.

'On the whole I think yes,' said Lefaux. 'I spent quite a time talking to him and I hope he took the point that to run the scare story about the Specials would be really irresponsible. Unfortunately, the Gillan quote touches the tender spot.'

It was Taylor the senior man who spoke. 'I think we've got to face it, sir, that the proposals from London, or a garbled version, are now common knowledge. Radio and television will have them. The *News Letter* have a scoop, and you can be sure that they've been ringing round all over the place for reaction. The opposition, once the Specials are mentioned, will be there like a shot. At least there is no sitting of the House tomorrow so we have a slight respite but, with respect, sir, I feel we must say something to dampen down speculation before it gets out of hand. And I think that the Carson line is as good as any. Admittedly he probably said too much, but nothing damaging.' Taylor stopped.

Packham nodded reflectively but without comment, helping himself to a piece of cheese. He turned to the Assistant Cabinet Secretary who had been eagerly waiting for a chance to speak. 'Well Ronnie?'

'In my view, we must get off the defensive and start making the running in uncompromising and positive fashion.'

There were ironic smiles on the other faces.

'You're sounding more and more like a politician every day Ronnie,' said Lefaux.

Fine coloured slightly but stuck to his guns. 'No, wait a moment. Hear me out. All these changes tend in one direction – greater integration with the rest of the United Kingdom. They fall into the same category as more Ulster seats for Westminster – the sort of thing which is totally consistent with Unionist philosophy. Yes I know we have always had our cake and eaten it on this whole question of devolved powers, but I'm saying in principle, in principle, this is the kind of change which a Unionist Government could legitimately have been pressing for.'

'Pressing to abolish the Special Constabulary?' There was a note of impatient incredulity in the Prime Minister's voice. 'Are you serious?'

Fine smiled resignedly, but seemed unabashed. He was used to his master's habit of seizing on the last line of a paragraph. 'If you'll bear with me, sir?'

'Go on. Get to your point.'

'I think we can, and we should, stand over the proposed changes in the administration of the courts. But on the question of the Specials, with all the overtones, I think that you, sir, have no choice if the situation is going to be contained. There has got to be a categorical denial that there is any intention of abolishing the Specials. Billy Dixon is right.' He paused, and the other three looked at him. 'In any case, what is proposed is not removal but renovation. Let's not get bogged down in semantics – the end result will be a force doing the job the Specials are doing now. It must be clearly stated, therefore, that the Specials will remain and, PM,' – he turned to Packham who was obviously impressed by the logic of what he had just heard, the more so since it chimed with the kind of thinking he had voiced earlier to Carson – 'I am sure that you are the person to say it *and* that you should do so on television as soon as possible.'

The mention of television brought an immediate response from the Prime Minister. He put down the glass he had been toying with and leaned forward, interested. 'Yes. Yes. I agree that we must meet the question of the Specials head-on. Certainly I am prepared to give serious consideration to a television broadcast. There is nothing to touch it for getting a case across to the greatest number. And,' he added with feeling, 'it is the most civilised medium.'

Lefaux, anxious to keep options open, broke in. 'I think, PM, we should certainly kept the possibility in mind. Meantime, we have got to get something out to counteract the Gillan statement and keep the temperature down.'

Fine, who had been scribbling sporadically on a pad during the course of the discussion, cleared his throat. 'I have something here, PM. You might like to cast your eye over it.'

He handed Packham a sheet covered in neat legible script. 'The first part is essentially the Carson line, that discussions have been taking place . . . putting the courts on a UK footing.' He waited while the PM adjusted his spectacles and starting reading.

'Yes, yes,' murmured Packham. 'I like that.' Fine shot a mischievous glance at the other two. Thank God they had, at last, a formula which might meet with approval! 'Ah, yes,' said Packham. 'What do you think of this Tom?'

He turned and peered at Lefaux over his glasses, then proceeded to read. 'The Ulster Special Constabulary holds a significant and vital sector in the overall security front against terrorism. The Government is determined that this sector will not be breached or abandoned.' The PM paused and nodded assent. Ronnie Fine was mouthing the words in unison, his eyes switching from one face to the other assessing the reaction. 'The threat facing our Province from street violence, and from sophisticated forms of subversion, has markedly changed during the past years. To combat this menace, the most up-to-date techniques and training are essential, both for the RUC and for the Special Constabulary. The Government will not shrink from making whatever changes in organisation and operational methods it believes to be necessary, both in the public interest and for the safety of the police officers themselves.'

The Prime Minister stopped reading, took off his glasses, and looked at each of his companions in turn. 'I think that's good. That's good, Ronnie.'

Fine, who had been twitching nervously as he waited for the verdict, broke into an embarrassed smile.

Lefaux turned to pat him on the shoulder. 'I must say it is a masterly piece of ambiguity. I *like* the bit about not breaching . . . what is it?'

'The Government is determined that this sector will not be breached or abandoned,' repeated Fine, grinning with pride.

'Yes,' said Lefaux, clenching his fists and laughing. 'I like it.' He turned to Packham and struck while the iron was hot. 'OK, PM? I want to get it out right away.'

'Better check it with Des Carson first.'

'Of course, he knows about it anyway. A straight Government statement which was felt to be necessary in view of the unfounded rumours which have been circulating – that's the kind of guidance I propose. I'll have another word with Ricketts.' He took the draft statement from the table and made for the door with a rueful chortle. 'So long as he doesn't ask me to be more specific about these essential techniques which are going to transform the Bs!'

He disappeared, bound for the suite of information offices which was centrally housed in the rear wing of the Castle.

Packham sighed as he poured himself another glass of port and pushed the decanter towards Fine. 'You deserve it.' He looked all of his sixty-seven years, a man aware that this was only the beginning. 'What about this call to the Home Secretary, Stewart?' he asked wearily.

Taylor was all bustling attention. 'The Private Office said he would have a word with you some time after nine – if you recall. He'll be at his home by then.'

'And Hedges will be able to help, you think.'

Earlier in the day, Taylor had spoken long with Sir David Hedges, the

Permanent Secretary at the Home Office, in an effort to gain time. The PM was now looking for reassurance. Taylor repeated his story. 'As I said, PM, he will do all he can to help with the cosmetics, putting a face on it. But on the substance,' Taylor shrugged apologetically, 'his master appears to be adamant. Hedges is convinced that they are determined to push us to the limit. But you'll be in a better position to judge when you've spoken to the Home Secretary.'

'Well, if they are prepared to play along on the timing, that, at least, is something.'

Fine came in, reluctant to introduce a more pessimistic note. 'The trouble is that the thinking behind this so-called initiative is to provide a sop for the opposition. So the Government may feel that if they start watering it down the whole impact and point of the exercise is lost.'

The Prime Minister frowned. 'If they are determined to push our backs against the wall, so be it. In which case we're wasting our time.' Taylor intervened on a more positive note. 'It's a matter of balance, sir, isn't it? Their priorities against ours. I gather from Hedges that the Opposition over there are pressing them hard, threatening to break the bi-partisan approach unless something is seen to be done.'

'The same bloody story,' exploded Packham. 'Keep the Opposition happy at all costs. Anything to prevent Ulster becoming a real issue at Westminster. Keep it as cosy and non-controversial as possible. No matter how many people are bombed and shot to hell over here.' His voice was full of bitterness. 'One of these days, someone over there is going to get hurt, badly hurt, and then they'll sing a different tune.'

The two officials waited to let the mood pass. Then Taylor tried again. 'Let's hope, then, the Home Secretary realises that the easier he makes it for us, the longer he keeps the Ulster issue at a distance. If ever – which God forbid – they had to take over and set up direct rule, then they'd be in it up to their necks!'

'That's what we need at Stormont,' said Ronnie Fine, 'the bi-partisan approach! – we could make common cause in bashing Westminster.'

The Prime Minister brightened. 'Craigavon used to say that all an election platform needed was one good plank.' There was a tentative knock at the door. 'Come in,' called Packham. Billy Dixon put his head round the door. 'Come in Billy. Have a drink. There's whiskey over there.'

Dixon put down his brief-case and went over to the sideboard. 'My God, it's a wild night, pourin' rain. Three places on fire, I hear – one just down the road there in Castlereagh – a furniture store and some other shop.'

'Anyone hurt?'

'No, not as far as I know. Incendiaries set to go off after closing time I suppose.' He shrugged his shoulders. 'What do you do? Get the bastards that make them, I suppose.'

There was no further interest in that night's acts of violence – they, like the rest of the people of Northern Ireland, had become so drugged on a daily diet of destruction that it required a massive mainline shot to produce any significant reaction.

'I asked you to drop up, Billy,' said Packham, 'because I want to go over a few things for tomorrow. We've put a statement out, by the way.'

'Tom just showed it to me, looks OK. You know that Gillan has leaked the lot to the papers?'

All round were cynical smiles. Taylor spoke. 'Tom Lefaux and Carson are in no doubt – it was Ricketts who got it.'

Dixon grunted. 'Don't you know?' His way of underlining a truism. He settled down on a sofa by the fire and took a folder from his brief-case.

The PM looked at his watch. 'Nearly nine. I'm sure you two would like to get away. I'm just going to mark tomorrow's card with Billy here.'

Taylor rose. 'I've got a few things to clear downstairs, PM. I'll hang on until you speak to the Home Secretary.'

'Damn it, I'd forgotten about that,' said Packham. 'Ronnie, if you could remember to jot down a couple of headings for tomorrow afternoon's meeting.'

Fine nodded. 'I'll be at home if you want me after sir. Good night.' As he left the room with the Cabinet Secretary he was sure that he had not heard the last of his master for that evening. Packham, especially when anything resembling a crisis blew up, had a neurotic habit of telephoning his Kitchen Cabinet at the slightest development. He expected them to be on call and ready to fly to his side at short notice. This was less onerous than it appeared since they all lived within walking distance of the Stormont buildings, a relic of the days when any official who hoped for advancement conformed to the unwritten code. The code said a modest life-style, an unostentatious car and a house 'over the shop'. This avoided invidious comparisons with less well-heeled MPs, and perpetuated the image of the Civil Service as not only an industrious but a disadvantaged sector of society.

Packham settled on the sofa beside Dixon; cut and lit his daily cigar. He was off his guard with the Party Secretary who represented no threat, no rivalry, no ugly question-marks as to why he acted in this way or that. Civil servants, however honest, perforce swayed from left to right and back again in the wake of those whom the electorate set over them. Colleagues? Well, Arthur Packham had, over the years, decided that there was no such thing as colleagues, only fellow-conspirators. But Dixon was different. He had reached his ceiling and was content. Packham had seen to it that financially, whatever happened, he would be well provided for. He had no divided loyalties. Dixon was a Packham man through and through. Now, two comrades-in-arms who had faced the flak together many times, they went down the strength of their forces for the morrow. One by one, Dixon went through the names of the Unionist Parliamentary Party, ticking off here, querying there, dismissing others as lost causes. The instinctive principles he followed in the art of political persuasion were, though he did not know it, precisely those laid down by old Niccolo Machiavelli, four hundred years before. But self-interest has many forms in politics. There are the ambitious who seek promotion up the greasy pole. The hedonists, who look for parliamentary trips to exotic places, invitations to official dinners, to receptions for visiting firemen, where the shorter the guest-list the higher the status. The inadequate, the vain, those craving recognition, who see a unique magic in the letters KMG, CBE or even JP. Lastly those of more modest wants, who desire a little extra shove with a planning application, a job for a relative, a judicious word to the right Police Officer about a delicate matter. In some cases, Dixon earned his reward for assiduous attentions over the years, in others, for past services, solid investment that carried continuing interest. Down the list they went. The inducements, the carrots, the sticks, the blunt threats which he had seen fit to employ, were related in detail. One of the secrets of the Prime Minister's success in managing his party was his familiarity with the political account of each individual member — whether the person concerned was in debit or in credit. Behind the air of patrician nonchalance was a shrewd student of the human condition, its weaknesses and its vaulting ambitions.

'I make it about five or six in our favour,' said Dixon, doing a quick tot on the list before him.

'Hmmm,' said Packham. 'Tight enough. We'll have to make sure that there are no backsliders. And we're assuming that we get enough help from London to put a reasonable front on the whole situation – which is assuming a lot. What else can we do?'

Dixon took a sip of whiskey and pondered a moment. 'What we need is to get the constituencies to come out and back us. I'll tell you what. Tomorrow morning I'll get one of my lads to ring round the chairmen of the constituency parties that we can trust, and get them to send telegrams of support for the Prime Minister's stand.'

'I'm not entirely certain what the Prime Minister's stand *is*,' said Packham ruefully. 'And surely they won't have time to consult their executive by tomorrow afternoon.'

'Never mind about that,' said Dixon, brushing niceties aside. 'They can deal with them afterwards. The main thing is to get the declarations of support coming in, so that we can feed them to the BBC – keep the pressure on, make the buggers think twice, if the Gillan lot start putting ideas in their heads.' The Dixon enthusiasm was infectious.

'Can't do any harm, I suppose.'

'Look PM. Once this whole story is really out in the open, and it looks as if you are standing up against Westminster and fighting for the Specials – the support will come rolling in. Don't you worry!' Dixon was emphatic. There were no nuances in his politics. As far as he was concerned, they were fighting for the Specials. He could see a future in that.

Packham was pensive. To inveigh against making concessions in the strongest terms while all the time quietly giving ground behind the scenes – this has been a Prime Minister's prerogative throughout history. But the essence of the tactic is time. The telephone rang at his elbow. It was Taylor. 'Home Secretary's on the line, sir. I'll just switch to scramble before I put you through.'

There was quite a collection of cars assembled that evening in the stable yard of the Gillan home in Co. Antrim, about twenty miles from Belfast. They had come through the driving rain from far and near. Two would drive over seventy miles home to Londonderry and East Tyrone that night. The large Victorian farm-house stood back from the main road about a quarter of a mile. Reached by a winding avenue, it was well screened by copses of mature timber. About a hundred yards from the house the avenue forked, one branch leading to a gravelled forecourt at the front door, the other leading round behind the lawn and pleasure gardens to the stable-yard. The yard was approached through an archway and surrounded by farm buildings.

James Gillan kept a small herd of beef cattle and was known as a gentleman farmer. The epithet was unnecessary, he was wont to declare at agricultural dinners, because he had never yet met a farmer who wasn't a gentleman! The cars tonight were instructed to drive round to the stables where there was shelter and a covered way leading into the rear of the house. The purpose was to conceal their presence from casual callers. As they arrived, the visitors were conducted into the dining-room for drinks and sandwiches or, for those whose principles forbade strong liquor, tea, with that wide selection of cakes and fancy breads which in the North of Ireland is the staple of country suppers. Gillan and his wife circulated, chatting and looking after their guests. The object of the soiree, despite the social trappings, was to win votes and influence people. The method had been consumer-tested on many occasions. Mun Martin was there, with two or three die-hard Gillan men who knew exactly what their roles were. Cecil McFee was there, under the flattering impression that he had been invited by his influential colleague for an intimate chat and a quiet meal in congenial surroundings. As the evening progressed and the true nature of the gathering became clear, he looked more and more uneasy. Those of his fellow MPs who were there had never been his political soul-mates. Some were there because they opposed the Prime Minister. They disliked him because of his upper-middle-class background, because of his air of superiority and because of his Englishness. But they hated him because they believed he was soft on the Fenians, because they believed that even the mildest reform was a betrayal of the Protestant cause. Others genuinely believed he was the wrong man at the wrong time, and looked to the able and energetic Minister of Trade as the most acceptable alternative.

There was another group of floating dissidents who were the main target for Mun Martin and his special service unit – these were the possible new recruits who were to be enlisted and committed to the Gillan cause. This last category were never left to talk among themselves, but were skilfully exposed only to selected Gillan adherents so that they gained the firm impression of a unanimous front among those present. The news from London had been broken by Gillan himself. He was now neatly exonerated of any charge that he was breaking Cabinet secrecy by the fact that he had been contacted by the press. Despite that, he and Mun did their utmost to ensure that their audience had the flattering sense of being taken into confidence, of being admitted to the magic circle. For a politician, the feeling of being 'on the inside' is the most potent of boosts for the ego. Yet, like Ramsay Macdonald at the top of the grand staircase in Londonderry House, the high-point of social triumph is the moment when defences are down. The case being peddled that evening was simple: the country needed a strong man to stand up to these intolerable demands. Packham was not that man. The race was to those who moved ahead of the inevitable public outcry and established their claim as the next administration.

Gillan and McFee were tete-a-tete. 'It's not my wish Cecil, God knows. I hope I've made that clear. But someone has got to give a lead. And if the party decide that the country needs my services at this moment, then I could not, in conscience, shirk my responsibility.'

McFee listened, feeling that he must at least salute such high- -mindedness, but all he could do was nod, conscious that even the act of listening to such talk was sucking him further into collusion. At last he managed to say half-heartedly and realising as he spoke that he was only damning with faint praise: 'Arthur has still got a lot of support in the country, you know.'

James Gillan didn't even change gear. His voice rang with sincerity. 'Arthur Packham has done a lot for this country and for the Party. No one knows that better than I do. But the man's tired, Cecil. He's tired. Look at what happened this morning. No decisions. No lead. The will's not there any more. After all, he's been in the chair for over fifteen years – he's not getting any younger.'

Mun materialised at their side. 'He's right Cecil. He's right you know. You were at Lisburn last night weren't you? Weren't you? Look at the reception he got. Is it any wonder? The IRA's tearin' this country apart and all Packham wants to do is give, give, give, to the people who are supporting them. And now, they're trying to ruin the police force, and all the Prime Minister does is offer to help?'

Gillan, who was showing signs of some uneasiness at the Martin hard-sell, intervened on a more statesmanlike tack. 'I believe that each of us has just so much to give and that's that. Arthur has given as much as any man can be expected to. These last few years have been rough.' McFee sighed agreement. 'The pace has no doubt told on all of us, and my honest belief is that Arthur has had enough. You can see it.'

Mun moved in again, looking past McFee and speaking out of the side of his mouth to underline the deadly secrecy of the information he was about to convey. 'I'll tell you something, Cecil, I think you should know. I have it on the very best authority that . . . whether this whole business had blown up or not, Arthur had made up his mind to go anyway. It was only going to be a matter of weeks. And that's the God's truth.'

He looked at Gillan for confirmation. The Minister of Trade nodded as one forced to admit a sad truth.

The effect of the revelation was rather spoilt by McFee showing a sudden deep concern. 'You mean he's not well, he's got . . . something?'

Mun's reaction was almost testy. 'No. No. Nothing like that, as far as I know . . . no, it's just that he's . . . had enough.'

'So . . . ' said Gillan, anxious to exploit what remained of the impact, 'where does that leave *us?* We've all got to think about that, Cecil. I'll be frank with you. I think you do a good job in Education. A very good job. You really have a grip on the department.'

McFee was only human. He found it hard to conceal his pleasure. 'That's very kind of you, James, I must say. I try to do a reasonable job . . . '

Mun piled in. 'You do more than *that*, Cecil.'

Gillan continued. 'If ever I had a say in the matter, I would like to see you stay there, or maybe . . . move on to better things. I want you to know that. But.' Gillan paused and looked his subject straight in the eye for a brief moment. Mun had meanwhile faded away. 'But naturally, Cecil, I would have an obligation to help those who had helped me.' McFee said nothing. 'I am sure you appreciate that.' He waited a moment. 'The trouble is, as you know, there's very little time. Think it

85

over. I sincerely hope, Cecil,' he fixed the subject once again with an unwinking eye, 'that we finish up on the same side.' He smiled and moved away to greet a new arrival.

McFee was left in a state of acute mental agitation. He was implicated, tainted. He knew that news of the night's gathering, with a list of those present, would inevitably be in the hands of Billy Dixon by the following morning. He swallowed hard as he pictured the scene in the PM's room at the Castle, when the nature of the event was revealed and Packham learnt that the only other Cabinet Minister present, besides Martin, was his Minister of Education, the man he had plucked from the back benches and placed in high office for one reason – his loyalty. It wouldn't matter, McFee told himself, that he had entered that room with no notion that his political future was in the balance. Now if he protested his innocence, would they believe him? He agonised as he looked around. Everyone seemed to be engrossed in intensely earnest conversations. A North Antrim MP, a close associate of Mun's, was leaning over a colleague who was writing on a sheet of paper – no, *signing* it, for he handed back the pen after a few seconds. 'Good heavens!' McFee muttered to himself. They were getting people to sign something, to commit themselves in writing!

There was only one way out for him. He had to say straight out that he had been brought there under false pretences, that he would support the PM through thick and thin, and that he was shaking the Gillan dust off his shoes forthwith. And yet, supposing that what he had been told was true, that the PM *was* thinking of retiring . . . Gillan was Deputy Premier and heir presumptive . . . wouldn't it be rather pointless to make an enemy of the next Prime Minister when one could have him as a grateful friend? He remembered his father's solution when his Baptist conscience was wrestling with some moral dilemma – 'Ask yourself son, what would John Bunyan have done?' John Bunyan was forgotten as Mun Martin once again clapped a hand on his shoulder.

The tormentor was not wasting time.

'Well Cecil, have you made up your mind? This whole room is for us, and they're only the start. Wait till you see – tomorrow when the people wake up to what's happening there'll be only one way to go, and that's our way. And in any case, Packham is going!'

McFee was getting desperate. 'Wait a minute Mun. I didn't know that this evening was . . . '

'Look, Cecil.' Martin took a tight grip on his arm. 'Either you want a future in politics or you don't. If you do, then you've got to stand up and

86

be counted. That's what the rest of us are doing. We're putting our money where our mouth is. Come on! Are you with us?' Not for nothing was Martin known as Gillan's hatchet man.

McFee was sweating slightly. 'Mun.' He was almost pleading. 'Give me a moment, will you? I really wasn't expecting this.'

Martin considered his man for a moment, weighing him up. Then he decided. 'Right. I'll give you a while to think it over. But I want an answer before you go. Right?'

Then he moved away to join a group which seemed to have become the main focus of interest in the room – the Rooster, Beatty Samson, QC, Member for Antrim SW, had just arrived and was talking to his host. He had a drink in his hand and was clearly making his presence felt.

'I don't know what you're making all this mystery about – every newspaper in the country seems to know. It can be assumed that I was not the only person who was rung up for a reaction.' There was more chatter of a general nature, and speculation about the source of the press leak. As they all moved in to the drawing room, Samson turned pointedly to his host: 'We'll have to make you an honorary Welshman, James – for a gentleman farmer it would be a most appropriate emblem!'

Gillan smiled sourly but did not pursue the jibe. He had never liked the Rooster's irreverent raillery. He had never liked the Rooster. But because of Samson's well known antipathy to Packham, Mun had thought it a good move to try and win over such a formidable campaigner. The Rooster would be a real asset if they could get him. On the way to the drawing-room, there was the usual breaking of ranks for the comfort stop in the cloakroom. By the time they reassembled, the Rooster was in close conversation with another lawyer, Sam Collins, a solicitor from Dungannon who was known as a hard-liner. Mrs Gillan had discreetly withdrawn, and in the large low-ceilinged room, its windows heavily shuttered behind the curtains, the groups of men disposed themselves on and about the chairs and sofas which fanned out facing the fire. The tactics, previously worked out by his caucus, was for Gillan, at the appropriate moment, to 'make his spiel,' using the presence of the faithful who had already declared themselves to exert maximum psychological pressure on the unconverted.

Thee was much loud laughter and banter as whiskey and orangeade were dispensed from a side-table. Cigarettes and cigars were handed round. Gillan waited for five minutes or so, until the smoke haze was forming and the atmosphere receptive. Then he moved to the middle of the hearth-rug. He began with the well-tried sales technique of getting agreement to a number of simple propositions to which there was only one possible answer. Do we face a crisis? Are we prepared to sacrifice the police? Carrying his audience along on a tide of affirmation, and making it progressively more difficult for anyone to withhold the final 'Yes' of total commitment.

All was going smoothly for the first few sentences until the Rooster, who had reacted sharply when Gillan started to speak and now was visibly restraining his growing annoyance, suddenly interrupted. 'Just a moment, James. Sorry! You're going rather too fast for me.' Gillan was frowning with anger. There was a growl of disapproval as his trusties turned ostentatiously in an effort to stare the QC into discomfiture. Samson took no notice of them. 'I have no wish to be here under false pretences. May I make my position clear, or would you prefer that I leave?'

'Typical of the bastard,' thought Gillan, 'but I have no alternative.' If Samson stalked out, the whole patriotic front which they had been constructing would shrink to a sordid conspiracy. He forced himself to assume the air of an impartial chairman whose only wish was to take into account the freely expressed views of all concerned. 'Of course not, Beatty. Don't be silly. We're here to speak our minds. I was only attempting to sum up the general feeling which has been conveyed to me this evening.' He spread out his hands, as an indication that he had no ulterior motive. There was a chorus of 'Hear. Hear. Of course he was.' Mun was clearly anxious to silence this importunate lawyer, but Gillan motioned to him to calm down and invited Samson to have his way.

The QC moved forward so that he could face his colleagues, and automatically placed his hands on his hips in approved forensic fashion. 'I intervened,' he turned courteously to his host, 'and I apologise for the abruptness of my action, but I felt I had no alternative. I intervened because I wished to make my position clear. I felt that my silence might lead some of those present in this room to jump to false conclusions.' His eyes took them all in. 'First, let me state that I am no admirer of the present Prime Minister. I consider him effete, indecisive and lacking in the mental toughness necessary to deal with terrorism once and for all.' Mun Martin's spirits rose. The Rooster was not such a cuckoo in the nest after all. 'Secondly, I do not believe that he has the nerve to confront Westminster in the situation in which we find ourselves. Let no one think I am advocating, at this time, a rejection of the authority of the Crown. Far from it. What I am saying is that our present Prime

88

Minister is no match for the British Government in a constitutional crisis.' Some of the Gillanites muttered, 'Hear. Hear.' The Rooster, no matter what one thought of him as a person, could certainly lay it on the line. 'Since I see that no one is leaping forward to his defence,' the Rooster smiled his ironic smile, 'I take it that you all share my views.'

The hapless McFee coloured, cleared his throat, as if to speak, but feeling like Peter in the Palace of the High Priest, held his peace. He hated, despised himself.

The Rooster went on. 'So let me not put a tooth in it! This is, in fact, stage one of a coup to overthrow the Prime Minister.'

His audience showed every sign of embarrassment at such bluntness. Gillan was moved to object. 'I must point out, Beatty, that this is not a matter of personalities, but of policies.'

'Of course, of course. I understand.' The Rooster was affability itself. Yet his voice had an edge. 'But if we throw out Packham's policy, we have to find a new policy and a new personality, don't we? The question is – *who* is that personality to be?' He looked at Gillan again with that infuriating, condescending smile. 'Clearly the mantle seems to have fallen on you – certainly as far as our colleagues here are concerned. In principle, I should be prepared to support that choice. I shan't embarrass you, James, by enumerating your sterling qualities.' Gillan demurred between annoyance at the patronising tone, and his hunger for flattery. Mun was congratulating himself on his insight. But there was more to come. 'But may I, since most of you are ahead of me, it appears, ask a few questions?'

'Fire away,' said Gillan.

'Good! I learn from my friend here,' he indicated Sam Collins, 'that a document has been circulating, a document, I gather, to which some of our colleagues have put their signature. May I see it?' He looked enquiringly at Gillan. Gillan looked at Mun Martin, who was clearly hesitating. 'I take it that is in order?' said the Rooster with elaborate politeness.

'Yes, of course,' said Gillan, who was less and less happy with the turn the meeting had taken. Mun Martin took from his inside jacket pocket a folded sheet of foolscap and handed it to the QC who had now taken charge of the proceedings. Neither Gillan nor his henchman could think of any plausible way of stopping him.

The Rooster opened the paper. 'Has everyone else seen this?' Several shook their heads. 'I'd better read it then. No heading. No date. Hmm. "We, the undersigned, hereby declare that we no longer have confidence

89

in the Prime Minister as Leader of the Unionist Party, and request the Chief Whip to make arrangements for a new leader to be elected forthwith." From a legal point of view, it might be more tightly drafted, but it's clear enough. Appended are seven signatures.' He looked up from the paper and fixed his gaze on Gillan and Martin in turn. 'I notice that none of the signatories here is a member of the Cabinet.'

Martin replied, muffing his words. 'We haven't had time. After all, we only knew this morning. But we'll get . . . there'll be Cabinet names there all right.'

'Including both of you, I take it?'

Martin hesitated just a second. 'You see, all that is required to summon a meeting of the Parliamentary Party to elect a new leader is ten names. We'll have far more than that.'

'You'd need to. But with respect. You haven't answered my question. Are you both prepared to sign this document tonight in our presence?'

Gillan's face was flushed. 'Look, Beatty, you're not in court now. There's absolutely no need for this aggressive tone. It must be clear where Mun and I stand.'

The Rooster was courteous, but very cool. 'I am sorry, but it is not clear and in a matter so grave as this, it is essential that all of us here know precisely where we stand.'

Someone said, 'Quite right, Beatty, quite right!' Others grunted agreement. The Rooster was now clearly voicing the views of the uncommitted. He addressed himself to them.

'If we sign this paper, we burn our boats. There is no going back. If, for the sake of the country, I take that chance, I expect others to do the same.' He turned to face Gillan squarely. 'You will be the chief beneficiary if this plan succeeds – I'm assuming that if we get rid of Packham, you will be his successor – therefore we have a right to demand that you take the same risk as we do, that you commit yourself as irrevocably as we do.'

Gillan was all righteous indignation in an effort to call a halt. 'Look Beatty, neither I nor any of my colleagues . . .'

'*Our* colleagues.'

'*Our* colleagues here, need to submit to your hectoring. If you do not wish to support us, if indeed you wish to go along with capitulation, then that is your privilege.'

Mun, who had been chafing at the bit, shouldered forward, face reddening. 'Yes, Beatty – you're either with us or against us. Stop confusing the issue. Come out into the open!'

'Right!' The Rooster's voice was tense. 'Let's come out into the open.'

He was speaking very deliberately. 'If you resign from the Cabinet and oppose Packham openly, I shall not only sign this paper tonight, I shall organise your campaign for the leadership!' He turned round dramatically. 'Is that a fair offer, gentlemen?' There was an excited burst of acclamation. One man even clapped his hands. Mun Martin stood nonplussed. Gillan's face tightened and turned a shade pale. The heat was on. 'Well?' asked Samson again. 'Will you resign?'

Gillan's mouth was working, like an animal chewing the cud. The words came out, clipped. 'No. I will not be blackmailed like this.' There was an astonished 'Oh!' from the uncommitted, which boded ill.

'What's holding you, James?' asked Collins the solicitor. 'There's nothing holding *us*. *I've* signed.'

Martin looked appealingly at his candidate. He would have to give some sort of undertaking . . .

'Will you resign?' repeated the Rooster.

Gillan tried to seize the initiative. 'No. I will not. It would be totally irresponsible to . . . stir up a Cabinet crisis at this moment, until we are sure . . .'

'Sure of what?' interrupted the Rooster.

'Sure that we have enough support to put him out.' Gillan blurted it out. Mun Martin closed his eyes in anguish of spirit.

'Aaah! So that's it,' exclaimed the Rooster, nodding his head slowly, as if a great light had dawned. With a sweep of his hand he included all the prospective signatories. '*Now* we know where we are.' He rounded on Gillan with withering sarcasm. 'You have a *neck!* We come down here, under the impression that you are prepared to stand up and be counted. You ask us to commit ourselves, to sign on the line . . . while you, the man who's supposed to be our leader – what do you do?' His voice hissed with fury. 'You wait to see which way the cat is going to jump! While your friends risk the lot, you keep your options open waiting for the goodies to fall in your lap . . . greater love hath no man!' The mocking tone changed to deadly serious. 'I came down here, Gillan, prepared to support you openly, believing you were a man with guts. I was wrong. You are *nothing* but an object of total *contempt!*'

Whereupon he strode out of the room. There was a shuffling, embarrassed silence. Then two others followed him. McFee, after a moment's hesitation, murmured something apologetic, and with thanksgiving in his heart, slunk out, almost on tiptoe, like a man leaving church in the middle of the service.

Gillan was very pale. Mun Martin broke the silence. 'I knew the bastard would make trouble. He always does. We're better off without him. Here, have a drink.' But the momentum of the meeting, the enthusiasm, had gone.

When he got back to his home on the outskirts of Belfast, Samson rang the Attorney General. 'Shane, I told you this afternoon that I'd let you know. I've changed my mind. Let's say that my eyes have been opened. I wouldn't touch him now with a barge-pole. Yes. I thought that would make you happy. Goodnight!'

Jo Scanlon arrived home that evening after eight o'clock. She lived in the converted gate-lodge of what had been a Victorian merchant's mansion. The Malone area was middle-class and affluent, free from the sectarian attacks and intimidation which had driven working-class Catholics and Protestants out of so-called mixed areas, into their respective ghettos. They had been lucky to find somewhere with secluded access and which dealt with her parent's objections to moving from the family home, some fifteen miles south, near Saintfield.

At first her sudden decision had met with stubborn opposition from her father, who was loth to see the youngest of his four daughters fly the nest. Surely it would be time enough when she got married . . . This was no time for a young girl to be living on her own!

But his prettiest daughter was also the most self-willed. She was twenty-seven. Ever since school in Ascot, she had managed to look after herself far from paternal surveillance. She had had her own flat in Brussels. Anyway it was a *fait accompli*. Her boss, Desmond Carson himself, had been good enough to contact a friendly estate agent, to make sure that a member of his staff was safely and suitably accommodated. That had been a daring stroke, though her parents suspected nothing. On the contrary, despite their instinctive antagonism to Carson's politics and to the public man himself, they were flattered at the high-level interest being taken in their daughter's welfare.

Now she moved from the kitchen into the L-shaped living room – two rooms knocked into one, with a fireplace at one end and lit by cream-shaded table lamps. She put a match to the fire and, leaning her head on the mantelpiece, watched the flames take hold of the chopped wood. Waiting. So many evenings spent in waiting. For Godot? No, hers was not some unattainable ever-receding Grail. Her Godot was flesh and blood. If there was some hold-up he would telephone. He would come, for sure, and she would come alive again. Constantly she felt the need for reassurance, telling herself that he would come. Something had happened today. Something had gone wrong. What had he said in the office? That they were trying to *crucify* him. The word was another twitch on the thread. Only the day before, she had found herself entering a strange Catholic church, instinctively seeking anonymous asylum from the demons of near despair that sometimes descended on her. She had sat, benumbed, her gaze fixed on the red flicker of the sanctuary lamp, her mind a turmoil. How could she hope to have luck? An adultress, living in mortal sin; denied the food of the soul. No Mass without Confession. And how could she confess, knowing in her heart that she intended to persist in sin. Caught in the Catholic trap. For a long time she had remained, head bowed. The words 'mortal sin', even 'immortal soul', were empty of meaning. To lose him was to lose everything, against what? The faint hope of . . . heaven? The familiar aroma of Catholic piety brought no comfort. She had no longer the old, sharp sense of guilt. The bond she had forged was so final, the gift she had given so irrevocable, that to deny it was the one transgression she could not commit. The altar on which her eyes were fixed offered no help. It was cold and lifeless as a marble tomb. Into her mind came a memory from her schooldays; a retreat conducted by a Redemptorist who had preached on the savage penances imposed by the Early Church – seven long years for fornication, fifteen for adultery. She had risen to her feet, automatically crossing herself, on her lips the ghost of a smile.

The fire had taken hold. A falling coal interrupted her reverie. She moved into the kitchen and busied herself with the preparation of supper, adding further ingredients to the copper pot already simmering. Deftly removing the stalks from mushrooms, slicing tomatoes on a heavy chopping board, coarse salt from the earthenware jar, caraway from the convenient row of Perspex containers – all was professionally and easily accomplished. At home there was always a good table – solid if unenterprising fare. But a Dublin uncle who had progressed through the construction business into hotels, had first sparked her interest in a wider gastronomic scene. In her final year at school, she had attended a Cordon Bleu course at Wingfield and discovered a talent and a recreation which more than made up for a failure to shine at lacrosse. Cooking was a challenge, not a chore. She tasted, ground in some pepper, tasted again and nodded, satisfied. Then she went into the other room to lay the table.

All was soft beige and browns. Carson knew nothing of such things. He had left it all to her, who revelled in shapes and patterns. End-on to the fireplace a downy settee covered in oriental cushions; a slab of glass on sand-coloured perspex formed a low table; a stone head from Italy, and a canvas of horses in umbers and dusky yellow by Basil Blackshaw; a chest in black bog-oak and bronze chrysanthemums in a plain, round jar. It was stylish, without being what the local interior decorator called, in his camp cosmopolitan way, 'piss-elegant'.

Idly she switched on the television for the nine o'clock news, vaguely hoping for a clue to her future. But there was nothing in the headlines. It might be an hour before he arrived.

She peeled off her clothes and shook her hair free. Critically she studied the reflection of her body. Outlining the pale breasts was still the faint, golden transfer of last summer's sun. Her flesh was the element in which he swam. She saw herself as an odalisque, awaiting her master, always waiting, waiting to be used, to serve. The thought was not distasteful to her. She closed her eyes as the benison of warm scented water enfolded her.

Coming home from the office, she had called to see her parents. Her mother, pressing food upon her, solicitous about her religious obligations. When had she last been to Confession? Whom had she seen at Mass? What was she rushing back to Belfast for? Her father, once again bitterly attacking the Army. One of his employees had been held for questioning. Let her ask her boss, Carson, why it was always the Catholics who were harassed and hounded! There'd be no peace till the British got out of Ireland! Faced with the flow of questions and complaints, she had lain low. She was becoming so enmeshed in falsehood that sooner or later she must slip up. What would her father say if the truth were out? He who had prayed for a German victory in 1940; who had told her how, night after night, he had listened to the broadcasts from Berlin of the notorious Lord Haw-Haw, and how, at each announcement of RAF planes lost, he and his friends had cheered. The intensity of his hatred had lessened with the years as business had prospered but she shrank from the thought of his reaction.

Carson and a Scanlon! If he got a divorce, what political future could he have? What future could they have together? It was hopeless. She had told him so a thousand times, but in his incurably romantic way he had talked of their marriage as a symbolic conjoining of the two communities; how the bigots and the hypocrites would be shamed into acceptance. And if they weren't – his mind was irrevocably made up. When they were together his confidence carried her with him, and all seemed possible. On her own, it was different. She tried to close out the dark thoughts, and, in a phrase of her mother's – count her blessings. They were spending more and more time in each other's company. Who knew what the morrow might bring! He would be here tonight. In the warm scented vapour of the bath, like some drowsy syrup, the harsh other world was less than real. Under the surface, her hands smoothed over the contours of her body, like spreading out a map. She stretched and felt a delicious frisson of desire, remembering his kisses. Gentle-skinned, her fingers probed beneath the dark delta where her limbs flowed together, finding the pink corolla stirring under its hood. A fluttering tantalising fire was licking up the inner surface of her legs. 'Bless me father for I have sinned.' 'And where did you touch yourself my child? Above the knee? How far above the knee?' Oh the prurient persistence of the older curate! In the years of her growing up when she had raked her mind for impurities. Impure thoughts. Impure actions. The tremulous awakening of young womanhood infected with guilt. 'Where did he kiss you my child? On the breast? Below the breasts? How far below . . . ' The catechism of trespasses would prove less venial now. In the thoughts was almost a malicious satisfaction. A hard and practised sinner – was that what she had become? Lying, deceiving the parents who loved her and whom she loved? Prepared to hurt them, to cover them in shame. The middle-class Catholic community was harshly censorious towards carnal sin. The Carson dimension would compound the offence a hundredfold. It was selfish, irresponsible – mad, mad! Her mind was turning in circles, always returning to the same terrible conclusion. Hopeless. This is what happened when one lost the faith. How often had she been warned of the slide into despair. She had experience of it now. She shivered and hugged her shoulders. The pricking in her loins had died. It was all in the mind; desire, love. All illusion. She felt desperately alone, alone in a silent, ruined world. Behind her closed eyelids she could feel the tears forming. Mary, Mother of God! – it was a cry from the depths. For minutes she lay motionless, trying not to think, soaking in self-pity. She could feel herself crouching in a dark corner, with her black sorrow. There was only one refuge. As a pigeon, released in some alien sky, after days of travail, finds her way home, so would she, after this bitter journey, end up with his arms about her. With nothing solved. She turned the hot water tap, as hope came seeping back. If only they were together all the time. He was so full of confidence, always telling her not to be afraid to win. Blast! The ends of her hair were soaking. It would all frizz up, and she wanted so much to wear it loose. The cream shirt? The striped briefs, he liked those . . . No bra . . . What was the time? She stood up and reached for the long green towel. No make-up . . . just a touch of eye shadow . . . body lotion from its frosted bottle . . . crème parfumeé Pour le corps – Christian Dior . . . neck, shoulders, breasts, thighs . . . hmm. I smell . . . délicieuse . . . funny how the words come back . . . Son haleine fait la musique . . . and his voice the perfume. Oh Carson, I adore you, but I wish your French was a little better!

The telephone rang. Tucking the green towel round her, she made for the living-room.

Brian Kedge's yellow BMW 525 pulled in through the Carson gate at about nine o'clock and drew up at the front door. The Halogen floods had been turned on and the whole of the front garden was brilliantly illuminated in the pouring rain. Kedge got out of the driving seat as one of the B Specials detached himself from the shadows at the side of the house and wished him 'Goodnight'. Kedge nodded and ducked his head into the car to mutter something to his passenger. Harry Harrmon got out, instinctively putting up his hand to cover his face and shield his eyes from the light.

Carson, who had heard the car arrive, was waiting at the front door. He led them into the room which served as study and private office. 'Wild night — did you get wet?'

Harrmon ran his hand through his bushy hair, which was tight and curly like wire-wool. 'No. Makes it grow.' He had exchanged the anorak for a jacket and a knitted tie, a possibly unconscious acknowledgement of the expectations attached to Kedge's invitation.

Carson seated his guests in two armchairs and offered them something to drink. Harrmon asked for a small whisky which he took neat. On being offered cigarettes, he excused himself, and lit one of his own small cheroots. Kedge was getting the drinks, and as he poured Carson another beer, the latter lit a cigarette and swivelled round in his old-fashioned desk chair to face the Commander of the UDF. They had already met on a number of occasions. Harrmon had led delegations to him, seeking to change certain prison regulations in The Maze. On one occasion, Carson had found the UDF man helpful in averting a confrontation with the Army. A Saracen had accidentally crushed two civilians during a demonstration one stormy night in West Belfast. Since then, Carson had accepted personal calls from Harrmon on prison welfare matters. Harrmon had been careful not to abuse this privileged access. The relationship between the two men was relaxed, but formal, and Carson had always been careful up to now to keep it on that kind of basis. Despite that, he had been attacked in the House on two occasions for being 'in cahoots' with the Protestant paramilitaries, a charge which he had always vigorously rejected. He now realised he

98

was treading on delicate ground. He determined, at the outset, to underline the basis of the meeting.

But it was Brian Kedge, who, after a brief exchange of small-talk civilities, broke the ice. 'Well, I had a word with Harry here about the UDF reaction if they start to muck about with the B's and the police.' At the mention of the B's, Carson gave a slight grimace. Kedge explained. 'The press already have the story you know – the *News Letter* are working on it.' He nodded towards Harrmon. 'He had a call just before we left my house.'

Harrmon enlarged with a half-smile. 'Yeah. We've got *some* friends in the papers, you know. They got in touch with my HQ. What's it all about? Brian, here, asks me what we'd do if they try to take over the police; doesn't mention the Specials. Then next thing we hear, it's all over the press that they're doing away with the Specials. Am I supposed to be a bloody mug?'

Carson hastened to smooth the prickles. 'No, no, of course not. I'm sorry it's all been a bit... muffled. But now that things are out in the open, I can speak more frankly.'

'I'm listening.'

'It is true that there is great pressure on the Government here to change the Specials.'

'From Westminster?'

'Yes. They want to bring them more under Army control, make them more mobile, better equipped.'

'Change the uniform.'

'I assume so: they'd be more like army.'

'And the personnel? Will they stay the same?'

'If they disband the force, they would have to re-recruit from scratch.'

'Where? Among the RC's?' said Harrmon, with heavy irony. Carson shrugged his shoulders.

'It's not on,' Harrmon was emphatic. 'The Protestants won't wear it. We won't wear it.'

'That's what I was afraid of. That in fact is why we got in touch. I wanted to forestall if possible any over-hasty reaction from your organisation.'

'It won't be over hasty, don't you worry.'

'I want to do everything I can to prevent a confrontation between the UDF and the police. That's only playing into the hands of the IRA.'

'What do you expect us to do? Sit back and wait till they hand us over to the Republicans? The Army's hands are tied. Now they're going to do the same with the Specials — if we let them. That's what's behind all this. Sure it's stickin' out a mile!'

'What would you propose to do about it?'

Harrmon looked at him coolly. 'We're a democratic organisation. The Central Council will make the decision.'

'If you behave responsibly, you will have public opinion on your side, I've no doubt. It's like soccer. There's a time to put the boot in and there's a time to play with the head. I hope you'll use the head.'

'We're a legitimate body and we operate within the law.' Carson raised a quizzical eyebrow. The UDF man was unabashed. 'We are blamed for a lot of things that have nothing to do with us, simply because some cowboy is looking for special privileges in the Maze Prison — so he uses our name.'

'We won't argue about that. Just so long as you keep your lads in check.'

'They'll do as they're told. It's taken longer than I thought to get some discipline. We're workin' on it. But we're not the Government. What's the Prime Minister doing? That's more to the point. If he lets the British Government do this he's finished. You're all finished. You know that?'

'There's no question of us accepting anything that we can't stand over. I've told you. No decisions have been taken. We're talking to them, and no doubt they realise that there's a limit to what this country will take. They're very aware of the danger of a backlash.'

Harrmon nodded with his ironic half-smile. 'Are they? A Protestant backlash. I wonder where that's going to come from? Hardly from the gin-and-tonic lot on the Malone Road, eh? So we fall back on the good old Rent-a-Backlash!'

'I don't think that will be necessary,' said Carson coldly. 'The mood of the ordinary decent Ulsterman will come through quite clearly enough.'

Harrmon threw up his eyes and smiled his cynical smile of disbelief. Carson coloured slightly, aware just how pompous and facile his retort had been. Like many others, he had doubted that the long-prophesied Protestant backlash would ever manifest itself. When it had come, when the marching men in denims and dark glasses first appeared, he had issued the expected condemnation of vigilante armies, however well-intentioned. But in private, he had harboured mixed feelings. It was no bad thing for the world to see that the Protestant community was not entirely impotent, despite the grave problems which the paramilitaries posed for the Government. Yet the standard-bearers were not the ones he would have chosen. These were not the men of 1912 who had come from farm and foundry and signed a Covenant to keep Ulster for ever British. In the Battle of the Somme, that compact had been sealed with their blood. Then, everyone had been in, the Movement-peers, mill-owners, shipwrights, linen workers, clergy, rich and poor, men and masters bound together and fired by the same high purpose. As a child, he had listened to his father and uncles tell the breath-taking tale of the 24th of April 1914, when 50,000 German rifles and 3 million rounds of ammunition were smuggled in to Larne and Bangor and distributed through the length and breadth of Ulster in the space of a single night. He could still remember the doggerel ballad they sang round the open grate in his grandfather's farmhouse near Banbridge. 'Who ran the guns when landed, From Larne, North, South and West, Through a vigil-keeping Ulster, That had known that night no rest? T'was the gallant men of Ulster, Then away with talk and cant. For all are of the self-same breed, who signed the Covenant.'

Now history was repeating itself. Again Loyalists prepared to rebel against the Crown to prove their loyalty. The old paradox remained, and the gun-runners were still buying in Germany. But there was a big saddening difference now. Gone were the eagles and the trumpets, gone the paladins of Passchendaele. As Carson saw it, today's defenders of the faith were hard men, venal, some with a record of crime. True, there were those who acted from a sense of tribal duty, imbued with the fervour we call patriotism. But bad money tends to drive out the good, and the man sitting opposite Carson was as cynical as most of his followers, and less certain about the nature of the 'final victory' which gives the initial impetus to every crusade. With the end-result unspecified, the power-game and its rewards were now the things that more and more engrossed him.

Harrmon now more deferentially, sensing perhaps that he had gone a little too far with the Minister of Home Affairs: 'If there's going to be a reaction of any kind, it'll have to come from us. You know that. The working class is the backbone of this province. If it hadn't been for us, we'd have been in a united Ireland years ago. If there's dirty work to be done – we do it! Why? Because there's nobody else. All your moderates, all your stuck-up fur-coat brigade — they're tucked up nice and snug in their bungalows down in Cultra watchin' the telly! While we're on the streets! But I'll tell you something.' Harrmon's mouth tightened. No deference now. 'We're not the politicians' mugs any more. If we're going to do the fighting, we're going to have a say in what happens when it's over. Some of your friends up there in Stormont spend their time sneerin' and givin' off about…the Protestant extremists. McFee, the other day — "thugs," he called us. He fuckin' didn't say that at the last election! It was a different tune then!'

'Take it easy. Take it easy,' said Carson, and leaned forward to pat the UDF Commander on the forearm. The latter shrugged away and took a deep pull at his cheroot, dragging the smoke into his lungs. Carson went on talking. 'What you people do is your own affair. Let's get this straight — my aim and object is simply to avoid any clash between the Unionist people and the security forces. The police especially have enough on their plate without having to deal with a lot of Protestant aggro. I understand the strong feelings on our side of the fence. Of course I do. But it's one thing to express those feelings in a legitimate way; it's another to take the law into your own hands. I've tried to make my position clear all along. And I think you'll admit that I have not been unhelpful…when you've had your problems.'

Harrmon was calmer now. He took a sip of whisky, dragged at the cheroot again. 'That works both ways.'

'Of course, point taken.' It was Brian Kedge, silent till now, who came in to ease the situation. 'That's the way it's got to be, isn't it? We're both on the same side. Only Des here is a Government Minister and I know you…appreciate his position.'

'Sure, sure!' Harrmon spoke directly to Carson. 'You've been fair with me. But some of those other buggers, they piss me off!'

Carson made no comment. Harrmon's words struck a guilty chord. He was only too conscious of the hypocrisy in Unionist attitudes, including his own. The whole battery of pious condemnation was brought into public play when the private armies brought off some deadly exploit, but secretly there was barely concealed satisfaction that 'our boys' could give those Republican bastards as good as they got. And when perpetrators were caught red-handed, the most withering contempt was reserved not for the deed, but for the inefficiency, the letting down of Protestant standards. It was a mirror image of Catholic ambivalence towards the most heinous actions of the IRA.

The UDF man drained his glass, and when Kedge moved to refill it, shook his head. 'Right,' he rose from the chair, threw one leg over the corner of the desk facing Carson, 'What do you want me to do?'

Carson smiled uneasily. He was not happy with this confidential approach. He was determined to keep his distance. He kept smiling. 'I've told you. I'm not asking you to do anything, except to keep the lid on. When this thing boils up tomorrow there'll no doubt be all kinds of wild rumours. We'll all be under pressure to do this or that.' Carson paused. 'Naturally, I have no desire to stop — I couldn't if I wanted to — Protestants giving vent to their feelings at what will no doubt be seen as unjustified interference by Westminster into our affairs. It's only right that the British Government should be aware of the strength of public opinion. All I'm asking is that there shouldn't be any trouble. That's why I'm having this discussion with you — and I don't care who knows it!' He was tying it up nicely, keeping the record straight. There had been, there would be, no collusion with paramilitaries. But had he withdrawn too far? Harrmon's face had tightened. Reassurance was needed or the whole exercise could suddenly go sour. 'You have a lot of influence, Harry.' It was the first time he had addressed the UDF man by his first name and the flattering effect was noticeable. 'You're a big man in this province. I acknowledge that. If you use your influence in the proper way, I'm prepared to give you support as far as I can. I'm certainly prepared to ensure that my colleagues give you co-operation, if and when the occasion arises. I can't say fairer than that, can I?'

Harrmon was not proof against this. He was no longer keeping up a front of indifference to the Carson blandishments. He handed his empty glass to Brian Kedge, half suppressing a smile. 'I'll have that one now, all right?' At last they were prepared to give him his place. And he, Harry Harrmon, would show them that the concession was overdue.

In the private apartment at the Castle, Packham was just finishing his telephone conversation. 'Very well. I'll let you know by tomorrow morning. Goodbye, John.' He put the receiver down, sat in silence for a moment, took up his half-smoked cigar which had gone out, re-lit it and turned to Billy Dixon who waited patiently, sipping his whiskey. 'Not good Billy, not good. You heard me tell him that we needed time, but as you probably gathered they are not being terribly co-operative. Ronnie was right, I'm afraid. They're determined to play up the "radical change of direction" bit. Downing Street — and you know what a stubborn bastard the PM is — is adamant that this big initiative of his — apparently the whole scheme was cooked up at Number Ten, not the Home Office — anyway it's his initiative, and he's going to make sure that it has maximum impact with the minority. It's the Catholics he wants to please!' Dixon shook his head in silent disgust. 'The Home Secretary is doing his best for us I know, but he's swamped in Cabinet. They're all toeing the PM's line. He did make one suggestion, though I can't see a lot of point in it.'

'What's that?' asked Dixon.

'If I wanted to come over to Downing Street, bring a couple of my colleagues, they would give the meeting the full PR treatment. He thought it might emphasise that this was a joint decision…make it easier for us to sell…' Packham's voice trailed away, clearly unconvinced.

'What's the point?' said Dixon, brusquely. 'If he is determined to rub our noses in it for the benefit of the Republicans, what's the sense in expecting him to try and save our faces? He really *is* a shit.' This last, muttered to himself, was charged with feeling.

There was a tap, and Stewart Taylor poked his head round the door. 'Come in, Stewart. You heard the lot, I take it?' said Packham.

'Yes, and I took a note, PM, for reference.' It was common practice for the Cabinet Secretary to listen to important telephone conversations and to note or tape them, except when requested not to.

'Well?' said the PM wearily, as he and Dixon looked expectantly at the official.

Taylor nodded grimly. 'Just as Hedges said, sir. It looks as if they're going to push us all the way. He wasn't very forthcoming when you asked him about presentation.'

'I don't think he's in any position to be.' said Packham. 'That's the truth of it. It's now pretty clear that the point of the whole scheme is not just to gather total control of security into their own hands. They want to make a public execution of the B Specials as "the hated symbol of Protestant oppression" is the phrase, I believe. At the same time they give credibility to the parrot-cry, "fifty years of Unionist misrule".'

'Christ, it makes you sick,' said Billy Dixon. 'If they think by knocking us, the only friends they've got, they're going to convert Republicans…by God! They'll soon find out their mistake. Perfidious bloody Albion…' There was silence for a moment as they reflected on the perfidy of Albion. Then Dixon snapped out of it. 'Well, there's only one thing we can do — take them on. Tell them we do it our way, or they can try and do it for themselves – and see how far they get.'

'It may come to that,' said Packham gloomily, looking at the Cabinet Secretary.

But Taylor was more sanguine. 'I don't see the situation as radically altered, PM. If we go ahead, we put our own gloss on it, present the changes in the way we have already decided. They can hardly accuse us of mis-representation. And even if they were silly enough to try and do so, who would the opposition believe? Both here and at Westminster, our opponents would be convinced that the Unionist Party was up to its tricks again, and that we'd simply outwitted Her Majesty's Government to get the best deal for ourselves.'

'Yes, by Jove!' the Prime Minister's face lit up. 'You've got a point Stewart. That's one advantage of having this Machiavellian reputation — alas entirely undeserved — even when you're in it up to your neck, your opponents still won't believe it — they think it's some kind of cunning ploy.' He grinned. 'Maybe the best thing to do, is to say that we are simply abolishing the B Specials. Nobody would believe us!' The other two joined in the laugh. The mood was lighter now. The Prime Minister nodded approvingly at his Secretary. 'Yes, Stewart. That's it. What about this nonsense of flying to London? I said I'd let him know by tomorrow. I honestly can't see any advantage.'

Taylor thought for a moment. 'Certainly not in the next few days. But I'd keep the offer open, sir. It might help to dramatise the situation. You never know…If you want to catch the headlines fly to London!'

'All right. Leave it. Tell them we shan't need lunch tomorrow! Pity! The food's rather good in Number Ten.'

Carson, too, had food on his mind. When Kedge and Harrmon had left after the nine o'clock news, he had telephoned Fred Butler to check how the round-up was going. Butler had reported a reassuring start — of the six he'd rung he'd managed to contact four, all of whom were OK. That meant they would support Carson in whatever line he took. In the politics of the back-bench, as Carson well knew, there were very few who made an independent judgement on any issue, whether of policy or power. The ordinary MP attached himself to a particular personality, usually a member of the Government, more seldom someone with enough character, charisma or popular following in the country to stamp him as a leader. He was probably identified with strong, even extremist, views. Moderates exerted little magnetism. The Law-and-Order man, the Protestant fundamentalist — these, as they fought their way up the ladder, might attract their quota of like-minded disciples. The group-instinct was strong, and a minister without his personal clique was doubly vulnerable to his Prime Minister's whims. Carson had come up on a tough no-nonsense ticket — the men around him were right-of-centre. Their views were conventional, respectable and static. Increasingly, Carson was finding himself trapped by their allegiance. More and more, he was being intuitively driven to the conclusion that only radical change could lift them out of the constitutional morass. Yet he was imprisoned by his own image, by what they automatically expected of him. During the past three months he had often quailed at the thought of their reacton when they learned of his love affair. He had faced up to the fact that it was 'when' rather than 'if'. But the sense of pre-destination which he had inherited from his Protestant forebears came to his aid. Life, like a labyrinth, was a series of dead-ends from which there was always a preordained way out. He was hungry. She would have prepared something special, despite his routine request for late-night scrambled eggs. The rain was still lashing down as he emerged from the side door of the house, pulling his raincoat collar round his ears. He had left no note for Janet — it only complicated matters — but followed his usual practice of telling one of the Specials on duty that he was going to make a few calls nearby. Later, to cover himself, he would get through on the R/T and ask the police to ring his home with a reassuring story for his wife. The police sometimes wondered why he didn't contact her direct on an ordinary line, but accepted the fiction that he was always on the move and that security forebade the Minister of Home Affairs to go borrowing a telephone at midnight. He had another card in the deception pack — an elderly uncle who lived alone not far from Jo, and who was delighted and surprised at how solicitous his famous nephew had become, dropping in for lightning visits at all hours. The whole shabby charade was wearing thin, and Carson knew it. A good Special Branch man would have torn it apart in a couple of hours, and probably had. But for the moment he had no alternatives. He got into the Merc. On a number of occasions he had come under fire from his own side because he possessed a 'Krautwagon' instead of buying British. His standard defence had always been that German guns were good enough for his namesake Sir Edward in 1912!

As a routine, he tested the R/T before he pulled out of the garage. The guard had switched on the floods again. As he swung into the road, they were turned off. He made a mental note to tell someone to omit that particular piece of ceremonial. She lived near Stranmillis and his way took him down through the centre of the city. After five minutes, he was crossing over the Queen's Bridge. Through the rain-splashed side window, he could see the lights of the Cross-Channel berths, Liverpool, Heysham, Ardrossan, memories of childhood during the war, journeys to a doctor uncle in Wales, snug cabins with brass and mahogany, and in the morning, slivers of toast soaked in butter, and tea that tasted too strong. The cry of the gulls over the Mersey and the two great Liver Birds pinioned and pegged down in the sky. Returning home in the grey wintry dawn, the water in the Victoria Channel iridescent with streaks of oil, and the Harland and Wolff shipyard ablaze with lights and loud with clanging hammers, the gantries like crucifixes nailed to the lurid sky. The gantries were fewer now and the huge Krupp crane bestriding the yard like a colossus was working tonight in the floodlit rain, fitting together the weldments, great chunks of ship weighing hundreds of tons, into another super-tanker.

Left at the end of the bridge, into Oxford Street. The bus station was still open, grey, dim-lit and cheerless, the scene of the IRA's most bloody massacre. A bomb in broad daylight, blowing a crowded queue to smithereens. Afterwards, they had swept up the fragments of decimated human beings and shovelled them into plastic bags. The televison cameras had been there to record it . . . Bloody Friday, the echo and answer to Bloody Sunday, thirteen mown down in Londonderry by army bullets.

Only recently had Carson admitted to himself that there was another side to the question, a case, however weak, occasionally to be answered.

Right, into Cromac Square, past the army post in the brick-built, former National School, the front protected against explosive missiles by a great tent of steel tube scaffolding and netting wire. Inside, beside a couple of parked 'Pigs' a soldier moved in the semi-darkness, his rifle sloping under his right arm, his left hand beneath the trigger guard. Wherever he was, crouched at street corners, sprinting across exposed intersections to take up a firing position, moving slowly back to back along dangerous pavements, gun and eyes together like a scanner swinging in an apprehensive arc, his was the classic silhouette of Ulster's unknown soldier. Here was the Markets area, one of the heartlands of the Official IRA. All around the square, gelignite, nail bombs, incendiaries had taken their toll. Where shops had been were yawning gaps, the ground roughly tarmacadamed to provide a makeshift parking lot. Most of the buildings were boarded up against vandalism, or awaiting the bulldozer. The Social Security building on the corner, its grimy grey cement gleaming in the wet, was grilled and shuttered like a blockhouse. Opposite in a butcher's shop — 'Flesher – Choice Cuts', announced the fascia — a single light shone morgue-like on the bare white tiles, a hopeful deterrent to marauders. There was blight and litter everywhere. A sodden piece of newspaper blew across his headlights. He slowed as a woman, her head covered with a plastic scarf, angrily scolded a child as she scurried with it across the road. There was no one else on the pavements. Even the battered cars parked in the middle of

107

the square looked abandoned for the junk-yard. Carson remembered sadly how, only two years before, a party of head porters from Dublin hotels — some tourist exercise — had told him of their most outstanding impression of Northern Ireland, the cleanliness of the streets. Now the dirt and desolation were deeply depressing. As he hit Cromac Street with the shadowy openings leading off left and right he accelerated, bumping over the ramps opposite what had been Mooney's pub. This was no place for a Unionist Minister in a private car. Apache country…Eliza Street, Matilda Street, Riley's Entry — he knew them by heart. The last time he had penetrated the squalid decaying warrens into which they led was in an Army Saracen. It was one of the regular sightseeing tours which he insisted on making to Republican ghetto areas in order to be able to pronounce with that air of first-hand knowledge which carried Parliamentary conviction. Long before the teeming estates of Anderstown and Ballymurphy had hit the headlines, the Markets, a tightly knit community, clustered round the mock-Tudor of St Malachy's Catholic Church, had been a Nationalist stronghold. Time and time again, the houses had been taken to pieces in arms searches. Joe McCann, one of the Republican heroes, had left his heart's blood on the street there, a few hundred yards from his family home. After his shooting there had been 24 hours of vicious rioting which had only stopped when the IRA had exacted revenge on some British soldier. The doctrine of 'an eye for an eye' so often invoked, operated in one direction only. A phrase used once by the Rooster came back to Carson. 'Before the soldier can shoot he must consult a yellow card: the terrorist has carte blanche.' He was out of Cromac Street, past the gasworks and Ulster Television, to whose studios he was a regular visitor. He wondered what were they cooking up for the ten o'clock bulletin — they must have rung through the story to ITN by now. So much depended on how they handled it initially. He would know time enough. He stopped at the Botanic Avenue traffic lights behind a grey RUC jeep on routine patrol. They would recognise the car if they were alert, and if they were doing their duty, they would report seeing it. A feeling of hopeless weariness descended. His confidence that all would be well in the end had deserted him. The old guilt complex, the old sense of sin reasserted itself. Could he hope to have luck? He switched the radio on. Radio One. Nice slow, beat stuff. He shook off the mood, telling himself that it was only natural at the end of a long wearing day to sag a little. A year from now they'd be laughing at the whole thing. Life was good. What in hell was he complaining about. She was waiting for him. He pulled off the road into what had been a rear lane leading to stables and was now the well-screened entrance to a parking space at the back of the lodge. Her Mini was there. As he locked the car and closed the farm-type gate behind him, the light beside the back door was switched on. She had heard him arrive. As he pushed the door open she was waiting. He took her in his arms.

'Oh it's so good to see you,' she said. 'I've been depressed all evening. I'm better now.'

She hung up his raincoat, and with his arm round her shoulder they entered the living-room. The fire burned brightly. The light was gentle, restful. He could feel the coiled springs inside him slacken already. Another world...The battered, bleak Philistine city had been effectively excluded — it was 'luxe, calme et volupté' all the way and for Desmond Carson the country doctor's son it was a different outlandish oasis that held a unique enchantment.

She made him Black Bushmills with ice. She took off his tie and loosened the collar of his shirt and lit his cigarette.

'My sister, Maire, just rang. She was coming over. She had bought me some things in London.'

'You stopped her. You're great!'

She kissed him. 'I said I was dead tired. I was going to bed!'

'Yes?'

'One track mind.'

When they had kissed long and deep he said again. 'Yes?'

She laughed, a laugh that was not unsympathetic, and pulled his ear. 'You're going to have some food. Relax. Now tell me about this awful hassle you're in.'

He took a drink of whiskey and stared at her. She was wearing tight jeans with a cotton shirt and a sort of waistcoat hanging loosely open. 'You're lovely.'

'Thank you.' She looked at him steadily. 'I'm glad. Glad you think so.' They sat silent a moment. 'Come on. What's it all about?' She sat on the sofa, her legs curled under her, all attention like a child.

He blew out a slow plume of smoke. 'The British want to clip our wings. Remove control of the police, all our law and order powers, *and* they want to do away with the — wait for it — B Specials.'

'Dear God! That hits *you* doesn't it? I don't know what to say. You know what I think of the B Specials. There won't be many tears shed over them on my side of the fence.'

'Not even a Requiem Mass?'

'Oh yes — a very solemn one concelebrated by the Cardinal and the Bishops *and* a few coadjutors!' They laughed and she leaned forward and pushed her head into the crook of his shoulder. He kissed her hair, no longer bound by the official ribbon of the afternoon. She was all concern, half-whispering, 'What are you going to do, love?'

'Flee the country. Are you coming with me?' She made a sad grimace. 'Why not? But seriously?'

'As Louis McNeice said: to ask the hard question is simple. I don't quite know. It's one of those situations where you have to make up the answer as you go along. Clearly we can't just lie back and say "come and take me, I'm yours".'

'Don't be coarse!'

'But you get my point. Nor can we really resist.'

'Why not?'

'Oh come on! Rebel against the Queen? We'd be worse than you lot. At least you don't pretend to be Unionists.'

'We'll let that fly stick to the wall. What are you going to do, today, tomorrow?'

He put the cigarette down and concentrated on what he was going to say. 'I have a feeling…that this is very much a crunch situation. It could blow the Cabinet apart. The old man hasn't made up his mind. He may huff and puff a bit, play for time to put a face on it, but he won't defy them. Friend Gillan is away out in front with his strong man act — "Ulster will fight and Ulster will be right".'

'And you?'

'I'm the pig in the middle. I don't see how I can preside over the removal of the Specials and remain in the Government.'

'No?'

'No darling, whatever my personal feelings, though I happen to believe they're a much maligned force.'

'But they're totally Protestant and anti-Catholic…'

Carson gently interrupted. 'Look! Let's not get het up over the Specials. They're a product of their time, and their time was the 1920s. I grant you — they're an anachronism. But they're symbolic, and now's a bad time to start ditching the household gods. That's all I'm saying. On the other hand, if we try to take the British Government on, I can't see a future. In 1912 we had the Tory Opposition on our side, so the Liberals caved in. Today we're on our own.'

'I'd tell you to get out, but I know it's hopeless.'

He chuckled, 'It might be sooner than you think. Don't you want to be a Prime Minister's wife?'

110

'Oh Des, that's not funny.' She spoke quietly, with sadness. Instinctively he put his arm around her.

'It wasn't meant to be funny really.' It was said slowly, almost as if to himself.

She was whispering, 'You're mad. You're out of your mind. I love you.' There was silence during which, with his free hand, he took up the cigarette, inhaled and put it down again. 'You really are smoking too much.' He tone was one of gentle but resigned reproach.

He began again, as if he were thinking aloud. 'It could come to that you know.'

'To what?'

'The old man seemed tired today, pumped out...and doing his Sphinx act. I couldn't quite make out what he was conveying to me, but it's very clear that if there's going to be any laying on of hands, friend Gillan is not the favourite. No. I think he'll back me.'

It took a moment to sink in before she twisted her body round to look into his face. 'Are you serious? Is the Prime Minister going?'

'Gillan's pushing like mad, that's all I know. His men were all over the bar this afternoon openly lobbying. He'll either have to get out of his own accord, or be kicked, and he won't go without making a bid, that's for sure.'

'So?'

'So maybe the old man will slog it out. I think we could still keep him there. It all depends on how big the wave of reaction is when the great Ulster public learn of today's proposals. Gillan could be riding high. If the old man decides to go — and I have a sort of feeling that he's fought the same battle too often — then your candidate — is he your candidate?' She put out her hand and gripped the back of his wrist tightly. He went on. 'I could be in with a chance.'

It was a moment before she said anything and then her voice was dead. 'And I could be out.'

Fiercely he grabbed her forearms in his hands as if about to shake her. 'Don't say that! Don't say that, Jo! Please! How often do I have to tell you?' He closed his eyes and his shoulders slumped like a beaten man.

In a flash she leaned forward and kissed him tenderly on the side of the brow. 'Sorry.'

Her voice was almost inaudible. He hugged her to him as if he would squeeze the breath out of her body. Slowly they came to. 'Alright?' she whispered.

He nodded and looked at her long and steadily. 'There is nothing

111

more important to me, nothing. Don't forget that.'

She smiled. 'No, sir!'

'Come here.'

'I thought we were eating?'

'Later, later. Please.'

'Easy! Take it easy! Let me help! Oh you are a hungry baby…These bloody jeans!'

'Two sizes too small!'

'Don't be cheeky! I don't know why we're not in bed. There. All right?'

'Yes. Yes.'

. . . .

'Oh dear God…thats heaven!'

. . . .

'Am I smothering you? Are you…'

'Hush! Don't say a word. Just flop.'

'Happy?'

'Oh Carson you silly, silly man.'

. . . .

'No, stay where you are. I'll get the food.'

'The sofa's a bit…'

'It'll brush off when it dries. Why not have a shower? Do as you're told. Or we'll never eat tonight.' He kissed her for the forty-ninth time that evening. 'Life is so simple,' he said, releasing her eventually, 'when you're around. Everything falls into place.' He moved into the bedroom off which was the tiny bathroom. Space in the lodge was concentrated enough to make conversation possible wherever one found oneself. 'I'm famished. Virtue has gone out of me. Brr, this water's cold…'

'I've made a special soup, so you'd better like it…' The kitchen was on the other side of the living-room and through the open door the hint of a savoury aroma sharpened his appetite.

'I can smell it…great! What is it?'

'It's got ox-tail and tomatoes and wine and onions and garlic and mushrooms…tiny ones…and paprika…and…oh, all kinds of delicious things.' She was standing leaning over the electric hob, tasting the rich brew in a two-handled copper pot. The cotton shirt came down to just above the incipient horizontal crease in her bare buttocks. She replaced the spoon on the bench and smacked her lips. 'Hmm . . . I really am a good cook! . . . Oh! What are you *doing?*' He had silently crept up behind her and flung his arms around her at her most

112

callipygian, hugging her to him, his face buried. Then he stood up and nuzzled and kissed the nape of her neck.

'Oh, that's lovely,' she murmured. 'I don't mind that at all.'

He turned her round so that they were face to face. 'Do you know what you look like? One of those titillating pictures in a girlie magazine!'

'Oh, so that's what you spend your time reading in the office. I'll put my jeans on.'

'Please don't. I find you very succulent.'

'You're a dirty old man.'

'Yes I am.'

She looked at him for what seemed a long time, her brown eyes grave, unsmiling. Then she kissed him very deliberately. 'I love you. Come on. Food.'

The oval table was the angle of the room. It had been meticulously laid with tawny pottery plates and horn handled knives and solid hand designed steel salts. There were napkins a lighter shade than the coffee coloured cloth and in a little majolica vase a posy of autumnal flowers. It had clearly been a labour of love.

'Darling, you take such trouble. It's lovely.'

'Thank the good sisters,' she said, 'my convent upbringing, what's left of it!'

'Thank you, good sisters!'

'I'm glad it pleases my lord! I feel a bit like when I was at school and the local Canon came to lunch and all the nuns fluttered around looking after him and he was the only one who ate, though the Mother Superior would go through the motions to keep him company!'

'I'll tell you something. Not only can you keep me company, but you can eat with me as well! The Canon is well pleased with you!'

'Seeing that he has just bedded me in very uncanonical fashion I should hope that he is not just pleased, but thrilled with me!'

'He is. He is.' He lifted her off the floor and spun her round. Then his face became serious. 'I'm afraid there's something I have to tell you — at the risk of repeating myself. I love you Miss Scanlon — boring isn't it?'

'You can bore the...pants off me any time you like!'

Carson laughed a full-blooded, joyous laugh. 'And she's witty with it.'

'Come on,' she said. 'Let's eat. Open a bottle of wine. See what you think of this masterpiece. Why do men always like soup?'

'Anything in liquid form. We're still psychologically on the breast.'

113

'But only for the first course.'

'Oh, we move on for the second!'

'Well, you're getting no second tonight, of any kind! It's very rich, very filling, and if you're still hungry after a couple of platefuls, there's cheese and fruit and I'll make you an Irish coffee — or do you still want scrambled eggs!'

'My child, I think the Canon will skip the scrambled eggs. What wine?' He went to the bookcase, the lower part of which served as a drinks cupboard. 'You can have Beaujolais or Beaujolais. Let me see. I think…we'll have the Beaujolais.'

'Get on with it. This is ready.' She brought the soup and ladled it out at the table. An orectic vapour greeted their nostrils. There was a loaf of wheaten bread. He poured the wine and lifted his glass:

'Here's to…land without rent to you, the man of your choice to you, to hell with King William and death in Connaught! Isn't that what you say?'

She laughed a long laugh. 'It's not what I say and I've never heard it in any Catholic house, but if it makes you happy…Slainte! Here's to us.'

He attacked the food hungrily. 'This is great, great.' He paused. 'Why are you looking at me like that?'

She was contemplating him almost objectively, as one would look at a stranger who excited interest. 'I'm thinking,' she spoke slowly, 'of the kind of person I thought you were before I knew you. You were a typical Protestant politician.'

'Is there one?'

'For Catholics, yes. Bigoted, in that you hate and – which is worse – despise Catholics: superior, always a touch of the Herrenvolk even where it is least justified, and…!'

'Go on! Give me hell!'

'Hypocritical, I'm afraid, pretending to be good-living you call it, more sober, more honest, cleaner, more industrious than us poor Papists – yet on all those counts just as bad as we are. Now, what do you think of that?'

'Quite an indictment. Have we no good points at all? Is there nothing to be said in our favour?'

She smiled reasuringly. 'Of course I exaggerate a bit and of course you can't generalise, but seriously, that is a pretty average view. I think it was lack of *respect* that hit hardest.'

'Darling. *You* felt like this? I can't believe it. You didn't suffer. You weren't oppressed in any way.'

114

'No, of course I wasn't. But I belonged to a community, a very close-knit commuity, that did suffer or sometimes believed that they suffered, because of their religion or politics. They felt aliens in their own country. And you must remember that I am only first-generation middle-class or whatever. My father's generation really saw itself as down-trodden peasants – trapped in the one part of Ireland that hadn't managed to shake off...'

'The yoke of the hated Sassenach oppressor.'

'Right. That was what I learnt in school – and the nuns weren't half as inflexible as the Christian Brothers – and very often on Sunday, too from the pulpit, so that all the influences on a young Catholic growing up in Northern Ireland: family, school, church, tend to perpetuate the same attitudes – more so because, as I say, we're such an inbred community, and all the more resentful because we can see and visit the Gaelic Catholic heaven just South of the Border. Does that make sense? You're always asking me, aren't you, about how we think, so there you are.'

'Here I am. And no doubt I'm still a Unionist bastard to everyone else.'

'If they knew you as well as I know you . . .'

'You're biased.'

'Am I?' She placed her hand on his. 'Some more?'

'Please. I really was hungry.'

As she went into the kitchen to replenish his soup-plate, he poured out some more wine and took a drink. 'I was going to say that you hadn't known many Protestants, but I realise that you, Josephine, are the only Catholic I have ever been on terms of intimacy with – maybe that's not the happiest expression – but it's true, alas. I knew of course quite a number at university, but there wasn't, in the nature of things, much socialising so, like you, I relied on the conventional wisdom – though with far less excuse than you had. So I suppose I am a Unionist bastard.'

She caressed him with her mouth as she placed the plate in front of him. 'You can fool me.' After a moment she began again. 'It must be hard for outsiders to believe that, after all these years, in such a small area, there was still, there *is* still such lack of contact, such segregation of the two communities, like Jews and Arabs I suppose, the Catholic quarter and the Protestant quarter . . . if we had all been atheists maybe . . .?'

'Oh it's not about theology, about transubstantiation, or the Real

Presence, or the cult of the Virgin, or that sort of thing. In any case this place is rapidly becoming a pagan country like the rest of the UK. The only people who are interested in theological niceties are the ecumenicals, and they're no problem. No, it's about traditions and allegiances and flags and social attitudes like the whole contraception, divorce, Catholic education, abortion mish-mash. You don't get rid of that overnight.'

'It's just the older people who have rigid ideas on things like that.'

'Unfortunately, it's the older people in established positions in the churches, education and so on, who are consulted about legislation. It's the older people who make the running and who are most vocal. The young tend to opt out or go along with the parental line.'

'It's changing.'

'Everything is changing, but not fast enough. Vino?' She nodded. Bottle in hand, he pursued a favourite theme. 'How often have I heard it at rugger internationals in Dublin. Afterwards at the Shelbourne, all pals together and full of the milk of human kindness and Arthur Guinness. "Sure when everyone's wearin' the green jersey there's no difference between us. Sure we're all Irishmen. And pray God one day we'll all be together again. We may not live to see it Desmond but pray God that day'll come in his own good time. Here, take your hand out of your pocket. It's on me this time. What'll ye have?" And we all get sloshed and sing "Kevin Barry" and "The Ould Orange Flute", and the Irish problem is solved. But in the grey dawn next day, it's still there, and the Fianna Fail and the Fine Gael politicians, instead of "pray God we'll be together again", are blessing themselves gratefully and saying "Thank God a united Ireland is still just a national aspiration and thank God that we don't have to cope with the problems of assimilating a million Prods from Ulster into our nice little, tight little Catholic Republic".'

'When you've finished the speechifying, Minister, perhaps you'd pour me a glass of wine.' She was ribbing him with gentle irony.

'Sorry darling,' he patted her hand apologetically, and filled her glass. 'I'm sure you've heard it all before.'

'At long-distance, yes, but I don't object to hearing it in close-up.'

'I get so tired of this hypocrisy from the South, eternally shouting about a "nation once again" but never a gesture, never a move to put their money where their mouth is and has been for fifty years.'

'Of Unionist misrule!'

'Sorry! We mustn't forget that . . . "Of Unionist misrule"!'

She smiled at him. 'I think you are being less than fair to our friends in the South.'

'How? Come on. Say your piece. Put me straight.'

'Well, you complain that they do nothing to make the South more acceptable to the Prods in the North, yet everything they attempt in that direction is treated with scorn. They are accused of interference in Northern matters which don't concern them. They held a referendum on the recognition of the "special position" of the Catholic church in the Irish Constitution – a very sensitive issue, mind you, and not the easiest thing for Southern politicians to tackle – and when this offensive phrase was removed, what thanks did they get? None. Not even token appreciation of the gesture. All you people said was that it should never have been there in the first place. So naturally they say, "What's the point? All we get is abuse. We'll wait till they're ready to talk. When they are, we'll endeavour to give these obstreperous and warring tribesmen in the North what they want, assuming they know what they want".'

Carson laughed, fondly. 'Not tribesmen – diatribesmen! You're turning into a real little politician, aren't you?'

'I still don't know what you're going to do – nor do you, as far as I can see.'

'I've told you. I'm waiting to see. As we say in poker – I'm waiting on the openers, Gillan and the PM.'

'You won't throw in?'

'No. It's taken me too long to get this hand together. I'll play it whatever happens. Only one person could stop me . . .'

'You know I won't. God help me!'

He put his arms round her and drew her close. They sat some moments in silence. He sighed. 'I'd better clock in, just in case some dire calamity has happened.' He looked at his watch. 'Let's see if there's anything on the News At Ten. I won't be a second.' As he went out to the car, she switched on the television set and cleared some dishes from the table. Slowly and thoughtfully she wriggled into her jeans. When he returned he was distrait, summoning up a wan smile as he noticed the change in dress. 'Closed the stable door have we?'

'The horse hasn't really bolted – just a little chilly. Everything all right?'

'Yes. Yes.' He was preoccupied. 'No panic. We've got till midnight or so . . . oh there we are.'

Big Beg was striking. A familiar face was saying, 'First the headlines.

The Middle East – a setback to the peace talks. Commons row over North Sea Oil. Northern Ireland – a new initiative on security. First the Middle East . . . .'

Carson bent down and lowered the volume. 'So, it's really starting. They should have the Government statement by now. There'll probably be a quote from it. We'll see.'

'Anything more to eat?' She waited for a reply. 'Come on, darling. I've lost you. What's wrong?'

He was staring at the box, seeing nothing. When he spoke, his voice was matter-of-fact, unemotional. 'Nothing really. When I was talking to the police just now, they'd just had word of a rather nasty killing, some lad who'd been worked over and then apparently left to bleed to death. They found him dumped in a car near the river.'

'Oh God! That's awful . . . *tortured?*'

'I'll spare you the details. It seems he's been giving the police information.'

'They're all the same, wild animals.'

'Yes. You're right. There are a lot of wild animals around, however house-trained they seem to be at times.' She looked at him curiously. 'Forget it,' he said and smiled at her. 'It's a different world out there. I really enjoyed that soup, darling. I do appreciate you, you know. How about that Irish coffee? I'll get the Irish.' The newscaster was on to the Northern Ireland story. It ran just as Carson had guessed. Rumours of a pending announcement of new security proposals followed by two excerpts from the offical Government statement highlighting the future of the Specials.

'Well, is that a relief?'

'I didn't expect a splash on the national news. We are not, despite what we like to think sometimes, the centre of world affairs. If they'd had the story of the killing, it would have got equal coverage. Initiatives are dull stuff compared with blood. No, it's the local press who will go to town. Wait till you see.' He went to the bookcase for whiskey. She was in the kitchen making coffee.

'There was a funny man here today.'

'Oh! Who was that?'

'Oh, I'm probably being silly, but you've made me so security conscious . . . .'

'No, you're perfectly right.' He was being ultra nonchalant. 'What was it?'

'Well, I'd arranged to skip lunch and do some shopping. I left the

118

office not long after twelve and on the way down I thought I'd call here and collect a pair of slacks to be altered.'

'Yes. Yes.'

'I parked the Mini on the main road, and as you know, I always use the back door. Well just as I came round the big laurel bush, I saw him standing, not at the door, but near it, looking at the house. He saw me at the same time, and I think he was just as taken aback as I was.'

'What sort of person was he? I mean, was he a workman . . . or . . . how was he dressed?'

'He was wearing a light sort of fawn raincoat and he had one of those plastic document cases under his arm. Like a salesman.'

Carson smiled, relieved. 'Well, wasn't he?'

She shook her head, uncertainly. 'As soon as he saw me, he said something like, "I'm sorry. I must have come to the wrong house". I said "Who are you looking for?" and he said, "Mr Doherty. I was told he lived just near here". So I suggested he might try the flats in the big house, and he seemed relieved and said yes, that was it. So off he went.'

Carson was gently but firmly dismissive. 'Darling. I'm sure it was quite innocent. If it hadn't been, do you think he'd be prowling around in broad daylight? And anyway, who's going to bother you? I'm never here except at night.' He went over and put his arm round her reassuringly. 'But you were quite right to tell me. Better to be safe than sorry.' They sat down together on the sofa as she mixed the coffee and whiskey. 'Well, what nice things did you buy?' She launched into a recital of the delights and deficiencies of the better end of the Belfast rag trade. Carson reacted as expected, but his mind strayed back to her visitor. He looked at the girl chattering beside him. The animation of the dark eyes, the pout and play of the lips, the unresting movement of face and hands and the currents of her fragrance that he was constantly aware of. He wondered at the way the whole array of bodily signals multiplied around him until they encompassed his world from the fringe to the centre, and he was left drugged and drifting in the hot inarticulate dark of human yearning. With an effort he tried to face the reality – he could be endangering her as much as himself. But as he reached out to draw her to him, reality was slipping away.

119

There were seven cars outside the Harrmon HQ at 10.30 that evening. Just a glint of light from a window in the house opposite revealed to the initiated that the guard was at his post. In the upstairs room of the HQ, Harrmon and eight of his commanders from the greater Belfast area were assembled. Most of them were wearing leather jerkins or padded anoraks. Two, like their chief, had jackets and ties, having been hastily summoned from a social evening with their women. Harrmon was wasting no time.

'I've told you what we're faced with. The whole British Cabinet is behind it. It's no use telling them it's not on. We know from past experience that they won't shift. So either we go on whining and belly-achin' like the rest of those bloody eejits, or we do something that really stops them in their tracks. The time for big protest rallies is over, finished, finito!' He was given to the odd exotic expression picked up from television. As he surveyed his band of brothers, they waited in some suspense for what was coming. He spoke slowly, biting off each word with emphasis. 'This time, we've got to show them who's in charge. This time, we've got to deliver.' He still held them transfixed, ready for the coup de grace. 'We've got to show them that we can close . . . ' He raised his voice and struck the desk once with his clenched fist. '. . . this country down.' He got the effect he had been building for.

It was Big Charlie from Carrickfergus who tentatively sought clarification. 'You mean . . . we take over?'

'If we have to,' answered Harrmon, without hesitation. He could sense that his confidence was not fully shared by all present. The feeling was confirmed as the shock effect of his words subsided and he was subjected to a flood of questioning, as his fellow officers looked at each other anxiously and exchanged cigarettes. 'Look at it this way. We need the power stations. We need the diesel and petrol tankers. We can probably get a lot besides, but the rest is jam. If we have the electricity and the oil – that's it. We're in control.'

'What about the Army? What are they going to be doing?' asked someone.

120

'Exactly,' said Harrmon, his face alight. 'That's the key question. To beat the Army we need public support – the kind of cause that puts us on the right side. And I believe we've got it!' He made no attempt to tone down the note of triumph in his voice. 'Once the people learn what's happening to the Specials and the police, once they hear that they're going to be left defenceless, then we'll have every Protestant in the country behind us. This will sort out the so-called moderates I can tell you.'

'Fuck the moderates,' said someone. 'All they're good for is letting the Fenians walk over them. There's not a decent Protestant among them.'

'And, if we have the public behind us,' continued Harrmon, 'the Army won't count. If the time is ever going to be ripe, then it's now.' The more he talked, the more conviction he carried, and the brighter the faces around him. 'You know Megs Kane? Well he has been working on a plan for some time. He's not a member of the organisation, but he's got the lads in the power stations behind him and he's with us all the way. So I thought it would be a good idea to ask him along tonight. Do you agree to have him in? He's downstairs.' There was loud and unanimous approval.

Reg, who had recovered his composure said, 'I wondered what Megs was doing here. I saw him when I was coming in.'

'He sits in my old lodge,' explained Harrmon, 'Megs is straight, I've been keeping in touch with him because, although in some ways he's a funny bugger, there's nothing he doesn't know about the power game – and I mean the power game!' Harrmon was pleased at his little verbal felicity.

A small, dark terrier-like man entered the room, nodding briefly and unsmiling as he acknowledged the greetings of the assembled UDF men. His eyes restlessly roved round the room as he took the offered chair next to Harrmon and accepted a cigarette with the automatic movements of a chain smoker. Megs Kane owed his nickname to his early preoccupation with megawatts. Without any formal training, he had acquired an astonishing working knowledge of the increasingly sophisticated power system. Although only a charge-hand in one of the Belfast stations, his position as senior shop steward, combined with his self-taught expertise, gave him a status and influence on a par with the station manager. During a work-to-rule, which had been called to back up a wage claim two years previously, he had glimpsed the awesome potential of political power, which resided in the Northern Ireland electricity industry. Fed by only four plants, and with no possibility of emergency supplies from either the British mainland or the Republic, it was tailor-made for a determined takeover.

Harrmon began almost formally, with a hint of deference. 'On behalf of the Force, I want to say that we appreciate you coming along and sparing the time, Megs. We have been discussing how we're going to run this campaign. It's got to be planned, and it's got to be tight, because there will be no second chance. So maybe you can fill us in on the power side.'

Hesitantly, Megs Kane began. But as he warmed to his theme, the words came faster and the thread of fanatic steel in his voice bound them to him. Behind him, as they well knew, was an unbroken union record of successful campaigning for a better deal. Men who are unsure like to stick close to a winner and Megs Kane had never lost a battle yet.

'Me and a couple of my mates have been thinking, thinking about this problem for some time. The Protestants don't know their own strength. They don't need an army. All they need is men who believe. Men with a faith that will not be shaken. The don't need guns or gelignite. "And they that dwell in the cities of Israel shall go forth and shall set on fire and burn the weapons . . . for they shall burn the weapons and they shall spoil those that spoiled them and rob those that robbed them," Ezekiel 39, Verses 9 and 10.' He paused as he sought out the eyes of each one of them. They were hard men but some of them looked away from his unwavering disturbing gaze. Not one attempted to draw comfort from an exchange of glances with his fellows. After a moment, he deliberately broke the spell by slapping the table with his hand. 'Brothers, let us never forget what wins battles is strength of spirit, not strength of arms. Right!' He leaned forward and his manner was much more matter-of-fact. 'This wee country of ours lives by electricity: factories, farms, hospitals, telephones, light, heat – the lot. We use about 720 to 730 megawatts a day. About a third of that is used by industry – the rest is farms, homes and services. If we cut supply down to about 400 megs, then there has to be cuts all over Ulster. That would give them a taste of just what we could do. If we screw it down further, then the whole of industry would have to shut down, so that the essential services are kept going. The limit is about 200 megawatts. Round about that point the whole system goes unstable, gets out of balance – what we call a cascadin' failure – and you get a complete black-out, not a spark on the whole grid.'

'The whole thing shorts-out?' asked someone.

Megs treated this simplicity with the nearest he ever got to a smile.

122

'You could say that. But there are two ways of stopping a turbine. You can ease her down gently like a bird coming to rest, or you can let her thrash her blades to bits in thirty seconds – one and a half million quid down the drain, and it takes months to repair the damage. You could wreck every generator in this country inside five minutes. We control the power stations. That means we control the country.' He remained silent, as the blunt assertion sank in. Harrmon nodded, unsmiling, exuding the satisfaction of a man who has produced the goods as promised.

Someone asked nervously, 'What happens if the Army move in and run the stations themselves?'

Megs looked at the questioner reproachfully. Then he intoned. '"Ye shall eat the flesh of the mighty and drink the blood of the princes of the earth".' Sensing perhaps that he had not fully satisfied the questioner he went on. 'If the Army moved in, or the Navy, for that matter – because they would know more about turbines than the Army – they wouldn't know where to start. If they put a foot wrong they could melt the tubes in the burner in thirty seconds! To give you some idea of just how complicated the control system is, there are nine manuals of over two hundred pages each – and that's for the boilers alone. There are six manuals, over three hundred pages each on the turbines, not to speak of books on the pumps and switchgear etc. Even a fully qualified engineer has to spend months in the station – on what we call familiarisation, before he's allowed to go on shift at the control console. No, there's no danger of the Army or the Navy takin' over. You can be sure of that.'

It was Charlie from Carrickfergus who pursued the matter, 'Supposin' some of the senior . . . er . . . engineers, the qualified people agreed to work on . . . couldn't the Army run the manual side, the boilers and on? I mean the management are goin' to side with the Government aren't they? And if they've got the know-how and the Army's got the muscle, what's to stop them.'

Megs looked at the speaker with interest. 'I can't see the engineers or middle management scabbin' with the Army. They know that when all's said and done, they'll have to work with us. But . . . ' he emphasised the conjunctive, 'if some of them decided to try and run the station with the Army, then they might be able to carry on . . . in *theory*.' He gave a wry twist of the mouth. 'In theory!'

'Grow up, Charlie, for Christ's sake,' snapped Harrmon, angry that the obtuseness of one of his lieutenants was letting the side down. 'They'd be blacked in every station in the country!' Megs gave a deliberate nod of agreement. 'Apart from that,' continued Harrmon, 'Do you think that we're going to stand by and let them? We'd get to them, don't worry, even if the whole bloody Army was guardin' them.'

Megs Kane had a faraway look in his eyes. When he spoke again it was like a patient schoolmaster repeating a lesson which he knew by heart. 'You see, it's all been foretold in the Book of Revelations, everything. Even the length of the first power cuts – eight hours. "And the third part of the sun was smitten, and the third part of the moon, and the third part of the stars so as the third part of them was darkened, and the day shone not for a third part of it, the night likewise." – Revelations Chapter 8 Verse 12. It's all there in the Good Book.' The dreamy tone in his voice took on a sharper edge and the mouth tightened as the eyes cut a flashing swathe round the room. 'I know some of you don't believe. But before it's all finished, you will — you will!'

'Thank you Megs,' said Harrmon after a pause. He turned to his colleagues, suppressing the note of triumph in his voice. 'You can see the possibilities. We can block off roads. We can get them out of the factories. But that's only boxin' for show, scoring points. This is the KO. No come-back. Mind you, there's a lot of planning to be done, a lot of detailed planning. We've got to keep the essential services in operation – food, water, hospitals. We've got to make sure that the people don't suffer, especially our own people. It's the British Government who have to go to school. They are the ones who've gotta to be taught a lesson.'

'In democracy!' said Reg amid a general chorus of approval.

Megs Kane took from the inside pocket of his jacket a thin school exercise-book folded in two. His manner was now subdued. The Old Testament visionary had given way to the union official at a branch meeting. Licking his thumb, he turned over the pages of the jotter, glancing up at Harrmon as he began to speak. 'What we need is a central council to co-ordinate all the different sectors of the stoppage. I've made a note of the key trades that should be represented.' He found the page he was looking for and continued. 'This is a list we have been workin' on – power, telephones, oil and petrol tankers, propane and Calor supplies, animal feedstuffs, hospital supplies. We need technical men who know their stuff to allocate supplies – not too much, just enough to keep the services running at a minimum level. Then we've got to be prepared to deal with some of the workers – and I'm not just talkin' about the Taigs – there's some of our own sort as well who'll try to back out . . .'

Harrmon help up a peremptory hand. 'That's our problem. We'll look after them,' he said.

'You're fuckin' right we will!" said big Charlie from Carrickfergus, and a growl from those around him assured him that he would not be on his own.

'Right!' said Megs again, with a glance at Harrmon, conveying the impression that he was really acting as the mouthpiece of the UDF Commander. 'There's another thing. We need a spokesman, someone who can talk to the press, somebody with the gift of the gab who can go on television and tell the people what we're doing and why we're doing it. Once the lights go off, people can get panicky you know. It's absolutely essential to bring the people along with us every step of the way.' Harrmon nodded his agreement. 'Harry here,' continued Megs, 'could do it, but he'll have his hands full.' Harrmon allowed himself a fleeting smile. He was not displeased.

'What about the politicians?' cried Reg, who had now recovered his self-confidence. 'Surely to Christ we're not expected to run this on our own. Aren't they goin' to back us?'

'Packham'll cave in,' said someone. 'Can you see him fightin' the British Government?'

'What about Mun Martin? He's a good Orangeman.'

'Wylie Mullins — he'll be with us all right.'

Harrmon slapped the table to still the babel of claim and counter-claim. 'Hold it. Hold it. I've good reason to believe that whatever Packham says or does, we can rely on at least one of his senior ministers — and that's not to say there won't be others. But you can rest assured. We won't be on our own.'

There was another interesting meeting taking place that night. Oliver Birch CMG, special Foreign Office representative in Northern Ireland, was entertaining a couple of visitors. The generosity of Her Majesty's Government enabled him to do so in comfort and in privacy. His official quarters, Loughside, was situated on that part of the southern shore of Belfast Lough known as the Golden Mile, because of the number of fine houses tucked away among the wooded policies which once formed part of larger properties. The original estates had belonged to the linen and shipping barons of nineteenth-century Belfast. Loughside is in some ways typical of the area. The house is approached through a maze of lanes and private roads. Its entrance is well protected by trees and a belt of rhododendrons that curves round on one side, hiding the kitchen quarters, garages, and the heating plant for the swimming pool. On this October evening the rainswept pool was stained with leaves and empty. In front of the house, where the lawns sloped away opening up a view of the distant sea, shifting clusters of lights sketched in the outlines of freighters anchored for the night. In the building itself a muffled glow from behind the heavily curtained windows revealed that many of the rooms were in use. For Loughside was more than a residence. It was a communications centre in the widest sense where on occasion the most unlikely people were assembled. Gunmen carrying weapons had come there and had not been searched by the brisk young Royal Marine who opened the door. Six soldiers in plain clothes were quartered in the house on permanent guard duties. Oliver Birch, if not all things to all men, was a number of things to the different political groupings. He saw himself as the catalyst bringing the most disparate elements together in search of the elusive common ground. Though he endeavoured to maintain the utmost impartiality in his attitude towards the different factions, his postings in the past, which had included Ghana and Nairobi, had conditioned him to think in terms of underdogs. All the more since, as a grammar school boy from Birmingham, he had always resented the top-hatted assurance of his public school colleagues in the Foreign Office. So tonight duty and inclination went hand in hand. His two guests were the leading figures in the Nationalist Opposition at Stormont, and there was a cosy camaraderie at the supper table as he elaborated on the good news he had for them. They were just finishing bacon, eggs, sausages and fried potato bread, accompanied by a plentiful supply of Guinness which Birch always referred to as the 'vin du pays'. This was his informal style of entertaining the natives. No fancy dishes. Give them what they're used to and promote a state of unbuttoned ease in which the chat flows indiscreet and unconstrained.

'There are a few more bangers here, Joe.' Birch lifted the cover of a metal dish and looked enquiringly at Joe Maguire, the Party leader, who was opening bottles of stout at a side-table.

Maguire's big square face creased in a grin. 'Don't worry lad. They won't be wasted.' He spoke in the unmusical throaty tones of his native Belfast. An ex-docker from the Catholic Lower Falls he had come up through municipal politics, a populist, working the system for his own advancement, exploiting it for the benefit of the people he represented. He instinctively avoided fixed positions. Rather he dealt in dimensions that overlapped and balanced each other: the Catholic dimension without being the hierarchy's favourite son; the Republican dimension without being too anti-British; the working-class dimension without scaring off the solid bourgeois publicans who gave so generously to Party funds. Maguire had a hand of pinkish-green cards, and he played them skilfully depending on the issues. He was a gut politician.

His companion Dr Patrick Keevy was different. He was the thinker with a theological cast of mind that saw things in black and white, a trait strengthened by the year he had spent training for the priesthood in Maynooth, before turning to teaching and then to politics via a County Council. From Omagh in County Tyrone, he wore the *fainne*, the gold ring of the Gaelic speaker, in his lapel. He had a ruffled academic air and kept shifting the spectacles on his bony nose as he peppered away at the subject under discussion, rarely pausing for a word, fond of throwing in Irishisms. Dabbing his mouth with a paper napkin, he continued his staccato delivery. 'Like I say, the Courts and the judiciary are one thing – you can get away with that, and anyway it's only the lower courts that are affected . . .'

'A very important area of patronage nonetheless,' cut in his host.

Keevy was dismissive. 'Oh, come on now! Whether judges are appointed from London or from Stormont, it's the same soup on different plates. The same men will get the jobs. After over fifty years of High Court judges being appointed by the Lord Chancellor, how many have we? One – and he's a West Briton, not a real Irishman at all!'

'He's a Catholic,' said Birch.

'That's about all you can say for him' grunted Keevy. 'The token Catholic. Isn't that right, Joe?' Maguire merely grinned and handed his colleague one of the bottles of stout which he had just opened. 'This major reform of the legal system, as you call it,' continued Keevy, taking the proffered bottle and expertly pouring it at just the right angle to avoid too big a head of froth. 'It won't make one button of difference. The old boy network will still function. Sure Crossley the Attorney General, and the Lord Chancellor are as close as two peas in a pod. He stayed with Crossley the last time he was over here. Crossley will go on making the appointments – he and Packham. Cosmetic, eyewash – that's all your proposals are. Give us credit for a bit of sense for God's sake!' Keevy took a long draught of Guinness.

Birch gave a resigned smile. He had not spent two years as First Secretary in Chancery with an African High Commission without learning how and when to give excitable natives their head. 'I'm sorry you feel like that about it, Paddy, and I think you're being a little unfair, but let's leave the judiciary – the move on the B Specials is surely unequivocal enough isn't it?'

'Your Specials now, that's a horse of another colour,' said Keevy.

'If it ever gets through,' chipped in Maguire looking hard at Keevy and then at Birch.

'It will go through all right,' said the latter, emphatically. 'The Prime Minister is quite determined.'

'We've heard that before,' said Maguire with some heat. 'He was determined to do something about Local Government. He was determined to do something about housing allocations. I'll believe it when I see it. Like they say in the States – Don't tell me. Show me!'

'I assure you,' said Birch stiffly, 'that this is a firm decision. Whether you believe me or not.'

Maguire was at once apologetic, all warm affability. 'Now, please don't misunderstand me, Oliver. I accept that the Cabinet have taken this decision. I know that you're being straight with us, otherwise we wouldn't be here, would we, Paddy?' He appealed to Keevy who gravely shook his head. 'If I seemed a bit sceptical, it's just that we've been led up the garden path so often. We have every confidence in you, personally, and I'll tell you this – and I hope you don't mind my speaking frankly. Of all the Englishmen who have come over here, civil servants, newspaper men, BBC, the lot, there's not one who's got inside the Irish mind like you have. There's not a sinner among them who even begins to understand the problem like you do – and that's the God's truth!'

Keevy nodded agreement. 'He's right, Oliver. We all think that.'

Birch smiled nervously, capitulating to this double-barrelled charge of flattery. 'My dear Joe, it's very kind of you to say so. One tries. One tries.'

'I don't know about the Unionists, but at least *we* appreciate the contribution you're making,' continued Maguire, a firm believer in the Disraeli dictum that when you lay it on, you lay it on with a trowel.

'You see,' Keevy now took up the running, 'what worries me about this scheme to scrap the Specials, is how you're going to avoid a Protestant rebellion – no, just a minute.' He waved a silencing hand as Birch was about to intervene. 'You see, in attacking the Specials, you're committing an act of desecration against one of the holy relics, or maybe,' he allowed himself a fleeting smile, 'to avoid a papish metaphor, I should say one of the sacred cows of orthodox Unionism. I cannot see how any Unionist Government could go along with it.' Maguire was signalling vigorous agreement, 'And that's why I share Joe's concern. If Packham tries to carry it through, he's finished. The grass roots would murder him. I can't even see him getting it past Cabinet, let alone the Parliamentary Party. So what we're talking about is a head-on confrontation with the Protestant population. Are your masters prepared for that, I ask?'

'If they were, I take it that they would have your support?' countered Birch.

It was Maguire who answered. 'We would certainly not stand in their way if they abolished the most blatantly sectarian force since the Black and Tans – Catholics will shed no tears over the Specials – a lot of bloody Orangemen with rifles!'

The Party Leader's face was red with anger.

'What Joe says is true,' said Keevy quickly, smoothing out the jolt, 'but surely the answer to your question would depend on what will fill the gap when the Specials disappear. Will the Army activity be expanded? Or will the RUC simply start recruiting ex-B Specials?'

'Or will they just be drafted into the UDF, seeing as half of them are probably in in already!' It was the sarcasm from Maguire this time, rather than anger.

Ignoring the remark, Birch addressed himself to Keevy. 'Since control of the RUC will be shifted to the Home Office, it hardly matters if some of the ex-Specials join it. In any case, I doubt if they would wish to join a full-time force where the discipline is pretty tight.'

'How will the gap be filled then? I'd like to know,' insisted Keevy.

The slight hesitation before Birch replied did not pass unnoticed. 'Present thinking is to have a sort of TA, a Territorial force under direct control of the GOC – really a kind of army reserve.' He had spoken casually, but his two listeners exchanged a swift glance.

'Ah! so that's it,' said Maguire, with heavy irony. Birch looked at him coldly. Diplomatic urbanity was slipping.

'Hold it a minute Joe,' said Keevy. 'Oliver's on our side, remember? Let's get this straight. The Specials will be disbanded and then . . . replaced by a sort of Territorial Army force? Which presumably would be composed of B Specials?'

'No, not necessarily, not exclusively. One would hope to recruit across the community for what would be an entirely non-sectarian force, under totally impartial commanders and subject to normal army discipline. I would hope that you both would see your way to encourage Catholics to play their part in getting the force off to a good start.'

Maguire could no longer restrain himself. 'And join up with most of the B Specials? About ten of them to every Catholic? Can you see it? I knew this whole thing sounded too good to be true!' Impatiently he waved down his colleague who had been about to speak. 'Look, Oliver. We've had several meetings over the past few months. It's been very pleasant and we couldn't ask for a better host. So whatever I say, there's nothing personal in it. But you're the only contact we have at the moment with the British Government. I understood from you that a new deal for the Catholic people here was on the way. That there was going to be an end to discrimination and injustice, that the Unionist clique that have run this place for sixty years were going to be stripped of their powers. This was to be the great new initiative for which we have all been waiting, the new deal that we had succeeded in getting for our people, to win them away from the IRA and along the road to co-operation instead of conflict. That was the theory. And what have we got? A few changes in the courts and the judiciary – nominal, nothing to alter the basic balance of power. It's still in Unionist hands. The Prods will still decide who sits on the Bench, just like they always have. Then the B Specials, this sensational move that's going to prove once and for all that the Prod supremacy is finished! And what happens? The Bees are dead! Long live the Bees in the TA or is it the 'BA'? The same old soup on a brand new plate! After all the build-up we have nothing to sell. You've left us naked.' There was a silence. Maguire sat down heavily at the table with no great sense of relief, despite the fact that he'd got it off his chest. Keevy toyed with the bridge of his spectacles and gazed into his glass.

Birch's face registered open dismay. When he spoke, his tone was formal and official. 'I hardly think that the Unionist Government shares your view. These are extremely radical proposals – radical, I believe, to the point of unacceptability. You yourself used the term "sacred cow" with reference to the Special constabulary. I think that sums up Unionist feeling, and I do not see how my Government could have gone much further, short of demanding the resignation of the entire Unionist Cabinet. You have repeatedly stressed that, from the minority's point of view, this force was the most obvious and most detested symbol of what you have called Unionist hegemony, oppression, dictatorship – your expressions have been wide-ranging. At the risk of grave confrontation with the majority population, the British Government proposes to remove that symbol and replace it with an instrument which will be as impartial as we can make it. Now, when the Cabinet decision has been taken, when the die is cast, you dismiss the very measure which origi-nated in your own representations – and nowhere else! – as a worthless

130

gesture. I must say I find it hard to follow your logic, and my masters will find it even more difficult, I assure you!' This last was uttered with no little bitterness. For Oliver Birch, Commander of the Order of St Michael and St George, one time Principal Private Secretary to the Secretary of State for Foreign Affairs, most recently Deputy Undersecretary at the Foreign and Commonwealth Office, veteran of half-a-dozen dubious deals in emergent Africa, political reactions in Accra and Lusaka were of Pavlovian predictability compared to what he was facing in Belfast. Still, one must keep on trying.

This time it was Keevy who held up his hand authoritatively. 'I'll deal with this Joe.' He swung round in his chair with his elbow on the table and squarely faced his host. After Maguire's bovine assault it was now his deputy's role to provide a subtler, more intellectual apologia for their attitude. 'Oliver, I can quite understand your reaction. You must think we are a graceless, ungrateful lot. You give us what you believe we have been asking for all along, and we throw it in your face. I'd just like to make two points which I hope will clarify our position. First, with regard to your proposals. Of course we have urged, and we welcome, changes of this nature, provided they have real political impact. Take the Specials. How is the ordinary Catholic going to react to that one? Exactly as Joe has just reacted – the same soup as before, *"plus ça change, plus c'est la même chose"*. I know, I know, that's not how you see it, but believe me, that's how our people will see it. Indeed I'm not so sure that Packham won't be able to get away with it. I can just hear him now, talking about upgrading the whole force, better co-operation with the army etc, etc. Sure as God I can see him finishing up by convincing all concerned that he's given the Specials promotion! You couldn't be up to him – he's a wily bird! So if the purpose of this exercise is to convince Catholics of your bona fides I'm afraid you've missed the target. That's the first point. The second follows on. If you really want to win acceptance by our side, you'll have to cut deeper, much deeper. You see, the kinds of things we have been discussing up to now, even if they worked, would only scratch the surface. What we want, what we demand as of right, is a seat at the top table.' Birch slowly poured himself another Guinness and made no comment. 'I seem to remember a phrase that was used at our last meeting: a permanent and guaranteed share in decision-making – that's the sort of of initiative we were looking forward to.'

'Now you're talking, Paddy.' Maguire in some excitement slapped his fingers on the table. 'Now you're talkin'.'

'It comes to this, Oliver,' continued Keevy. 'If you want us to take a real interest in the business and to have some confidence in its future, you'll have to see that we get a share in the management. It's as simple as that.'

'When we get that,' cried Maguire, 'then the courts and the Specials and the rest of it will take care of themselves.'

'Much more than that,' added Keevy, his voice rising. 'We shall feel at long last that we can assert our own Irish identity, follow our own culture, without the feeling that we need a special dispensation from his Most Pompous Excellency, the Governor of Northern Ireland – God save the mark! – every time we speak the language of the Gael on a public occasion!' Keevy gave a forced and unconvincing laugh to counter the alienation he sensed his words were producing. But his host had slipped on the diplomat's mask again. This blow hot, blow cold of fulsome phrase, however agreeable, alternating with boorish bluntness, was rapidly turning off Her Majesty's FO representative. He was also uneasily conscious of the fact that present Whitehall policy had been constructed, to no small degree, on the basis of his own detailed reports of political feeling in the province. That knighthood, the 'K' at the end of the day, was receding all the time thanks to the arrogant expectations of these bloody Irish peasants. He was growing more and more Blimpish by the minute.

'I'm afraid, gentlemen,' and his smile had no warmth, 'that I can't help, much as I sympathise with your aspirations. As you know, I can only transmit, imperfectly sometimes I regret to note, the general thrust of present policy. On a share in Government, all I can say is that we'll have to score a lot more runs before we can put that one in to bat. I've told you of the firm decisions which have been made and which will be announced tomorrow. I'm sorry that apparently they don't go as far as you would wish. Can I take it that at least you will give them a qualified welcome? I am convinced that when you see the Unionist reaction you will feel rather better about everything than you do now.' Training was now reasserting itself. Despite himself, he was persuading them again. So many hours of hard hospitality, so many hours spent in building a rapport, so many bottles of bloody stout for which he had never acquired a taste, it would be stupid as well as unprofessional to blow it now. This was the only material he had to work on. It wouldn't go away. He smiled, more warmly this time. 'You really would think, lads, that we were acting against your interests instead of falling over backward trying to be helpful. I can tell you off the record that the Prime

Minister didn't have it all his own way in Cabinet when he pushed this through. I think he has a right to ask for your co-operation in getting as good a press as we can for it. I'm sure you'll agree?'

Maguire got up from the table and reached for another bottle of stout. Then he swung round, all forthcoming. 'For you, Oliver, we'll do what we can. You know how we feel about it, but, as you say, it will depend on what the other lot do. We've had a really frank talk tonight and that's good, that's good. Tomorrow's another day.'

'Don't worry, Oliver. We'll do our best for you,' said Keevy.

'Of course we will,' said Maguire, putting his arm on Birch's shoulder. 'Sure he's the only Englishman worth a damn I ever came across.'

'I wonder, Oliver, does that lot in the Foreign Office really appreciate the great job you're doing here. I was just saying to the Taoiseach in Dublin last week . . .'

The double act of the Blarney Brothers slid into overdrive. Despite himself, Oliver Birch CMG began once more to see *la vie en rose*.

In the Gillan farmhouse in Co Antrim, the lights in the drawing room were still on, well past midnight. The other guests had gone, leaving only Mun Martin with the host. The post-mortem on the Rooster's assassination job was not yet over. Gillan, gloomy, in contrast to his usual brisk self, was still licking his wounds. He poked at the fire, leaning forward in his chair, and let Mun do the talking.

'I bet a pound to a penny it was Crossley put him up to it. Shane and he are very thick – that's why he got the Crown Prosecutor job, and that's worth a few quid. He was out to wreck us from the word go.

'He didn't do too badly,' muttered Gillan. He looked up at Mun Martin. 'If what you say is true, he was taking a bit of a risk, wasn't he? When he said he'd come out against Packham if we resigned?'

'Bluff. Bluff,' said Mun, and could not help noting that he had now been included in the resignation demand. After tonight's hammering, James was looking for cover, spreading the load. Loyally Mun pressed on. 'At most, we lost a couple of votes tonight, but don't worry, they'll come back. But we can't hang around now the cat's out of the bag. Did you see the way McFee sidled out? He's probably on to Packham at this minute with a blow-by-blow account – that's if Shane Crossley doesn't get there before him – you can be sure the Rooster's been on to *him*. What a crew! We're well bloody rid of them – and our own lads are solid as a rock. You saw that when the others left.'

'Not enough,' said Gillan, quietly. 'They're not enough. We have no hope of carrying the Party tomorrow – not a hope in hell. Even if the reaction tomorrow morning is in our favour. We need time to let the message get across.' He stared into the fire for a moment. Then suddenly he brightened. 'What about Mullins?'

'Yes,' said Mun, perking up. 'We know what line he'll take. Why don't I give him a ring?' He looked at his watch. 'He's up till all hours, and he's bound to know by now what's happening. You know, he could swing three or four our way if he wanted to. Macrory and his pals.'

'Just a moment. Let's not rush it. Isn't he pretty friendly with Carson?'

'*Was*. They don't seem to like each other any more. Carson

134

apparently said something that offended him. No, there's no tie-up there.'

'What line do we take?' Gillan was thinking aloud. 'Tell him simply that Packham is going to cave in on everything — courts, police, Specials, everything. We are going to stand firm, but we need more support in the Parliamentary Party. Once he knows that Packham's trying to get the British Goverment to agree to a smoke-screen, that will be the end of that! Why weren't Macrory and Co here tonight? – just as well they weren't, but we should have asked them.'

Mun laughed 'What! They run a mile from a bottle of whiskey – the devil's buttermilk!'

Gillan smiled for the first time. 'Of course, stupid of me.'

'But I'll say this for them. They may not be drinkers but, by God, they're workers. Every single one of Wylie Mullins' congregation is a potential political activist. When the word goes out that he's backing a candidate, my God! They're like beavers, canvassing, driving, addressing envelopes. Hail, rain or snow, they're out there working away and they won't take a penny piece for it, not like our lot. I wish to God we had a few like them – that last election I never had my hand out of my pocket – I reckon I'd no change out of four hundred quid.'

Gillan gave a scornful grunt. 'You people out in the country don't know you're living! In Belfast it would cost you twice that!'

'Anyway if Wylie Mullins ever decided to stand he'd have no problems in that direction. I've a feeling he's just waiting for the right moment to throw his hat into the ring.'

'I think it suits him at the moment to stay outside and pull the strings. In that way he has the best of both worlds. He can exercise political influence *and* get on with his crusades, building up a bigger following all the time. I hear he's giving up the tent?'

'Oh yes. He's got a site for a big new gospel hall – the People's Temple he calls it – on the Lisburn Road and the money's pouring in. He told me he raised twelve thousand pounds at one service alone! Praise the Lord! Make no mistake. Pastor Mullins is going places. And he hates Arthur – hates him!'

Gillan brightened. 'He does, doesn't he? I gathered in Cabinet that they gave Arthur a rough ride in Lisburn.' Gillan did not conceal his pleasure. 'Right! Give him a ring. It's just . . . five to twelve. I want to hear what they're saying on the late news. The phone's next door.' He moved over to the television set which stood in the corner of the room.

Martin rose from his chair. 'I know that Mullins is holding a big revival meeting on Saturday night in the Ulster Hall. That'll be a great platform for him just when he wants it.' Mun rubbed his hand in anticipation.

Gillan had a moment's doubt. 'You're sure he won't bring me into it in any way. At this point I don't want any open association of that kind.'

'I won't even mention your name. Though mind you, the same man won't be slow in putting two and two together. But don't worry. I know how to handle it. As a matter of fact . . . ' Mun paused significantly, 'I've been in touch with his younger brother fairly recently. He has a garage out my way and he was having a spot of bother with a planning application.'

'You were able to fix him up?' Gillan's question was purely rhetorical.

Martin just grinned as he left the room.

Carson was taking his leave. When he left her at night it was always a protracted process. He kept finding reasons for lingering a few more minutes.

They were seated together on the sofa in front of the waning fire. 'Tomorrow's going to be very difficult, darling. I'll have to contact you when I know the form. Cabinet in the morning. Party meeting in the afternoon. God knows what kind of crisis we'll be into by the evening. Anything could happen.'

'What are you going to do? – We never really got round to that.'

He looked at her with a half-smile. 'I've no regrets.'

She shook his arm with mock impatience. 'Come on. What happens tomorrow?'

'I promised I'd ring Arthur first thing . . . I'm going to back him. For two reasons. I believe he's backing me *and* I see no future in a head-on collision. It will only play into the hands of the trogs. And even if we won on a technical knock-out by making the place ungovernable, it would be a very short-lived triumph. They'd kick us out of the UK in no time.'

'UDI? United Ireland? Take your choice.'

'Don't start me on those buggers in the South again. They really have a lot to answer for, and I'm not just talking about the fact that half of them are crypto-Provos!'

'All right. We've done that for tonight. But where do we go?'

'Stay with the Union for the moment, even if the price of membership goes up and up in terms of swallowing pride and tolerating this eternal pussy-footing round on security. But, as an old uncle of mine used to

136

say: you don't like to pay *and* pray!'

'When you say pussy-footing around, what you mean is you want the Army to hammer the Catholics?'

'The Catholic thugs, the Catholic gunmen, yes – I don't think there are many Prods in the Provos. Wait a minute,' laughing, he put an arm round her shoulders, and hugged her, 'let me finish! You're right. I used to think of security, I suppose, as keeping Catholics firmly under the thumb – that's the side the threat came from and that's the way one looked at it. But I've changed. You've changed me. A thug is a thug and a gunman is a gunman and murderous vermin are murderous vermin, and there can be no question of theirs or ours. But the old tribal feeling isn't easy to shake off, darling, especially when the deathlist is very one-sided, and decent men trying to do their duty are cut down without a chance. But I try. And I look at you, and I think so many of the things I say, and automatic reactions I express to this or that, must be shocking and maybe deeply hurtful to you because of your family background and the way you've been used to look at things, and yet you put up with me . . . and love me.' He took one of her hands in both of his and spoke very softly. 'I can only try to tell you how grateful I am darling. I'm at your feet.'

They sat in silence and her eyes shone with an enormous tenderness. She brushed the back of her hand across them. 'How can I argue with you when you talk like that. It's unfair to a girl.'

He took her in his arms and they kissed for a long time. Then he said, 'I've never asked you – are you a fatalist?'

'In what way – in religion? About us? Or do I follow the stars in women's magazines? All I know is – I'm a Libra.'

'You won't belive this – I'm a Capricorn!'

'My randy goat!'

They laughed, and he continued, 'No, I wasn't thinking of the stars nonsense. But I actually feel that it's all pre-planned – my Calvinist upbringing, I suppose.'

'We have a sect called Jansenists who went in for the same sort of thing – they were heretics actually.'

'Friends of mine! What I was trying to say was' – and he spoke very seriously – 'I'm convinced the next few days will shape the future. There'll be big, possibly historic changes. And I'm determined – this is the important thing – that whatever happens on the political front, you and I are going public.' She was about to speak but he cut her off. 'No darling, please. There's nothing to discuss. In any case it's too late

137

tonight. You know we just can't stagger on as we are. Apart from the fact that it gets more and more difficult leaving you like this . . . any day now the balloon could go up. I'm quite sure my police know . . .' He stopped speaking as it sank in. 'All right?' She nodded and rubbed her cheek against his hand as they rose. Then she led him to the door.

Sir Arthur Packham KCB was standing in his bathroom brushing his teeth, preparatory to getting into bed. He was distrait, and still wearing his trousers with his braces slipped over the shoulders and dangling at each side. His unbuttoned shirt was half in and half out of his trousers, with the tail hanging free. This surprising form of deshabille went back to desert days with the Eighth Army when one's toilet was often a very rushed and makeshift affair. It had been a wearisome day and he had just finished a final nightcap with Billy Dixon fifteen minutes before. Billy had taken the call from McFee on the unlisted line, a worried McFee, falling over himself to justify his presence at the Gillan soirée, and terribly anxious to speak to the PM personally so that he could assure him of his unwavering loyalty and support. But Packham remained aloof – 'tied-up' had been Dixon's phrase – leaving the party Secretary to listen to a somewhat breathless account of the Rooster's onslaught.

McFee would be no problem. 'He's learnt his lesson,' had been Dixon's comment. 'He knows which side his bread is buttered on.' But what was to be done about Gillan? It was not the first time he had intrigued against his Leader. But at least appearances had been preserved. Now it would be common knowledge that he was openly compaigning to depose the Prime Minister. The list of signatures was damning – the press would go to town. Faced with another 'leadership crisis' how could any semblance of Cabinet unity be maintained? Just when a public show of solidarity was essential.

He could forgive Gillan his ambition – had not he himself manoeuvred his predecessor out of office? – but he could not forgive a caddish disregard for the proprieties in pursuit of that ambition. *Pas devant les enfants* – in politics, as in the conduct of an affaire, breeding showed. What else could one expect from a lemonade bottler? . . . His first impulse had been to confront the little bugger and sack him. But Dixon's counsel had prevailed. 'Now is not the time for the hatchet. Sleep on it boss. Sleep on it.' He would. As he faced himself in the looking-glass, what concerned him was not the disloyalty, not the possible defection of some of his colleagues. It was the image of the

138

sinking ship that was driving them to desert it. Despite all the denials and ingenious justifications, the message would come through loud and clear – his government was being stripped, stripped in public.

He finished brushing his teeth and automatically rinsed his mouth with a glass of water. Then he moved back into the bedroom .The lamp on the table by the bedside shone warmly on a copy of *Phineas Finn*. Like other Prime Ministers, he had an affection for the political novels of Anthony Trollope. What he found attractive in them was the solid assurance of the society which they reflected, a world in which your money was as good as gold, and the standards of public life were accepted and rigidly adhered to, whatever the delights of the bedroom corridor during country house week-ends. He moved to the window and drew the curtain back. The rain had thinned and the outlines of the hills, pin-pointed with lights, were clear enough. This city and this scene he had dominated for sixteen years. He had known the good times. Away once for nine months on a Commonwealth tour, and not a cheep of criticism, not a murmur about dereliction of duty. The shop had gone on doing business as usual, good prosperous Unionist business, no crises, no mention of Civil Rights and the only demonstration had been a rousing welcome home and a Lord Mayor's banquet for him at the Belfast City Hall. Since then, it had been uphill all the way. Minority expectations aroused by demagogues and agitators and still unsatisfied, indeed not capable of being satisfied, without the destruction of all he had ever stood for. He was losing stomach for a battle that he knew could only be prolonged but never won. Over the next week or so he would give it one more try and then . . . well, life was not entirely devoid of other satisfactions. He pulled the curtain closed and started to undress. He looked forward to escaping even for all too brief a space, to the grave concerns of Phineas Finn and of Plantagenet Palliser and to the darker European charms of Madame Goesler.

'All right Billy. Look after yourself.' Harry Harrmon waited a moment as his minder pulled away in the Ford Cortina. It was well after midnight. Then he entered the modest semi-detached house which had been his home since his days in the Sirocco works as a turner. It stood on the edge of a housing estate, just outside the city, in a solid Protestant area. But as an extra precaution, the gates which gave access front and rear were wired with a simple buzzer device which was activated after dark. The twin semi was occupied by another member of the organisation, as were the adjoining houses. Harrmon lived a dangerous

139

life, but on security he always endeavoured to play the percentage shots.

He could have lived in grander style, but he was never to lay himself open to the charge that he had grown too big for his boots. He was leader of a democratic organisation in which all were equal, only some were more equal than others. His wife Maisie was waiting to open the door. She never enquired. She never complained. The only perks she enjoyed were a comparative freedom from financial pressures and the deference paid to her when she and her husband had a night out at one of the organisation's approved drinking clubs.

'Cuppa tea? Are ye hungry?' she asked, as she closed the door behind him.

'I could take a fried egg,' he said as she moved into the kitchen, a new extension which had been built at the back.

'Young Evans was here lookin' for you.'

'Who. Walker Evans?'

'Aye.'

'What did he want?'

'Didn't say. Said he'd give you a ring tomorrow. He works for Wylie Mullins, doesn't he?'

'That's right.'

The subject was not pursued any further, but the UDF Commander had a fair idea of why the messenger had come.

When the PM slept on the premises, it was always more trying for his personal staff in the office. He had a tendency to be up and doing at an early hour. Already by nine o'clock the following morning the rooms on the ground floor of the Castle were humming with activity. The telex was ticking. Stewart Taylor was on the blower to his counterpart Hedges at the Home Office. As expected, the media had splashed the story. The BBC on the seven o'clock and 7.55 news bulletins had led with the proposed changes, mentioning a replacement force for the Specials. The Protestant *News Letter* had led SPECIALS DISBANDED? and the Catholic *Irish News* SPECIALS SCRAPPED. WHITEHALL ACTS AT LAST! The official release from Lefaux had been given good placing in both papers, but in the *News Letter* Gillan had got a two-column head with GILLAN STANDS FIRM heading a whole list of defiant protests, the most prominent one from Wylie Mullins. It was all as they had foreseen. The main drift of the reports was negative – this was bad news. And comment was no more helpful, being especially critical of the way in which major proposals were still only leaks unconfirmed by any sub-stantive official statement. That was why, after a brief consultation with his master, Taylor was on the telephone trying to get agreement to an immediate release. It would, they hoped, be a bald outline of the proposed changes beginning, 'The following changes in the fields of legal administration and security have been jointly agreed by Her Majesty's Government and by the Government of Northern Ireland . . .' To use 'jointly agreed' in advance of the two crucial meetings yet to take place, was, as Taylor pointed out, taking a major risk, but on the instructions of the Prime Minister he was going ahead on that basis.

Packham had decided that he might as well be hanged for a sheep as a lamb; either he got his line accepted by his Cabinet and party – and he was confident on Dixon't tot that he would – or the situation was past redemption anyway. By the time he went into the Party meeting in the afternoon, his approach would already have been endorsed by the Cabinet and could be presented as a fait accompli. Over his coffee at 7.30 that morning, after a sound night's sleep, and two boiled eggs, he had thought it all through. Was it Sydney Smith who had said, 'Success

141

in politics is a good digestion?' Carson's call just after 8.15, assuring him of support, had finally clinched it. Young Carson was not the worst. Not a schemer. Ambitious, a bit too impetuous sometimes, but not two-faced. No, Carson would not regret it.

Lefaux came into the room as Packham was leafing through *The Times*. 'Good morning, PM. Nothing much in that. Just a couple of paragraphs, written early in the day, forecasting possible changes. May be more in the later editions. Well . . . ?

Packham put the paper down and pulled off his glasses. 'As we expected. No better no worse.'

'Ricketts gave Gillan a headline, blast him! I must have spent twenty minutes trying to shift him last night. I've been talking to the *Telegraph* people . . .'

'Yes. Yes.' Packham interrupted.

The niceties of newspaper balance and exegesis bored him. You got a headline or you didn't. So far as he was concerned that day's press was a lost cause. Television was the thing. 'I've been thinking about this, Tom. I've *got* to go on television this evening. There's nothing else for it if we are going to stop the rot. I've been trying to jot down a few headings. I think we should have a little pow-wow. Is Ronnie in yet?'

Lefaux remembered that it was always a pow-wow when the heat was on. 'I'll tell him. I better get on to the BBC and UTV right away then. Between six and seven if we can fix it. Later tends to clash with news on one channel or the other.' Lefaux didn't waste time arguing the toss. The old man was clearly pinning his hopes on the 'box', the approach personal and direct. At least you got an immediate feed-back. Within an hour of the broadcast they'd have a fair idea of the response across the country.

Henry Wilson, the Principal Private Secretary, a withdrawn studious type with a First in Classics, hovered tentatively till he caught the PM's eye. 'Mr Dixon's on the line, sir.' He indicated the telephone on the sidetable.

Packham spoke to Lefaux. 'I'll tell Billy. Immediately after Cabinet. We must get it right. Stop the rot.' Lefaux nodded and left. Packham walked over and lifted the telephone. Watson quietly closed the door leaving him alone. 'Yes, Billy.' A brief exchange on the press reports; the planned television. But it was Dixon's little confidential piece of news which really excited interest. 'Did he indeed? Maguire and Keevy? We really must *do* something about Birch. It's monstrous. Of course. He's told them the lot. And with his own angle no doubt. Yes. Yes. Never mind. We'll fix him one of these days. We'll fix him. After Cabinet then.' He replaced the telephone frowning.

Watson came back in with a folder of letters. 'Sorry about this, sir, but I thought we'd better get them out of the way. The ones on top are a bit tricky. Perhaps you'd glance through them, sir. The rest are routine – there's one from your constituency Vice-Chairman – I thought you'd like to add a personal note to it?'

'Leave them. I'll do them in a moment. Ask Sir Stewart if he has a moment, would you?'

'Right away, sir. One other thing. The Ulster Week dinner in Birmingham. I don't think we can get out of it. I promised to confirm today . . .'

Packham sighed. 'Very well – it's six weeks away, isn't it?'

'November 27.'

'God knows what will have happened by then.' Watson smiled and chanced his arm again.

'Finally, sir. I've cleared the day as you instructed – apart from what we agreed – but Bishop Keele is terribly anxious to . . .' He got no further.

'God! Will no one rid me of these turbulent priests,' groaned the Prime Minister. 'The answer is *no!* Some other time.'

'Of course, sir. He was so insistent . . .'

'Well find out what he wants and don't come bothering *me!*' The Prime Minister was as near to anger as he allowed himself with his officials.

'Yes, sir.' The Principal Private Secretary hurriedly withdrew.

The Prime Minister gazed out of the window. He had little time for clerics, Protestant or Catholic. He divided them into Trollopian categories. Nowadays the place-seeking Proudies and sycophantic Slopes had given way to the publicity seekers. He had a special distaste for those who for every sermon had a press release, for those who specialised in clandestine meetings with the IRA, basking in the limelight as self-appointed authors of peace and lovers of concord. Of a notable Protestant divine, active in ecumenical politicking, Packham had been heard to say 'He spends so much of his time rendering unto Caesar – he might as well become a Roman and be done with it!' But that was in a very private gathering.

Outside beyond the window the evergreens were heavy and autumnal. Along the path from the direction of Speaker's House came the two men on RUC guard duty, walking with deliberate step, engaged

143

in steady conversation, their Sterlings as usual slung casually over the shoulders of the heavy black rain-coats. As they neared the French window, he opened it on impulse and walked out to meet them. Hurriedly they snapped to attention and saluted.

'Morning, lads – you just came on at eight o'clock I suppose?' After a few brief enquiries about their duties and family – one of them was from Tyrone – he got to the point. 'You've heard the news I suppose?'

They looked at each other uncertainly, not knowing quite what to say. One spoke up. 'Just what it said on the BBC, sir. It's not true, sir, is it? They're not doing away with the Specials?'

Packham gave his most reassuring smile. 'Of course not. We have some changes in mind of course – the whole force needs to be modernised – but tell your friends not to worry. There will still be a job for the Specials to do.'

Their faces showed their relief. The one he knew said, 'I knew it was a lot of nonsense sir. It's always the same with the BBC – always knocking us.'

'I intend to speak on television this evening, explaining exactly what's happening, so I hope that will put an end to all this speculation.'

'It's good to hear that, sir,' said the same policeman 'because, as you well know, sir, as another County Tyrone man, if they touch the Specials that would be the last straw.'

As he left them and returned to his room he reflected on his ad hoc opinion polling – he could hardly have expected it to be any different. It was a measure of the problems that lay ahead.

Stewart Taylor was waiting for him with the statement. 'Well, I think we've got it agreed. As good as we could hope for. Hedges has promised me that they will leave us to do the talking – on their side they will not go beyond the factual announcement.'

'We've heard that before,' said the Prime Minister, taking the copy handed to him. Taylor pursed his lips and nodded in reluctant agreement. He knew well that despite the most solemn assurance, 'unofficial sources' had a way of getting coverage for their own interpretation of goverment statements. For 'unofficial sources' read 'the ever-active PR machine in Whitehall'.

'It means, PM, that we have to get in first. The holding statement last night was a start.'

Packham handed back the statement. 'Fair enough,' he said without enthusiasm. 'But we need the television. It's the only answer. I've just told Tom to set it up for this evening.'

Taylor did not demur. He'd known it was coming. And he shared the PM's belief in the potency of the personal presence in the sitting-room. If they were going to pull it off he saw no alternative. Already the telephone messages and telegrams were coming in from the public, from the Party officials, from relatives of members of the police forces. Protests, demands for a denial of the rumours, anxious queries.

Lefaux came back – he was the only one in the government who had access to the Prime Minister without formality. His office as Minister of Information gave him a hybrid status half official, half politician. And more than any other, he was a Packham trusty, like Billy Dixon. 'The press conference, PM, I forgot to mention it.' Packham looked blank. 'When the joint statment comes out . . . It's now timed for midday – and I know they'll want you. After all, it's very big – the biggest thing we've had for a long time.'

'Yes, yes,' Packham was unenthusiastic, 'but I don't want to pre-empt what I'm saying this evening. If I face a full press conference, I've used up all m'ammo haven't I?'

'No more than the Chancellor in a Budget broadcast after he's already given the details in the House. I think they are two different approaches, equally important.'

'The House is different,' said Packham. 'One can't avoid that, but a press conference and then over the same ground again . . . ?'

Taylor cut in, diffidently, 'I know there will inevitably be a measure of repetition, but it is so important, I do urge you, sir, to consider taking the conference.'

The PM was getting testy. 'But the television cameras will be there, won't they? They always are. It's the same thing.'

Unabashed, Lefaux made a suggestion. 'Why don't we simply say – no filming. They'll know you're going on both channels later.'

After a pause the Prime Minister conceded with none too good a grace. 'If you insist then. If you insist.'

Lefaux caught Taylor's eyes. They were both wondering the same thing. It wasn't like the old man to try to avoid the camera – on any pretext. Reserving himself for the big one maybe. The set script and the safe studio. Or did they detect withdrawal symptoms? A lack of fight? It was unlike him and a little worrying. They passed on to the coming Cabinet.

'Where's Ronnie?' asked Packham irritably. 'I want him to be in on this.'

'I'll see if he's there,' said Taylor and hurried out.

145

'I don't think we'll have too much difficulty now that Desmond is all right,' said Lefaux. 'Fred will fall in behind him. Gillan and Mun will growl but I can't see them opening their mouths too wide with the kind of support they've got at the moment.' One of the girl secretaries came in with a tray of coffee things. She was followed by Taylor and Ronnie Fine who smiled his apologies.

'Sorry PM. I was just making a few notes for your broadcast.'

'Clairvoyant of you!' said his master cryptically. Fine smiled even harder. 'We're just wondering what Trade will do this morning,' went on Packham. He spoke to Lefaux. 'A new situation has arisen which I'd better tell you about. I only learnt about it after you left me last night. Close that door. We had a call from Cecil McFee – Billy took it. He'd just come from Gillan's house. A little supper party. Well chosen guest list . . . ' Packham smiled grimly. 'They were openly canvassing against me . . . and touting for names.' He briefly recounted the Rooster drama. The two officials looked uneasy and embarrassed and said nothing.

Lefaux went straight to the point. 'Well! We knew what he'd get up to but *that* makes it *very* difficult. If you sack him he automatically becomes the Champ – leading the troops in the cause of Ulster.'

'Exactly,' said Packham. 'I'd be kicking him into the saddle. Mun would have to go too. Hardly the moment for a re-shuffle. On the other hand, his stock can't be very high after the Rooster fiasco. My hunch is that he won't be quite so bold as he might have been.' Stewart Taylor had been diffidently trying to catch his master's eye. 'Yes Stewart?'

'What had been worrying me, Prime Minister, was that, after the very hard line he took at yesterday's Cabinet, he might have seen himself as having no alternative but to resign. He's not a natural resigner and after last night I think he'll be even more reluctant. *And* more open to a firm reminder of the doctrine of collective responsibility.'

The Prime Minister gave a noncommittal grunt. 'He has it both ways. In the situation we're in, if I sack him, he's a hero. If he resigns he's sacrificing all for principle.'

Lefaux spoke up again. 'Stewart's right about him not being a resigner. And if last night's carry-on proves anything it proves that he's not a gambler either. He shied away from the risk didn't he?'

'Not without ambition but without the illness should attend it . . .' murmured Ronnie Fine.

'So I turn a blind eye for the moment?' the PM was addressing Lefaux, who in response merely pursed his lips uncertainly.

'There's another possibility PM,' said Fine and waited for encouragement to continue.

'Well, what is it?' said Packham wearily, with the air of a man who would not be easily surprised.

Fine gave a twitchy half-grin. 'Yesterday PM you said something in jest. I think we might consider it seriously.' His grin disappeared. 'We need something radical, some kind of quantum leap. If we're going through with this, Desmond Carson must be moved. Right, he takes Trade and you put Gillan in Home Affairs – the strong man, the man who will stand firm, takes over security.' He paused for reaction. The other three looked at him blankly.

'Can you see him taking it?' said Lefaux. 'And becoming the government fall-guy?' he went on incredulously.

Stewart Taylor was of the same opinion. He looked hard at Fine. Unorthodox solutions were one thing, but for heaven's sake let's keep our feet on the ground. He spoke without his usual self-effacement. 'PM, I really don't think this is on. Move Carson into Trade's job by all means. But surely you can't believe that those in the party loyal to you would countenance for one moment moving Gillan into Home Affairs, especially after the story of last night's dirty tricks gets around.'

'It must be around already,' said Lefaux.

'But Home Affairs will be downgraded,' said Packham defensively.

'That's not what *we'll* be saying,' rejoined Lefaux, with unusual sharpness. 'PM . . .' he was appealing to his Leader. 'Stewart is right. We decided our strategy last night. Des Carson has agreed to go along with it. Despite what I said earlier I'm forced to the conclusion that, if Gillan doesn't fall into line, then he must go. Either he resigns or he's sacked.'

Taylor nodded sadly. 'I see no alternative, PM.'

Ronnie Fine sat silent and morose, licking his wounds. Packham turned to him with a wry smile. 'It was a good try, Ronnie. But they're right, I'm afraid. Blood may have to be shed.'

Fine shrugged good-humouredly, 'You know how I hate the sight of it, PM, especially bad blood!' Ronnie Fine's resilience was well known.

'We'll have to see what happens,' said Packham. 'He may wait until the Party meeting before he shows his hand. Now. I want a few minutes to think about this television.'

'Right. I'll get the press conference set up. You've no objection to the sound people . . . something on tape?' said Lefaux.

'No. No. If they must. What about those notes you mentioned, Ronnie?'

'Would you like me to fetch them?'

Packham nodded.

'That security meeting, sir,' said Stewart Taylor, 'General Boydell will fit in whatever time you want him — a working lunch perhaps?'

'Good idea. Make sure Desmond knows. I'd be curious to find out just how privy our friend Boydell was to all the Downing Street discussions. He never gave any hint?'

'Nothing. But I'm quite sure he must have been consulted. After all, the new force to replace the Specials is very much on his patch.'

The Prime Minister shook his head. 'Sworn to secrecy, I suppose. You know, Stewart, sometimes I find it hard to believe that we are still part of the United Kingdom.'

Desmond Carson was up and dressed that morning before his wife Janet. When she appeared, he was already in the kitchen making toast. She whisked in, still in a dressing-gown, brisk and capable. They exchanged a perfunctory peck on the cheek. 'Leave it darling. What do you want. Scrambled eggs?'

'Great,' he said, willingly surrendering his culinary activity.

His wife's upbringing had left her uneasy at the idea of a husband having to prepare his own food. She had not yet adjusted psychologically to a world without cook-housekeepers. 'You were very late last night,' she said, busying herself with kettles and crockery.

'You heard the news?'

'Westminster is attacking the Specials or something? I heard the ten o'clock in the car. I wasn't really paying attention, because Sylvia was with me, and you know how she chatters away.' He told her just what was afoot. She went straight to the point. 'I think you'd be mad to start fighting the UK government. We wouldn't have a single friend at Westminster on any side. And the whole British public would be behind them. You stick with Arthur, darling. Otherwise the next thing you know you'll be in the same boat with that fellow Mullins.' Carson, whose attention was divided between his wife and the *Belfast News Letter,* looked up thoughtfully, but said nothing. 'I know this whole police thing is very difficult,' she went on, 'but I see no future, none whatsoever, in trying to defy the rest of the UK. And I feel sure that most decent people here would feel the same as I do. It would just be sinking to the same level as those Republican ruffians on the Civil Rights.' Carson nodded and continued to spread butter on his toast, with the concentrated care of a confectioner icing a cake. She had always been an accurate barometer of middle-class Unionism, unswerving in her

148

attachment to the Queen, suspicious of Catholics because of their Nationalist allegiance, but with little time for anti-Popery.

He was encouraged by her unhesitating endorsement of the position which he himself had, only on balance, decided was the right one. But his conscience gnawed when he compared her total dedication to his interest with his own duplicity. How would she take it when he broke the news? How much harder would be the blow if it entailed the destruction of the political career to which she had devoted so much of her life? Could he himself face up to that prospect despite his passionate insistence to the girl he loved that his priorities were immutably fixed? There were times when he wasn't sure, yet it needed only a separation of twenty-four hours from her presence to bring home the totality of his obsession.

'Coffee darling?'

The calm accustomed tone of the familar morning routine was another twist of the knife. Defensively he lit a cigarette, and, with an effort, faced the day ahead. Check with Fred Butler? He could do that before Cabinet. He took out his daily programme which Robert was constantly amending to keep up to date. Today had been cleared except for essential meetings. A name at the bottom of the sheet caught his eye. It was underlined twice and followed by an exclamation mark. *Mrs McKeown!* He knew what Robert meant. He really *had* been very lax.

'You *will* be sensible, darling, won't you?' His wife did not seem to realise that this was much more than an internal party crisis, and he saw no purpose in spelling out the implications. She would know soon enough. 'Don't worry. I'll play it by ear,' he said. 'I shall not be resigning!'

As he was going out to the waiting car she called, 'The Dungannons have a party tonight. I can't go. Anyway, I don't like their set. Let me know sometime what you're doing.'

'Sure. I'll ring you.'

'Just like her,' he thought. 'My conscientious and unselfish social secretary, not wanting me to miss a chance of influencing people in the right places.'

The Dungannons were rather unorthodox members of the local aristocracy, who had reputedly several tenuous lines to the British Cabinet. But their party was today not very high on Carson's list. Nor for the moment was the British Cabinet. It was 8.30 when his cars moved off. As he exchanged the usual greetings with his escorts, he knew they were waiting for him to broach the subject. But at that hour he had no stomach for more specious justifications. He contented himself with simply, 'All this rumour about the force. Don't let it worry you. Things are very firmly under control.' Then he buried himself in ostensibly important papers fished from his brief-case. After a moment, he relented enough to add, 'There will be a statement today, which I think will settle things.' They were too polite and well-disciplined to do other than signal their appreciation that he had vouchsafed even this brief comment. 'I want to call in on old Mrs McKeown – Shorland Street,' he said.

'Yes sir.' The man in front lifted the R/T and notified the change of course.

As the cars stopped in Shorland Street, small back-to-backs with the doors giving on to the pavement, there was a flutter of interest from some of the neighbours. Several were leaving for work. Carson greeted, waved, joked and fended off the anxious enquiries, pooh-poohing any talk of concessions. His presence seemed to reassure them and he felt, as he always did on such occasions, a sharp sense of his responsibility to simple unlettered people who trusted him to carry them through. There were roughs, of course, and harridans, the mean and the grasping, for whom he had only concealed contempt. But the mass of his constituents were undemanding, kindly, steady folk whose cheerfulness and fortitude, often in the most discouraging conditions, left Desmond Carson, despite his own self-knowledge, feeling anything but superior.

Mrs McKeown was a lively old soul in her seventies. Carson was welcomed with delighted surprise. She ushered him into the tiny living-room-cum-kitchen, unceasing in her flustered apologies. 'Och, Mr Carson. Imagine you coming at this time and finding me like this. And me not even dressed! Och, I don't know where I am. Would you like a cup of tea? I'm just makin' Billy his breakfast.'

Carson reassured her, and gently brought her round to the reason why she had wanted him to call, apologising profusely for his dilatoriness in answering her request.

Minnie McKeown and her late husband had been, since Carson's first appearance in the constituency, among his most loyal and hard-working supporters. Of the old school, brought up in the tradition of hard work and self-reliance, she had 'wrought' as as she was always proud to recall, twelve hours a day in the Belfast Ropeworks for thirty shillings a week, and every evening when she came home, it took her fifteen minutes at the jaw-box – the all-purpose stoneware sink that served in Belfast back-to-backs, to wash dishes, clothes *and* bodies – to scour the tar from her hands. The cause of her concern was Billy, her only son and apple of her eye. An unskilled labourer, Billy had been paid off at Short's aircraft factory and for the past few weeks had been seeking work. Would Mr Carson have a wee word with him and maybe advise him what to do? Of course Carson would, gladly. His mother confessed that Billy was still abed. It was his nerves, she confided. He needed his sleep because he wasn't really strong. Billy was produced, unshaven, red-eyed, tucking his shirt into his trousers. In his fifties, plump and ingratiating, he had the complexion of a man who enjoyed his glass. After a repeat of the ritual apologies for troubling her MP, Mrs McKeown smiling benignly, withdrew to the tiny scullery, leaving her son and the Minister to their serious male deliberations. Having commiserated on the loss of the job, Carson enquired the reason. Redundancy?

'Oh no, Mr Carson. It was the nerves . . . me nerves in me arms.'

'Oh?' Carson showed acute interest.

'Yes, you see. I couldn't put me hands in cold water. Every time . . .' Billy stretched out his arms dramatically and gave a catatonic shudder, accompanied by an agonised groan which would have melted the heart of the hardest foreman. 'Every time I put me hands in cold water the pain goes right up my back . . .' His face contorted, 'and me arms can't move. It's the nerves, you see, it's the nerves.' He relived the gesture with electrifying realism, choking back the pain.

'I see,' said Carson, after a moment. 'Awful for you. You've seen a doctor?'

'Three,' said Billy stoically. 'They can't do nothin' for me.'

'Well,' said Carson reflectively, 'it's clear that we'll have to try and get you something that doesn't involve wetting your hands.'

'A storeman, maybe?' suggested Billy, warily. 'Something light, no heavy work.'

But Carson had already sized up the situation. 'I'm sorry Billy, but there's no point in raising your hopes. It's going to be very difficult. Of course, if I hear of anything, I'll let you know, but I'm afraid I can't hold out much hope.'

Billy received this sombre assessment with massive relief. 'That's very good of you, Mrs Carson. I know you'll do your best, but God's will be done.' He summoned his mother and related the news.

'Well, we'll just have to hope for the best, Mr Carson. Anyway, he's not really fit yet – he's still on the sick, you know. It's only his pigeons and the bowls that keep him going.' She beamed fondly on her battered lamb.

Carson took his leave. Amid the most lavish professions of gratitude, Billy pressed his Member's hand in both of his, the nervous condition momentarily quiescent. They understood each other. Carson understood. The McKeown family had over the years deserved his grateful thanks. Their relationship would not be soured by any unthinking act of his. The evening of Mrs McKeown's long, honest and hard-working life would be gladdened by the company of a happy contented child. From Billy, the cloud had passed – the threat of employment had been lifted, indefinitely.

At about 11.30, as the Prime Minister followed by his two officials left the Cabinet room, he spoke quietly to Stewart Taylor. 'Catch Desmond, will you, before he leaves. I want to talk to him.' As the double doors closed behind them, Billy Dixon rose from the chair where he had been awaiting them. His face was anxious.

'Relax, Billy,' said Packham. 'There were no surprises, and the Cabinet is still intact, but I suspect only just.'

'Tell me,' said Dixon.

Packham motioned to the decanter. 'A stiff one please.' He sat down heavily and stretched out his legs. 'Well, pretty much to plan. I'd a word with Desmond and he opened up. Good stuff. Pointed out that whatever action outside bodies, such as the Orange Order or the UDF or whatever, saw fit to take, we as a government, could have no part of it. On balance, any popular protest would help us by making the British Government more amenable to our methods of presenting the whole thing. On presentation, he followed the line we decided yesterday. We have got agreement from Westminster – and this was a nice new touch – that they will provide us with extra funds to refurbish and modernise the *second* line police force – that's the reconstituted Specials, and he saw no reason why all those fit and ready to serve should not be simply transferred to the new force.'

Dixon was looking more cheerful. 'If we can do that, we're half-way there. What did friend Gillan say to that?'

'Well, Desmond finished by stressing that no decent Protestant, despite misgivings, would do anything to endanger the Union, especially when it is already under heavy attack from the IRA. Gillan intervened then, I remember – what did he say?'

Ronnie Fine spoke up. 'He said that it was not the Union, but democracy that was in danger when London, against the will of the majority, attempted to strip us of control of our own defence.'

'That was it,' said Packham. 'And, of course, he knows that *control* . . . is the ticklish one. We're vulnerable if the army are clearly seen to be assuming overall direction of security. I don't like that.'

'I've been thinking of a possible way round,' said Fine, handing him a whisky.

'Good. Good. But let me finish this first,' said Packham. 'Very briefly, Butler and Tom piled in, supporting Carson. I didn't think it was necessary to bring Shane in. The constitutional issue wasn't raised again. Willie havered and wavered. He seemed to come down on our side, but he was full of dire premonitions that the silent mass of Protestants would rise up and smite us. At the end, he was clearly hedging his bets, though he did graciously confess that up to now he has always had the utmost confidence in my judgement.'

Dixon snorted 'Still playing it both ways. He probably hasn't heard about the Rooster row. When he does, he won't know whether he's on his arse or his elbow! Don't worry – I'll make sure he goes the right way this afternoon.' He looked to Packham, who smiled indulgently. Billy's confidence wasn't always justified in the event. The Prime Minister sipped his whiskey and put it down, rocking the glass gently on the table as he considered.

'I really can't make up my mind just what our friend Gillan is up to. He took the same tough line as yesterday: we must stand firm against a Downing Street Diktat, suicide to give way on the Specials. He was very cocky, despite the hammering he took from Beatty Samson last night. So was Mun, who came in after him – not at all subdued. Gave the impression that they had a lot more fire-power than I could detect. Was that your impression Ronnie?'

Fine assumed his judicial face. 'It was, PM. They appeared to have something up their sleeve or perhaps they believed they had something up their sleeve. And I did notice one thing which I thought was significant. When Mun was getting heated about the Party speaking for all Unionists . . . wait a moment, I made a note of the phrase . . . ' He flipped over a page on the clip-board which he was still holding. ' "If this Cabinet thinks it has a mandate to speak on behalf of all Protestants, it's making a grave mistake." As he said that, he looked round sharply at Gillan, who, I'm sure, had just kicked him under the table. Gillan didn't catch his eye, just kept looking ahead with his chin in his hand, but I noticed that Mun changed tack very swiftly.

'I must confess I didn't see that,' said Packham.

'You wouldn't sir, with Gillan between you and Mun, but I'm

looking straight across at them from my table.'

'What do you make of it?' The Prime Minister's eyes swung from Fine to Dixon. 'Is he talking about the Orange Order?'

Dixon shook his head emphatically. 'No. No. I spoke to Jack this morning. The Orange is OK.'

Fine shrugged 'Unless they're hoping for some link with the para-militaries? But I don't think Gillan would risk it.'

'We're probably reading too much into it,' said Packham. 'The important thing is, that despite all the fighting talk, he accepted the joint statement – with reservations, as he put it.'

'What was that?' asked Dixon blankly.

'The statement we're putting out – we had it in front of us.'

'Oh yes. That was a bit of a climb-down, wasn't it?' said Dixon.

'I'm afraid I gave him no choice. It was that, or resign. When he spoke, he didn't really commit himself for or against the statement, so I made a point of giving my little homily on the collective responsibility of the Cabinet. It was clear that a majority were in favour . . .'

'McFee?' asked Dixon quickly.

'Oh yes, very definitely. So I spelt out very clearly that those who felt that they could not go along with their colleagues, had better speak up there and then. Mun remained silent and sullen. Gillan repeated that he accepted the statement with some reservation, and that depending on the attitude of the British Government over the next few days – an attitude which I think is all too clear, but still . . .' Packham smiled ironically, 'depending on their attitude, he reserved the right to reconsider his position. I thanked them, and that was it.'

'No mention of last night?'

'Nothing. It was all a bit of a charade. We all knew what had gone on. Cecil McFee was clearly terrified that someone might bring it up. Tom did get a dig in – how at a time like this one depended so much on the loyalty of one's colleagues! The little bugger didn't twitch a muscle, but he can't have failed to notice a number of smirks round the table! But that was all. We'll wait until after the Party Meeting. There's nothing to be gained by sacking him now. We'll give him a bit more rope and see what happens.'

'After last night I think he'll pull in his horns a bit.'

'I don't know,' said Packham, anxiously. 'He doesn't give up easily. are you sure we're all right?'

'Should be OK. I've been in touch with most of them personally, including as many of the constituency chairmen as I could get hold of.

Several telegrams of support should be on their way. The BBC will have them by lunchtime, so the members concerned should know what's expected of them. Tom, as acting Chief Whip, will be in the chair and he'll bring Des Carson in early on, to set the tone. I'm hoping, now that the Rooster is backing us, that he'll be able to neutralise Macrory and Co. They'll get their riding instructions from Mullins and you wouldn't know what Mullins would do at a time like this. Certainly, if the Specials seem to be at risk, he'll do his nut. Anyway, we don't need them, and if they abstain, it's a bonus. It's not the Parliamentary Party that worries me at the moment. It's the party in the country. That's the people you've got to get tonight, on television.'

'I've got something drafted, PM, on the basis of our discussion this morning,' said Fine.

'That was quick. You did it during Cabinet, I suppose.'

Fine grinned like a naughty schoolboy. Putting words together swiftly was his 'thing'.

'I'll look at it this afternoon, and we'll have a session; depends how long the meeting goes on. We must get it right,' said Packham. 'That reminds me. You said something earlier on, Ronnie, about this question of *control* of the police . . . that *does* worry me.'

'Yes, PM. It struck me . . . .'

Stewart Taylor peeped round the door apologetically. 'Desmond's in my room sir. I wondered if you were ready for him?'

The PM hesitated a moment. Carson had never been one of the Kitchen Cabinet. But now it looked as if he would have to be co-opted. 'Yes. Bring him in. This is very much up Desmond's street.' Packham rose and waved Carson to a chair as he entered. 'Well done, Desmond. Good work this morning. Most grateful.' All around him the kitchen cabinet beamed with bonhomie, nodding agreement. 'We're just looking at this question of control.'

Carson looked mystified.

Fine explained. 'The transfer of control over security to Westminster is very much our Achilles Heel.'

'Yes,' said Carson stiffly. These officials were always prone to start cooking up something behind one's back.

'Simply this. We thought one might make the situation more acceptable by re-vamping the security committee with,' Fine hesitated, looked at Packham, 'you yourself, or whoever is in Home Affairs, the GOC, and the top policeman, but *chaired* by the PM himself. By doing that we might divert attention from the sorry and denuded state of

Home Affairs. We could make quite a lot out of this new top-level council – rather like a war cabinet – with the PM as Supremo. At least it would disguise the reality.' Fine stopped, looking anxious. It sounded thin. The PM looked at Carson for first reactions. The latter had decided that this attempt to apply cosmetics to a corpse was not for him. Mentally he was already clearing his desk in the Ministry of Home Affairs.

'All very well,' he said, 'if Downing Street agrees. But, from their point of view, it would seem to blunt the whole point of the exercise. If they did agree, such a committee would only be allowed advisory powers. We'd have to carry the can without being able to influence policy or decisions. Could be the worst of both worlds.'

Ronnie Fine looked very unhappy. This was the second of his bright suggestions to hit the deck with a dull thud in the past twenty-four hours. Nor did the Prime Minister either see much merit in the proposal.

'I agree, Desmond. The situation is messy enough. I think, for the moment, we'll have to hide behind some loose portmanteau phrase like "Responsibility for security in the widest sense will of course continue to be a matter for the Government of Northern Ireland" . . . that sort of thing. Sounds good but says . . .' He stopped abruptly as Lefaux came rushing into the room.

'There's been a raid on the Specials Armoury at Larchfield. They got away with a lot of stuff. Could be a hundred Sterlings and they don't know how many rifles. A load of ammunition as well, mostly nine millimetre. They loaded up a ten-tonner.' His listeners faced him in shocked silence.

'Damn!' said the Prime Minister. 'That's all we needed. If the Specials can't look after their own weapons, in their own armoury . . . .' He groaned and shook his head. Everyone started talking at once.

'I'd better get down there right away,' said Carson. 'These IRA bastards are getting cheekier all the time.'

'No,' said Lefaux, his face tight with anxiety. 'That's the trouble. they think – though it's a bit too early to be sure – they think it might be a Protestant job.'

'Good God! They haven't wasted much time,' said Carson, jumping ahead.

'Surely not,' murmured the Prime Minister. 'What makes them think that?'

'The RUC chap who rang from Brooklyn – Knox is down there – had only a first report. But all the signs; the timing just when a depot truck normally arrives; their knowledge of the lay-out . . . it all smells. There were four of them in Specials uniform and apparently they were inside before the man on the gates realised.'

'How many were on duty?' asked Carson. 'There should have been four.'

But Lefaux had no further details.

'At least,' said Carson, 'if it's . . . not the IRA that's some comfort.'

'I wonder,' said Ronnie Fine gloomily. 'I wonder.'

The PM looked at Carson hard. 'You think it is our side then, Desmond?'

Carson nodded, grimly. 'That's what it certainly looks like. And I fear that this could be the beginning of the backlash. I'd better get back to the office right away.'

'The GOC is coming for lunch,' said Packham.

'I know. 12.45.'

'In view of what's just happened you must be here. Leave Knox to handle Larchfield. He's had plenty of practice at bolting the stable door . . . .' The PM had none too high an opinion of the Inpsector General.

Lefaux broke in, 'PM. We've only got ten minutes before this press conference. It's an ill wind. This latest news will probably take some of the heat out of the joint statement. I'm sorry PM, we really must have a few minutes to go through it. They're all there already having drinks, and my lads will try to ensure that we get a couple of decent questions – to start with anyway.' Lefaux was only too aware that, despite the efforts of his growing staff of press officers, sympathetic coverage for the Unionist viewpoint was harder and harder to get, as the national and international papers piled into the Ulster hotbed.

'All right. All right,' said Packham resignedly. 'I'm sorry Billy – we'll have to forget about the broadcast session. I'll get Ronnie to send you down a copy.

'I'll be down at the studio,' said Dixon, combining duty with an appreciation of the BBC hospitality provided on such high-level occasions.

As Carson was leaving the room Packham drew him aside speaking in a hushed confidential tone. 'I want to have a word with you, but we haven't time now. I want you to know that I appreciate very much what you have been doing.' He put his hand on Carson's shoulder before turning back to the others. It was not what he had said that mattered, but the fact that he had taken Carson aside for their brief tete-a-tete. Here, in the heart of his Kitchen Cabinet, this was, and was intended to be seen as, a special mark of favour from the chef de cuisine. Carson could not restrain a glow. The water was getting warmer.

Harry Harrmon and Wylie Mullins had fixed a meeting for 11.30 that morning. The two men had much in common. They had both clawed their way up by their own efforts. For both, the ladder had started in a gospel hall. They shared that blend of showmanship and self-confidence which is essential in a popular leader. And they were both uncompromising and unashamed Protestant fundamentalists. They did not need to agonise over niceties of doctrine or theology. The world was divided into sheep and goats. The goats were Romanists. It was as simple as that. Since their origins, Harrmon from Belfast, Mullins from a fishing port in County Down, their paths had come together, diverged and were now converging again. They had always been distant rivals. As one of the many part-time evangelists in Protestant Ulster, the trade-union stream recognising his talent had engulfed Harrmon and carried him up the class. Mullins had been, from the outset, an entrepreneur, selling first dress fabrics and then, on a full-time basis, God. In the business of winning converts and healing by faith he had been marvellously successful. To a heckler who had once accused him of placing too much emphasis on the collection boxes he had thundered, 'I don't preach for money. I preach for souls, but if my family had to live on souls, it would take a good many of the size of yours to make a decent meal!'

Recently, he and Harrmon, as two influential voices on the same end of the Protestant spectrum, had found themselves increasingly on the same wavelength. They professed a common aim – the assertion of the Protestant way and purpose. And since Harrmon's interests were now totally secular and since neither had openly entered politics, areas of possible friction appeared minimal. The trouble was that neither was content just to influence – they wanted to command. It was on this basis, as commanders seeking a mutually helpful alliance, that they had gravitated towards each other at that moment.

The meeting place was in Mullins' private office at the rear of the building in which his organisation was housed. At 11.30, as arranged, Harrmon's Consul parked round the corner and, unremarkable in a jacket and with an unaccustomed trilby pulled over his wiry thatch, he walked quickly down the path between gardens which led to the large

Victorian building, originally two semi-detached houses.

In the office, Wylie Mullins was waiting, hand outstretched. 'Good of you to come brother.' His voice had that mid-Atlantic rotundity which is common to most English speaking evangelists. He was forty, with a large head covered in thick well-groomed sandy hair. The eyelashes were remarkably blond, focussing attention on the deep-set light blue eyes which their owner used like miniature searchlights, beaming them unwinking, full on to the person he was addressing. It was the disturbing hypnotic quality of the eyes which literally bowled over female converts, in a dead faint, during his faith-healing crusades. Wylie Mullins was not unaware of their potency. He had been know to compare them, giving full credit to the Almighty, to Pentecostal flames burning out the sickness and the sin. The rest of the bodily equipment given by the Almighty was less remarkable. He was burly, smoothly plump and not very tall. He waved his visitor to a well-designed armchair, one of several in the comfortably furnished room ranged round an open fire. Only a large modern desk, complete with talk-back console and telephone, hinted at official activity. There was a bookcase, an impressive stereo system and a television.

'Sit down, Harry. Make yourself comfortable.' And seeing his visitor's eyes take in the scene. 'This is where I come to think and charge the batteries.' He pointed to the stereo.' When I play Gospel music, I like to be able to hear it properly. A member of my church gave it to me. Cost nearly one thousand pounds.' He spoke into the console, and turned again to his guest. 'A cup of fresh coffee will be here in a moment.' He leaned forward, nodding for emphasis. '*Proper* coffee. I got used to it in the States and I can't drink anything else now.' He wagged an admonitory finger at his guest and smiled broadly. 'You'd feel far better, Harry, in every way, if you stuck to the bean!'

Harrmon lit a small Wintermans cheroot. 'You remember, Wylie, a little wine is good for thy stomach's sake!'

The finger wagged again. 'Don't you bandy Scripture with me. You're too rusty – and well you know it!'

They both laughed, especially Mullins, who had difficulty in composing himself again.

Then Harrmon said, 'Well, what do you think? Bad isn't it? Can't go on.' The eyes were directed at him, like a blow lamp, full beam.

'Yes. It's time we did something. The Protestant people are being treated like dirt. A blind man can see what's going on. Sure the present British government is full of Papishes. They won't stop till they leave us defenceless!' He leaned forward. 'We have got to put a stop to it once

160

and for all. We have got to show them that we are the masters in our own house – in a way they won't forget.'

'What are we talking about?' asked Harrmon coolly.

'If we want to stop the British Government, we have to stop the British Army.'

'Who's going to do the fighting – us?'

'Who's talking about fighting the army? That's Republican talk! Stop playin' games Harry. We're not wee boys. I may be a country lad – but let me tell you something: I didn't come in on the last load of hay! What we're talkin' about is,' Mullins paused, 'a *total shut-down.*'

Harrmon gave a quizzical tilt of the head. 'Who've you been talking to? Megs Kane?'

'I know Megs Kane. He's a born-again Christian and he's a good man. But he isn't the only one, you know. I've got men in the power-stations too, and in the water service, *and* in transportation – any service you name – who can deliver, when the time comes!' Mullins spoke deliberately stressing every key word as in a sermon.

'I'd back Megs in the power stations,' Harrmon said, smiling, 'but let's not fight over it. You know we have a plan?'

'So have we. And I've got several good lads, members of my church – one's an accountant, one's on computers – all very bright boys. They've been working on a control system for essential supplies to hospitals, farmers, food stores and so on. Special passes, fuel vouchers – they've got it all worked out.'

Harrmon was impressed. 'You've been at it for some time then?'

'We have been in contact with various groups – very privately – because it has been clear to me for many months that sooner or later we would have to call a halt; probably sooner. As you well know, they have been deliberately setting out to demoralise the RUC. Not only have they been pushin' Papishes into the key jobs, but they've given the army the final say in all the so-called operations against the IRA. The police have to play second fiddle now. What these changes will do is to make it legal. That we cannot have.'

A pretty, fresh-faced girl came in with coffee and chocolate biscuits. 'This is Mr Harry Harrmon, Betty,' said Mullins, 'one of the future leaders of this country. My eldest daughter.' He waved a dignified hand in introduction. 'No time for chit-chat now, dear. You'll meet him again, never fear!' Smiling shyly, the girl withdrew. Harrmon helped himself to coffee.

'I've been promoted then!'

Mullins was in no mood for facetiousness. 'That's up to you. Are you

161

prepared to accept your responsibilities? The Protestant people are adrift, leaderless. It's no good looking to Arthur Packham and his clique. He'll go on licking the boots of the British Government, and at the end of the day when he's given away everything he *can* give away, he'll end up with a peerage like the rest of them. The working people are crying out for men they can trust, real Protestants who are not afraid to stand up and fight for their Protestant heritage. Are you ready? If you're not, we're wasting our time here this morning,'

Mullins was walking round the room like a caged panther as he talked. Harrmon looked at him steadily. The preacher had a reputation for takeover bids. Any organisation with which he associated himself tended in a short space of time to become his. Harrmon could feel his hackles rising. This was the Mullins he had encountered in the past – too big a mouth.

'Look, Wylie.' and Harrmon's eyes were cold. 'You do a lot of talking. You've got it all worked out. I've got eleven thousand men under orders. What have you got?'

The lighthouse gaze was beamed into his face as the preacher stopped in front of him. 'I'll tell you what I've got. I've got a *hundred* thousand who will eat grass before they surrender their birthright. I've got something else. I've got the *will* to *win* – have you?' The question was not so aggressive as the statements. Like two mastiffs prowling round in circles, each with a healthy respect for the other, they had established their positions. An honourable compromise was now on the cards. There was a silence. Mullins recommenced his pacing round the room. Then he spoke. 'When do we start? There's no time to lose.'

'Rightaway,' said Harrmon. 'Just as soon as we can get the word round – Monday at the latest?'

It was Mullins who was now taken aback. 'Just a moment. There are a lot of other people involved. Megs Kane and the trade union lads.'

'Megs agrees. We had a long session last night. The workers are organised. What we need is a central co-ordinating council. I'll come clean. That what I came here to tell you, providing of course . . .' he shrugged and looked hard at Mullins. 'We've summoned a meeting for tonight – representatives from all the organisations involved.'

'You've what?' Mullins was very angry and suspicious. 'You'd no right to do that without consulting other interested parties, no right!'

Harrmon was unperturbed. 'Did I know *you* were involved? Not until Megs told me last night. Look Wylie.' The UDF man was all sweet reason. 'Somebody has to kick off.'

'Who's chairing this council?'

Harrmon smiled, his face conveying what he was thinking. 'I don't think it would be a good idea if you or me was in the chair. The council can decide democratically. Megs maybe or one of his mates. It's not important is it? The main thing is to get going.'

But the preacher was still in the mood to cavil. 'These other organisations you're talking about. What are they?'

Harrmon replied almost casually, but choosing his words. 'Oh, certain sections of the loyalist institutions and . . . a couple of organisations which are affiliated to us.' Mullins raised his eyebrows, but he was not answered directly. 'You realise, Wylie, that once this strike gets under way, there's no turning back. If the government – I'm thinking of the British government – start to get heavy, we might need more than microphones to see us through. And it could be,' he paused again, looking for words, 'it could be that appeals will not be enough to get some of our friends to come out.'

Mullins decided not to press the matter further. 'Well, that's up to you. If the end is right – and the end *is* right, brother – the good Lord will justify the means.'

'Amen,' said Harrmon.

'It's no joke Harry. It is essential to carry the public with us.'

'That's where we're going to have to rely on you, Wylie. And they've played into our hands. The whole Protestant population will be on our side, wait till you see.'

'What time is this meeting called for?'

'7.30 at the wee Orange Hall up in the hills behind Dundonald. Its tucked away – easy to get to and neutral! You know it?'

Mullins nodded. 'I'll bring my lads along.'

'Only one, if you don't mind. We don't want it too big, for several reasons. Each of the groups concerned are sending two.'

'Politicians?'

'I don't know – if they happen to be delegates. They could be useful.'

Mullins gave a sceptical toss of the head. 'In my experience, they are very sweet when they need you, when they can use you. When you need them, brother, it's a different matter. Here, have one,' he offered the plate of chocolate biscuits which he had been voraciously disposing of during their exchange. Harrmon refused. The preacher helped himself to another and grinned. 'Got to have my carbohydrates to keep me going, you know!' His manic energy, which often encompassed a sixteen hour day, was well-known. He was now in expansive mood again. 'I had a very interesting telephone call last night at a late hour – from a

163

politician, a well-known politican. Oh yes, they know where to come to when they're looking for something.' He was very pleased with himself. 'Have a guess.'

'Not . . . Carson?' said Harrmon, thoughtfully.

The suggestion was dismissed indignantly.' No! I have no time for him – two-faced!'

Harrmon said, 'He's not the worst. He could be very useful.'

'To *who*?' Carson was clearly out of favour on the gospel circuit.

'Come on, who called you?'

'Mr Edmund Martin called me, the Minister of Agriculture – and he wasn't trying to sell me a heifer! . . .'

'Oh, Martin?' Harrmon was interested 'What did *he* want?'

'What did he want? He wanted to knife his leader and he wants me to get John McCrory and our little group in Stormont to help him.'

'They think they see a chance?'

'Oh yes! There's a party meeting this afternoon. Packham and company will try to sell the changes – as a wonderful new deal for the police forces. The Specials will be re-equipped . . . reincarnated! – anything but the truth!'

'You got this from Martin? Gillan's behind it of course. You can't see Mun running for Prime Minister.'

'You never know! No, I won't hear a word against Mun Martin. His heart's in the right place – he's a good Protestant. If he and Gillan come out against concessions – that's a big plus. Make no mistake. They're both well thought of in the country.'

'I thought you said that the politicans were only out for number one?'

'That is what I said brother. But if they are of any use to us at this time, let's use them. Two can play at that game! But give Mun Martin his due. He can see that this is no time for Protestant disunity. If we don't stand together we go down together. That will be my message tomorrow night – I have a big Rally at the Ulster Hall,' he chuckled. 'You wouldn't like to come along for a guest spot? We'd give you a big welcome!'

'Wylie! You do it your way. I'll do it mine.' Harrmon got to his feet 'I've got a lot to do. I'm sure you have too.' They shook hands formally.

'Let us not forget, Harry that we are just the transmitters. The producer is,' the preacher threw his head back, 'up there.'

The press conference was not going well. The long, low-ceilinged room in the rear wing of the Castle was crowded with sweating bodies. The

164

Prime Minister had arrived fifteen minutes late. The extra drinking time had not made his inquisitors any more deferential. Besides a full turnout from the national dailies, there was a large Dublin contingent, attracted by the prospect of finally burying the B Specials. Packham was trying to get it across that reports of their demise had been greatly exaggerated. The TV reporters, informed only at the last moment that there would be no filming, were proving especially difficult.

'Can you tell us, Prime Minister, why, when nearly all the changes affect his department, the Minister of Home Affairs is absent?'

The Prime Minister was muttering something not very coherent, when Lefaux moved in quickly to the rescue. 'The intention was that he should be here, but he was called away because of the very serious situation at the Larchfield armoury.'

Packham recovered his aplomb. 'The important statement you have before you conveys a number of *government* decisions which affect *all* Ministers equally. As head of the Northern Ireland Government, I am here to answer for them. In this, I have the whole-hearted support of the Minister of Home Affairs and the rest of my colleagues. Next question?'

The Prime Minister was determined to avoid a reporter from the *Irish Times*, a cocky, fair-haired young fellow who was trying to catch his eye and whom he found particularly objectionable. Instead he pointed to the *Daily Telegraph* who sat next to the *Irish Times*. 'Yes?'

'I think, Prime Minister,' said the *Telegraph* reporter, who despite his Hoorah Henry voice was a very shrewd operator, 'that my distinguished colleague here was in before me,' and he nodded to the *Irish Times*.

'*Have you* a question?' persisted the Prime Minister.

'I have,' said the *Telegraph*, 'but I am prepared to give way in favour of my colleague here.'

Packham was trapped. 'Well?' he snapped at the *Irish Times*.

The reporter was holding the press release in his hand. 'I'd like clarification, Prime Minister. Your statement says, "the B Special Constabulary, *as at present constituted* will be stood down".'

'Stood up!' cried a clear Irish voice from the back of the room. The *Irish Times* turned round appreciatively, amid a ripple of general laughter. It was a couple of moments before he could continue, still grinning. The Prime Minister's face had reddened with anger. How right his instinct had been! He should never have exposed himself to these yobbos! Like a baited bear. The insolent voice continued "as at present constituted will be stood down, *to be replaced* by, etc".'

'*What* is your question?' snapped the Prime Minister. Beside him,

165

Tom Lefaux looked far from happy.

'My question, Prime Minister, is this. Have we or have we not seen the end of the B Specials? Are they being scrapped or are they not?'

There was a frisson of expectation in the room. This was the sixty-four thousand dollar one. Not because anyone expected an affirmative answer, but because over the past twenty-four hours the feed from the Home Office in Whitehall, both on a Lobby basis and in less direct ways, had been unmistakably clear. The government was determined to end a situation in which part of the police service of the United Kingdom was alleged to be sectarian. And many of the journalists in that room were aware that Joe Maguire, Leader of Her Majesty's – active, if not loyal – Opposition in Northern Ireland, had received discreet assurances to the same effect. Was the Prime Minister going to directly contradict his overlords in Westminster? Already the 'insight pieces' and 'lid off' features were being lined up. They watched him closely. Stung by what had gone before, he spoke with unusual heat.

'The answer is, no. Firmly and unequivocally, no. No government of which I am the head will throw on the scrap-heap a body of men who, over sixty troubled years, have given such sterling service to this Province. What is intended is, I repeat, a necessary measure of reorganisation. The B Special Constabulary is, one might say, being pulled out of the line for a re-fit, which is long overdue. The name we recognise is out of date, a relic of the pre-RUC days, when there were three categories of Special police, A, B and C. The force will be reorganised and renamed but the men – the men – will be the same, joined, we hope, by the new generation, resolved as their fathers were, to meet and defeat the threat of the IRA, and to uphold our Constitution.' The peroration had been automatic, repeated so often over the years that it was out before he was aware of it. At the last moment he spared them the final ringing phrases about, 'our British way of life and the Ulster we love'. As he stopped, Lefaux looked at him approvingly. Good stuff! Firm denial but leaving plenty of water for a change of tack in the future. It was clear from reaction in the room that the pros were feeling baulked. That was not quite what they had hoped for.

The *Irish Times* was trying to come back. 'That's not what Downing Street is saying Prime Minister . . .'

Packham cut him short. 'You've had your turn . . . yes Billy?'He pointed to the BBC, then swung back quickly to the *Irish Times*. 'You forget this is a joint statement from ourselves – *and* Downing Street. Yes Billy?'

The BBC voice, polite and subdued, began innocuously enough. 'I wonder if you could help us, Prime Minister, on this matter of control. If, as the statement says, overall control for security will be in Army hands – and that means MOD in London – what guarantee is there that the B Specials will continue as a separate force?'

The PM hesitated. This was tricky.

'*There's* the guarantee,' he said, taking up a press release and striking it with the back of his hand. 'The two Governments are agreed.'

The BBC persisted. 'Yes, Prime Minister, but all it says is that the Specials will be replaced by a new force.'

'Under army control,' it was the *Guardian* who had been well briefed from London, chipping in uninvited. Packham looked in his direction, unintentionally giving him the floor. 'A new force which could be just another TA Regiment Prime Minister. There's no guarantee that the Northern Ireland view will be accepted.'

'No guarantee at all,' said the *Irish Times*.

There were all piling in now, protocol forgotten. The lack of respect made Packham even angrier. Ill-mannered young pups! He was still Prime Minister.

'I assure you, gentlemen,' and his voice was stretched, as he struggled to control his temper, 'that in this case the view of the Northern Ireland government *will* prevail. As long as I am Prime Minister.'

An American voice, the *Christian Science Monitor*, called out clearly. 'Even if the British Government take a contrary view Prime Minister?'

He had been goaded enough. He was not going to be humiliated in front of this rabble. 'Yes!' That would shut them up. It did. An excited buzz crackled like static round the room. This was news. As the follow-up came, 'In the case of a major clash with Westminster then . . .' the Prime Minister had turned to Lefaux and whispered in his ear, 'Just a moment please.' Lefaux waved a hand for silence as he continued sotto voce with his Leader. Then, as he ostentatiously consulted his wrist watch, the Prime Ministr nodded an impatient assent.

Lefaux addressed the reporters 'I'm afraid gentlemen, the Prime Minister must go now – he's already late for an urgent security meeting.' There was a rumble of protest. 'I'm sorry,' said Lefaux. 'I shall remain for any further questions.'

The Prime Minister rose, and with a baleful glare and a muttered imprecation which did not sound like thanks, left the room. Lefaux accompanied him to the door. Half of those sitting down had stumbled to their feet in the usual gesture of deference. Others had remained seated, still protesting about the abrupt curtailment of their kill. Thomas Lefaux, Minister of Information returned to the familar chore of picking up the pieces. This clash with Westminster – that had to be toned down by hook or by crook – no matter what was on the record!

Carson had wasted no time in getting to his office. The Specials had always been a law unto themselves. As a part-time force mobilised only during the periodic IRA campaigns, they were paid a mere pittance when they turned out for drill or rifle practice at the butts. After the Second World War they had been held together by the sporting and social attractions of shooting competitions and gun clubs. Many of them were farmers working the irregular hours dictated by the demands of stock and weather. During the periods of peace in Ulster, attendance and discipline had not been too strictly enforced. The freebooting traditions of their origins in the lawless Twenties, when they had stood between the infant state of Northern Ireland and anarchy, still lingered. Carson felt sure that they would not take their dissolution lying down, especially since they regarded themselves as not only the oldest but as the last line of defence.

In his office, Robert was waiting with a list of messages and telephone calls, protesting about the changes or promising support. The phrase 'No surrender' occurred often. Arthur Jones, the Permanent Secretary was waiting for him too. The Larchfield raid had been pieced together.

At 11.15 a.m., its normal time on Fridays, the service truck from the Omagh depot had arrived at the Larchfield perimeter gates to draw supplies of ammunition and replacement weapons. The grey-painted ten tonner, with the usual canvas awning, registration number as advised, two Specials up in front, was authentic enough. The guard on the outer gate, with no reason to be suspicious, went through the drill, glanced at the police pass and the requisition order, presented by the driver's mate who had climbed down from the cab. Then he had gone to the rear of the truck to be reassured by the sight of the regulation two guards seated one on each side, their weapons across their knees. A brief exchange of names and greetings. All in order. The outer gates were opened and the truck drove into the security tunnel. The gates closed behind them and the guard signalled to his colleague to open the inner doors and admit the vehicle on to the forecourt of the armoury, where the guard-room was located. The two guards and the driver jumped out. Suddenly the two men on the gates were told to keep their mouths shut and face the wall with their arms spreadeagled.

The remaining two guards looked up from their Nescafe in the

168

guardroom to face a sub-machine-gun. All four finished up locked in one of the strong rooms used for ammunition storage. It had all been too easy. With hindsight, had the first man on the gate looked more closely at the pass presented, he would have seen that it carried the picture of someone else. The truck had been hijacked fifteen miles out of Omagh, and its original USC personnel held at gun-point until midday in a nearby barn. It had just now been reported, once again empty, abandoned near the M1. Everyone's story fitted. But Arthur shared his master's misgivings. Would the guards recognise the raiders again? Apparently descriptions were not good – a cold day, and the raiders had their collars up and their hats pulled down. Carson was not unduly surprised.

He was aware of conflicting interests, and in front of his officials, found himself having to feign a sense of outrage which he knew, as a Minister of the Crown, he ought to have been feeling. But the umbilical thread back to the gun-runners of 1912 was still there. Whose side was he on?

Jones was urging an immediate review of security for all arms depots and suggesting that the Army be involved. This Carson turned down without hesitation and noticed, as he did so, an approving nod from his private secretary – Robert's gut reaction in sensitive areas was much sounder than that of his senior English colleague. Relations between the Army and the local forces were delicate enough. The CID would be investigating in any case. Meantime there would be a switch-round of all regular security personnel at USC depots, just in case anything else was afoot.

Carson's days at the Ministry might be numbered, but his prestige was at stake. The raid would be juicy meat for the media. They had already telephoned the office for comment. Arthur Jones had a possible statement ready. It gave the facts deadpan with no precise details of the losses. The identity of the raiders left open but no reason to suspect IRA involvement. Urgent review of security arrangements in train.

'Fine, Arthur,' said Carson. 'Put it out right away. But, of course, it leaves the big question open . . .'

'We certainly can't point the finger at this stage,' said the Secretary.

Carson was mulling over the political pluses that might accrue from the affair. It had been sparked off by the British proposals. One could now be sure of that, in the absence of any claim from the IRA. They would not have failed to capitalise on such a sensational coup. Here, on the other hand, was the warning salvo across the bows of Westminster, perfectly timed and without bloodshed. It was better than he could have hoped for. There were certain links between the Harrmon crowd and some former members of the USC, but on the whole the Specials tended to steer clear of the paramilitaries. There was, to use Kitson's term, another 'foco' at work. And one which clearly could go into action at very short notice.

Arthur Jones had always held the theory that the backlash, if it came, would stem from the fusion under intense outside pressure of a number of nuclei which up to then had been independently active. The resultant release of energy would be explosive. It was a neat little academic conceit as far as Carson was concerned – Jones had read science way back at Cambridge – but nothing more. Now the Secretary was convinced that another nucleus was on the boil. A report just in from Special Branch drew attention to growing political activity in the power stations. They had evidence over the past months of a number of confidential meetings on and off the plants, called by shop-stewards and devoted to non-union business 'of a political nature'. Sources on this 'non-union' business were not very precise but indications were that discussions centred on the attitude of power-workers in the event of civil war. Some kind of emergency blue-print was being drawn up by two union officials who had vsiited all four Northern Ireland stations. The officials concerned were little known except in their own union, both Orangemen, one a lay-preacher, and neither active in Unionist politics. This kind of development, Jones argued, was much more worrying than the vocal street politics which took various forms in the Protestant community. It was the quiet pigs, he maintained, that did the rooting. Was the army aware of such developments? It was hard to know, since they kept all their own intelligence activity under such close wraps. Where was the common data bank that would enable the Government to identify and contain the elements in a sudden popular backlash if it occurred? Jones felt the Minister should put the matter squarely on the table at the security meeting which was about to take place. On the general security scene there were several agencies, duplication of effort which they in Stormont were unable to eliminate, despite repeated efforts, and a total lack of co-ordination. With the changes announced, the next few weeks could be critical. This lack of rapport between the army and the police; on a minor scale it was the old story of inter-service rivalry which one might normally tolerate but not when a war was on. The Secretary had attended a number of courses at the then Imperial Defence College and proudly showed the letters 'IDC' after his name.

When he started talking in strategic terms Carson lost interest. Robert caught his Minister's eyes raised vaguely heavenwards. 'Yes Arthur,' said Carson. 'I take your point about lack of co-ordination between us and the Army, but I feel it may very well resolve itself if these changes go through. Just what the future relationship will be, we shall have to see. Certainly I intend to bring up the whole question with the GOC – no doubt there'll be a few cracks about Larchfield – we'll just have to grin and bear it!'

'You could remind them, Minister, of the IRA man on the Malone Road,' said Robert. This was a reference to an IRA hide-out which contained a whole collection of taped conversations tapped from the military network – army security was not impenetrable.

'What's on the agenda, Arthur?'

'Not too heavy, Minister. Re-routing of the Orange parade on Tuesday. A Cross-Border road at Newtownhamilton – they've opened it up again – Army says it's our pigeon. The housing estate at Suffolk – Protestants are complaining that the Army are not giving them proper protection.' The Secretary handed Carson an open folder, heavily tabbed. 'That's the route we've suggested for Tuesday . . .'

'Yes, yes,' said Carson. 'Surely this can be sorted out by Boydell's Number Two? It's the new situation which I want to talk about and I know that's what concerns the PM.'

'As you wish, Minister. I can easily have a word with the Brigadier. But last time, after the petrol bomb incident, you remember, you wanted all routing decisions to be tabled.'

'Of course I did, Arthur. You're quite right!' Carson was all charming apology. 'But please – save me from myself today!'

'You'd better be getting down there Minister – it's 12.40,' said Robert.

Carson rose from the desk. 'You'll be glad to know: I *did* call on Mrs McKeown.'

'She's happy?'

'Very!'

'Good!' said Robert. 'That takes care of Shorland Street!'

Coming up to one o'clock the Tavern was three-quarters full. It did a lunch-time trade, serving the lower end of Sandy Row, the symbolic heart of Protestant Belfast. It smelt of damp clothes and smoke and hot pies. The barman wasn't the talkative kind. He served without thanks or comment. Half seated on one of the chrome bar stools was

171

Reg Nimmo, Quartermaster of the UDF. He was waiting for someone. In the intervals of sipping his stout and riffling through the *Mirror* he kept glancing at the door. Each time it opened the cold air blew in and you could hear the noise of the railways engines behind. Downstairs the Tavern was essentially a male preserve. It had tradition. The battered oak bar-counter and the elaborately carved oak woodwork behind, on which were ranged a variety of bottles and ornaments, dated from the early part of the century.

The various notices and bric-a-brac attached to the reredos gave, for the informed observer, clear indication as to the nature and interests of the clientele. There was a faded gaudy illustration of King Billy on his white horse, a coloured photograph of Glasgow Rangers Football team for 1959, a wooden plaque with the Red Hand of Ulster, a symbol preferred on many Loyalist banners to the Union Jack, and a notice roughly printed in ink which said that 'RAOB LOL 134 meets here every Tuesday'. There was as much chance of finding a Catholic in the Tavern as there was of finding feathers on a frog's back, or – as the locals had it – Holy Water in an Orange Lodge. The Catholic Lower Falls was only five or six hundred yards away on the far side of the railway line, but in terms of allegiances, it was the Gaza strip next door to the Promised Land. Nimmo finished his stout just as the other man arrived. He was well-built, very fit-looking, with short fair hair and thin oriental eyes. Under his jacket he wore a white roll-top sweater. He might have been a PT instructor. They exchanged no greeting as he took his place beside Nimmo at the bar.

'What'll you have?' said the UDF man.

'A rum.'

They took their glasses and moved to a small table at the end of the bar. Nimmo took out cigarettes and held out the packet. The man shook his head. 'We've got the stuff for distribution,' he said. 'We're spreading it around. Could you take thirty?'

'The short jobs?'

'Yeah, yeah,' said the man impatiently. 'Nine mill.'

'All right. When?'

'Between seven and eight. Here's the address.'

The man scribbled on a piece of paper and handed it to Nimmo. 'OK?' He knocked back his drink and left.

Nimmo looked at the scrap of paper, crumpled it up, and threw it on the floor. If this had been a film, he thought, I'd have burnt it or swallowed it. He smiled grimly. Then he remembered the bloody electric drill.

172

The security committee met once a week in Stormont Castle. Normally it was chaired by the Minister of Home Affairs but latterly, because of the political implications of every move on law and order, the Prime Minister had become a regular attender. After the meeting, the usual form was a press release listing the successes of the security forces over the previous week – the number of those arrested and charged, arms and explosives recovered, sticks of gelignite, so many hundredweight of nitrate and sodium chlorate.

Increasingly, these discussions had been dominated by the Army in the person of its GOC Lt General Sir Frank Boydell MC KCB, a gunner who had served in Kenya and Borneo. After staff appointments at Sandhurst and in the Ministry of Defence he had come to Northern Ireland as a man who was fully aware of the kind of political tight-rope he would be called upon to traverse. Bombarded on one side by the local politicians who thought he was not doing enough and from the other side by those who thought he was doing too much, he had to be as scrupulously fair to the part of the community that loathed his troops and all they stood for as to the part that regarded him as their shield and buckler. Not to speak of assuaging the whole echelon of pro- and anti-British sentiment in between. Soldiering in Northern Ireland required political nous rather than fighting skill. The battle was a battle of wits. It had not suited Boydell's predecessor who, on leaving Ulster, had been heard to echo the words of the cavalry officer after the First World War, 'Thank God that's over: now back to proper soldiering again.'

The GOC's civilian counterpart was a native. Crosbie Knox, Inspector General of the RUC, was a quiet-spoken professional police-man who in the Fifties had been District Inspector of B Division in West Belfast, the cockpit of sectarian rioting. Knox had come up through the ranks and he was proud of his force. He had not taken kindly to the way the army had assumed the dominant role on the security scene. In theory the army was 'in aid of the civil power', that is, in a supporting role to the RUC. In practice, over the years the army had been taking over more and more of the police functions for the simple reason that the police were not equipped to operate in the heavily armed IRA heartlands.

173

Today in the Cabinet room at the Castle, friction had been absent so far. Carson had arranged that routine matters be dealt with by their deputies in an adjoining room. He wanted to concentrate on his own private strategy. The four men were alone. The Prime Minister had just been speaking of the grave implications of the raid on the armoury. If members of the USC were themselves taking up arms in defence of their own survival, so to speak, then the outlook was grim.

'We're sitting on a landmine, gentlemen,' was how he put it.

Boydell, who was wearing his informal gear, khaki webbing belt over a woollen pullover with leather elbow patches which conveyed, he felt, that 'active operations image', put down the spectacles with which he had been studying the list of stolen weapons. 'In which case, Prime Minister, we'd better start de-fusing it. One, it would be a help if we recovered these arms. It might convince whoever was responsible that crime doesn't pay, might even stop them trying it again! If it's any help,' he turned to Knox, 'my Special Investigation Branch people are at your disposal.'

'I trust that won't be necessary, General!' said Knox, with a frosty smile.

The General was blithely undismayed. 'Anyhow. They're there, old boy, if you need 'em. Two, if you think if might be a good idea, we could, if you wish, transfer all the hardware to our central magazine in Lisburn. No problem in looking after it there. Gives you a breathing space to look at your security and take whatever steps you think necessary.'

It was all very helpful and reasonable. Knox had a vague feeling he was being finessed again, but he didn't want to appear too dog-in-a-manger, since he himself had at that moment no very constructive suggestion to make. It was Carson who came in, easily. He had always got on well with Frank Boydell. He liked the soldier's unpompous approach.

'At any other time, Frank, I think that would be very helpful. But just now, with this big question mark hanging over the Specials, to start moving their arms into an Army store. . .' he laughed and threw out his hands, 'I hardly think it would do a lot for morale!'

'Point taken,' said Boydell, smiling. He went on, speaking first to the Prime Minister and then turning to the IG. 'I think we really have got to get down to this one. I'd be glad to hear how you see it, Prime Minister. You'll appreciate my position. Ministry of Defence is my boss and if Her Majesty's Government – and your good selves of course,' he smiled, and included Carson and Packham. 'If you go ahead with this, and I

174

assume, after today's joint statement, that you will, then clearly certain adjustments will have to be made. We'll still all be in the same boat, pulling the same way and I don't anticipate any great upheaval. But we face a new situation and at a time when anything could happen. There's a lot going on.' He nodded at the IG. 'Saw that Special Branch report of yours on the power stations . . . interesting!'

'I don't attach too much weight to it,' said Knox. 'There's a lot of these doomsday plans around.'

As he spoke, Carson reflected on how quickly the report had got to Boydell's desk, while his own men had the devil's own job getting sight of even low-grade army intelligence. It was suspected in the RUC that the tab 'UK eyes only" did not include Northern Ireland eyes.

'Maybe. Maybe,' replied the General, apparently not convinced. He was waiting for the Prime Minister who was taking his time. After a moment's spectacle play and a quick glance out of the window, Packham looked at the two men opposite – Carson was seated beside him – and grasped the nettle.

'I can't pretend that we gladly embrace these changes in what I might call security management, but we understand the present thinking – with Westminster involvement and with your present strength on the ground here it's natural that MOD should wish to have overall control – and I think Crosbie here would agree that the RUC have not now the weapons to fight a guerilla war – not and remain a civilian service. I regard the changes as only temporary and we should be addressing our minds to the task of enabling the police to assume full responsibility again. Meantime, I would hope that we can devise some form of effective liaison.'

'I'm quite sure we can,' said the soldier, relieved at the Prime Minister's tone.

'There will, no doubt, be protest, even resistance in political circles, but I feel we can handle it,' went on Packham. 'But,' he spoke more emphatically, 'the whole emotive USC thing . . . is a different kettle of fish. Already today, we've had bad public reaction. My Cabinet's not too happy and at 2.30 I face the Parliamentary party – they undoubtedly will reflect the feeling in the country. We shall do our best – we've spent a long time,' he motioned to Carson, 'the Minister and I, trying to work out the best way to present the switch into a new force. It's not easy, and the press don't make it any easier. I've just spent a very bloody half-hour trying to get a polite hearing.' His colour mounted at the recollection. 'And now I've got to make it sound convincing on television this evening. Otherwise the groundswell of opposition may grow too fast and too strong. I can't believe that Downing Street realised just what a hornet's nest it was stirring up. Today's raid should be a warning.' He paused. 'Crosbie, how are you finding reaction?'

The IG rapped his half-closed knuckles together and leaned forward on his elbows. 'Very much a sense of shock Prime Minister. Very close ties, as you know, between the Specials and the parent force – very often a man leaves the regular service for some reason and joins the USC for the sporting side. I gather that initially the effect of the news was two-fold, a feeling of being let down. And secondly, indignation at what one of my officers regarded as a "sell-out" by the British Government. They feel sure it must have been forced on us. This morning, long before the official statement, no-one doubted that the press reports were true.' Packham opened his hands and looked at Boydell. Comment was unnecessary.

The General was lookng pensive. When he spoke, it was with some hesitation. 'That's bad news. We knew it wouldn't be easy, and I thought that since quite a number of USC members are quite clearly gentlemen in their fifties, that a brand-new force might appeal. Obviously not. The trouble is — and I'm only telling you what I know. At this level, I don't take decisions. I just take orders. The trouble is, MOD regard the whole thing as a *fait accompli*. I have to tell you that I've already been instructed to think in terms of raising seven battalions for the new force, which is in fact very similar to a TA Regiment: one battalion in Belfast and the other six on a county basis.' The other three men were looking at him.

'So it's got as far as that, has it?' said Carson, as if to himself. 'And the USC?'

'Taken off everything except static guard duties and phased out over six months.'

'It would have been nice to have been told something of this, PM,' said Carson. 'Not that the details matter once the decision was taken. Just the courtesy.'

'I was not in a position . . .' began Boydell.

'Of course not. You're not to blame. I suppose I needn't ask when you were first brought in on the discussions? Early on I imagine.'

The GOC smiled wanly. 'I do what I'm told. We're always being asked to consider all kinds of options . . .'

'Of course. Of course. We fully appreciate your position,' said Carson, rescuing the GOC from his embarrassment. 'But you must see that we now carry the can. We'll run as far as we can with it, of course.

But the longer we run with this one the less likely it seems that we can deliver.' He caught the Prime Minister's eye for a moment and looked away. 'I think it only fair to warn you Frank. Your masters may find themselves in a head-on confrontation with the greater part of the Protestant community. Perhaps they are prepared for that. I dunno. And perhaps you have made your plans accordingly. Even if you have, I don't envy you. The Prods can be just as vicious as the IRA and there's a lot more of them.' Carson noted the reaction to his words so far. The PM looked grave. Twice it had seemed as if he were about to interrupt, but he had kept his silence. The GOC was keeping his cool. His head was down and he was doodling with great concentration on the pad before him.

The IG was sitting rigidly, his elbows on the table, his chin resting on his hands, joined as if in prayer. He felt uneasy at this blatantly political discussion, especially with the Prime Minister present. It did not accord with his ingrained sense of protocol, acquired during all those long years when a Cabinet Minister was a being apart and the top table at which he now sat, an impossible dream.

With hardly a pause Carson went on. 'We shall all be sucked in. You can rest assured that the Prime Minister,' he included his chief with a glance, 'and I and most of our colleagues' – there just a hint of emphasis on 'most' – 'will act responsibly, but – and here I can only speak for myself – in the crunch situation I am talking about, there is bound to be a conflict of loyalties. Who knows?' With a bleak smile he shrugged his shoulders in a gesture of stoic agnosticism.

'Well,' said the Prime Minister in the resulting silence, 'perhaps my colleague has painted the picture in more lurid terms than I should have used, but I must say . . . I share his pessimism at this moment. I say that purely for consumption at this table,' and his glance at the Inspector General was invocation of the Official Secrets Act. 'I don't think we can take it much further today. All we can do is await events.'

'Prime Minister!' The GOC had roused himself. He was smiling again. 'There's just one thing I'd like to say, and I don't know whether you will find it reassuring or not. We have *no* contingency plans to take on the IRA *and* the Protestant community!' There was a relaxation of the tension round the table.

Carson was satisfied he had made his point.

'Let's have the others in, Stewart,' said the Prime Minister, 'and we'll see how they've grappled with the big problems like the Junior Orange Parade! We can do it over a bite of lunch. What can I offer you to drink?'

It was 2 p.m. The two guests had just left. The Prime Minister looked at Carson. 'Well, you set the cat among the pigeons with a vengeance. I wish you'd warned me.'

'I'm sorry, Arthur. It was on the spur of the moment. It may have some effect.'

'I realised at once what you were getting at and it was better it came from you. MOD will have it within the hour, I'll be bound. It will give Number Ten food for thought.'

'I believe friend Boydell if he's saying they don't want to get caught in the middle, but when he says that they have no contingency plans I take leave to doubt. Don't you?'

'They have a military plan, Desmond, to cope with what they conceive of as a civil war situation – they'd be bloody fools if they didn't – but what they don't realise is, that in this God-forsaken country, nothing is cut and dried. The thing you need to forestall is the thing you haven't foreseen!'

As he drove back to the office, Carson wondered about the process of political decision-making. The outsider, the man in the street who paid his taxes and worried about his family's future, would like to believe that his leaders balanced all, brought all into account and, having gravely and rationally steered a critical path between the pros and the cons, had come to the only responsible conclusion. This was how Carson, with the aid of his officials, attempted to make his administrative decisions. Yet even from those, prejudice and personal preference could not be excluded. But the forces that came into play when a man was faced with the kind of political choice that now confronted him, were much more complex and more arbitrary. In his mind fermented a must of motives and emotions. A climate quickened by all the thermals he had ridden to rise to where he was. Genes and dreams contending with the id and ethics: self-interest with self-respect. And always aware that one day, as the earth clattered down on the wooden box, he would want them to say that he had left a mark that would not lightly be erased.

Yet why, in his thoughts, should a woman's face loom as large as the public weal? He had no idea which way he was going – that was the truth. His pronouncement at the security meeting had been the result, not just of a considered tactic but of an impulse to get under the English skin, to inject the chilling thought that cosy containment of the Ulster condition might not last much longer. He had allowed the PM to rationalise it for him afterwards. Now he was going into the Party meeting still dithering and swithering. Even if he resigned, the dilemma

178

would not be resolved. He would still face the question – do I rebel agains the Crown? In the loyalist world in which he had existed since the day he had been born, it was a cosmic question.

Joe Maguire and one of his cronies were having a lunch-time drink in the Europa Hotel after a meeting. The Europa, much bombed but still in business, was the unofficial rendezvous and clearing house for the international press corps. Many a vivid eye-witness story of riot, shootout and explosion had been typed in its bedrooms to enliven the pages of news sheets from Frankfurt to New York. Inevitably it was said that some of the front-line newsmen had seen no more of Belfast than the Europa Bar. Against that, certain of the English journalists had built up an enviable reputation for reliable inside knowledge of the Ulster political scene. At least two were full-time Belfast correspondents for London dailies with offices in the Europa. In Fleet Street the hotel was as well known as El Vino's.

'John, c'mere a minute.' Maguire had hailed a bespectacled, clerical-looking figure who had just come up the stairs. It was John Seal, the very astute and respected correspondent for the *Sunday Times*. 'What'll ya have?' It was clear that Maguire had information to impart and Seal was a good listener. He accepted a Harp and there was the usual chit-chat. Then Maguire said, 'We've just been having a Party Executive meeting about these changes. Load of eyewash, isn't it?'

'Is it?' said Seal. 'I'd have thought it amounted to rather more than that.'

Seal, who had the entrée to the Downing Street offices was aware of the agonising that had preceded the launching of the long-awaited initiative.

'The only thing that means a light, is doing away with the B Specials – good riddance to bad rubbish!'

'Can I quote you?' asked Seal, half in earnest.

'As often as you like. You can also say that every Catholic in Northern Ireland will breathe a sigh of relief to see the last of a discredited force which was nothing but an instrument of Unionist domination.

'You're happy about it, then?' asked Seal.

'Happy, so long as the British follow through. They say they intend to. It all depends on what Packham gets up to.' Maguire moved closer to impart a matter of great secrecy. 'That's what I wanted to tell you. Packham's running round like a blue-arsed fly.' he chuckled. 'He

179

doesn't know how he's going to sell it to his party. So the Cabinet are going to try and do a white-wash job – deny they're being scrapped, say they're simply being re-formed, bigger and better than ever. That's the God's truth – I have it from the horse's mouth. John, we mustn't let him get away with it. We gotta nail him John.'

Seal didn't light up with the expected interest. He'd already heard the story from another source, close to James Gillan's press officer. He didn't believe it. Arthur Packham was far too shrewd an operator to attempt anything as naive as that. 'Thanks, Joe,' he said to Maguire. 'I'm grateful for the tip.'

Billy Dixon was at his desk in the Whips' office. This was the form before a Party Meeting of any consequence. The faithful, that is those who supported the Prime Minister, dropped in to register their allegiance, if they had not already made it unequivocally clear. Like a satrap, he received them with degrees of warmth according to the tribute they had rendered in the past. In the concentric circles of Unionist MPs surrounding Arthur Packham, the one furthest from the warm sunshine of the Chief's approval was reserved for the unreliables. Dixon's definition was simple. A man was unreliable if you didn't know for certain before the meeting how he was going to vote. Today there had been a disturbing number of absentees among the back-benchers. Dixon had not been unprepared for it. In his telephonic swing round the constituency chairmen to drum up support, he had not found the response encouraging. The usual excuses; they would have to consult their executive et cetera, but when he had pinned them down they had made no bones of the high level of feeling in their areas.

As one man put it. 'We've had two funerals here in the last four weeks. Two good men. The people are in no mood for this reorganisation carry-on!'

After the Cabinet meeting, he had not revealed to the PM the true state of the party wicket. There was no sense in lowering morale before a battle and, in any case, his master did not take kindly to bad tidings these days. Dixon was finding him increasingly moody and given to arbitrary changes of mind.

McFee came through the door, making assurance doubly sure. 'Everything going all right, Billy?' he said brightly.

Dixon nodded, 'Fine. We'd like you to come in early? OK? Get things moving in the right direction.'

McFee beamed. 'Of course.' He was accepted again!

'Have you seen Willie about?' asked Dixon casually.

'No.'

'He's probably down in Room Ten.'

Dixon looked at his watch. 'Time we were getting down there.'

Room Ten was down the long corridor in the south-eastern corner of Parliament Buildings. It was the usual venue of Parliamentary Party meetings. Its long red-leather-covered tables, ranged in a rectangle, had been the arena for many a bitter and historic party struggle. Here the votes were taken which deposed and elected leaders. Not only leaders, but behind them the old or new guard of ambitious men whose hopes of preferment are either dashed or realised. Outside the room where the corridor turns at right angles were several little knots of Members, some engaged in close and earnest conversation, others in apparently carefree banter. Dixon eyed them closely as he approached. Years of experience told him that the jokers knew what they were doing, had already made their minds up. The earnest ones were undecided, still looking for guidance or worried about backing a loser. He noticed that Willie was hovering on the edge of a very attentive group who were listening to Joe McCrory, a dedicated adherent of Wylie Mullins and his church.

The Rooster was there, laying down the law on something or other. Mun was involved in a quiet but sizeable little gathering and the booming voice of Marcus Kilmurray was fulminating as usual against some act of official lunacy.

'I tell you, *this place* is a bloody mad-house! They're just like *lemmings . . .*' Every word was given a conclusive emphasis. He was a baronet of distinguished lineage whose forebears had served in the Parliaments of both Stormont and Westminster where he himself had been a Member for some years, before returning to the family estate in Co. Fermanagh. He saw himself as one of the last advocates of sanity, despairing and isolated in a society where unreason was drowning out the voice of moderation. Still, noblesse oblige. One must struggle on with the kerns and peasants that surrounded one. For Dixon he was the prototype 'unreliable' except that he was impervious to both blackmail and bribery.

Lefaux came hurrying up the corridor and pulled Dixon aside. 'Did you see the ITN midday slot? First a piece on the PM – defying Downing Street. Then a clip of Gillan. Much harder than yesterday. *No way* could the Ulster people accept any weakening of their defences! They made a pretty twosome!' said Lefaux chuckling.

'Talk's cheap,' said Dixon, grimly. 'We'll see what Gillan does when the chips are down.'

The Prime Minister and Carson had already arrived. Behind came Shane Crossley and Fred Butler. Gradually the whole assembly trickled into the room and took their places. They distributed themselves round the tables, those of like mind sitting as usual all together, members of the Cabinet dispersed among backbenchers, without any ceremony. A Party meeting was the great leveller. At the table to the left of the door, facing down the room, was the Chair, distinguished from the others by its wooden elbows and occupied by the Acting Chief Whip, Lefaux. On his right was the Prime Minister flanked by Carson; on Lefaux' other side Billy Dixon and the Attorney General. Mun and his cohorts, along with McCrory and his two associates, were on the left. On the right was a strong Packham contingent, including McFee and Fred Butler the Minister of Labour. Willie was nearest Fred Butler but, as it happened, just round the corner on the end table facing the Chair. Others on the table which might be thought of as a cross-bench were Sir Marcus, Beattie Samson – the Rooster, George Patterson the doctor who was friendly with Willie, and Sam Collins, the solicitor from Dungannon who had been a prominent guest at the Gillan home the night before. For the practised Stormontologist the cross-bench presented an intriguing mixture. As it filled up Carson and the PM were engaged in close conversation. At the last moment James Gillan hurried in, nodded to the Chair and took his place beside Mun.

Lefaux wasted no time calling them to order. The meeting had been called to consider certain decisions taken by the Cabinet jointly with her Majesty's Government. The Prime Minister regarded it as a matter of confidence that they be endorsed by the Parliamentary Party. Lefaux congratulated them on a full attendance, thirty-two members present – the only absentee the Chief Whip, through illness, and the Speaker. It reflected the gravity of the situation. 'First, I know you would like to hear from the Prime Minister himself what has been happening and why these decisions had to be taken so quickly.'

Packham, speaking from notes, gave a factual account of how the Cabinet had first learnt of the proposals, and how they had reached agreement with Downing Street on the joint statement. He referred repeatedly to the British Government's insistence that what they were putting forward was not a paper for discussion, but firm Cabinet conclusions. He drew attention to the advantages of unified control of the security forces. He pointed out that one result of the changes would be a new-look police force, better designed to work side by side with the army and equipped with the most modern weapons. *That* they would insist on – he had made that clear at his press conference. 'The media, of course, would interpret it as confrontation with Westminster!' . . . Mention of the media evoked the usual growl of disapproval. The PM continued.

'Gentlemen. Whatever our personal feelings about certain aspects of these changes, two things stand out. First, looked at objectively, these changes will mean a strengthening of our forces. Second. Westminster has a right to make them. It *is* the sovereign Parliament. The Union is a two-sided covenant, and our fellow citizens have given generously, not only of their treasure but of their blood . . .'

'What about Ulster blood? . . . there's been a lot more of that shed than English!' It was Joe McCrory, his face red with anger.

There was a chorus of indignant support from the whole of the left-hand table. 'What about the war?' '*Two* wars!' came another angry voice. Carson groaned inwardly. If only the PM knew when to stop. He had been doing well. But the blood bit . . . !

'Please, gentlemen, please! Order! Order!' Lefaux knocked the table with his gavel. The rumble reluctantly ceased.

Whatever momentum, whatever sympathy the Prime Minister had been gaining, was being lost. After repeating that the joint statement had the full backing of the Cabinet, he made a final lack-lustre appeal for their support, and sat down.

Several people were jumping in to speak, including McCrory and Marcus Kilmurray. Lefaux took McCrory, and indicated to the baronet that he would be next. Let McCrory get it off his chest right away. Joe McCrory was in his late thirties, fresh-faced and hair prematurely grey. He stood up with the awkward aggressiveness of a man to whom words don't come easily, and hitched his right thumb in his belt in the manner of a countryman. His voice had the strong North Antrim colour which to the outsider is totally Scots. 'I won't keep you too long, Marcus.' He waved towards his colleague.

'Please, my dear chap. . . please. . .'

McCrory looked down at the table and then at the Prime Minister. 'I'd like to know one thing, Prime Minister. Why are the British pushing these changes down our throats . . . *now!* You say it's because they want to improve security. Well, how will it improve security if the Specials are taken over by the Army? We all know the Army's hands are tied by Westminster.' His voice assumed a heavy sarcasm. 'They

183

mustn't be hard on the poor IRA, because that would worry all the nice Roman Catholics. So instead of having one man with his hands tied, you'll have two men with their hands tied.' He began to speak more quickly, his voice trembling. 'Is that going to stop the murders? Is that going to stop the bombings and the killing of innocent people? Two more slaughtered last week in my own town! I'll tell you why they want to get rid of the Bs – because the Roman Catholics hate them. And why do they hate them? Because they put the fear of God into the IRA. That's why. They stopped them in 1920. They stopped them in 1960, and they could stop them again – if they were given a free hand. But no! Just to please the Catholics, they're going to be sacrificed. And I hear, too, they're talking of disarming the RUC. Why? To keep the Republicans happy! Appease! Appease! We've done nothing but give, give, over the last few years, and for what? For what? Have the murders stopped? They've got worse, far worse! And now you're asking us to hand over our last defence! I say, No! No!'

Right you are, Joe. Right!' The vehement voice was Mun Martin's.

'I swear by the Almighty, Prime Minister.' continued McCrory with emotion, 'and I'm a Bible Christian – I don't take His name in vain – I swear that if you don't stop Westminster doing this, the ordinary working Protestants of this country will stop them! – and I'll be there – among them!' He spat out the last words in challenge towards the Prime Minister, and sat down to a chorus of table-banging 'hear hears' from the group around him, and to snorts of disgust from several members around the room, notably Sir Marcus Kilmurray. The Prime Minister sat Sphinx-like, his pen tapping the pad in front of him. He hardly reacted when Carson muttered something in his ear.

'Thank you Joe. Order please, gentlemen,' said Lefaux, knocking the table with his gavel and nodding to Sir Marcus. The latter rose to his feet. With his fleece of hair round a bald pate, he looked like an amiable sheep. 'Chief Whip, Prime Minister, gentlemen, I am sure we are all acutely aware, faced as we are with a most difficult and potentially dangerous situation, of the need to speak with the utmost restraint,' he looked round expansively 'and to do nothing which might exacerbate . . . sectarian feeling either inside or outside this room. Far be it from me . . .'

'Get to the point!' It was one of the McCrory henchmen who interrupted. 'I am endeavouring to do so – if you will allow me,' said Kilmurray, nettled. 'The point is, that I am appalled at the sectarian tenor of the previous speaker – *appalled!* To imply that the entire Catholic population is supporting the IRA is monstrous!'

184

'Is it? Is it?' cried the same interrupter. 'When were you last up the Falls?'

'Please gentlemen. I must ask you not to interrupt, otherwise we shall never get through.' Lefaux was appealing directly to the McCrory group.

'All right,' said McCrory, 'then let him stop calling me sectarian. I speak for the loyalist people – the people he *doesn't* represent!' It was a shrewd thrust, since Kilmurray had been heavily involved in the ecumenical scene. It was greeted with savage satisfaction on the left-hand side of the room.

'I refuse to get involved in this cheap exchange,' said Kilmurray stiffly. 'Sometimes I depair, when I hear some of the views expressed – on both sides of the House, both sides are equally entrenched – I concede that. There is a kind of damnable stalemate between the extremists – seventeenth-century religion has ever been the only common denominator in this country . . .'

'He's now launched on one of his Parliamentary utterances,' thought Lefaux. 'Still, nothing like boredom to bring down the temperature.'

'When, therefore, our friends, in another place . . . er Westminster, who have shaken off the clerical strait-jacket, and can see things rather more clearly than we sometimes can, make certain proposals in the larger interest of the United Kingdom as a whole, surely it ill behoves us, without the firmest evidence, to reject them out of hand as being directed against one side of the community or the other, against Catholic or Protestant.' At the words Catholic and Protestant attention in the room quickened noticeably, but Kilmurray was moving on to another line. 'Surely, as Unionists, we should welcome any measure which re-integrates us more closely with. . . what one might call the *mother ship*. As loyal subjects of Her Majesty, we should embrace such proposals, not oppose them. In any case, gentlemen, let us be honest.' He waited for effect. 'Unless we are going to get ourselves into a completely untenable situation, occupying the same ground as the IRA, then we have no *alternative* but to accept.' He sat down, suddenly, to a few low-key 'hear hears'.

Lefaux was taken by surprise. But, on reflection, he remembered that the baronet never did have the stomach for a verbal rough-house. The barracking at the beginning of his speech had subdued him. It was not his voice, but his vote, that would count. Round the room, half a dozen hands were claiming Lefaux's attention. After left and centre, he went right. He indicated George Patterson, the bluff family doctor from

South Belfast. Patterson's attitude would be a good barometer of Willie Burton's commitment to the morning's Cabinet decision, for Willie would certainly not be getting to his feet, if past form was any guide.

'I'm just a plain GP,' began Patterson, in his best homespun manner. 'I'm afraid I can't follow my learned friend back to the seventeenth century – I find it hard enough to cope with the twentieth. By the way, I notice he didn't refer to the only part of the seventeenth century that some of us are familiar with, the Battle of the Boyne – 1690! Maybe that's a wee bit too sectarian for you, Marcus! Though my friend the Minister, there,' pointing to Carson, 'informs me that the Pope had his finger in that one as well – can't keep him out, can you?'

'All genial bedside manner stuff,' thought Lefaux. 'When does he get to the point?'

'You know, lads, as just an ordinary back-bencher, whenever I'm faced with a big political problem – and by God, you can say that *this* is a big one – I tend to listen to my constituents, and since a lot of them happen to be my patients, I don't have to go very far. So what are *they* saying?' He leaned forward and his face hardened. 'They are saying, Prime Minister, that *they've* had *enough!*' From the table opposite, came a rumble of satisfaction. 'They are saying, – Joe McCrory hit the nail on the head – that they have made a lot of concessions already and that it hasn't made a button of difference to Catholic attitudes, and it certainly hasn't cut down the violence. One man said to me – he's an oldish man, but he's no fool – "You must stand up to them," and when I said, "That's easier said than done – we're British too you know," do you know what he said? "What have we got to lose? Sure, if we go on like this, they'll have us in a United Ireland anyway!"' The growl of approval grew. 'Now, I may be just a simple GP, but I do know this.' He looked slowly round the room and then he fixed his gaze on the Prime Minister 'There are some conditions, and if you don't catch them in time, then all the medicine in the world won't help you. PM, the prognosis for this wee country of ours is still reasonably good . . . but the treatment has got to start right away.'

The left hand table was jubilant. This was a convert they hadn't counted on. In the buzz of conversation that rose as Patterson sat down, Lefaux had a hurried word with the Prime Minister. 'It's not going too well, PM. I'll keep Desmond to the end, to sum up. Gillan hasn't caught my eye. Maybe he's going to sit it out.'

Carson was busy doing his sums. Dixon was doing the same, in his heart a black hatred for Willie Burton. After Patterson's contribution it was practically a cert that both he and Magee were gone. A switch of two made an overall difference of four votes. If anyone else should defect . . . Dixon's heart beat faster. He hadn't dared look at the PM. It was getting far too close for comfort. The Rooster was on his feet. Lefaux breathed with relief, that here at least was one loss to the Gillan camp.

The QC was just getting into his stride. 'Our deliberations today have, for me, a certain unreality. No one yet has considered the world outside, the world of cold reality, as distinct from hot air. No, George,' he looked down at Patterson beside him. 'I don't count your surgery, instructive though it was. I'm talking about the wider world, the press, British public opinion, what's happening in this Province at the moment. For twelve hours now, these very radical changes have been bandied around, first as a press leak, from which quarter I shall not speculate on now, and then, as decisions apparently already agreed by both governments. On that basis, the public has no doubt made up its mind, one way or another. A whole chain of events has been set in train. Decisions as to how to deal with this new situation are already being made. One example is, undoubtedly, the arms raid on Larchfield armoury. What else has already been decided we do not know. But we do know that we, as the elected representatives have been given scant opportunity to take *any* decision in this matter. We have not been consulted in any way. Now, presented with a fait accompli – very much as the government itself was – we are being asked to endorse or reject these measures in toto, in the full knowledge that if we reject them, we leave the Prime Minister no alternative but to resign. So now we have not only the responsibility at this meeting of deciding whether or not these very far-reaching changes in our legal and security systems are desirable, or indeed acceptable. We have also to make another very grave decision – whether or not we wish, at this fateful moment in our affairs, to change our leader.'

As always, the Rooster was addressing a jury, remembering the advice of his tutor, the Attorney General who listened to him now with a certain pride. 'Always treat your jury as intelligent eleven year olds, Crossley had said, 'and you won't go far wrong!' The eleven year olds were following his argument with rapt attention.

'What concerns me, is that our freedom to choose is being unnecessarily restricted. There may be some here, who would wish to reject the decisions without throwing out the leader and, of course,' he smiled, 'vice versa. It would be hypocritical to pretend that certain events of last evening are not common knowledge in this room. Prime Minister, as you are aware, I have never been an uncritical admirer of yours. That is still my position . . .'

Lefaux had risen to his feet, rapping the table as he did so. 'I'm sorry. Would you give way?'

'Of course.' Samson sat down.

'I have to remind you that we are here to consider the joint statement, to approve it or otherwise. This is not a meeting to select a new leader. I've allowed you a lot of latitude already.'

The Rooster rose again. 'I accept your ruling, Chief Whip, but you must see that the two are inextricably linked. Indeed, I get the impression that, in the minds of some of our colleagues here, the main issue is the leadership one. However, my own position is this. I am not happy with the proposed changes. On the other hand, given your probable successor, I should be happier to see you, Prime Minister, continue to lead the Party for the moment.' Gillan coloured angrily, but no one said anything. 'Since these two aims appear to be incompatible, I intend, therefore, to abstain. One final thing, if I may presume, Prime Minister. Given the principle of collective Cabinet responsibility, I take it that any of your colleagues who, today, or in future, depart from that principle, will be tendering their resignations!'

'Trust the Rooster,' thought Carson, 'as cussed as ever!'

When Samson sat down, there was again muted hubbub, as the effect of his words registered. Gillan was sitting in sullen silence, reacting little to overtures from the group around him. The Rooster had made it finally impossible for any of the Cabinet to speak, even obliquely, against the decisions, and it was clear that neither of the two openly dissident ministers would speak in favour. Lefaux would resist any attempt to vote by ballot – it would be done, as usual, by a show of hands, eliminating any chicanery. Whatever the final voting, Carson had the feeling that Gillan was looking less and less like a leader. Lefaux was ringing the changes, two more back-benchers, mercifully short and predictable, one from each side. Then McFee, with a quasi-religious exhortation to support the appointed leader.

The Prime Minister turned to Carson 'I've a feeling we're wasting our time,' he murmured with a sigh. Carson waited for further elucidation, but none was forthcoming, so he continued making the odd note of what was being said. In summing up, he always liked to quote by name, from as many speakers as possible. The speakers liked it too, but by now the list had almost dried up.

Sam Collins, the solicitor, was on his feet. Like most of the hard-liners, he was neurotic about the press. A late convert to the view that it was, on balance, better to talk to them, he still believed that throughout the media there was a built-in bias against the Unionist standpoint. His mentor, the Rooster, had tried to convince him that what the QC called the 'underdog syndrome', the sympathy for minorities, had significantly diminished in the UK and was now confined to the overseas newsmen who filed the same story from Vietnam, Africa and Ulster. 'They'll be outside there, like vultures, waiting,' Collins was saying. 'Waiting to hear that the Unionist Party is split down the middle, waiting to hear that we no longer have the will to protect our own vital interests. Our people are confused and deeply worried by the suddenness of these changes, and by the secretive way they appear to have come about. What are they going to think when they hear that we are now split – and you know what happens to a house divided! And it's no use, Chief Whip, pretending that the leadership is not an issue. It may not be on the official agenda but when the Unionist Party sees its leader knuckling down to these outrageous demands from Westminster . . .'

'Nonsense!' cried Fred Butler.

'I hope it's nonsense. All right, all right. I'm nearly finished.' – this, as Lefaux was rising to his feet again. 'May I just say this, Prime Minister: you would still have a lot of support, more than you think, if you'll only *stand firm*. Before I sit down, I would like to know this – what does the Minister of Home Affairs say about all this? It's his Ministry which is most deeply affected, and yet we're still in the dark about his attitude. Let me say that I, and many others, have nothing but respect and admiration for the way he has handled a very difficult department over the past few years.' Carson kept his head down for the gratifying swell of approval that greeted these words. 'So don't misunderstand me.' He addressed the last directly to Carson. 'But we'd like to have the benefit of your views on the whole matter.' This, too, met with general approbation.

'Your timing, Sam, as always, is bang on the button,' said Lefaux, smiling broadly. 'Since, apparently, none else wishes to speak?' He waited a moment. 'Right. I now call on the man himself. The Minister of Home Affairs.'

Carson felt his heart quicken. He knew the importance of making an impact now. This was his launching pad. The PM had fallen. His rival was muzzled. He had to sound like a leader. He had already decided to keep as many options open as possible. He was confirmed in this approach by a Delphic remark of the Prime Minister's.

'Don't burn too many boats,' he whispered, as Carson rose to speak.

He began by reminding them of the case made by the Prime Minister, and reinforced by Sir Marcus – the basic obligation imposed by the Union. He understood and sympathised with the depth of feeling expressed by Joe McCrory. He not only sympathised: he fully shared Joe's feelings of anger and frustration at the continuing carnage. He accepted what George Patterson had said about the feelings of his constituents. As he touched on Beatty Samson's misgivings and praised Sam Collins for reminding them of the paramount need to avoid the wrong headlines, he was at the same time subtly underlining the fact that they were all in the same boat – nobody was happy about the content of the joint statement before them. The Cabinet was committed to what was in the statement, but no more. How the changes would be implemented, in what time-scale, the exact nature of the force that would replace the B Specials, and the system adopted to enable Specials to transfer to the new force – all this had yet to be agreed. And indeed, given the views expressed at the meeting, and the hostile feed-back he was getting and, he was sure, they were all getting from their constituencies, it would be dishonest to exclude the possibility of indefinitely postponing implementation. When this possibility was greeted on the left-hand table with open scepticism, Carson went on. 'I assure you. That is no empty threat, undertaking – call it what you will. And I make it, fully aware of the implications. We have accepted *this*,' he waved the joint statement, 'in principle. How it is put into practice must be a matter for us. From now on, it is our views that must prevail. The Prime Minister made that clear at his press conference and indeed, Chief Whip, that could be the crunch. Speaking for myself,' he paused, and then he spoke very deliberately, 'I am prepared to go the whole way to ensure that our views *do* prevail. It is on that basis that, on behalf of the government, I ask for your support today.' The reception he got as he sat down showed no great surprises. The 'antis' were still on the left and the 'pros' opposite. But there was warmer approval than he had expected from the cross-bench, led by the Rooster.

'Very well, gentlemen,' said Lefaux, 'we can now proceed to the vote. Unless . . .' He turned to Packham and said something. 'No, the Prime Minister has nothing to add. The usual method – by a show of hands.'

Immediately, George Patterson was on his feet. 'Chief Whip, on a very important question like this, I think it's essential that we vote by ballot. Only in that way will we get a true picture of how the members of this Parliamentary Party really feel. I move that we vote by ballot.'

There were raised eyebrows as Mun Martin stood up. But it was immediately clear that there had been no collusion. 'I'm sorry George, but I don't agree. I think we should have an open vote. This is an issue on which members will have to be seen to stand by their convictions. I propose that we stick to the normal procedure.' At the top table glances were exchanged on each side of the Chairman. They were not slow in getting the message. Mun was obviously acting for his candidate. Gillan was shying away from a head-on collision. It would have been too transparent to have supported a secret vote. Gillan and Martin were biding their time, letting their supporters make the running. The two tellers were Fred Butler and McCrory. The hand-count did not take long – there were thirty-three members present in the room. Dixon had marked the card eighteeen to twelve in favour with three doubtfuls. After a brief check with the two tellers, Lefaux banged the table and announced the result. 'Approving the statement, eighteen: against, thirteen.' Patterson, Willie's friend, voted against. The Rooster and Collins abstained. As expected there were no defectors from the Cabinet. 'Thank you, gentlemen. I declare the meeting closed.' Lefaux turned to his right. 'Well, PM?'

Packham had risen slowly and heavily to his feet. 'Well, Desmond?' he said, looking, in turn, at Carson. They were all thinking the same thing. Eighteen/thirteen sounded reasonable enough as a majority. But take away Gillan and Martin and just one other and it was fifteen/sixteen. It was not a base from which to launch a highly controversial policy. 'We'll have to talk about this,' said Packham, 'but not now. I've got this wretched television to think about.' He did not sound like a crusader leading his army, bright with banners into battle. His paladins escorted him out of the room. Carson could not help but note that the McCrory crowd were cock-a-hoop.

Eight of the twelve-man Army Council of the IRA were meeting south of the border that evening, in the back room of a wine and spirit grocer's in Monaghan town, just off the Diamond with its fine parish church.

They were assessing the latest bombing campaign in the North. The supply of 'stuff' – gelignite, siphoned off from the main explosives factory in Drogheda through various legitimate channels such as quarry blasting, was being choked back by the Irish Government under constant pressure from the British to introduce stricter controls. They were having to rely more and more on nitrates and chlorate – fertiliser ingredients.

On the agenda, too, was the perennial problem of funds, not only for supplies, but for the living allowance of each full-time Volunteer. Routine business.

But there was one item which provoked unusual interest. The Chief of Staff had received from the OC Belfast Brigade a copy of an intelligence report dated three days previously. Desmond Carson, the Northern Ireland Minister of Home Affairs, was closely involved with one of his office staff, a Catholic girl called Scanlon. The relationship was at least three weeks old. Her mother's family, the McElroys of Cushendall, Co. Antrim, had been associated with the Movement in the Twenties. Josephine Scanlon lived alone in a secluded bungalow near the Malone Road in Belfast. She was visited by Carson several times a week, usually after dark between 20.00 and 22.00 hours. Apparently he was without escort of any kind. He left the bungalow at a late hour – on the last occasion, Tuesday, at 01.45 hours. He drove his own car, a Mercedes 280SE, metallic grey, EPT620. He parked at the rear of the house which was approached by a short lane. The Intelligence Officer of the 3rd Battalion, who had submitted the report, would, during the next few days, recce the location personally. A further report with sketch map would follow.

The Chief of Staff, a thin sharp-eyed man who chain-smoked, spoke to the OC covering the South Armagh/Newry area. 'This could be big. It raises the whole policy issue once again. Do we or don't we?' Some months before, the question of assassination of public figures had been discussed. No conclusion had been reached and more urgent operational matters had intervened.

'I can't credit it.' said the Newry man. 'Does he really drive round at night without an escort? How do we know the Branch don't have a tail on him?'

'We'll just have to find out, won't we? I've got to talk to Liam about this.' Liam was the Belfast Brigade commander. 'I can see why the bastard might give them the slip. Catholic girl, dropping her knickers for the big boss man.' He spoke bitterly. 'Christ! If that got around . . .'

'Make sure it doesn't! I wonder how many people know about this already.'

The Chief of Staff spoke to a junior. 'Get Liam down here! As soon as you get hold of him.' He lit another cigarette. 'I don't know. I don't know. It could be the answer.'

192

On the way down to the BBC on Ormeau Avenue, Packham had turned to Ronnie Fine, who was sitting beside him in the Daimler. 'I suppose this bloody man, Holroyd, will be fussing around as usual. Every time I meet him it's one long self-justification – why he's allowed this one or that one to appear – he never stops talking about "the Corporation". He seems to think we run this country expressly to provide him with controversial interviews. So keep him away from me, will you?'

Fne smiled. 'I'll do my best, sir.'

The old man was *not* in good form. The Party meeting had depressed him. As they drove into the courtyard through the security gates, the Controller came forward to receive them.

Holroyd was a fleshy, pink-faced man who, as a news expert, had been sent to Northern Ireland where, it was said, everything was happening. He was feeling the strain of keeping both sides happy and of maintaining his own place in the Corporation rat-race to the top. Hence his neurotic desire to share his problems. 'Tom Lefaux and Mr Dixon are waiting upstairs, Prime Minister. Would you care to join them for a drink before . . . ?'

'Let's get on with it,' said the Prime Minister. 'We can have a drink afterwards.'

'Right, we're all ready for you. Just a touch of make-up first.' As they walked down the corridor towards the lift, he said, 'You should have a very big audience Prime Minister. There's a lot of opposition to the proposals. Our news people tell me they've been getting it hot and heavy all day. I'm looking forward to hearing what you have to say.'

The Prime Minister grunted. 'Can I have a pee somewhere?' he said.

Upstairs in the Controller's room on the second floor, Lefaux and Dixon were having a drink, and discussing the *Belfast Telegraph's* report of the press conference. Lefaux's last minute efforts had borne some fruit – the Prime Minister's remarks were interpreted as 'firm determination to press the Northern Ireland Government's point of view.' That was the line he would take in the broadcast. Since the Prime Minister was being videotaped to go out later on both Channels, they would not yet be able to see him in action.

Below in the control cubicle, Ronnie Fine alone, as the script-writer, would stand behind the technicians, fingers crossed, eyes glued to the monitor, mouthing each word his master spoke, praying the old man would pull it off. Riding on the PM was not just the fate of the government, but the life-style of his entourage.

But Arthur Montgomery Packham was not thinking of his

dependants. As he sat at the impressive walnut desk, a prop wheeled in for ministerial occasions, he was overcome with an unworthy desire to be back in County Armagh. To poke his fattening buttocks with a blackthorn as he walked his fields with the yardman; to stand in the stables talking to his two brood mares, sniffing the scent of hay and horse-dung. What in God's name was he doing here? The pretty young thing dabbing powder on his face, the lights, the voice of the floor manager, 'Thirty seconds to go. Good luck sir.' He could do with it tonight. 'Five, four, three, two, one,' the finger stabbed at him. It was all so unimportant. He squared his shoulders and looked at the autocue.

'Good evening. I'm speaking to you tonight because, after a day of rumour and misrepresentation, I think it is time you knew the facts.' In the cubicle, Ronnie Fine followed every word.

Lefaux and Dixon rose to their feet as Packham came through the door of the Controller's room followed by Fine and Holroyd. To their unspoken question, the Prime Minister answered, 'Could have been worse I suppose.'

The two men behind him were loud in praise for his performance. 'That phrase at the end, Prime Minister,' said Holroyd, handing him a glass of whiskey. "Before we jettison the certainties of sixty years" – superb! And then you went on, "Let us not forget, that for us, the Union is no *dead word* on the Statute Book – it is our way of Life!" You see! I remember! Stirring stuff, Prime Minister.' Fine's face lit up.

'I wonder,' said Packham. 'I wonder.' He drank his whiskey. 'I feel more and more that rhetoric – which is essentially language at white heat, leaves this generation cold. In the past I have enjoyed speaking on television, but tonight I never really had the feeling that I was communicating – that I was getting across.'

'You're probably tired PM – it's been a hectic day – I'm quite sure you'll be very good,' said Lefaux confidently.

'Yes, PM. You get out of it for a while. Don't worry – we'll look after the shop,' said Dixon mechanically. He'd come down to the BBC for a wee bit of a party. It was becoming more like a wake.

'I am weary,' said Packham. 'I've decided to go down to the country tonight. I had intended to stay until tomorrow, but I really must get away. Tell Stewart to ring me in the morning.' He finished his whiskey and the Controller escorted him out of the room.

At once Lefaux turned to Fine. 'Well – how *did* it go?'

Fine made a grimace. 'It could have been the words – I wasn't mad about them – but we did the best we could. Nevertheless, on occasions like this, he's usually . . . pumped up. Down there tonight, I'm sorry to say, I had the feeling he's pumped out. Not just that, but earlier on, when we were trying to stick the thing together he just wasn't . . . with it.'

'You think it's the Party meeting?' asked Dixon anxiously. 'I know it wasn't a good result. And now they've requisitioned a meeting of the full Standing Committee – you can imagine what that'll be like – bloody murder!'

'I shouldn't worry, Billy,' said Lefaux. 'When's it summoned for?'

'A fortnight's time.'

'Oh, we'll have reached the crunch long before then, believe me!' As Dixon looked bewildered, he went on, 'I'm not joking, am I Ronnie?'

'I don't think you are,' said Fine, unsmiling. 'I don't know how the Cabinet has held together – certainly during the next few days something's got to give.' Fine hesitated then broached it. 'If the PM goes . . .' There was a silence. 'Desmond?' said Lefaux.

'Could be.' said Dixon. The subject was not pursued.

'Thank God I'm going out tonight,' said Lefaux with forced heartiness. 'I'm going to get full.'

'So am I,' said Dixon, struggling to his feet. It looked as if the wee party was over.

Desmond Carson left the party meeting with mixed feelings. He was reasonably happy with his own performance and with the reception he had received. But he was acutely aware of the significance of the voting figures. It had been touch and go.

Only Gillan's ultra-cautious nature was keeping him in the squad – but for how long? Then the PM's attitude, so remote from it all. Later in the office, he had watched the television broadcast. Well enough put together, but lacking all Packham's usual warmth and persuasive authority. It was a performance – routine, bloodless, no balls! Even the final sentence, 'The future of this province within the United Kingdom lies not with politicians or with Parliament – it lies with you!' sounded more like an abdication than a call to arms! Carson had switched off the set and looked for reaction to Robert, who was watching with him.

His secretary hesitated and then said quite firmly, 'Well I got the impression Minister, that the PM didn't really have his heart in it.'

It was an impression, Carson was convinced, that would be widely shared. He himself, though he had subscribed to the joint statement, was gradually edging further and further away from it. At the Party meeting he had kept his options open, with the PM's unexpected encouragement. It was clear now that the attempt to sell the British proposals had foundered even before it was under way. For better or for worse the Government had only two alternatives: either resign in protest or spearhead the opposition. To dither on was to lose all credibility. It was vital he see Packham as soon as possible and tell him straight. Robert was back with another list of reminders and items for information and for action. Requests for TV interviews.

'Stall them!' The Police Federation Chairman and Secretary wished to see him urgently. 'Make it Monday,' said Carson. By then he would know what to say.

Tomorrow morning, he was reminded, was his monthly date for pistol practice at the RUC range in the old Belfast Ropeworks. The theory was there was no point in carrying a weapon unless one could use it with reasonable efficiency. They had changed the method from one he had learned in his days with the Territorials. Instead of the Webley revolver sideways on, with cheek down on the shoulder, they now had you crouching, feet apart, and holding a Walther PK automatic in both hands, square on to the target. It was very light on the trigger and blazed off rounds like a movie cop at the cardboard cut-outs of head and shoulders. Carson found the twenty minutes of sound and fury, only partially muted by ear-muffs, exhilarating. But at this moment it was far too frivolous a pastime. 'Cancel it,' he said to Robert. 'I don't think the IRA are gunning for me at the moment. More likely the Prods are after my blood!'

He left the office after seven o'clock and was driven to his home. Everything seemed to be in the melting pot. He toyed with the idea of going straight down to Armagh. The telephone was no good. No, tomorrow morning. Both he and Packham had had enough for one day. He found himself in an unusually febrile reckless mood. He'd arranged to see her that evening. There was nothing like a woman to unbend the mind. He would take her to the Dungannon's party and to hell with the lot of them. They had never been out together in public. The Dungannons were an unconventional couple, and their parties had a way of dictating their own terms of reference. What harm to drop in for a while with an aide? Who cared? His wife was spending the night with her sister in Tyrone.

There was a note. Crissie, his daughter had phoned. The stab of remorse went deep. The child who adored him and what was he doing to her? The guilt he had always felt because he had never given her enough of his time; because her homecomings, built up so strenuously, too often crumbled into disappointment, so over-anxious were they to communicate the pitifully little they knew of each other after fifteen years. His own flesh and blood and yet – he was ashamed to think about it – so far away from his world compared with the heart-stopping immediacy of the erstwhile stranger. He sat down there and then and wrote a letter to his daughter, telling her things were difficult but that all would be well. But as he penned the words, he knew that all would not be well. How would she feel when the scandal of his affair – for scandal it would be – became known? How would this child, insecure enough, stand up to the agony of her parents' divorce?

She would go with her mother of course. How much would he miss her? How much would she miss him? It could scar her for life. Was the future he kept predicting with such confidence, really anything more than an escapist dream? Against all the omens, could he go through with it? Was he lying, even to himself? Were the questions that kept intruding, rhetorical. To brood on it – that way did madness lie. He had passed the point of no return. Like Macbeth – a part he had once played at school – 'he was in blood stepped in so far, that should he wade no more, returning were as tedious as go o'er.' With his fondest love, he enclosed a cheque for twenty pounds and he was under no illusion as to why he did so.

Then, his mind made up, he rang Jo and told her he was taking her to a party, overcoming her objections with a mixture of cajoling and logic. 'You must allow a little male chauvinism now and then – I'm in a macho mood!' He wanted to pick her up at the lodge – there was no point in cloak and dagger any longer. But she insisted on being collected from a friend's house, where she could leave her car.

He had a shower and was changing when the phone rang. It was John, the Ministry Press Officer. He had just heard: a group of Protestant organisations had announced a general strike from midnight on Sunday. The proclamation on behalf of a body calling itself the Ulster Loyalist Council had been signed by W. Sproat, Chairman and P. Osborne, Secretary, but John had heard that Harry Harrmon and Wylie Mullins were also involved. According to the Press Officer, it all looked like a bit of sabre-rattling, though the demand for a referendum was new. Protest strikes up to now had been without any specified objective and usually for one day only. That was all he had at the moment, but, no doubt, there would be more in the bulletins once the reporters got on to it.

197

As he hung up, Carson was already putting two and two together. A connection between this and the arms raid? Is this what Harrmon had been thinking of yesterday when he talked of UDF decisions? In which case there could be something more than a protest strike. Then he remembered the intelligence report on the power stations – another part of the jig-saw? Of course, against all the hypotheses he was throwing up, was the fact that no such co-ordinated effort could possibly have been mounted since the publication of the British proposals. The raid possibly, but the rest, no. Yet something significant was afoot – he felt it in his water. And he was all the more conscious that he was so near the summit and yet being bypassed by events. Despite the impression he gave of knowing just where he was going, nothing was further from the truth.

To fill in the awful blank in his mind, it was imperative to speak to the PM. He reached for the telephone again. Packham himself answered. He was matter-of-fact. 'Glad you rang. I want to speak to you. Come down in the morning, will you?' Yes, he knew about the strike thing. Lefaux had just been on. He would not prolong it now. Ten-thirty in the morning. All very crisp and to the point. The PM sounded like a man who *did* know his mind.

Earlier that evening they had arrived singly or in pairs at the small Orange Hall on the hills south of Belfast. Some had come a long way. The meeting place had been specially chosen to avoid undue attention, although apart from Mullins and Harrmon, none of the men who walked through the small porch into the shuttered room would have been known to the general public. Yet on only two occasions were introductions necessary and even then those concerned were known to each other by hearsay. Predominant were the trade unionists, from the shipyards, the foundries, the new industries on the Castlereagh estate in Belfast – industries where the workforce was overwhelmingly Protestant. There were other inter-connections, membership of the loyalist institutions like the Orange and Black, service together at some time in the police force or in the Army – there were several ex-servicemen from the Second World War. Two men had played together on the same Old Boys' football team, formed from past members of the Boys' Brigade, a youth organisation associated with the Presbyterian Church.

For several years, anger and frustration had surged in waves throughout the Protestant working class – fury at the ceaseless loss of life and livelihood, at what was universally regarded as a frontal assault on the Protestant way of life and on the state which guaranteed it. Frustration at the reluctance or incompetence of Government, British or Stormont, to hit back, to make an end of it. Double frustration at the apparent inability of the Protestant community to create for itself a counter-weapon. Sporadic attempts had been made to form militant groupings, not only for self-protection – there was no No-man's-land between the Protestant Shankill and the Catholic Falls – but for self-respect.

Some particularly revolting murder such as that of three teenage soldiers, would spark off a mass protest with various organisations in improvised uniforms taking part. But when the anger subsided the marchers would disappear from the headlines. Only paramilitary bodies like the UDF seemed to have a continuing existence. Others existed, purely as a skeleton presence in a journalist's cupboard. But behind the scenes, away from the headlines, dedicated men were beavering, re-organising, for a day as yet undetermined, for an aim as yet unclear. Now and then they would publicly flex their muscles with a lightning protest strike. They were learning their lessons all the time, most valuably from their failures. Recently, their efforts had acquired an urgency caused by their deepening sense of being cornered in a cul-de-sac of history.

In the back-to-back houses of the fiercely Protestant Shankill, where sometimes the only picture was a coloured photograph of the Queen, the feelings of rejection that the covenant between her and her Ulster subjects had been scribbled over, defaced by her Ministers in Whitehall, had grown stronger. How else could they interpret the secret parleying between British Officials and the IRA killers? Oliver Birch and his predecessors – Protestant activists were only too well aware of their guest lists – had a lot to answer for.

But tonight, in this unprepossessing setting, there was the unspoken sense that it was all beginning to gel. At long last, as Carson's Permanent Secretary had foreseen, the elements were beginning to fuse under the heat of events. There was as yet no justification for euphoria but as each man entered the room he had the feeling not just of attending a meeting, but of becoming part of a crusade. Mullins arrived with a young man wearing tinted glasses whom he introduced as Peter Osborne his computer expert, and who at once started chatting with one of the trade unionists who had come with Megs Kane. At a trestle table there were sandwiches and cakes and soft drinks. Mullins frowned slightly when he saw a second table with beer and spirits, but he had learned to live with the human frailties of those who did not share his own strict Puritan views. He had a piece of cake and a glass of lemonade and turned to an unmistakeably military man, tweed-suited, with a Sappers regimental tie who had been a commandant in the Specials. 'Did you hear Packham just now, Major?'

There were now ten men in the room. Harrmon and with him Big Charlie. With Major Humphrey Bennett DSO, was another ex-B Special and Borough Councillor, Geoff Simpson. Megs Kane was busy checking a list of names with Billy Sproat, a powerful voice in the Confed – the Confederation of Engineering and Shipbuilding Unions. Peter Osborne was talking to Jim Patton, a convenor at Shorts aircraft works, and an active member of the Orange Order. A good looking young man who had cut his teeth in the American firm of Dupont was helping another guest to rum. This was Denny McNamee, the articulate champion of the Protestant workers on the big industrial estate of Maydown near Londonderry. The man with him was known to all as Jacko.

Jacko spoke little, but wielded in paramilitary circles a far-reaching and frightening influence. He was no stranger to killing, having first learned the knack with the Royal Marines special service unit in Aden. He wore the same white roll-top sweater as he'd worn at lunchtime in the Tavern.

A late arrival was Hugh Reddy, a big paunchy man with sparse greying air – he was a transport worker and had organised several Loyalist protest marches. Behind him came Brian Kedge, Carson's part-time agent. As soon as he caught sign of Kedge, Mullins frowned heavily and pulled Harrmon and Megs Kane to one side.

Clearly he took exception to Kedge's presence. Harrmon was anxious that the power worker should deal with it.

'Right lads,' said Megs, rapping a table. 'We haven't elected a chairman yet, but a little matter of credentials has come up. I know you won't get me wrong, Brian,' all eyes turned to the latest arrival, 'but it was agreed at the first informal get-together that we were not going to affiliate to any political party . . .'

'Just a minute, Megs,' said Jim Patton the Shorts convenor, 'Brian's with me – we're the two Orange delegates.'

'Then that's fine,' said Harrmon. 'The Orange are entitled to two.'

'Hold on a second,' said Mullins ominously. 'I've got nothing against Brian – he knows that – but he *is* a close political associate of Desmond Carson, and with him here, we might as well have Carson himself here!'

'Can I say something,' said Kedge. 'I am here entirely under my own steam, as an Orange delegate. I think you all know where I've stood and where I stand. I support Des Carson – he's a friend of mine – but I'm not here as his spy or to speak on his behalf. But I'll tell you one thing. If he was in this hall now, I think you'd find that he would not be opposed to what we are trying to do. *He* didn't tell me to say that but I'm telling you!'

'That's good enough for me,' said Harrmon quickly. 'I've got nothing against Carson.'

'Look, Wylie,' said Megs. 'We're doin' this for ourselves, all right? *But* we'd be stupid to turn away support, and if any politician wants to come along with us. . . on our terms, I say, let him! He's welcome.'

'This whole thing has got to be thrashed out . . . ' said Mullins.

'You're happy enough then?' said Megs.

'All right,' said Mullins with a magnanimous wave of the hand. 'Get the meeting started – before some of these fellows are intoxicated.' He motioned with a wry smile towards those helping themselves at the drinks table. 'Just a second,' he raised his voice.

'Before we sit down, lads, we need a chairman. I propose Megs.'

'I second that,' said Harrmon. There was unanimous approval.

'Thank you, boys,' said Megs. 'I am prepared to do my bit, but I'd rather not be in the chair. I think Billy here is the man.' He caught the arm of Billy Sproat, the slow-speaking likeable shipyard worker from the Confed. Like a new House of Commons Speaker being dragged reluctantly to the Chair, Billy allowed himself to be drafted. Two trestle tables were pulled into the centre of the room end to end. He sat in the middle and others ranged themselves around him six to each side and one at the end.

'Nobody superstitious I hope,' said Sproat.

'What do you mean?' said Denny McNamee. 'Wasn't it the *thirteen* Apprentice Boys that shut the gates of Derry against the traitor James II?' The parallel drew a delighted response. The meeting was off to an optimistic start.

'I'm not going to waste time talkin' about why we're here. If we didn't know before Packham spoke, we know now,' the Chairman began. 'I believe we have a just cause that will carry the people with us. They've seen what's happened since the Army came in. If they take away control of the police and the Specials, we're wide open. But just what are we going for?' His listeners looked at him, puzzled.

'We're going for a complete shut-down – that's what it's all about, isn't it?' said Big Charlie indignantly.

'All right. We close the place down and the British Government says, "OK. Forget about it. As you were!" Can you see any government cavin' in like that, in public?' asked Sproat incredulously. Several shook their heads. Others protested heatedly that they weren't beaten before they started.

'I see what Billy is getting at,' said Mullins slowly. 'It's not realistic to expect the British Parliament – because make no mistake, all the parties will close ranks on this – to be seen to give in to threats.'

'They've done it before,' said Major Bennett, clearing his throat self-consciously.

'Yes, yes, but we've got to give them a face-saver.'

'What about a referendum? All we want is a democratic decision. Put it to the people whether *they* want the changes. Whether, specifically, they want control of the police forces to remain in Ulster.' It was Jim Patton again, bright, self-assured, well known for his dialectical skill in tough negotiations.

202

'How about asking for new elections here?' said someone.

'How would that change the *British* Government? No that only confuses it,' retorted Sproat. 'A referendum's what we want – it's simple and people can see that it's fair!'

'That's it!' said Mullins, as if he'd just thought of the idea. 'A referendum. It's an absolutely reasonable demand – *and, and,*' he wagged his finger left and right, 'it gives us the initiative. It shows that *we* call the tune.'

'I'm with you,' said Harrmon. 'That makes sense to me. Megs?'

'I always say – before you come out make sure you know exactly what you're coming out for. It's got to be clear-cut. I accept a referendum.'

Sproat looked round the table, inviting comment. 'All right? Good. That's settled. A referendum on whether *we* control the police forces or they do.' He shook his fist exultantly. 'It's a bloody good issue!'

Megs was chuckling, muttering grimly to himself. 'And He delivered them into the hands of the spoilers.'

Sproat tore a sheet of paper off Meg's writing pad, and poised his Biro. 'Now! We've got to have an agenda, otherwise we're talkin' all over the place. Suggestions?'

'We need to fix a date.' It was the hoarse uncompromising voice of Hugh Reddy. 'If we start getting bogged down with details, we'll never get goin'.'

'Can I say something?' It was Peter Osborne tilting his tinted glasses nervously. He looked the crisp young executive with his well-cut suit and blue-striped shirt, out of place among the older and established hands who didn't feel the need to impress with clothes. Only Dennis McNamee rivalled him in the fashion stakes. He was conscious that with these hardened campaigners he would have to win his spurs.

'Sure,' said the Chairman. Mullins nodded encouragingly at his protégé.

'I go along with Hugh here,' said Osborne. His strong Belfast accent had lost none of its edge. He spoke deferentially to the huge jowly face staring at him. 'We don't want to get bogged down in the software too early. But before we can fix a date we have to know what has already been done in the way of preparation – the state of readiness of our different groups.' He looked enquiringly at the chairman who gave him the nod to continue. 'We've been workin' on this, as you know,' he looked at Megs, 'for several months. I have a check-list here of the things that have to be decided.' From a folder in front of him he took a number of copies and passed them round the table. 'It's not complete, I'm sure, but it may be a help as a basis for discussion.' There was silence as his companions studied the three-page document with interest. It outlined, under headings, the different areas of responsibility for which a director or controller had to be chosen. Admin covered provision of a headquarters, transport and a system of rationing vital suppleis such as bread, milk, drugs, petrol, animal feedstuffs. There was a heading for Press and Public Relations. Under Operations was a diagram breaking down the stoppage into key sectors: power, transport, engineering, light industry, with a man in charge of each. 'This,' explained Osborne, 'is to make sure that production is properly monitored during the run-down. Obviously Megs here has got the electricity situation tied up, but in the continuous process fibre plants like ICI, Monsanto, Enkalon and so on, if the run-down is not properly phased, the machinery can gum up and . . . it's a write-off. That's what the experts tell me and some of them are here.'

Denny McNamee and the Chairman nodded agreement at this reference. 'We've got to see too,' wheezed Hugh Reddy, 'that enough men are detailed to keep fuel, gas, propane and stuff moving – you gotta think of the old folk.'

'That's essential,' said the Chairman, 'from every point of view. We've got to make sure that any hardship is minimised, though to tell you the God's truth, some of the old ones could teach the youngsters a thing or two about true-blue Loyalism.'

'You've got two headings here, "Security" and "Enforcement" with nothing underneath?' said Harrmon.

Mullins broke in to explain. 'That's really you and . . . Jacko.'

'Can you, perhaps, be a little more explicit?' asked Major Bennett, an unorthodox member of the county gentry, who ran his own very efficient organisation of rural vigilantes but who was not so au fait with the less scrupulous methods of the hard men of the city.

'"Security",' explained Mullins, 'is simply protection of the Protestant areas and property, commercial and industrial. Our Republican friends could very well seize the opportunity when the strike begins to bite. When things get a bit chaotic they might think our guard was down. But this is all for discussion, isn't it?'

'What about "Enforcement"?' asked Simpson, the other B man, his mind clearly running on a legal connotation.

Harrmon laughed, 'Oh come on now, George! Pickets are enforcement aren't they? A few barricades if necessary. A little friendly persuasion, eh Jacko?' Jacko smiled a mirthless smile. 'We can't mess around. Gotta show we mean business.'

'I must say,' said the Chairman, lifting the top page of the check-list and letting it slowly subside. 'This is first-class Peter, first-class, and I think that's the feeling of the whole meeting.' There was a spontaneous murmur of assent.

'I told you,' said Mullins. 'He's put a lot of work into it. I think he's the obvious man to run the admin for us.'

'Christ!' said Harrmon to himself. 'He's at it already, pushing his men into the key jobs.' Several others at the table had exchanged glances, even though there was an unspoken recognition all round that Osborne was clearly right for the job. Mullin's methods were often counter-productive.

'We'll get to the business of selecting people in a minute,' said the Chairman, diplomatically. 'This list seems pretty comprehensive, but are there any other items anybody wants to add?'

'On the PR side, Mr Chairman.' It was Brian Kedge, who hadn't spoken before. 'There's bound to be RUC and maybe Specials covering picket-lines and barricades – in case of aggro. It's going to be very difficult. They're going to be torn two ways – and *we* can't draw back. I was going to suggest that the Major and George might be able to think of something – maybe a flying squad of ex-policemen who could be wheeled into potential trouble spots, to keep things sweet. Whatever happens, especially in the first few days, we don't want to find ourselves taking on the RUC. It would look terrible, apart from the fact that their sympathies will be with us.'

'I take your point, and it's a good one,' said the Major. He nodded. 'We'll put our heads together, and see what we can devise.'

'I'll make a note of that,' said the Chairman. He turned to Osborne. 'Maybe you'd act as secretary for the moment, and keep a note of all the decisions?'

'Certainly. Anything I can do to help, just say the word!' said Osborne anxious to undo the effect of his patron's over-zealous pushing.

'By the way,' said Jim Patton. 'We've got a very comprehensive register of volunteers with special skills, or knowledge – or just thick skulls!' he added to general laughter. 'We let on we were getting names for a petition, but in fact we did a very good canvass right through North Belfast – I know South and East Antrim have done the same.'

'Good lad!' croaked Reddy. 'You can't have too fuckin' many on the

205

streets the first few days – that's the make or break time.'

'There's one very important thing we've got to settle,' said the Chairman. 'What we do about Roman Catholic areas like the Falls? Do we try to get them out? The big Protestant firms will be OK, like Mackie's and Corry's, but what about the rest? And the shops and pubs?'

'You won't bloody well close the pubs on the Falls, that's for sure,' said Big Charlie. 'I don't see how we're going to shut our own.'

'There's a little public house, that everyone could close,' sang Denny McNamee, grinning, as Mullins smiled approvingly, 'And that's the little public house, that's underneath your nose!' Reddy and Kedge joined in, chanting the few lines to the tune of 'Auld Lang Syne'. It was a time-worn rhyme beloved of Temperance preachers and always good for a laugh.

'It's the very best of advice, and if you took it to heart you'd be the better for it,' said Mullins, half-chiding, half joking.

'Seriously, now,' admonished the Chairman, looking at Harrmon as the man who would be at the interface if it came to enforcement.

'We'll have to play it as it comes,' said the UDF commander. 'It's not on to try and close down Roman Catholic yards or shops without a full-scale war. I mean, that's the position – you can take it from me. It's just not worth the candle. But,' he emphasized, 'if the IRA – Provos or Officials – decide they're going to try and use the opportunity to have a go at the Prod areas, then that's a different ball-game. In any case, we don't need to shut down shops by closing the doors. If we choke off supplies – that's it!' He gave a smirk of finality.

'We've got to remember what we are trying to do,' said the Chairman, speaking very firmly. 'We're not in this to starve out anybody. A lot of the left-footers are just ordinary working people who have done us no harm.'

'Not hell they haven't!' grunted Big Charlie who found this doctrine too heretical for his liking.

But Sproat persisted. 'Our objective is to screw down this country until the British Government gives us our democratic rights. The Catholics will have to take their chance of shortages with everybody else, but,' and he spoke with some heat, 'women with childer, and old people are the same in my book wherever they are!' He stopped, his face flushed with determination.

Megs jumped in with equal emphasis. 'As a trade unionist, I agree, and I don't think anybody here disagrees.'

Mullins decided to lower the temperature. 'Look, lads, there's no *question* of letting children and old people starve. The strike will bite across this community – light, heat, food. We're not going to go out of our way to look after the Republicans – that's for sure – but they take their chance with everybody else. On the other hand,' he wagged his finger, 'if they attempt to take advantage of the situation, then that is *their* funeral! Right Billy?' He turned to Sproat, implying the Chairman's automatic agreement. There was a relieved growl of general acceptance all round the table. Both Sproat and Megs Kane combined a fierce hatred of Popery with an astonishing humanitarianism which knew no barriers. On a matter of conviction they were seldom crossed.

'If you like, we can find out just what they're going to do.' It was Jacko who now gripped the attention of his fellows. He spoke quietly, looking at no-one in particular. 'I mean the Provos. We can make it clear that their areas will be treated the same as the rest, provided they keep their noses clean.' Harrmon nodded vigorously. 'No question of a deal, just make it clear where we stand and leave us free to get on with the main business. And I can tell you, if the Army decide to protect the scabs and keep the streets open, we'll have our hands full.'

'Right. That's settled,' said the Chairman, all passion spent and very glad that they had come to an amicable conclusion. 'Now let's get down to the business of electin' men to head up the different sections. It being understood that this council will keep a firm grip on the overall situation – we'll have to meet at least several times a day. OK? Nem. con.' The choice of directors was quickly made since they mostly selected themselves according to the industrial sector in which they were active. Mullins was designated 'council co-ordinator'. This gave him a free hand and conscience and kept him near HQ which, it was agreed, would be in premises on the Antrim Road loaned by a sympathiser. McNamee was an obvious choice as official spokeman for the council. When the posts had been allocated, it was he who returned to the fateful question of the deadline.

'The sooner the better,' said Hugh Reddy. 'Our lads are rarin' to go.'

Osborne pointed out that extra telephone lines would be needed. . . the Strike HQ would have to be manned full-time. . . it couldn't be organised overnight.

'Why not?' rasped Hugh Reddy through his cigarette. 'You don't get notice of a train crash or an Act of God.'

'Or a bomb,' added someone.

'I don't think there's any argument,' intervened the Chairman. 'The decision was made for us, at midday, when that official statement was put out. The government are doing nothing – you heard that waffle of Packham's about an hour ago. The people are lookin' for a lead. It's not enough to say "No". We need to back it up with action. Right away.'

'Billy's right,' said Harrmon. 'We gotta go public at once. In any case, it will take a couple of days to build. What about midnight – tomorrow?'

'Start on Sunday? Sure we're off anyway,' said Patton.

'We cannot begin on the Lord's Day!' said Mullins. 'What sort of talk is that?'

'In a good cause, Wylie?' said Reddy, teasing.

Mullins shook his head angrily.

Out of the question,' said Megs. 'I vote we start Monday.' Most favoured Monday.

'We announce it right away,' said the Chairman. 'The deadline is midnight, Sunday. Agreed?'

It was agreed. The newly appointed spokeman was instructed to issue a press statement right away. The first words would be the same as in the Ulster Covenant of 1912; 'Being convinced in our consciences . . . '

In County Armagh, where his forebears had lived for four generations, Arthur Packham was having dinner in the breakfast room of the run-down family mansion where he had spent his boyhood years and where now, in the evening of his political career, he spent as much time as possible. On this cold October evening, the inadequacies of the primitive heating system had dictated the choice of room in which he was entertaining his guest. A wood fire blazed warmly in the wide-barred grate and the circular table had been pulled closer to the hearthrug. On it gleamed silver and china, white and gold. With the frayed and faded red curtains drawn, the old Donegal carpet and the Victorian button-back chairs in blotched crimson leather the effect was one of scuffed and shabby opulence. A standard lamp drew a circle of enclosing snugness round the two diners. Opposite the Prime Minister sat Shane Crossley summoned at short notice for what his host on the telephone had called, 'a little pow-wow on something rather important'. But there were compensations for the hour's journey at the end of a tiring day, and Crossley, no mean trencherman. was one to appreciate them. After a bumper of fino sherry they had eaten collared eels, mopping up the juice with wheaten bread. The Toome eel fishery on Lough Neagh was glad to indulge the Prime Minister's predilection for their produce. The eel was followed by a roasted pheasant shot over the fields outside.

Now the Attorney's glass was being recharged with a '52 Pape-Clement, 'Quite decent booze and good value – I wish I'd bought more of it,' said Packham.

Crossley, who was attacking a Welsh rarebit which had just been set in front of him, gave a grunt of total approval. 'A first-rate dinner – as always, Arthur,' he said, putting his knife and fork down and fingering his glass.

'Good. The least I could do, old chap. I do appreciate your coming down like this.'

Slowly Crossley twirled the stem of the glass in his fingers, took a sip of wine and set it down. 'I really don't know, Arthur. You're pretty sure in your own mind, I can see. Yesterday, when we were talking, I didn't take you seriously.'

'Twenty-four hours in politics . . . a long time!' Packham smiled. 'I suppose it's anno domini, I'm sixty-seven. I haven't the stomach for it any more, and that's the truth Shane. My first instinctive reaction was to fight, but what's the sense in battling on? An expense of spirit in a waste of shame! I'm no rebel, whatever they say about me.' He poured himself some wine, the last of the decanter, smiling ruefully. 'I think we've seen the last of the big vintages, in more senses than one.'

'Has the situation changed so very much since yesterday? Are you sure you're not just feeling . . . a bit down? You know, that's not the state of mind in which to consider such a final step.'

'Dear Shane. You're saying what you think you should say, not what you are intellectually convinced of!' The Attorney shook his head, half dubiety, half denial. 'I've got a glass of port for you which I trust you'll approve of.' As Packham moved to a side-table to fetch another decanter, he pushed a dish of apples towards his guest. 'Try it with one of these apples. They're Sykehouse Russets – we've got a couple of trees. I like a good russet, got aroma as well as flavour. Hardly ever see them now. When I was a boy we had a dozen varieties in the orchard – remember the Pearmains, and Irish Peach, and Nonpareil and the Duchess of Oldenburgh? Lovely names – and Blenheims and all the other pippins? Now there seems to be nothing but the wretched Cox's Orange! Where are the apples of yesteryear?

'Où sont les pommes d'antan?' said Crossley, sententiously.

'Along with the politicians of yesteryear – on the rubbish heap! . . . Here!' said Packham pushing the decanter of port towards his guest.

'"Get a glass of that down you and you'll begin to believe in God again!" as a friend of mine used to say.' He helped himself to an apple, and started to peel it with fastidious care. 'You asked me just now what has changed since yesterday. I'll tell you. First the Parliamentary Party was within an ace of voting against us – if Gillan had had the guts to go, he could have swung it. Tom was on the phone just before you arrived. He's been taking soundings round the newspapers on my television speech. Reactions tomorrow will not be good. "Packham plasters over the cracks!" That will be the gist of it. He also told me that Billy has received a requisition for an emergency meeting of the full Standing Committee for next week. You can imagine what sentiments will be expressed at *that!* About six hundred members with the hardest liners in the party in full cry. Some of them may well have been involved in that very significant gesture of protest we saw this morning – at Larchfield! There is also the public outcry we have already taken on board during the past twelve hours.' He paused. 'That, my dear Shane, in a nutshell, is what's happened since yesterday. Do you wonder that I've decided to call it a day?'

'What about the succession. I'm sure you've thought of that.'

'I have. Very carefully. Desmond is the only possible choice and he's been loyal, very loyal. You agree?'

'I don't think there's any question. If you want to block friend Gillan, he's the only one.'

'Of course I want to stop Gillan, but that's not the important thing. I am very conscious that I am leaving the ship at the height of the storm. I believe that Desmond Carson is the only one with a chance of pulling her through. *My* hands are tied. I have no room for manoeuvre. But if I went now he would be released from any undertaking I have entered into. He could start afresh. And indeed, my very departure would serve to bring home to the British Government just what can happen if they push too hard. If we are going to stop the lunatic fringe taking over in this Province I believe it is *imperative* that we face up to Westminster and make it clear that there are limits to what they can impose on the Unionist community.'

'This amounts to defiance, prima facie rebellion,' said Crossley.

'Precisely. As I've already said, my temperament and my convictions would not allow me to carry such a policy through. *I* am not the man. I believe Desmond is.' He put down the napkin he had crumpled in his fist and emptied his wineglass. His hands were shaking. His friend looked at him for some time.

210

Then he said quietly, 'How do you propose to break it?'

The Prime Minister was composed again. 'I've asked Desmond down here tomorrow morning to have a word. Then I'll tell the Cabinet. I would say the election meeting will be on Tuesday or Wednesday – as early as possible. What do you think?'

Crossley considered for a moment. 'Yes. If you've really made up your mind, then I'm sure it would be best to go right away. It makes it easier for Desmond to announce his policy and get a grip on the situation. From the country's point of view it's essential that a new administration be seen to know its own mind and to act without hesitation. A vacuum can be dangerous. It sucks the strangest creatures out of the woodwork. That's another reason to move fast – I am convinced that Gillan is likely to go at any moment. He resigns office to save the country! A magnificently unselfish gesture! Think of the kudos! But your pre-emptive strike cuts the ground from under him. There's no answer.'

'Why is he waiting?'

'To make doubly sure that the tide is flowing against us. He always dithers on the brink. He likes to bet on certainties.'

Packham struck the table lightly with his fist. 'That's it, then. Come on. Let's go into the library for coffee. You might even take a brandy, eh?' He put his arm round Crossley's shoulder. 'I'd better look after you, hadn't I? After all, the next time we dine you will still, I trust, be Attorney General, while I shall be unemployed.'

They were walking across the gloomy hall when Crossley stopped. 'If you go, what official reason will you give?'

'The real one. I disagree with their policies and I am resigning to bring home to all concerned the realities of the present political and security situation.'

'You realise that the implied criticism of HMG will not go down too well. That kind of plain speaking is not the way . . . to the House of Lords.'

'Bugger the House of Lords,' said the Prime Minister with vehemence. 'Too many already have sold their birthright for a mess of peerage.'

His friend looked at him hard and nodded. Then they resumed their walk towards the library.

Gillan was on the telephone to Mun Martin. The conversation tended to be rather cryptic since Mun lived in constant fear of eavesdroppers, either by accident or by design. Gillan was saying, 'I'm not convinced that it was the right decision to remain where we are. I know you'll say that I've changed my tune since this afternoon. Maybe I have. But, with the resistance building up all the time, I feel now that we should be identified with it, and the sooner the better.'

Mun, who had been on tenterhooks that names might be mentioned on the line, went into his unwieldly code routine. 'Tell your friend from *Antrim*,' he said, emphasising Antrim, Gillan's home base, 'that I would tend to agree with him at this moment. But tell him that a couple of days is not going to make any difference. It gives more time to make preparations for his departure, if you understand me.'

'You mean you think that . . . er, he shouldn't consider going tomorrow?' said Gillan, who found this method of communication both confusing and unnecessary.

'It's not easy. But when he didn't go today I think Monday's time enough. Look, I'll drop down and have a word with him tomorrow on my way into town. Just before lunch-time. Then he can finally make up his mind one way or the other. All right? See you tomorrow then, about one,' said Mun absurdly relapsing into 'clear' as he put the phone down.

212

The Dungannons lived in a Victorian castle near the southern shore of Lough Neagh. In the 1840s the then Earl had countered the drastic reduction in his rent-roll caused by the potato famine, by marrying an English heiress. With just under nine thousand pounds of her dowry, he had enlarged and remodelled the plain seventeenth-century house of his forebears into the bastard baronial then in fashion. Togged out with candle-snuffer turrets and massive machicolated corbels in Mourne granite, the Castle had survived the arson of the Land League Agitation and the troubles of the 1920s. It had surmounted the more insidious threat of inflation, thanks to the continuing family policy of judicious marriage. The present Earl, himself the product of an alliance with an American dynasty, had married the daughter of one of the steel barons of the Ruhr. Liesel Dungannon, lingering in her thirties, was unconventional, artistic and intent on shutting out the sound of the winged chariot. She and her husband, Alexander, spent most of their time in London or on the Continent. Perhaps it was a survival of the German Romantic attraction to Ossian and the Celtic myth that drew her back to the bleak shore of Lough Neagh where she had no roots and few convivial friends. She had far too great a sense of style for the mock-British pretensions of the Ulster gentry. Every autumn they spent at the Castle, ostensibly for the shooting. They brought their own mixed bag of guests. But entertainment was more cosmopolitan than confined to country pursuits.

Something of this background Carson tried to convey to his mistress as they drove down to County Tyrone. His firm had handled Dungannon legal business for three generations now, and he knew them both, though not intimately. There was little danger, he once again assured Jo, of eyebrows being raised at their appearing together in such a gathering. Conventional couplings were old hat. Figuratively speaking, the beast with two backs no longer excited comment in the menageries of the metropolis.

'I don't know that I'm going to like this. It sounds vaguely sinister,' she said. 'Why are we coming here anyway?'

'I've told you,' said Carson, lightly kissing her cheek. 'To show you off. To take you away from the kitchen sink! You can do a little opinion research – how the affluent society in Ulster is reacting at this time of crisis, and report to me! It's a few hours away from it all, darling! God knows, we both need it and I'm sure you'll find it amusing to see the Third World at play!'

She clutched his arm and smiled at him as they swung through the entrance gates. In the lighted doorway of the lodge, a man in shirt-sleeves waved his hand in greeting and then closed the door as the two cars disappeared round a bend in the avenue.

'Don't stray too far from me,' she said with a nervous smile, as the car stopped under a lofty porte-cochere.

Quickly he took her hand and looked at her. 'They are not worthy to touch the hem of your garment – whoever they are.'

'Politican's talk!' she said, and her eyes were bright. On each side of the entrance doors stood electric lamps in tall wrought-iron torchères. They lit up the driving rain blowing in under the stone canopy of the porch. Beyond was the barely detectable grey-black presence of the Lough and the faint swish of wind-whipped waves. The doors opened immediately on a dim-lit hall. A Filipino manservant in white linen jacket bowed briefly with a murmured greeting, and ushered them inside. As the door closed behind them, shutting out the sound of the wind, they were at once aware of the insistent heavy throb of amplified music coming from some distant upstairs. 'Deesco,' smiled the Filipino, seeing their reaction as he took their coats.

'It's all right, thank you. I know the way,' said Carson, taking Jo by the arm and leading her through double doors into a much larger inner hall, the walls of which soared up to shadowy vaulting, thirty or forty feet above. The air was heavy with the smell of burning wood smouldering in the great stone fireplace. The only light came from the glass globes of two massy chandeliers suspended high above them.

Jo took hold of Carson's hand. 'My!' she said as she gazed around her. 'It's like a museum!' And indeed they were environned by a bewildering profusion of objets d'art, baroque curiosities and the booty of empire. The stone floor was chequered with Eastern rugs. Two magnificent elephant tusks mounted in silver stood crossed like swords on a wooden plinth. In a glass case, crouched on a simulated rock against realistic jungle grasses, was a majestic tiger, the re-creation – so ran the ivory label – of Rowland Ward, Grosvenor Street, London, 1898. Next to a bronze temple bell a Chinese warrior carved from a single trunk gleamed red and gold. Under a sumptuous Stubbs of two

214

racehorses stood a Florentine caisson richly inlaid in precious woods. A whole wall patterned with the martial glitter of shields, halberds and damascened swords. A terrestrial globe, dark yellow with the patina of centuries, was incongruously allied with bottles of Campari, whiskey and glasses on a very fine parquetry commode. Against the wall sprawled several bags of golf clubs and a guncase – the debris of a varied day outdoors. In the centre of one of the end walls of the chamber was a two-manual Willis organ, the pipes enclosed in a frame so that it resembled a piece of modern sculpture. Jo leafed through the music sheets on the stand. 'Widor– Toccata. And film themes!' she exclaimed. 'By Michel Legrand! That's catholic taste for you!'

'His lordship fools round on the organ. He's aparently quite good,' explained Carson. 'Come on! we're very late. I could do with a drink. I told you you'd find it different here.' Together they raced up the broad staircase as the sound of music grew louder.

The public rooms of the Castle were on the first floor or the 'piano nobile' as the present mistress called it, a direct reference to the Venetian custom of keeping the living quarters well above water. But the periodic floods of the early nineteenth-century were no longer a danger now that the level of Lough Neagh had been substantially lowered through the demands of industry and farming.

The staircase led to several interconnecting chambers fanning out from an oval assembly room. Here the general level of lighting, though diffuse to the point of obscurity, was entirely theatrical in its effect, consisting of concealed up-lighters and low-voltage spots which spangled the darkened walls and floors with splashes and jets of colour, picking out the golden head of a portrait, the mask of a wild beast, the vivid crimson of a carpet and the flash of Fabergé bibelots on a table. The dramatic atmosphere was heightened by heavy velvet drapes round the doorways and a concentration of spotlights on the centre of the floor, leaving the rest of the room in the shadowy wings. It was a comfortably full house. The cast were already on stage declaiming, debating, booming, bitching, being witty, waggish, scandalous, flattering, outrageous. The decibel level of babble and laughter kept peaking above the monotonic thump of the music.

'A mixture of exotic imports and selected natives,' said Carson as, from the head of the stairs, they surveyed the company around them. Another white-jacketed manservant was beside them holding a salver with two glasses and deftly pouring champagne. Their hostess, flushed and effusive, was not far behind.

'Desmond! How good of you to come – in the middle of your crisis!' She extended a cheek to be kissed, her pert lively face framed in frizzy curls and, as she talked, swinging her body in layers of trendy ethnic gauzes.

'Liesel!' said Carson, making appropriately gallant noises as he took her hands in both of his. 'This is a friend of mine – and colleague . . . Jo Scanlon.'

The Countess was at her most charming. With a graceful nod of the head she lavished a patrician smile on the guest. 'You are very welcome to the castle,' she said. 'A colleague? Are you . . . political too?'

'A civil servant,' said Jo, smiling unsurely.

'She organises me,' said Carson.

'Of course,' said the Countess abstractedly. 'That is what women are for. You know Shamus, Shamus Conway?' She indicated the plumpish elegantly-tailored man beside her. His pepper-and-salt hair was carefully coiffured. He wore dark glasses and an open-necked blue silk shirt.

'Desmond!' he burst out, controlling himself no longer. '*What* is happening? The PM on the box tonight – the country at the cross-roads! The army are taking over the police – that's what they say! Then this announcement of a strike! Is it a coup? Is it to be the barricades? Are they going to shoot us?' He put his hand to his breast dramatically. 'I must know what to *wear!*'

'Stop it, Shamus!' said his hostess. 'It's no laughing matter.'

Carson was laughing himself. Conway was well known to him as an arts critic for all seasons and as the garrulous host on a TV chat show.

'You should be telling *me*, Shamus,' said Carson. 'You're the prophet, after all! No! No!' He put up his hand to silence the pundit. 'Pax. I've had enough of politics for today.'

'Yes,' said his hostess. 'Come along and have some food. No, it's a drink you want, isn't it? Shamus, look after Jo.' She took Carson by the arm and led him towards the dining-room. 'Explain. What *is* happening? This B Specials thing. You demobilise one army and then recruit another. It's just like Germany after the war. The Wehrmacht goes and next day we have the Bundeswehr! *Plus ca change . . .*'

'Different control,' said Carson. 'That's the theory.'

'But why all the fuss? And what's Arthur doing? We saw him on the television. Is he *resigning?*'

'Why do you say that?' asked Carson sharply.

'He was so apathetic, so old. Is he going?' she insisted, intuitively seizing on Carson's reaction.

216

'Not to my knowledge.' But he had hesitated.

'I think he is,' she said triumphantly. 'You needn't comment! So we have the battle for the succession. Ha! Ha! Delicious intrigues! Can I poison some of your opponents? Or seduce the handsome ones! If Paris was worth a Mass to Henry IV my bum must be worth a vote or two. I'm told it's my best feature.' She twirled her hips coquettishly, swinging round her silken gauzes with one hand.

'You're a loose woman, Liesel,' laughed Carson.

'No, tight! At least I think I am. I *hope* I am. Do you smoke?' From a soft leather pouch attached to her belt she produced an étui of cigarettes. He recognised them.

'No, not now, thank you.' He lit the one she placed between her lips. The sweet sharp smell of cannabis hit his nostrils. She looked at him mockingly.

'You're an accessory after the fact – but I shan't give you away. It's quite harmless and very liberating in a bourgeois gemütlich way. I'd miss my little highs! Oh, you look so disapproving!'

She was laughing at him and he was finding the whole performance a little irritating – it was much too public. His puritan hackles were rising but he raised his glass and drank to her. 'Champagne is sufficient for me.'

'Of course. But then you have power, the one great aphrodisiac they say.'

This time Carson's smile was unforced. 'You don't know how ironical that remark is at this time! But there is an even more potent aphrodisiac.'

'Yes?'

'Aphrodite herself!'

The Countess beckoned to a servant to replenish Carson's glass as she looked him in the face. 'So you are in love! So! Can she help you? Is her body essential to you?'

But Carson was in no mood for a prurient inquisition with his hostess as mother confessor. He had talked too much. They entered the dining-room through one of the curtained doorways. People were milling round the long table with its tantalising display of food. 'I am in love, Liesel, yes! In love with my work, with life and with you! That leaves me, at the moment, emotionally drained and very hungry! It looks delicious!'

'Poor darling. You must eat.'

She motioned to a white-coated servant behind the tables as she

217

hailed another late arrival. Carson took a quick look back through the doorway. Jo was talking happily with Shamus Conway and several others. He was about to reclaim her when the Rooster detached himself from a group who were eating in the semi-gloom beyond the spotlit buffet. He was not wearing his glasses and he screwed up his eyes to focus on Carson as he waved the champagne bottle in his hand.

'Desmond! What in God's name are you doing in this den of iniquity? Bloody good food. Try the koldouny – this one.' He indicated a large entree dish on one of the warming plates. 'Sort of Polish ravioli. Speciality of the house! Will you take wine with me?' Unsteadily he topped up Carson's glass and re-filled the one in his other hand. His blood-level was clearly on the high side.

Carson grinned at him. 'Cheers. You're in good shape, Beatty, I see.'

'Superlative. I love the high life.' He smiled with a sudden disarming shyness. 'It's the peasant in me. You know what I mean.'

'Of course I do. But your first-generation peasant is too obsessed with the cost to enjoy it. You've passed that stage, I'm afraid. You've lived too high on the hog too long!'

'You're right. But the Protestant bit still lingers, the puritanism – the worm at the heart of the fruit. We Unionists are doomed, Desmond. Doomed! We're a race of Flying Dutchmen, condemned to roam the seas forever, seeking a spiritual and political home.'

'I wonder was the Dutchman an Orangeman?'

'He made a pact with the devil, didn't he? No, his Institution was the Black!' Suddenly the Rooster's voice dropped. His face was serious. 'Do you know that we're among the few people here who are not smoking pot? These people I'm with,' he jerked his head towards them, 'they're staying here with the Dungannons and they're all at it *and* God knows what else. At least one is sniffing cocaine. It makes me uneasy. I can't help it.'

'I know. It could be awkward. Though I must say that my objections are practical rather than moral. With unsolved murders daily it's hard to get worked up about a little cannabis. And we'll hardly be raided tonight! I must go and find my companion.'

'Just a second Desmond. Here – have some more.' He held out the bottle again and peered at Carson short-sightedly. 'He's going, isn't he? Arthur?'

'People keep saying that, but I assure you I have no inside knowledge.'

'He must. He's finished. His bottle's gone. You can see it as well as I can.'

Carson pursed his lips and made no answer.

'I just want to tell you that I'm backing you – for what it's worth. You're the only choice.'

In silence Carson sipped his champagne. Then he put his hand on the QC's arm. 'Thank you, Beatty. I realise a change is on the cards. As a matter of fact I intend to ask him tomorrow just what he proposes to do. I can't tell you how much I appreciate your support. If he goes it'll be rough.'

'Will you face up to them?'

'I've thought about it and I can't see any alternative. If we don't we may as well pack it in. But it's a gamble.'

'Right!' said the Rooster emphatically. 'I'm with you. And I won't be the only one. Packham's bound to back you, if only to scotch Gillan. What about the hard men?'

Carson held out his hand palm down, and in the classic gesture tilted it from one side to the other. 'We'll just have to see. Let's leave it there, shall we?' he murmured as another group edged closer to the table looking for food.

'You'll let me know,' said the Rooster moving away.

'Just as soon as I hear tomorrow.'

In the oval room, Shamus Conway had been regaling Jo and a number of other guests with his past life and future hopes. 'Come on, dear. I was told to get you some food. I'm on a diet myself.' He patted his stomach. 'Just a lettuce leaf and a piece of *very* lean fish! It's hell. If it weren't for this TM I'm doing, I just couldn't carry on.'

'Like yoga, isn't it?' asked someone.

'Trans-continental meditation – that's what I call it! It's American and it's terribly sedating and we all do it together. I love doing things together, don't you! I've decided I'm a people's person. We're all people's persons in the TM class. And terribly ecumenical. As a Catholic it's shaken my faith in Holy Church, it really has – the prettiest boys are *all* Protestant. *Anyway* this friend of mine who induced me or introduced me or whatever you do, he explained that what most of us are doing – those of us, that is, who lead an intensely active intellectual and dare I say, *emotional* life!' He threw up his eyes. 'Wishful thinker that I am! *?Well, what* we're doing is putting a thousand volts through a two hundred and forty volt plug. You see! The plug, that's the body, this frail vessel of clay just ain't up to it. Hence all the ills that flesh is heir to – insomnia, impotence, enervation, constipation – the lot! That's where TM comes in – total relaxation. Deep deep sleep – we all hold hands and just drrrrift away . . . restoring the body to all its vigour! And it's so good for Larry – he *adores* it!'

'And who is Larry?' asked Jo.

'Larry the *liver* dear. You must look after Larry. He's very important. Larry was being rather tiresome recently, especially in the morning, but after two weeks of TM he's a new boy. Re-born. Like our – what do you call them? – born-again Christians.'

'Don't talk to me about born-again Christians,' said a very loud Belfast voice. 'It's a pity that some of them were ever born the first time!'

A heavy hand slapped Conway on the shoulder. 'Oh Bodsy! Don't do that. I didn't see you.'

'Well, why the hell don't you take off those sunglasses. No wonder you can't see.'

'Take off my shades! I couldn't do that dear. I'd feel indecently exposed!'

'One of these days I'll have to do you.'

'Promises! Promises!'

'Give you a bit of *decent* exposure for a change!'

The newcomer was Basil Bowman, known as Bodsy, a local sculptor whose reputation owed as much to his flair for self-promotion as it did to his artistic talent. His was the earthy full-blooded approach, defying the establishment and horrifying the *bien-pensants* of all sides. He was a big man, the reddish-brown face framed in masses of unkempt black hair, shirt open to the waist revealing a chest like a dark rug. Jo Scanlon had not met him before. Shamus did the introductions with the rider, 'Jo is here with Desmond Carson and I'm chaperoning her. So keep your distance you great shaggy dog!' But Bodsy was already turning his luminous eyes on the girl. His gaze was long and unblinking.

She smiled. 'Am I getting the sculptural treatment? Do you see me as a great round Henry Moore or as an elongated Giacometti?'

'I see you as a Bowman. No, that's a lot of balls,' said Bodsy. 'I see you as a lovely girl. Don't listen to what Conway says. I'm just a workin' class Protestant who cuts stone for a living. I'm harmless . . . You could take me anywhere!' He grinned broadly, grabbed a bottle from a passing tray and filled their glasses. 'Is Des Carson your man?'

The directness of the question made her laugh. 'My boss,' she said.

'Yes, but is he your man?'

She capitulated, avoiding his gaze. 'You're too inquisitive!'

Philosophically he emptied his glass and refilled it. 'I've got a woman here somewhere. She's in wonderful shape. Rich and moist as fruit cake.

220

But . . .' he sighed. 'She's too attainable. No challenge. No excitement.'
He tapped his head. 'It's all up here. Sex. Too early for me yet. It's only
when I'm full that woman becomes mysterious again. Ah, here's your
man.'

Carson, who had been waylaid again, was coming towards them.
'Sorry, darling.'

'I'm being well entertained, don't worry.'

'We were ambushed,' said Shamus, 'but I've been looking after her
like a Mother Superior.'

'My mother's a great fan of yours,' said Bodsy. He and Carson had
met only fleetingly on public occasions.

'Is she? That's nice,' said Carson politely.

'She's seventy. Unionist party all her life. She met you once when you
were speaking at Larne. As far as she's concerned, you make all the right
noises.'

'Long may it continue. Give her my best wishes. I didn't realise you
were . . .' said Carson automatically falling into his constituency
manner.

'God no! Not me,' said Bodsy firmly. 'Politically I'm a mixed-up kid.
All this kowtowing to a moronic monarchy gets up my non-conformist
nose. All this Papist mumbo-jumbo and blood sacrifice for Ireland's
freedom makes me puke. And the last thing I want is the good-livin'
born-again boys who would like to turn this province into a Methodist
monastery. So what can I do? I Protest. I'm the only genuine Pro*test*ant
left.'

'Now then, you great hairy bigot,' cried Shamus, 'enough of your
sectarian filth!'

'I'm only explaining my position,' said Bodsy mildly. 'Look!' he
turned to Carson and his tone become confidential. 'I just want to say
one thing. From what I can gather, big brother in London is putting us
in our place, taking our privileges away from us . . . yes?' Carson
nodded non-committally. 'Well, I have no great feelings about the
Specials but we don't like being treated like bloody bare-arsed
aborigines. So we stand up to the buggers! We've got to keep a little
self-respect.' He grinned. 'The oul mother comin' out eh?'

'Be sure and give her my warmest regards,' said Carson. He took Jo
by the arm and led her back towards the dining-room, exchanging
greetings and the odd badinage with the few people he knew well,
nodding to acquaintances in the semi-darkness. En route he added sotto
voce comments for Jo's benefit. 'Harry Glinn, made a mint in the motor

business' – this was a very fat man in a gleaming mohair suit. 'Owns horses – don't know who the popsy he's pawing is. Hullo Hugh. How's the battle?' This last was addressed to a tall balding young man who shook a friendly fist in answer. 'Our militant peer,' murmured Carson, 'now fighting hard to stop Gillan's people cutting down a stand of beech trees to widen a road – he's a fanatical tree man. On the National Trust. Just divorced.'

'What a mine of information you are.'

'All useless.' He kissed her lightly on the head. 'No shortage of characters here – that's certain,' she said.

'The Ulster disease! Especially prevalent in politics. No shortage of characters but a shortage of roles for them to play. The fight for jobs used to be confined to the ruling party. Now your lot want a piece of the action!'

'Why not?'

'Why not, indeed? I always liked the remark of Balfour's when he was Chief Secretary for Ireland. Some Irish Member had shouted, "All we want is justice". "Justice be damned!" yelled Balfour. "There isn't enough to go round!"'

'A typical piece of Unionist arrogance. And yet it's *your* lot who go on about law and order and meting out justice!'

'Mea culpa!' said Carson with mock contrition. He drew her into the shadows and kissed her.

'You're being very daring tonight,' she said.

'At this stage of a party, people, like justice, are blind – anaesthetised with liquor or lust.' He took her elbow. 'It's funny how the finest words become two-faced – like "justice". When I hear the phrase "peace with justice" – which on the face of it no-one could take exception to, my hackles rise. Like Herman Goering when he heard the word "culture" I reach for my revolver.'

She laughed incredulously. 'In God's name, why?'

'It's become a specious justification for violence. It's a way of putting lawful authority in the dock. It's now an IRA slogan. It's double-talk for murder.' She stopped and looked into his face. He smiled uncertainly. 'Goes deep, doesn't it?' She was silent. 'Can you cope?' He searched her face anxiously. Her lips brushed his ear.

'Have I a choice?' she whispered. He hugged her to him. The tension melted. 'Come on! Either take me home or feed me.'

Most of the guests had been served and they were now almost alone before the long table arranged with bowls of flowers and epergnes of

222

fruit set among the galantines of fowl and chaudfroids of fish, marbled green and white, couched on their beds of ice. There were dishes of smoked eel and salmon, cold sirloin, Italian salamis, smoked Kassler ribs and Westphalian ham, a circle of Brie that overflowed its platter in creamy waves. Viennese gateaux and luscious Genoa cakes on silver stands interspersed with ornate ice-buckets holding still and sparkling wines. Decanters of claret flanked hot-plates bearing gently steaming entree dishes.

The white-coated Italian in charge beamed at Jo. 'Cold or . . . hot, madame?'

'Someone mentioned Polish ravioli?' ventured Carson.

The Italian made a moue of disapproval. 'Too heavy, too much onion for madame . . . I have a salmi of pheasant . . . excellent! And to start perhaps . . . a gravelax? It is very light, madame.'

'What's gravelax?' asked Carson.

'Sort of pickled salmon – Swedish,' explained Jo. 'Try it.'

'Wine?' said the major-domo indicating the choice with a sweep of his hand.

'Let's stick to champagne.'

He installed them at a small supper-table set in a corner and brought them the food they had chosen, with a fresh bottle of Bollinger.

'To us,' said Carson, raising his glass. 'On our first real evening out. Let's be anti-social. I'm going to keep you to myself from now on. Are you glad you came?'

Unexpectedly she paused, frowning, sipping her wine. 'Oh, I love all this,' she gestured with her hand, 'the atmosphere, the luxury. What woman wouldn't? But it all seems rather unreal. Not just the Castle, but the whole situation. I just can't believe that outside it's Friday night in County Antrim, with the country on the brink of – you know better than I do.'

'Fiddling while Rome burns us?' She hardly smiled. 'Who's the puritan now? It's just time out for a few hours, darling.' He was jollying her along.

She put her hand in his. 'I'll be better when I've had some food. I think I'm just a little overwhelmed.'

'Forget it, love. It's been a rather sudden exposure.'

She smiled, 'To your social life!'

'You mock me,' he said. 'I'm just the boy from Banbridge and under no illusions as to why I'm here.' The pheasant appeared and as they ate he told her of the Rooster's declaration of intent.

223

'I'm glad for you,' she said, 'but the more I think of it the more terrifying . . .'

Gently he cut her short. 'We agreed – that is no longer for discussion!'

There were only a few other people left in the dining-room. Enough conversation for confidential comfort. In the rooms outside, the pulse of the music beat on relentlessly, and the level of voices and laughter seemed even higher. A sense of release and well-being was creeping over Carson. 'My father always said that champagne got into the bloodstream faster than anything else. It's the bubbles. To him of course it was something he prescribed as a tonic – for his private patients.' He poured some more Bollinger. 'Are you having any of that luscious sweet stuff?'

'Yes. To hell with it! Get me something creamy. I'm going to look for the loo.'

As she was leaving the room, their hostess appeared accompanied by a ruffled teddy-bear figure, with the slightly intense air of the academic. 'Gerry's been looking for you,' said the Countess and led Jo away.

'What a pleasant surprise,' said Carson, grasping the newcomer's hand. 'What are you doing in the Black North?'

It was Gerry Ryan, a senior minister in the government of the Irish Republic. One of the more intellectual of the Southern politicians, he made great play with a Presbyterian grandmother who not only acted as antidote to a strongly Republican background but allowed him to claim a special instinctive knowledge of how Ulster Protestants felt.

'Family business. I go back tomorrow.' Ministers from the Republic did not make official visits to Northern Ireland. A few tried to preserve the myth that Southern Ministers had an up-to-date and personal knowledge of conditions in the Northern part of their sundered island. These relied on 'personal business' as a cover for their rare excursions into what the majority of their constituents regarded as alien territory. Gerry Ryan, under the distrait exterior a very astute political animal, made the effort oftener than most. Carson had met him on a number of occasions but he was very sure that the present encounter was no coincidence. They sat down at a table. Whiskey was procured – Ryan didn't drink champagne. After a brief exchange on the Dungannons, who had close connections with the Republic, Ryan ran his hand through his tousled locks.

'You must be worried about the present situation. Do you think you can carry it off?'

'I don't see why not.'

224

'You mean your people will accept the transfer of security? They'll let the Specials go? Without a fight?' It was clear that Ryan had already been in touch with Joe Maguire and his colleagues.

'They're not going.' said Carson. 'They're being re-formed, expanded and strengthened.'

'That's hardly the intention of the British Government.'

'Maybe not, but it's ours.'

Ryan stared at him. 'I'll be frank with you. If it comes to a clash between the Government here, and Westminster, the Catholic community here is very much at risk. In that kind of situation there would be enormous pressures on us to become involved. That's the last thing we want and I'm sure it's the last thing you want. But naturally we're very concerned at the turn events have taken over the past couple of days.'

'I appreciate your position, of course. But you must see that we haven't a lot of room for movement. You, with your special knowledge of the North, will see that more clearly than your colleagues.'

Ryan demurred but purred. 'Of course I do, of course I do. But what happens if the British Government insist on their pound of flesh?'

'Then there'll be blood on the saddle. It's as simple as that. No doubt when you people in Dublin were urging the Foreign Office to produce a so-called political initiative,' Carson allowed a fleeting smile to cross his face as he reflected on the irony of the situation, 'you must have pointed out the dangers, if the initiative produced nothing but a bitter reaction from the Protestants!'

Ryan shifted nervously on his chair and ran his hands through his hair again. 'I admit, I admit that we have pressed for some kind of political movement but we certainly did not envisage this kind of proposal, which, no doubt, acts as a sop to Catholic feeling, but is hardly going to make it easier to give Catholics a significant role in government which is what they and we have been asking for. And that's a fact!'

'I believe you,' said Carson, and he meant it. Ryan's reaction was the same as Joe Maguire's would be. It made sense. 'So no-one's happy,' continued Carson. He lit a cigarette. 'What a cockup! The trouble is *we* are left to pick up the pieces.'

'It's Poynings' Law all over again,' said Ryan brightly. 'We suffered under it. Now it's your turn!' As Carson looked blank, 'Sir Edward Poynings, Viceroy about 1490 . . .?'

'Remind me,' said Carson. 'My memory of the history of English oppression is not as vivid as yours.'

'No Irish Parliament was allowed to pass anything that hadn't first been approved by the English. Might I, without offence, draw the analogy with . . . Stormont? Westminster tells you what to enact but you carry the can when it goes wrong.'

'Responsibility without power – the harlot in reverse,' grunted Carson. 'I assure you the thought has occurred.'

'Why don't you come in with us?' smiled Ryan. 'Sample a taste of real independence. You'd find us easy to deal with. How could a million Protestants go wrong? You'd take the place over!'

'You could have a point,' said Carson, 'but I don't think it's a runner just at this moment! We'd have to prepare the ground first – there's a few changes we'd like to see in your constitution . . .'

'No problem!'

'Extradition?'

Ryan laughed. 'In a United Ireland it wouldn't exist! To be serious though,' he dropped his voice, 'I hear there might be a possibility of Arthur Packham going . . . ?'

'Pure speculation.'

'I know. I know. But if he did go . . . I suppose Gillan would be the man . . . ?'

'He's the deputy.'

Ryan's eyes were on him, vigilant, unblinking. 'You wouldn't have a go yourself?'

'I've got enough problems!'

'What do you make of this strike call? I heard it on the news tonight,' said Ryan, changing tack.

'You know as much about it as I do. Could be nothing. Could be bigger than we expect. There's a lot of feeling among the Protestant grass roots and a number of very determined gentlemen. This strike is a straw in the wind and if I were in Whitehall I'd go easy on this initiative.' He rose from his seat. 'Forgive me, I'd better find this girl of mine. She doesn't know the lay-out of this place.' They parted on the understanding that he would be Ryan's guest next time he was in Dublin. He was reasonably sure that his hints of a back-lash would be taken seriously in the Southern capital. But the unthinkable kept returning to his mind. *Real* sovereignty. Yes, that would be worth a battle.

It was 2.30 a.m. Many of the guests had gone. He was with Jo in the long gallery that served as a library. The sole illumination came from two bluish spotlights in the centre of the floor, which had been cleared of rugs for dancing. The ceaseless music from the stereo throbbed, all-pervading, but more subdued. It was difficult to tell how many people were in the room. In the deep alcoves down each side between the bookcases the sofas were occupied by bodies. In the semi-darkness was the odd gleam of naked flesh. It required no great imagination to decode the moans and breathless entreaties – the imbecile earnestness of lust. The air was heavy with sweet noxious smoke and every now and then a bottle rolled across the floor as someone stumbled against it. Carson was slumped on an ottoman, one leg on the floor, Jo huddled against him, curled up on the cushions. They had danced together and kissed and felt each other's bodies and talked aimlessly and endlessly, as lovers do.

Across the patch of brightness on the floor drifted, every now and then, two figures locked together, almost as if they were in the last stages of exhaustion, like an old newsreel of a dance marathon from the nineteen-thirties. Bodsy Bowman, after a frenzied solo performance when he sang some tuneless ballad of his own, had collapsed on the floor, his head on the lap of a pretty creature with hair drawn back like some serene and plump Madonna. Slowly she stroked his face. Carson had drunk too much and had lost the will to make the effort to leave. He was half-asleep when he was roused by the prodding finger of his mistress. 'Look! Look!' she whispered.

A new couple had appeared in the spotlight, two figures in long low-necked evening dresses. The shorter was wearing high-heeled shoes, the other was in stockinged feet. They moved with a supple, swaying languor looking into each other's eyes with fluttering lids. The tall one had a finely chiselled face. The broad shoulders were smooth and golden, marred only by the deep salt-cellars under the collarbones. The blonde hair was caught behind the ears with a clasp and shining with lacquer. The smaller one was paler, the bare shoulders fleshier, the dark eyes heavily made up and the ears starred with diamonds. But the chin was too square and the ankles under the long skirt too thick. They stood, pelvis and bosom pressed together, undulating in the eerie bluish light. For a moment the face of the smaller was turned towards the alcove.

'My God!' said Carson. 'It's Dungannon.' It was their first sight of their host.

'Let's go,' said Jo, dragging Carson to his feet. 'This place. Oh! Let's go.' Without leave-taking, they made their way down the stairs through the hallway and out under the portico into the night. A chill wind blew from the Lough. The cars were waiting, engines running to keep warm. The escorts greeted him, cheerfully as always. These men, thought Carson. decent policemen, family men, have been waiting here for hours to look after me. Protectively he put his arm round Jo's shoulders as they sank into their seats. The feeling uppermost in his mind was one of self-disgust.

First thing next morning, Lefaux was in his office with his chief Press Officer preparing to ring the Prime Minister's home with a quick roundup of press reaction to the events of the day before. So much had happened. The PM's press conference. The Party meeting. Then his television broadcast, quotes from many of the leading political and public figures and then, finally, pushed away on a centre page and clearly regarded by the papers as very low priority, the announcement of the strike. The media were clearly suffering from news indigestion. Local views reported were split into two camps, those who accepted, even with reservations, Westminster's right to dispose of security matters, and the hardliners who repudiated such a right and regarded the new proposals as a sell-out. Gillan was still the front-runner on the 'no surrender' line, but leaks from the Party meeting, coupled with the Prime Minister's outburst at the press conference, had so confused the issue and the commentators that most of them fell back on phrases such as 'only when the government's intentions have been clarified will it be possible etc.' Meantime they would wait and see.

Reaction in the Catholic papers North and South could hardly have brought much comfort to Oliver Birch and his masters. The initiative, they seemed to say, had been so blurred and blunted by conflicting interpretations as to be meaningless. It took no account of minority aspirations for a say in government and for a recognition of the all-Irish dimension to Ulster affairs. Joe Maguire was quoted as saying that 'the British Government might as well have saved their breath to cool their porridge.' For Arthur Packham personally, it was not a good press. He was criticised for lack of clear leadership and for allowing his Cabinet to speak with different voices. His performance on television received few bouquets. One paper, in a thinly veiled reference to the meeting at Gillan's house, ran a conspiracy story without naming names. Though conclusions were not openly expressed, the drift of the reporting was all too clear – the Prime Minister was losing the confidence of his colleagues. The English papers had no Ulster headlines but confined themselves to factual reports of the changes, and to quotes from party spokesmen and 'informed sources'. Only the *Daily Telegraph* pointed up the danger of a clash arising from the depth of Protestant feeling in the province.

It was with some trepidation that Tom Lefaux lifted the telephone. His fears were not realised. The Prime Minister heard him out with hardly a question or a comment. Then he said simply, 'I didn't expect anything different, did you?' When Lefaux was apologising for the failure of his department to produce better coverage his regrets were brushed aside. 'Say no more, dear chap. I accept full responsibility. I am only too aware that the whole issue has been a monumental balls-up from the word go. All I can say is that I intend to make my position unequivocally clear before the day is out. Ask Stewart to give me a ring will you? I want a Cabinet this afternoon. It's rather important. If we have it down here we might escape the press. About three o'clock I propose. See you then and . . .' There was a pause. 'Thank you Tom, for all your help.' Then he rang off.

'He took it far too well,' said Lefaux thoughtfully. 'I think he's put it all behind him.' He looked at his press officer. 'Maybe we ought to prepare the ground a bit, eh?'

Carson was awakened by the telephone at 9.15 a.m. With difficulty he found the receiver. An aching head, a foul mouth and the unwelcome memory of the previous evening already crowding back. It was Stewart Taylor. His appointment with the PM had been changed. There was a Cabinet meeting at the PM's home. Would he go down beforehand for lunch at one o'clock? Were the others invited for lunch? No, just Carson. As his head fell back on the pillow, he realised his pulse was beating very fast. He tried to control his elation. There couldn't be any other explanation, surely! This was the pick-me-up he needed. He scrambled out of bed and gave an exultant shout as he entered the shower.

Mun Martin arrived at the Gillan farm just before one o'clock. He found his colleague in his study on the telephone. Clearly stalling some journalist. With a deep sigh he put the receiver down. 'That was the BBC. They think Packham's going. They know about the Cabinet Meeting.'

'Well!' said Mun. 'That's a turn-up for the book. I wondered why Packham had called a meeting for Saturday afternoon. It's one of his shooting days.'

'He's shot us down, that's for sure,' muttered Gillan.

'Why do you say that?' asked Mun in surprise. 'It opens the door. No more behind the scenes. We're out in the open.'

'For God's sake!' said Gillan irritably. 'We've missed the boat. I can't resign *now*. It would look bloody ridiculous if *he's* going. We had a great platform: "Keep security in Ulster hands". You heard Carson yesterday at the Party meeting. He's saying practically the same thing now! He's stealing our clothes! And Packham's setting it up for him.'

'You think he's leaked this resignation?'

'Of course!' said Gillan impatiently. 'They guessed I might go and they've spiked my guns.' He turned angrily to Martin. 'I *knew* I should have gone yesterday.'

'All right. All right!' The Martin temper was rising too. 'But you weren't saying that in this house two nights ago!' There was silence as Mun strode up and down the room. Then he spoke more coolly. 'We can still make it.' He perked up. 'Look at the voting yesterday afternoon! Carson's not eveybody's cup of tea. He wouldn't be Mullin's choice – and Wylie swings a few votes, I can tell you. You could get every Loyalist with you if you play your cards right. I'm telling you!'

Gillan looked more cheerful. 'You're a hard man to beat, Mun.'

'Look! There's no time like the present. Let's make a wee list of all the doubtfuls, all the possibles. If he goes, there'll have to be an election within a couple of days – the Party can't be left without a Leader at a time like this. We've got a head start on Carson, despite everything. Here! Gimme a sheet of paper.'

Carson had just arrived, in good time, at the Prime Minister's home. He had talked to both Butler and Kedge and was clear in his mind as to what he had to do. He stood now in the library, drinking a glass of beer while his host, in an old cardigan with leather patches on the sleeves, was endeavouring to find the BBC one o'clock news on a battered transistor. 'My wife keeps moving it to the music station,' he said testily. 'Ah, got it.' The voice faded up. 'First the headlines. Reports as yet unconfirmed that the Prime Minister, Sir Arthur Packham, is about to announce his resignation. A suspect bomb on the main Belfast–Dublin railway line.' Packham switched the radio off. He turned to Carson with a sad smile. 'Well. That's it. Sorry to be so dramatic but I honestly didn't know if they were going to say anything.'

Carson was pale. 'It's true then Arthur?'

'Yes. That's what I want to talk about. I'm at a loss to know how on earth the BBC got wind of it. They rang here twice this morning. Shane was the only one who knew and he wouldn't breathe a word. Never

231

mind. I'm just sorry that our colleagues have to learn about it this way. Sit down.' He settled in his chair and briefly laid before Carson, as he had to the Attorney the night before, the thinking behind his decision, and his hopes that it would alert the British Government to the real danger of a constitutional clash. Then he said, 'Why am I telling *you* all this? Because, as Minister of Home Affairs, security is at the very heart of your responsibilities.' Packham paused for a moment. Carson's heart missed a beat. Christ! Had he jumped to conclusions too soon? No. Packham was smiling. 'But also, and more importantly, because I would like to see you take over.'

Forewarned though he had been, Carson still found himself stammering like a young MP being offered his first government appointment. 'I don't know what to say . . . Prime Minister.' The official title slipped out instead of the usual Christian name. 'I shall do my best . . . not to let you down.'

Packham held up his hand. 'Please. I'm going to support you, Desmond, because I believe you are the right man. But you realise that the leadership of the Party is not in my gift? And I shall, of course have to remain neutral.' He smiled broadly. 'But I think . . . we can help. Our friend Gillan's stock is not quite what it was, I gather. But he's a formidable campaigner and he and Mun Martin have already been at work. But we can talk about that later. What concerns me is the next few days. Wednesday is the earliest we can have an election. I shall, of course, tender my resignation today after Cabinet, but the Governor won't formally accept it till the new man is appointed. I shall be in the saddle till then. And I'm very conscious that we have got to get a grip on the situation at once. I don't know how you feel, but if we're going to keep the Party from falling apart we've got to dig our heels in.'

'Standing up to the steam-roller?'

'Yes. Reluctantly I have come round to the view that the timing of these changes and the manner of their introduction must be left entirely to us. Unionist reaction − right across the board − during the past forty-eight hours, the Larchfield raid, the announcement of this strike − whatever its effect − this all convinces me that there is no alternative. It's not a prospect I relish.' He looked at Carson, almost tentatively it seemed, as if already authority was slipping from him.

Carson reassured, chose his words. 'I think you must have already gathered − especially after what I said yesterday − that I am in total agreement.'

'I know you are aware of the implications and of the possible consequences.'

'Of defiance? Yes. We shall need to play rough. We shall, in fact, be relying on, even mobilising anti-British feeling to strengthen our hand. We could find ourselves siding with the strikers.'

'I know. I know,' said Packham grimly.

'At best, it will be a war of nerves.'

'That's why I want *you*.'

Carson shifted self-consciously in his chair. He hoped he was looking suitably resolute. But as he spoke the reality of the situation facing him was only beginning to break through.

'I think you'll just have to play it by ear,' Packham was saying. 'The beauty is that Gillan will have to go along with you – he's in a cleft stick!'

'Supposing we get through this? What do I do with him then?'

Packham laughed. 'I'm glad it will be your problem. Leave him in Trade – that's his proper milieu!'

'You're raising this question of policy this afternoon I take it?'

'I think so, don't you? It will give you a chance to establish *your* views – *and* your claim!' The Prime Minister stood up. He put his arm on Carson's shoulder. 'Come and have some lunch. Here, take a glass of sherry with you.' He poured two generous bumpers. 'You'll enjoy it Desmond. I've enjoyed every moment of it. It may look black now, but we'll get through. One thing I *can* do this afternoon.'

'What?'

'Make sure, whatever the niceties of Cabinet etiquette, that none of my colleagues is in any doubt as to where my vote is going!'

That afternoon the strike HQ of the Ulster Loyalist Committe was taking shape. Essential office furniture such as filing cabinets, a duplicating machine, typewriters, were already in situ. Sympathetic ETU personnel were busy installing telephones. Peter Osborne, the admin manager, was well down his check-list of items 'For Action'. The dramatic news of Packham's resignation had been received with grim satisfaction as vindication of the decision to go ahead – if the Prime Minister was resigning for the reasons given in his official statement 'to bring home to Her Majesty's Government the realities of the present situation' then the Ulster Government really was under pressure. All the more reason to stop the rot as soon as possible. The three journalists who had turned up at the first of Denny McNamee's press conferences – most of their colleagues had been dispatched to the Prime Minister's home in County Armagh – were surprised and impressed by the efficiency of the organisation at this early stage, and by the professionalism

233

of the press handout. Already it was 'on the stone' at the *Belfast Telegraph* with a two-column heading in the early edition. Denny McNamee and his friends at the Ulster Loyalists' Committee – the ULC – were satisfied that from now on their efforts would be taken seriously. He had been booked for a BBC piece that evening despite the enormous pressure on air-time from the resignation bombshell. Preparations were paying off – the press handout had been put together that morning by an anonymous member of the NUJ, aided by a university lecturer.

There was no shortage of well-qualified volunteers rallying to the cause. Brian Kedge was talking to Peter Osborne in a small inner room. He had already spoken to Carson on the telephone and was aware of the delicacy of his position on the Committee now that his friend's hat was openly in the ring. The BBC's political correspondent, reporting from Armagh, had tipped Carson as favourite for the succession and reported 'official circles' as believing that his successful tenure of Home Affairs had won for him the Prime Minister's personal preference. In an interview Packham himself, though scrupulously refusing to speculate on his successor since that was now a matter for the Parliamentary Party, had pointedly stressed security as the crucial area for the incoming administration. Kedge however was still convinced of the need to win the support of the Mullins faction for his candidate or, if that were not possible, to at least neutralise them. The antipathy went back several months to a widely reported speech of Carson's in which he had castigated those 'on the lunatic fringe of the Unionist Party who have a miracle cure for everything except our real problems'. This assumed reference to his faith-healing Mullins had never forgotten. Kedge had tried the bandwagon approach but without cutting much ice.

'If Carson's such a cert then why are you worried,' jeered Osborne who echoed in everything the views of his master.

'Look,' said Kedge trying another tack, 'I admit I'm biased, but Des Carson is the sort of man we need. And he's got nothing against Wylie. In fact if Wylie is thinking of a seat – and don't tell me he isn't – we might be able to do you a lotta good.'

'You mean we might do *you* a lot of good!'

Kedge laughed. 'All right Peter, all right. Just do me one favour – ask Harry Harrmon about Carson.'

'What do you mean?'

'Get an *unbiased* opinion. Just ask Harry what *he* thinks of Carson. That's all. OK?'

'I will,' said Osborne. 'He'll be in later. They're workin' away like niggers his lot. On Monday morning there'll be barricades on every main route in and out of this city and in most of the other towns in the province.'

'Good. Good.'

'What's more Megs reckons they'll have power output down 40 per cent by Monday evening, so the squeeze will be on from the start. You'll have the permits ready, won't you?' Kedge was responsible for the printing of ULC permits to enable those on essential services to collect petrol. As he was leaving, Osborne called after him. 'Wylie's got the Rally tonight in the Ulster Hall. That'll really get us off the ground!'

Others were active that afternoon. At Loughside, Oliver Birch had just sent off a lengthy telex to his Permanent Under Secretary at the Foreign Office. It made melancholy reading. The initiative had run into really heavy weather with the majority, and the minority response had been ambiguous and on the whole disappointing. Carson, the Home Affairs hard-liner, looked like the successor. He would not make things easier. A strike announced by a group of Protestant trade unionists would probably peter out like previous similar exercises. But he had already spoken to the GOC about the dangers of the Army becoming involved in a confrontation with Protestant workers. The GOC would play it very low-key while ensuring that essential services were maintained and that there would be minimum disruption of economic activity. He, Birch, would arrange to speak to Carson as soon as possible.

James Gillan had had a bad day. The shock of the resignation had been followed by news that two of his original supporters now appeared to be doubtful. As he had expected, Carson had, with Packham's connivance, hogged the Cabinet, taking an uncompromising line, coupled with a plea for party unity which Lefaux had referred to as statesmanlike. Gillan was now pinning his faith on the Wylie Mullins connection.

235

The Saturday night counter-attractions of pub and club had no effect on the attendance at the Ulster Hall. For those who thirsted after the pure and heady spirit of old-time Bible fundamentalism, Wylie Mullins had no competition, even from the powerful tug of television. Long before seven-thirty, the huge blue and yellow chamber was packed. The floor, the U-shaped galleries, the amphitheatre behind the platform, were crammed with expectant faces. This same hall had seen, during the past hundred years, the recurring pageant of Ulster's history. Sir Edward Carson, arming for rebellion against the Crown, fist outstretched with the cry 'Home Rule is Rome Rule'. Churchill, in those days a Liberal, preaching independence for the whole of Ireland, pelted with stones, refused a hearing and rescued by police from the howling mob. And Craigavon, granite-faced Prime Minister of the infant state of Northern Ireland, thundering 'No Surrender' and 'Not an Inch'. They had all stood on that same platform. Tonight – Wylie Mullins, preacher, healer, quasi-politician – a lesser Savonarola calling a people to arms.

An organ started playing softly, not the great pipe-organ behind the podium, but electric, heavily and effectively amplified. A young man in his twenties, fresh-faced, bespectacled and sober-suited, opened the proceedings at the microphone. 'Brothers and sisters – welcome! A warm welcome, a deep welcome, a very-glad-to-see-you welcome, old friends, new friends, whoever you are, wherever you come from – welcome to this great rally of praise and witness tonight. But first – Praise the Lord! – let us sing!'

They rose to their feet, some clutching Bibles, two thousand of them, and filled the Ulster Hall with their voices. A Gospel song from the Deep South appropriately entitled, *'He is Here! He is Here!'* And suddenly there he *was* on the dais as the ceiling lights were doused and two specially installed arc lights hit the lectern draped in the Red Hand of Ulster flag. Thunderous applause and hammering with feet on the floor. Mullins raised both hands above his head and turned from side to side in greeting. Gradually, silence was restored.

'Thank you, my friends. God bless you. God bless you,' he intoned. 'My friends, I'm taking as my text tonight Joel 3, verse 14. "Multitudes,

multitudes in the valley of decision. Multitudes, multitudes in the valley of decision." Tonight brothers and sisters, we stand, Ulster stands, in the valley of decision. Our Protestant heritage is in danger. We are menaced by the enemy from without and from *within*. The Ulster Special Constabulary, our strong shield and buckler throughout the years of peril, has been sentenced to a lingering death.

'No. No!' came the response.

'Make no mistake! For all his talk about re-grouping and re-forming, the Prime Minister knows the bitter truth – the Specials are not being *re*-formed. They're being *re*-jected! – that's why he's *re*-signing!' A great roar swept the hall. 'And why? Why is one of the finest forces in the world being swept into the dustbin? Why must we endure this latest surrender in the long series of surrenders and humiliations that month after month, year after year, whittles away our Protestant way of life? Why? Why? I'll tell you my friends. To keep the Roman Catholics happy! To fill the insatiable maw of Rome!' The last sentence, despite the microphone, was almost drowned out by the frenzied bellow of defiance which greeted the reference to Rome. 'For one thing is sure. Rome never gives up. She is working day and night to undermine the liberties of Protestants, aided – may the Lord forgive them! – aided by so-called Protestants riddled with the poison of ecumenism, the delight and joy of Satan himself. Aided and abetted by those same men who, at their ordination, subscribed to the Confession of Faith which sees the Pope of Rome in his true light – that anti-Christ, that man of Sin, that son of perdition!' Mullins raised his arms in imprecation. 'Save us, O Lord, from the curse of Popery, whose name is Babylon, the mother of harlots, the great whore that sitteth upon many waters. Her golden cup is full of abominations!'

Again came the roar of approval and shouts of 'Hallelujah!'

'Multitudes, multitudes in the valley of decision. Ask yourselves tonight, who will help us to decide? Where does salvation lie? Let us not, my friends, look to Westminster! Let us not look to Stormont, to an ecumenical Prime Minister whose time is up!'

Laughter and shouts of 'Traitor!'

'No, my friends. Salvation lies not there. But I'll tell you where salvation lies. It lies in you, yourselves. It lies in the ordinary, incorruptible, invincible, inviolate, Protestants of Ulster!' The storm of applause broke like a massive wave. 'I bring you good news, my friends. Our present troubles are but the shadows of the deliverance to come. The time for action is at hand. The time to say: Enough! Not another inch! My friends, the Loyalists of Ulster are on the march. While the false prophets have slept, some of us have been planning for this day. The world has seen the pomp of Rome. Now it shall see the power of Protestants. On Monday . . . we shall bring this whole Province to a standstill!' The drumming of feet and swelling voices rose in crescendo. 'We ask nothing but the right to defend ourselves. We ask only that the security forces are controlled by Ulster men and women.' Amid mounting excitement he continued. 'Will you help us? Will you help Ulster?'

'Yes, Yes,' they roared in answer.

'On Monday we want the support and the prayers of every Protestant in Ulster. In the words of the Protestant martyt, Latimer, as the Romish priests burnt him at the stake: "Let us this day light such a candle as will never again be put out"! If we stand together we can bring the craven spirits of Westminster to their senses. We can silence the factories. We can darken the sky. We can stop the rot once and for all. Yes! Multitudes in the valley of decision . . . The hour is late. The cohorts of Rome are massing against us. Fellow Protestants! Will you make your decision now, to stand up and be counted?'

Two thousand voices roared back fortissimo 'Yes!'

'Will you remain strong and steadfast come what may, until our goal is reached?'

'Yes! Yes!' came the thunderous response.

Mullins raised his arms high above his shoulders and tilted back his head. 'Let us pray to Jehovah, the God of our fathers, that layeth the beams of his chambers on the waters, that maketh the clouds his chariot, that walketh upon the wings of the wind. O Lord! save Ulster, we pray. Save us from the Irish Republican Army, save us from Popery, save us from the arbitrary power of Westminster and the tyranny of politicians. Give us strength, O Lord, to fight for our liberties and to keep Ulster Protestant. Save us from the scarlet iniquities of Rome and from the curse of ecumenism . . .' The voice ebbed and flowed like a tide. On and on the litany rolled.

Outside, through that October night, across the Province, from the coastal plain of Limavady to the sea-port of Larne, from the lake-land of Enniskillen to the industrial concrete of Castlereagh, the night-shift was going on duty. Grim-faced men, who had heard the appeal of their shop-stewards; some of them elated at the thought of the coming battle, joking and hectoring their fellows; others morose, far from

238

enthusiastic: another bloody political strike, what was the point? A few days loss of wages, then back again, nothing changed. On Monday, not everyone would be absent from work. But like it or not, unknown to them, the charge had been laid. The strike, in Osborne's words, was already off the ground. It would fly higher than any one of them had foreseen.

All day Sunday, Packham remained in Armagh, withdrawn like a bishop *in partibus infidelium,* already gelt of power – without a throne. Billy Dixon, when he rang up to report on the latest state of play in the leadership contest, was met by a bland uninterest in the impending strike, the Mullins' rallying call, in everything, except the over-riding need to block Gillan and get Carson elected. So that afternoon he found himself at Carson's home where Fred Butler was already narrowing down the list of those undecided MPs on whom pressure had to be exerted. None of the three men in the room was in any doubt as to the most effective form that pressure could take. Appeals to past loyalties, even refined blackmail of a personal or financial nature – these had been employed in similar contests before now. But in the end it was bribery, the capacity of one side to outbid the other with promises of promotion, which turned the scale. Carson was aware of this, aware also, as a former Chief Whip, of the danger of over-eager lieutenants committing their candidate to a degree far beyond his capacity to deliver. In forming a government, maintaining a balance between ability and reward for services rendered constituted a recurring headache.

'No,' he said firmly to Butler, who had been urging the need to promise the doctor, Patterson, some minor post. 'Let the bugger go if he wants to. He'll go along with Willie, whatever you say. In any case, I wouldn't put it past him to vote for Gillan and then, when he's backed a loser, to pretend he voted for us and claim his job. I wouldn't trust him or Willie as far as I could throw them!'

'I'm afraid you could be right,' said Dixon.

'All we need,' said Butler, 'is to convince Willie that we're going to win!'

'Exactly,' said Carson. 'Exactly!'

'What about the Mullins crowd? McCrory and that lot?' asked Dixon.

Butler shook his head. 'Brian was in this morning. He's on the strike committee *with* Mullins. No good he says. We can forget Mullins and Co.'

'We can do without them, thank God,' said Carson with such unusual vehemence that the other two looked at him. 'If I'm in charge I'm not going to be tied to their coat-tails. Protestants, yes, but these bloody bigots, no!'

The other two looked at each other this time. Butler spoke quickly, 'According to my sums I make it nineteen for us at the moment.'

'How do you make that out?' asked Dixon.

'Look,' explained Butler. 'We had a solid eighteen at the meeting? We lose Gillan, Mun and let's say, Willie and his friend Patterson. That leaves fourteen. We gain – the Rooster, Sam Collins, the Speaker, who had agreed – and that's firm – to attend, *and* Magee who is now with *us*.'

'Is he? Is Magee definite?' asked Dixon.

'Yes,' said Carson. 'We had to promise him Agriculture!'

Dixon grinned. 'Pricey bugger, isn't he?'

'That makes eighteen,' continued Butler. 'And. . .? The Chief Whip! He's out of hospital and we've checked with the doctors. They'll let him come – for about an hour, but that's enough! Nineteen!'

'Well!' said Dixon turning to Carson with a beaming smile. 'That's a turn-up.'

'Isn't it?' Carson beamed back. 'Apart from that, you go along with Fred's arithmetic?' he continued. 'Out of a total of thirty-five – that's including the Chief Whip – it would give us a majority of three?'

'At worst,' said Dixon. 'At very worst. Because I still believe that once it's clear that we are going to win, and once it's clear that the PM is backing Des, then a few more of the bastards, *including* Willie, will come our way. And I'll tell you one thing. I'll have someone next to friend Willie on Wednesday to make sure he puts his X in the right place. Because either he does it openly or as far as I'm concerned he hasn't done it at all.'

'Tom's giving a little lunch party, very private, for the senior press boys tomorrow,' said Butler. 'That should get the band-wagon moving.' He winked at Carson. 'All the press fancy you this morning. We'll have you odds-on favourite by tomorrow night!'

Carson looked dubious. Dixon laughed and clapped him on the shoulder. 'Don't worry, Desmond. Don't be afraid to win! You're home and dry!'

That same afternoon, in the town of Cavan, where the main streets are named after dead Republican heroes, ten members of the IRA Army

Council were meeting for the second time in three days. Just off Pearse Street, in a room above a busy newsagent's shop belonging to a sympathiser, they were discussing policy. One of the documents on the table before them was the latest report from the Intelligence Officer of the Third Battalion in Belfast which had been keeping the home of Josephine Scanlon under surveillance. The report dated from Friday and attached was a detailed sketch map of the location of the lodge and means of access.

The Belfast Commander, a noted hawk in the Movement, had brought the situation right up to date on the basis of the latest intelligence received in Belfast that morning. The regular pattern of the Unionist Minister's visits had not changed. There had been one exception. The lodge had been empty from 18.30 hours on Friday until 04.25 the following morning, when Scanlon had arrived home alone driving her own car. That night, Saturday, Carson had arrived at 21.00 hours as usual, driving his own Mercedes and unescorted. He had left at 00.35 hours. The Intelligence Officer on the spot was now satisfied that on these visits there was no police cover for the Minister, either with or without his knowledge. On the instructions of his Brigade Commander he had checked in every direction including a tail on Carson as far as his home. The arguments for and against had been debated, often with heat, during the past two hours. The probability that the man concerned would be Prime Minister of Northern Ireland within a few days sharpened the need to come to a decision before his lifestyle radically altered. It also made him an even more prestigious target. The Chief of Staff, his eyes screwed up against the smoke of the cigarette which seldom left his mouth, summed up, without wasting words.

'Right. You've all had your say. We've been through it all before. But an opportunity like this will not come again. The timing and the circumstances could not be better. This man is not only a sworn enemy of the Republican movement. He is in charge of the machinery of Unionist repression – the police state, in whose prison so many of our soldiers have suffered torture and degradation.' He looked round the table. 'I make it seven to three. My decision goes with the majority. Liam!' He turned to the Belfast Commander. 'He's yours.'

241

All through the early hours of Monday morning the change was taking place, inexorably, unnoticed as yet by most of the Province. Some factories silent, only a few lights ablaze, not so many vehicles on the roads, buses hardly at all in evidence. By seven o'clock, the beginning of the normal rush-hour into Belfast, traffic was much lighter than usual. As the Liverpool steamer docked near the Queen's Bridge there were no stevedores to meet her – two of the management had to handle the mooring warps. Train services were badly disrupted – half of the personnel had not turned up for duty. All over Belfast the forlorn queues, waiting for buses that did not come, grew longer.

Carson was on his way to the office well before eight. His escorts were tense. News coming in suggested that the strike was far more widespread than anticipated. They decided to avoid the city centre and take the Knock Ring Road. On many of the side-streets makeshift barricades – old furniture, scrap cars, oil-drums filled with bricks – had been erected. At one point they were stopped by a posse of youths wearing improvised uniforms of khaki anoraks, denim or leather jackets. They were carrying sticks and iron bars. 'Easy does it!' warned Carson, as two of his Special Branch men jumped out of the escort car. After a brief exchange, the group stood aside to let the cars pass, their leader waving Carson through with an elaborately ironic gesture.

'Bad boys, sir,' said his driver, shaking his head. As they drove on they could see an un-cooperative bus driver being swiftly assisted from his cab while his vehicle was driven across the road to form a further barrier. R/T reports were coming in all the time. Main roads into the city were still clear, but access roads in the working class areas and in the densely populated council estates were becoming increasingly impassible.

The two cars reached Stormont without further hold-ups, just in time to catch the eight o'clock news. For the majority of citizens the BBC bulletin was the first intimation of the ordeal before them. The first bulletin of the strike committee – the ULC – was given in full: the call was for a complete shut-down of all business and industrial premises until the British Government granted a referendum on the constitutional changes.

242

There followed detailed reports of the ways in which strike action was already biting. For the past five hours at the three main power stations, there had been a controlled reduction in output. As demand increased to the usual mid-morning peak of over 700 megawatts, power cuts would be inevitable – Megs Kane and his fellow-workers were wasting no time. From Londonderry, Balymena, Craigavon and other principal towns of the Province, it was reported that only half the labour force had turned up for work in the big industrial plants. Most of the smaller factories and business premises were carrying on as usual with between thirty and forty per cent absenteeism. But from all areas came stories of very active picketing. Workers were being urged to stay at home and shop-keepers to stay closed. There was no evidence, said the BBC, of strong-arm tactics – picketing was as yet good-humoured and well-controlled. At the crowded strike HQ on the Antrim Road the Chairman, Billy Sproat, listened with Harrmon, Osborne and several of their henchmen in one of the inner rooms. From the outset they had been aware of the propaganda value of avoiding ugly incidents. All the UDF units had been emphatically told to avoid open intimidation which could lead to clashes with the police. Tactics might have to be changed later, but, for the moment the image was to be one of men determined, but peacefully persuading.

'It's goin' all right,' said Sproat with marked satisfaction. He emphasised the point to Harrmon by beating a fist into the palm of his other hand. 'You've just got to keep them in check Harry, until Megs gets control – once the real cuts start, our work's done for us. Wait! Listen!'

He held up an urgent hand. Another BBC voice was reading out verbatim the blueprint for the conduct of the strike prepared in that same HQ the day before. It was a list of instructions that touched on every field of the community's life. Those who would be permitted free movement on the roads: doctors, nurses, hospital and welfare services, fire brigades, post office, bread, animal feedstuffs vehicles. GPO telephone and BBC personnel were allowed.

Forbidden to operate were public transport, all commercial vehicles, petrol, oil and gas lorries, restaurants and pubs. To maintain essential services, two oil companies would supply a number of points throughout Ulster – all permitted personnel would require a ULC pass to draw petrol. There was also a list of advice centres to deal with queries and to attend to the special needs of the old, the pensioned and the sick. For this last announcement Sproat had a special nod of approval. When the bulletin finished, they looked at each other with

243

unconcealed jubilation. It was the kind of recognition they had not dared to hope for. Read out in the formal tones of the BBC announcer, their hastily drawn-up directions had been given almost the status of official regulations.

Carson was listening in his office with his Permanent Secretary, Arthur Jones.

'Disgraceful!' said Jones. 'What are the BBC up to? Are they siding with the strikers?' Carson muttered something non-committal, aware of his own ambivalence. Later that day there would be bitter criticism of the BBC and heated discussion inside its walls over the initial handling of the strike news. But the news editor on that first fateful morning maintained he was acting in the public interest in giving full coverage to matters likely to affect the daily life and welfare of the province. Whatever the controversy – it was water under the bridge. From now on, the strike and the ULC would be taken seriously. Six full bulletins that day and numerous flashes would reinforce its gravity in the public mind.

Already in the Stormont ministries Arthur Jones and the other Permanent Secretaries had been calling meetings of their top officials to consider their attitude and to make contingency plans. The Prime Minister had decided not to call a Cabinet, but to confer individually with those of his colleagues directly involved. As soon as he arrived from Armagh, he summoned Carson down to the Castle. Stewart Taylor was there to represent the official civil service view.

'The most worrying aspect of this strike is maintaining order,' said Packham. 'It must not get out of hand. I've got Crosbie Knox and the GOC coming later and we'll see what they have to say, but we must at all costs avoid a clash between the Army and the Protestants. If that happened and the IRA pitched in . . . we'd have real civil war!'

'I hope that the Army are aware of the danger – I know the police are,' replied Carson. 'We've already told them to keep as low a profile as possible, until we see how the situation develops. We'll see what the GOC says.'

'You know, Desmond,' continued the Prime Minister to whom the strike seemed to have restored something of his old combative sparkle, 'this strike is really a godsend from our point of view. Instead of us being forced into confrontation, the strikers are making it more than clear to HMG that, however they rate appeasement so far as gaining the goodwill of Roman Catholics is concerned, without the consent of the Protestants, this place is ungovernable!' Stewart Taylor cleared his throat nervously. 'Yes Stewart,' said Packham recognising the signs.

'While accepting what you say, Prime Minister, I feel we should leave Downing Street some . . . honourable line of retreat – a face-saver. We cannot in reason expect complete capitulation, especially under duress.'

'What then do you suggest?' asked Packham, a touch testily.

'Desperate situations require desperate measures, PM. I was thinking possibly of – since the issue seems to be one of popular consent – of a general election?'

'An election?' said Packham impatiently, 'in present conditions?' He looked at Carson. 'This is one for you Desmond, I feel.'

Carson pondered a moment. 'Mind you, I don't dismiss it as a bargaining counter – we might feed it into the Downing Street computer and see what comes out – but,' he smiled at Taylor, 'I feel there's a limit to what the public will take.'

'I agree,' said the Prime Minister emphatically. 'Let the British Government stew in their own juice for a while – after all, they've insisted on asserting their supremacy. Let them try it on for size! I predict that they will emerge chastened and much more amenable. When it's all over you can hold your elections – you'll be in a stronger position then.'

'On present showing, we'll probably have a clutch of paramilitaries elected!' said Carson.

When Frank Boydell and Knox arrived, it was soon clear that they were not going to rush their fences. 'I assure you, PM, the Army is very happy to stay in barracks, but I fear that we shall not be permitted to. My chaps tell me that we're up against a bunch of very well organised gentlemen – the position with electricity is especially dicey. MoD are worried. They're exploring the possibility of getting a hundred standby generators from Rhine Army but that would only cover the top priorities – government and security networks and possibly hospitals.'

'Your REME people wouldn't tackle the power stations?' asked Carson.

Smiling, the GOC shook his head. 'Much too big, much too sophisticated. A Valiant class nuclear sub is the nearest equivalent, but I doubt if even the Navy boffins could handle it. In any case we'll be stretched to the limit. We shall have to keep our guard up in the Catholic areas just in case our IRA friends see an opportunity. Crosbie here will need more back-up than normal if only to keep the roads clear and to protect vital installations. We shall have our hands full, I assure you, without taking on the Prods.'

'We've discussed this,' said Crosbie Knox, 'and we think it's best to keep my lads at the inter-face, road-blocks and so on: Protestants seem to find the police less provocative!' He permitted himself a wry smile.

'I think you're acting wisely,' said Packham. 'We would urge you both to intervene only when it's absolutely necessary. Let them blow off steam. Let it burn itself out. Any attempt at strike-breaking by the Army or police will only fan the flames and could, I am convinced, have the most disastrous consequences.'

About midday the first power cuts were announced. All consumers were asked to exercise the strictest economy. But soon in all areas it was four hours on and four hours off. Throughout the afternoon the situation worsened. An Electricity Board spokesman warned that with only sixty per cent on the grid, industry would have to close down to enable essential services to continue. Such an instruction to close down industry would require a Government decision. But Packham had decided to sit tight. If Downing Street was going to run the country, let them get on with! Only when there was a sign of 'give' would he throw the Stormont machine behind them. Carson, though he did not like the idea of the Government standing impotently by, agreed it was the chance of getting Downing Street to bend.

About four o'clock, he visited two of the RUC operations rooms in Belfast. Radio reports were streaming in with details of the growing extent of the strikers' control. The police attitude was as equivocal as his own. A new development in road blocks was the human chain which, if broken up by the RUC, reformed immediately they left. More and more shops were closing down, encouraged by the bands of youths roving through the city and making it clear that strike-breakers were not popular. The official UDF stance was still 'no intimidation' but the Enforcement section were in no doubt as to the nature of their task. From the strike HQ came a bulletin giving the permitted hours of opening for chemists and food stores. Those shops still open were using small gas-lamps, but the main gas system and supplies of butane and propane were firmly in the hands of the strikers' committee. By the end of the working day the coal squads on the quays and merchants' yards were no longer working. Milk was in short supply and the shelves in food-stores were rapidly emptying as housewives stocked up against an uncertain future.

At the strike HQ there was a queue of business men, representatives of big industrial concerns, professional men, farmers, all seeking ULC permits or special concessions for those enterprises on the 'forbidden' list. Chambers of Trade had asked to send urgent delegations to the

246

strike leaders. The writ of the Ulster Loyalist Council was extending all the time. As Carson drove that evening through the darkened city to see his mistress – the shortage of petrol progressively reducing the need for barricades – he was deeply worried about this transfer of power. A new de facto government was in being. It would not just fade away.

Elsewhere, the reality was reluctantly being faced. At Loughside, Her Majesty's representative from the Foreign Office was finding life far from easy. Not only his masters at the FO but a Deputy Under-Secretary from the Ministry of Defence had been pressing him for information on the Loyalist Council's intentions. Apparently Army HQ at Lisburn was woefully short on this kind of political intelligence. He had been forced to admit that the significance and impact of the strike had been under-estimated but that he was engaged on an urgent re-assessment. He was sharply informed that Number Ten took a grave view of the sudden worsening in the situation. His Permanent Under-Secretary looked to Birch, as the man on the spot, to leave the strikers in no doubt as to HMG's attitude and policy. From his colleague's tone it was clear that Nigel Birch was very much on the spot. In desperation he had contacted the ULC. The Shorts convenor, Jim Patton, had been delegated to meet him on behalf of the strike committee who at once assumed that this was an opening move in negotiations with Whitehall.

At about eight o'clock Patton arrived, accompanied only by Harrmon's driver, who knew the house. The interview did not begin auspiciously. Patton refused refreshment of any kind. He had not come here to socialise with this two-faced smoothie who had entertained, probably in this very room, bitter enemies of Ulster! Stony-faced, he listened to Birch's carefully rehearsed introductory remarks; his masters' feeling that this meeting would be helpful in clearing the air, that dialogue had to begin sooner or later in a situation of this kind, that HMG, while certainly not seeking confrontation, had, nevertheless, the duty to ensure that essential services were preserved. He, Birch, had been instructed to warn the ULC of the very grave consequences of the course on which they were embarked. He would hope that having made their protest they would see the futility of expecting Her Majesty's Government to yield to this kind of unconstitutional pressure and . . .

'Just a minute!' interrupted Patton, his face reddening. 'Just a minute!' He brushed aside Birch's attempt to continue. 'Look! *You* asked to see *us*. We didn't ask to see *you*. I didn't come here to listen to a lecture. You can save that for Maguire and your Republican friends. As far as we're concerned, the dialogue has started. Our offer's on the table. We'll call off the strike if you agree to leave control of security to be decided by a referendum of the Ulster people. What's *your* offer?' As Birch sat tight-lipped, he went on. 'I'll give you time to ring up your bosses.'

'Thank you, that will not be necessary,' said the Foreign Office representative, momentarily nettled. 'I'm afraid the British Government is not in the business of making deals!'

'Say that again,' Patton's voice was as hard as carborundum.

'I said, I'm afraid the British Government is not making any deals,' repeated Birch with less assurance.

Patton cut him short. 'Right! I thought I heard you the first time. You'll change your tune before we've finished with you.' He jumped to his feet and quickly left the room.

With mounting misgiving, Nigel Birch listened to the sound of his departing car.

At the strike HQ, Billy Sproat the Chairman, Megs Kane, Harrmon, his lieutenant Charlie, and Osborne were all waiting. Within the past hour there had been evidence of a hardening in the British Government's attitude: three UDF members had been arrested by the Army for obstruction outside the Belfast East Power Station. Megs Kane had ordered an immediate walk-out of the power-workers and the station was closed down. The ULC members were in militant mood, reinforced by a whisper from a police contact that the Army were about to take over the oil refinery at Belfast harbour, giving them control of all petrol supplies. A collision seemed to be inevitable. They listened grimly to Patton's account of his meeting at Loughside. It was Megs Kane who spoke up when he had finished. 'This is where we stop messin' around. Now it's a fight to the bitter end.'

'What are you going to do?' asked Sproat uncertainly.

'I'm going to run the system right down until nothing in this province moves.' He waited till the words sank in. 'The Lord hath given and the Lord shall take away.'

His voice held a chilling quiet. From the men around him there was no answering growl of confident defiance. Each had, for a moment, glimpsed the nightmare that haunted them – a city, a whole community, totally without electricity. No power, no radio, no telephones. In the hospitals no life support systems, no kidney machines. All the electrical devices on which society depends, the pumps that prime existence – water, sewage, petrol – all useless. No light. Darkness at noon, nor any spark at midnight.

248

At eleven that evening a full meeting of the ULC was held. It went on for a long time. The eventual decision was unanimous – to announce that all essential services would cease within twenty-four hours. The list included, besides electricity: telephones, gas, water, sewage and petrol supplies, fire brigades, security guards, bakeries, abattoirs and grave-diggers. The dead would have to bury their dead.

The next day broke on an Ulster virtually immobilised and cut off from the rest of the world. Steamship services to Belfast and Larne were suspended. Trains from Dublin were no longer running. The civilian airport at Aldergrove was almost at a standstill. At the RAF airfield Hercules transports were unloading green standby generators. But Megs Kane's grip was already throttling life in the Province. With only forty per cent on the grid, industry was sliding to a halt. Bakeries were closed. On the farms, the useless ventilation systems meant heavy losses of chicks and broilers through suffocation.

The police had ruled that it was too uncertain for Ministers to travel by road. So Carson was driven to playing fields near his home and thence by Wessex helicopter to the Castle.

The strike had acquired a dynamic of its own. At a meeting with his senior advisers the mood was one of profound pessimism.

No-one could see a way out. The prospects, both economic and social, if the strike continued, were appalling. Carson was faced with the grim possibility that the inheritance he had so long desired and striven for might, in the very moment of possession, prove inoperable.

Despite the views expressed to Crosbie Knox at the security meeting, it was now clear that the police would have to get much tougher in dealing with the growing anarchy. That meant more and more confrontations and provided no solution to the escalating electricity crisis.

Civil servants, many of whom had walked to their offices, were desperately trying to provide against the worst. Once the pumps stopped, whole areas of low-lying Belfast would be flooded with raw sewage. The health hazard did not bear thinking of. Though the ULC had in theory guaranteed safe passage for hospital supplies of oxygen, blood and drugs, transport of any kind was now at risk. Hi-jackings were becoming more and more frequent, the UDF on the streets more and more lawless. As food disappeared from those shops still allowed to open, gangs in the working-class Protestant areas were helping themselves. There was something of a reckless Mardi Gras atmosphere. The streets were crowded despite the October chill. Bonfires and sometimes burning barricades functioned as cooking fires for communal barbecues – the steaks cut on the spot in a commandeered meat truck. Candles became a scarce black-market currency. Scuffles between strikers and the security forces were becoming more and more commonplace. On several occasions shots had been fired without anyone being injured but the writing was on the wall – much grimmer than the usual graffiti. In the Catholic areas such as the Falls and the Ardoyne, life was more normal – stocks of food and fuel within the enclaves were still plentiful. The Commander of the Belfast Brigade of the IRA had decided to lie low during the strike. The UDF arrayed against the hated Brits suited his book perfectly. In any case he was short of explosives and the respite was welcome. That day he alerted his Battalion Commanders to the need for a defence perimeter – the role, for the moment, was to guard the Catholic ghettoes against a sudden Protestant onslaught. Only his adjutant and two others knew of the imminent possibility of such a reaction. The operation had been kept tight as a drum.

From early on that Tuesday morning the telephone lines to Stormont Castle had been jammed by angry callers demanding Government action. The initial shock caused by the sudden escalation of the strike had given way to something approaching panic, as the seriousness of the situation dawned. The Confederation of British Industry; Chambers of Commerce from Londonderry, Omagh, Newry and several other towns, most of which had a non-Unionist majority and who were totally opposed to the aims of the strikers; those sections of the trade union movement which were either Nationalist or whose officials were committed Socialists; hostile local councils. They were all pressing for an immediate meeting with the Prime Minister. Delegations and individuals who had attempted to make contact unannounced were turned back by the heavy police cordon which had been hurriedly thrown around the whole area of the Government Buildings. In Packham's room that morning was a harrassed Stewart Taylor. The Cabinet Secretary had just finished a brief meeting with the Permanent Secretaries of the various ministries. Their forecasts of what would happen if the electricity system were allowed to collapse could not have been gloomier – the province would face appalling hardship, and, in the case of the sick and the elderly, almost certainly deaths. Their recommendation was, Sir Stewart Taylor reported, couched in the strongest terms he had ever heard officials use – someone must start negotiations with the strikers, at once. The Prime Minister listened in silence, nodding in a detached way at the end of Taylor's recital.

'I've asked Desmond to come down right away. Anything else?'

'Yes. I've had Maguire on – for about twenty minutes!' The Secretary made a wry face.

'Emergency debate this afternoon?'

'Oh no! From what I could gather he feels we're long past the stage of debate. He was most abusive, hysterical almost – Government a charade, Catholics could be murdered in their beds . . . heading for anarchy . . . I understand he's off to Dublin to try and get the Republic's Government to intervene.'

'Intervene?' said Packham sharply.

'Put pressure on Downing Street, I imagine.'

'I hope that's all they do,' said Packham shaking his head. 'In a heated situation like this, they're capable of sending troops up to the Border, anything!'

'All the more reason, sir, for us to take a firm grip on the situation right away.' Taylor was getting his point in quickly.

'Easier said than done,' said the Prime Minister calmly, tapping the table with the tips of his fingers. Then, 'What do you propose we do, Stewart? I can see that our present posture of waiting for the strikers to soften up Downing Street is rather too Fabian? We've got to act at once – that's clear. By the way, what did you do about all these CBI and commercial gentlemen who are after my blood?'

'Put them off for the moment. Told them that the Government was fully aware of the gravity of the situation and that a statement of its intentions would be issued just as soon as possible.'

'All right. What do we do? The trouble is, Stewart, that we are irrelevant. That's the damnable thing. The strike is not against us, but against Westminster. What pressure can we bring to bear on Westminster? All we can do is threaten to resign and leave them to pick up the pieces.'

The door opened and Carson's head appeared.

'Come in, Desmond. I was just saying that the only weapon we have is the threat of resignation. I'm not suggesting we use it – they might only be too happy to accept!'

'Resignation is out of the question. If we walked out now none of us could ever hold our heads up again.' Carson had not smiled at the Prime Minister's little quip. 'This electricity is really serious,' he went on. 'They tell me that if the system collapses it could be weeks before they could get it started again.'

251

'Surely they wouldn't do that. They'd be playing straight into the hands of the IRA. They're bluffing,' said Packham.

'I don't know,' said Carson. 'They may be. But if the load on the generators is run down below a certain level, then there's a danger of them "tripping" automatically. You get a cascading failure and that's it. Blackout. By this evening they'll be down to twenty per cent capacity, right on danger level.'

'You're very knowledgeable.'

Carson gave a bleak smile but he did not mention Brian Kedge nor his membership of the strike committee. 'No, we have no option, Arthur. We get on to Downing Street and tell the Prime Minister straight that if this part of the United Kingdom is not to slide into chaos then we must be given a free hand to talk to the strikers and get them to call it off. That means leaving control of security here. They'll *have* to climb down. Lives, and the whole economy, are at stake.'

As Carson spoke with heated conviction, Stewart Taylor kept nodding his head. 'I agree entirely, PM. We must do it at once.'

'Yes. Yes,' said Packham abstractedly. 'But let's look at this thing quite clinically. How do we make common cause with the strikers without abdicating all responsibility for governing this country? The answer is – we can't. We should be dragged at the heels of the Harrmon chariot! We fall back, therefore, on persuasion. But what happens . . . if the British Government refuses to capitulate?' He looked at Carson, who hesitated. 'It won't be my pigeon,' continued Packham. 'It'll be yours. But I'd like to be sure that you've thought this one through.'

Carson found himself blustering. 'They've got to see sense. In the last resort expediency always prevails in British policy. They can't let this place fall apart . . . losses in millions, people dying! They are ultimately responsible.'

Packham nodded deliberately. '*That*, Desmond, is the hard reality. Tell me, what *would* you do in the final analysis?'

'If it came to the crunch?' Packham nodded. 'I suppose I've never really faced up to it because it always seemed so remote. But in this case.' Carson paused. 'If I were to retain any self-respect I think I would find myself with the strikers, in the last ditch.'

The Prime Minister smiled sadly. 'In the words of King William III, of glorious, pious and immortal memory, "I shall die in the last ditch". I sincerely trust it doesn't come to that. If it does, your next deal would not be in London, but in Dublin – about a United Ireland.'

'PM, we must get a statement out and we'd better have a Cabinet,' said Taylor anxiously.

'To hell with Cabinet,' said Packham. 'Let's get this settled. Then we can get the Cabinet to OK it.' For a moment he was his old brisk masterful self. He wagged a finger at Carson, 'Don't forget, Desmond. The function of a well-run Cabinet is to form a quorum! Come on, Stewart. Get me Downing Street. I'll speak to him right away.'

'I'll call Cabinet, then, for this afternoon, sir,' persisted the Cabinet Secretary.

'All right. Provisionally. Keep them on call.' As Taylor left the room, Packham drew Carson to the side-table. 'Here, have a glass of sherry. There's no point in wearing sackcloth. We'll do what we can and hope for the best.'

'Have you heard from Gillan?' asked Carson.

'No. But I'm not surprised. He's sitting tight, gambling on the hope that we come a cropper. Then at the selection meeting tomorrow – which is what he has his sights on – he can pop up, clean and pure as the driven snow, the great mediator who can pull the country back from the brink. I'm told he has a line out to the striker's committee through Mullins.'

'I hear that, too,' said Carson casually. 'But what can he do that we can't do?'

'Nothing. Absolutely nothing. But by tomorrow he won't have been tried and found wanting, as may well be the case with us.'

'All the more reason then . . . . I'll leave you to it. Good luck!'

He left the room and went in search of Lefaux. The building seemed to be full of scurrying officials. The Minister of Information was in his office on the first floor. As Carson entered, he put down the telephone and dramatically wiped his brow. 'My God! What a shambles, Desmond! The country's going mad *and* the press – when they can get through. That was the BBC again. Tell me, what's happening? I could get nothing out of the PM earlier. He's doing his cool-as-be-damned act. If you can't stand the heat stay out of the kitchen! I'm completely in the dark and the bloody heating's been off all morning. What's happening for Christ's sake?' Carson told him. 'So that's it,' said Lefaux. 'It all depends on the boss man in London. You don't think he'll try and use the Army to break it?'

'Never!' said Carson. 'The Army knows its limitations – Boydell is far too shrewd a soldier. He's got enough on his plate.'

'What about the strike committee? They won't push it to the brink will they? It's their own people who'll get hurt, after all.'

'Your guess is as good as mine. They are Ulstermen you know. If we can offer them a way out they might take it. But it will need to be a real concession.' Brian Kedge had been keeping him informed of a less intransient mood in the committee. Carson had kept the Prime Minister in the dark, believing that Packham's advocacy would be all the more convincing if he believed the strikers to be hell-bent on a complete shut-down.

'What do you think they'd settle for?' asked Lefaux eagerly. But Carson shrugged his shoulders.

'We'll have to wait and see,' he said, and moved on to something else. 'What happens about the House this afternoon?'

'Oh,' said Lefaux off-handedly. 'Maguire and Co are in Dublin. We can make sure on our side that there isn't a quorum. So the Speaker will open the sitting and adjourn immediately. That's the least of our worries.' They went on to discuss the Cabinet meeting. Lefaux had no anxieties. 'They're all so punch-drunk. They'll go along with anything that offers a way out.' The telephone rang. He lifted it and nodded to Carson. 'It's Stewart. The old man wants you down. Me too.' Together they went downstairs.

They found Packham looking pensive and puzzled. He waved them to seats by the open fire and sat down in his own armchair. 'The answer is that the position is still not clear. The PM didn't say yes and he didn't say no. At the outset, he told me that he had intended to telephone me in any case. I talked to him for about twenty minutes. He listened to the arguments I put to him. He assured me that he and his colleagues were fully seized – that was the phrase – of the extreme seriousness of the situation and that, in fact, they had just been discussing it in Cabinet before I rang. He accepts that the Army is not equipped to take over the power stations. He recognises that any attempt to use military muscle would be counter-productive. In fact, for much of the conversation, I found I was pushing on an open door. But – and this I find worrying.' Packham waited for a moment before continuing. 'When I asked him what he proposed to do he couldn't or wouldn't tell me. They had several options under consideration but had as yet come to no conclusion. He stressed again that they were aware of the urgency, and that another Cabinet had been called for this evening – Boydell the GOC has been summoned to London for consultations. After this evening's cabinet, he would be in a position to tell me what they intended to do. All very cryptic and all very . . . unsatisfactory.'

'You can certainly say that,' said Carson who had listened with growing misgivings. 'And the transfer of security – are they sticking to that?'

254

'Oh yes,' answered Packham. 'Apparently so. When I put our proposals he said he was sorry but at this juncture he was in no position to give us any undertaking whatsoever. No sign at all of any give. He was sure that we would do everything possible to get the strikers to stay their hand. And I gathered, though he wasn't explicit, that they were doing the same through their own channels – that means friend Birch, I take it. He finished by promising that he would telephone me this evening personally, immediately after Cabinet, and inform me of their conclusions. It wouldn't be much before 10.30. That was it.'

Stewart Taylor had slipped into the room. He was looking very worried. 'I've just managed to get Hedges at the Home Office. Wouldn't say a thing. Tight as a clam. Out of his hands.' Packham threw out his hands in a gesture of hopelessness.

It was Lefaux who broke the silence that ensued. 'What in God's name are they up to? Do you think they're about to do a deal over our heads?'

'I do not know,' said Packham wearily. 'I just do not know.'

'It wouldn't make sense,' said Carson. 'Bypassing the elected government to negotiate with a group of militants and trade unionists? It's not their form!'

Packham gave a sceptical twist of the lips. 'That we shall know by this evening,' he said.

'The leadership election . . .' said Lefaux tentatively. 'Surely we should put it off for a day or so . . .'

The three men looked at the Prime Minister. 'Leave it,' he said. 'We can talk about it in Cabinet this afternoon. My feeling is to leave it until tomorrow morning.'

Lefaux sighed. 'Now, all I need is some kind of holding statement . . . for the press.'

'Let's have a drink,' said the Prime Minister. Outside the window the two policemen in their black raincoats paced up and down.

That evening Carson slipped out of the house earlier than usual. He knew he had to be back by 10.30 to take Packham's call. Outside, all was darkness. No floodlights tonight. With a muttered excuse to one of the security men he got into his Mercedes and drove away. As he sped along the darkened avenues and on to the main road, there was scarcely a car to be seen. His brain was buzzing with unanswered questions. So near to his goal and suddenly everything uncertain, so many factors unknown. Like the king of a rainy country, he felt at once rich and yet very old.

She was waiting for him as she always was. He had not seen her for two days. The only illumination in the lodge came from candles and a small cheap oil lamp. 'The lights went off hours ago. But I've just heard on the radio that your friends are graciously pleased to let us have a limited supply for this evening. So it'll be four hours on, four hours off, depending on what area you're in.'

'So they've agreed!' said Carson, thoughtfully. She looked at him enquiringly. He put his arm round her shoulders. 'Come and sit down.' On the sofa in front of the bright fire, they sat for several minutes in silence. 'Brian Kedge was on to me about an hour ago. Birch was meeting – at his own request – three of the strike committee, Harrmon, Mullins and Billy Sproat, the chairman. He must have given them some kind of assurance to get them to stop the run-down.'

'You mean, the British Government are prepared to give in?'

'Not just like that. But they'll cobble up some highly devious formula, neither one thing nor the other – British officials are very good at that. The bitter truth is that we're being completely ignored. We *are* only a puppet regime – our opponents are right.' He turned to face her, and spoke from the heart. 'At times like this I'd give anything, anything, to be in a *real* government.'

'*Any* government?' she asked, half-smiling.

'Almost. Only with sovereignty is there self-respect. You make your own mistakes.'

'But you still want to take over, don't you?'

He was silent a moment before replying. 'Yes. I do. And if I do, I shall

256

aim at that self-respect, no matter what the hell direction it takes us.' He smiled self-consciously and kissed her lightly.

'I'm your best audience,' she said. 'Let me get you a drink . . . Are you hungry?'

He shook his head. 'It's been one of those sandwich days. I'm up to here with tinned ham!'

She lay against him like a child, her head in the crook of his arm. As they sipped whiskey he told her all he knew: of the facts, of his chances, of the blanks still to be filled in. 'Kedge tells me the committee is not as solid as it was. There's a growing feeling that Megs Kane is pushing too far, too fast. He has a fanatic total faith in what he's doing. But the rest of them: Billy Sproat, Harrmon, Hugh Reddy the transport man, McNamee, Patton, Mullins himself – they're no fools. Most of them represent working people. I think they've looked down into the abyss and they don't like what they see. Brian believes that they'll settle for half a loaf rather than no bread. And there'll be no bread for anyone if they smash the power system.' Suddenly the lights came on. They laughed. 'Typical!' said Carson. 'We've got all the light we need. Turn them off . . .'

Jo was at the record-player behind the sofa. 'Culture tonight. Listen to this. I thought I wasn't going to be able to play it for you.' She lay down beside him again in the half-light and kissed him. Pianissimo it began, a long-drawn-out, throbbing chord on strings, music of ethereal tenderness. 'The love-duet from *Tristan and Isolde*,' she whispered. 'I'm a sentimental kid. Hush!' 'O sink hernieder, Nacht der Liebe,' the voice of Tristan invoking the night of love. Softly, like a protective cloak, the music enfolded two singers, two human beings. The myth and the reality became indistinguishable. 'Liebestod,' she murmured. 'That's what they call it. Love *is* a kind of death.'

But for Carson, Wagner was only the catalyst, the elixir that heightened the senses. All day, exhortation, argument, demands – talk, talk. He had emptied the weary ash-can of language. Now he was lost in a drowsy other world where words had nothing to say. With his mouth on the woman he loved there was release and oneness and peace. As her lips sought him out, over and over again, he gave himself up, like a voluptuous child, to this being who so completely absorbed and contained his deepest needs, mother and mistress in one. This dreamy foray into the core of life's sweetness – if only it would never end. They were the only realities. No more Tristan, no more Isolde, each the other, ewig, einig, eternally. She was murmuring in his ear and he could not hear what she was trying to say. But her voice was at once an aphrodisiac and a lullaby. Not passion, but an infinite tenderness. The old deep-seated doubts were in suspension. No misgivings. Round them the music, no longer earth-bound, eddied and swirled in mounting tumult. Now he could distinguish what she was saying. 'I love you Carson. I love you. You are my God.'

'I worship you,' he whispered and tightened his arms about her.

At a quarter to ten, earlier than he had expected, Arthur Packham received the promised telephone call from the Prime Minister of the United Kingdom. He took it downstairs on the scrambler. Stewart Taylor was on the extension.

'Arthur,' began the plummy voice with the shop-soiled vowels, so familiar to millions . . . 'I'm afraid I've got bad news for you, but let me first assure you that our only interest is to bring the Province back to normal as soon as possible . . . and, above all, to preserve the Union between Ulster and the rest of the United Kingdom. Our decision is final, and taken only after the widest consultation. The leaders of the other two major parties are in full agreement.' Packham listened dumbly. The exchange was one-sided and did not take longer than twelve minutes. As he emerged from his room with Taylor, whose face registered his shock and disbelief, Lefaux came bounding downstairs from the flat.

'Well?' Then he saw their looks.

'Tell him, Stewart,' said Packham. 'I'm going up for a drink.' Slowly he walked away.

'They're closing us down,' said Taylor, unconsciously lowering his voice. 'Suspending the Parliament here for a year. Direct rule from Westminster. They're rushing a Bill through tomorrow – all parties agreed.'

Lefaux' eyes searched Taylor's face and moved away. 'Christ! I never thought of that,' he muttered. 'Bloody hell.' He swung round, appealing with both hands. 'But why? What about the strike? They can't do it, can they?' His voice had brightened.

Taylor's face remained unchanged. 'They can do it all right. They hold the power and they hold the purse. We've just never faced up to it – Unionists have *no choice*.' Taylor spoke with bitterness. 'As for the strikers,' he went on. 'They'll be bought off. London's offering a stay of execution on the Specials and fresh elections to a new Stormont at the end of the period of suspension. They'll accept.' Taylor was in no doubt.

'They won't like it, but it gives them something, and leaves them with no clear-cut overwhelming reason for refusing. Vintage Whitehall. The place is full of spoilt Jesuits! They'll accept all right.' He spoke with the unemotional admiration of one professional for another.

The two men walked up the stairs in the strangely silent building, empty of all staff, except the duty officer and the telephonist in the rear wing. 'Did he offer any justification?' asked Lefaux.

'Oh, the need for radical action to arrest disaster, and, of course, their responsibility as the sovereign power to show the world that this part of the UK was being fairly and impartially administered! Et cetera.'

'The smack of firm government. God help us!' said Lefaux.

When they got to the flat, Packham was standing, back to the fire, with a glass in his hand. 'You know,' he said, with an almost childish resentment, 'The man *is* a bloody hypocrite. His deep regret that we had not been able wholeheartedly to accept his security proposals. If we had, what difference would it have made?!'

'None, PM. None,' said Taylor, soothingly.

'I'm sorry, PM,' said Lefaux. 'Nothing we can do, is there?' They waited for Packham to answer. He nodded to Taylor.

'Better ring the others, Stewart. They'll be waiting. Tell Desmond I'd like to see him tonight.'

They lay for a long time, holding each other. The duet climaxed and came to an end. The world began to seep in again. They were once more aware of separate identities. As they moved apart to look at each other, the door-bell rang. They jumped to their feet. It was a rude awakening. Carson could feel his heart thumping. He swallowed and forced himself to speak lightly.

'Who the hell is that?' Automatically he looked at his watch. It was almost ten.

Jo watched him, white-faced. 'I'd better answer it. Shall I turn the lights on?'

'No, wait a moment . . . .' The porch, which opened directly into the living-room, jutted out about five feet in front of the house. From the bedroom window on the left, there was a sideways view towards the front door. Quickly he slipped into the unlit room and lifted the side of the curtain. There was just enough reflected light from the street lamps. He bit his lip with relief. 'It's all right!' he called. 'It's some woman. You can turn the lights on.' The bell rang again. 'No, leave it to me. I'll answer it,' said Carson as Joe, nervously smoothing down her hair, opened the inner door to the porch.

'She could recognise you.'

'Never mind.' He would have been glad of the reassurance of a gun. He was about to ask Jo to take another peep from the bedroom, but stopped. She looked so frightened. He smiled at her and patted her cheek. 'It's all right, darling. She's probably got the wrong house.' He opened the front door. A girl was standing there, her face hard and white.

She blurted out the words in the tight-lipped accents of back-street Belfast. 'Can I use your phone, please?'

As Carson hesitated, she moved quickly to one side and the first bullet hit him. Its force knocked him back against the wall. Two more, and, with a groan, his knees gave way and he was on the floor, his hands clutching his shattered chest. Then the gunman, who had stepped forward from behind the blind side of the porch, took deliberate aim and fired two more rounds into the twitching body beneath him. Jo, who had watched in mesmerised horror, found release at last in a scream that tore her heart out. The gunman lifted his face towards her, wild-eyed with hatred. 'You British whore!' He hissed the words. Then he was gone, and she heard the running footsteps down the lane.

Sobbing, hardly seeing, she staggered towards her man. The hands pressed to his chest were covered in bright blood. Blood spurted from his neck and trickled from the side of his mouth. His breathing was a fitful gurgling. His eyes no longer saw her. Crying his name over and over again, she kneeled down and tried to lift his head. Five minutes later the soldiers came and found her sitting there, muttering broken prayers, the head of the dead man still on her knee.

As Taylor left the room to break the news of their summary dismissal to the rest of the Cabinet, he could think of no way to soften the blow. Packham turned to Lefaux. 'No, Tom. There is nothing we can do. Rebellion or UDI is certainly not for me. Nor, I trust, for anyone. We'll let Her Majesty's Government get on with it – God damn them!' For some minutes the two men gloomily pursued their post-mortem.

Then, for the second time that night, the telephone rang in the Prime Minister's sitting room. Lefaux lifted it. 'Lefaux here. Oh, hullo Crosbie.' He swung round briefly to Packham. 'It's Knox.' Then his plump face sagged with horror. 'Oh, God! No!'

'What is it?' cried Packham, jumping to his feet.

'They've killed Desmond.'

The Prime Minister swayed as if struck. His eyes were staring through Lefaux. Then he recovered.

'Give me the phone,' he muttered. When he had finished, he replaced the receiver with unsteady fingers and sat for a time with his head on his hand. Eventually he looked at Lefaux. 'That makes the political news very unimportant.' Speaking painfully, he repeated the brief details that the Inspector General had given him. 'Did you know about the girl?' he asked.

'I had heard the rumour.'

'I blame myself,' said Packham. 'I intended to talk to him about it. I never dreamt he was being so stupid.'

'Mad, at a time like this,' said Lefaux. 'But he had this reckless streak.'

'I'm going down right away to see his wife. I hope she's heard before I get there.' He rose stiffly and looked uncertainly at Lefaux. 'There could be trouble when this gets out. Boydell has an extra battalion flying in as a precaution. Little did he know . . .'

Stewart Taylor came into the room. 'I've heard,' he said, and his eyes were full of tears.

Within half an hour the news had spread across the land. In the Catholic ghettos there was open savage satisfaction tempered only by the fear of the retribution that might come.

For the Protestant majority it was a double sledge-hammer blow. They had lost both their Parliament and a popular leader who, for many, had symbolised the will of the Ulster people to resist the IRA campaign to bomb them into submission. Desmond Carson, unlike his illustrious namesake, Sir Edward, had been Ulster born and bred, and, as the man in charge of law and order, a steadfast defender of the faith throughout the bloody years of trial. Only much later, despite the discretion of the authorities, did word seep out that he, like the rest of them, was human, with feet of clay.

That night, heavy rioting broke out in Belfast and in towns throughout the Province, as Protestant crowds gave vent to their random fury against the elusive and barely identifiable forces that seemed intent on destroying them by stealth. But the Army had been forewarned, though on false assumptions. From out their fortresses of concrete and steel wire-mesh, from Hastings Street, Musgrave Street, Glenravel, Mountpottinger, the Saracens and Pigs flooded the darkened riot areas.

261

The ironically named 'peace line' dividing the Protestant and Catholic areas in Belfast was subject to specially heavy attack long into the night. Soldiers with blackened faces, steel helmets and bullet-proof vests swarmed through the side-streets. Armed with truncheons and rubber-bullet guns, peering through their Macron shields, their rifles strapped to their wrists, they met the hail of stones, petrol-bombs and sometimes bullets. In the mobs they tried to hold at bay, the women and the young boys were often as numerous and as vicious as the men. The IRA Belfast Brigade Commander, for the most part, kept his head down. The irony of a situation in which his people were being defended by the British Army while it, in turn, was beating off assaults from British Loyalists, did not escape him. As the first light of dawn broke over Divis Mountain the cost was counted. Five civilians dead and one soldier; whether the victim of an IRA marksman or of a stray bullet would never be known. When the bleak October morning was well advanced, whole tracts of the inner city were still shrouded in the clouds of smoke from burning buildings. Desmond Carson had been accorded a fitting funeral pyre.

At the strike HQ where some of the Committee had gathered on hearing the news, there was shock and bewilderment. Then there was anger, confused, and changing its focus from the IRA to London, and back again to the IRA. Billy Sproat of the shipyards was there. Megs Kane was miles away at Ballylumford power station, the sole remaining source of electricity. Harrmon was somewhere in the riot areas, having long given up any pretence of controlling his forces that evening. McNamee was at home at Derry. Mullins and others came and went. They wandered from room to room arguing, accusing, despairing, getting nowhere.

The communique from Downing Street announcing Direct Rule of the Province had cleverly stressed that Ulster was an integral part of the United Kingdom, further eroding the already shaky moral foundation on which the strike was based. As the night wore on, they felt more and more rudderless. The collective will of yesterday was fragmented. Megs Kane had withdrawn into his own inner world. They could no longer agree on any definable goal, unless they were prepared to take power unto themselves – and then, whither? They were punching cotton-wool. Stewart Taylor had been right. Nigel Birch had offered them just enough. They would call it off and settle for the crumbs of half a loaf.

In the following days, the rhythms and responses of ordinary life

262

reasserted themselves in Ulster. There would be new men and new measures, new assemblies, new initiatives, and always, new graves.

They gave Carson a grand funeral with all the trappings of state. In Belfast cathedral an archbishop spoke the funeral oration. In the front pew on one side of the aisle sat the new ruler of Northern Ireland, Her Majesty's Secretary of State. Opposite him, on the other side, sat Carson's widow, his only daughter and his kin. Security was strict. Admission was by invitation only. A junior civil servant, Josephine Scanlon, was not invited.

They laid him to rest in the family plot in the churchyard familiar since childhood, near Banbridge in County Down. Earth to earth, ashes to ashes, dust to dust.

She had hovered on the outer fringe of the crowd of mourners. Now, as they dispersed, leaving behind the churned-up earth with its carpet of dripping flowers, she moved forward to the graveside. A solitary girl in a black headscarf and dark glasses, she stood in the light drizzle for a long time. Willing him back, trying, trying in vain to feel again the touch, to see again the look in the eyes of the man whose love had been only for her.